The Reluctant Assassin

By Richard Scott

Winter Island Press
Salem, Massachusetts

Also by Richard Scott are the following e-books:
Lonely at the Top (a mystery in corporate America)
The President Has Been Shot! (Mystery about President Garfield)
Salem (Historical fiction)

For Jeanne

The Reluctant Assassin

Chapter 1

In two days his comfortable life would come to an end. He had an ominous feeling that the change would be permanent.

It was June, the time of the year he liked the most. He was sitting on the broad, sunbleached porch of the modest two-story dacha overlooking *Ozero Placeevo*. It was a small lake, about 130 kilometers north of Moscow, on the road to Vologda. Some of his most relaxing moments were spent just after sunrise, when he took his small rowboat out on the mirror-smooth surface of the lake. He'd pretend to fish, but it wasn't fish he was after. It was time with his thoughts.

He appreciated the bite of the chill morning air, surprisingly cool for this time of year. The dense birch forest that surrounded the stolid old house had in just the past few days seemed more welcoming. The little things meant more now. So often in the past he had felt this same way, this nostalgia for home before actually leaving home.

At times the serenity of the place got to him. He'd always been a man of action. Until today, he'd often missed the activity and energy of Moscow. But not today. Today, realizing that he would not be here much longer, and might never be here again, he felt a special closeness to these quiet woods so redolent of earth, dried leaves, and that indefinable smell you only noticed in the forest, especially after a warm rain. Today more than any day in the past he felt close to this comfortable place the two of them now called home.

Vladimir Vyugin had been enjoying his retirement these last five years. He'd earned it—at least by the standard of his profession, which was survival.

In Vyugin's line of work the survival rate had never been high. Certainly not during the Cold War years—the years he'd been active. At worst you could die. And even if you weren't killed, you could end up in some foreign prison, or be exposed and sent home in humiliation. If none of this happened to you, at best you were a survivor, not a hero. Never a hero, for spies were never thought of as heroes. Vyugin was a survivor, and he'd grown content accepting that fact.

Today, he supposed, the survival rate would be higher. He closed his eyes and ran his hand through his thinning gray-brown hair as he reflected on how dramatically things had changed in just a few short years. Now that Russia and the West were on speaking terms, the life of an intelligence operative had to be less risky. That is, until now. What he was about to do was very risky.

"Volodya, what's the matter? You don't look happy." It was the liquid voice of Ludmila, his devoted wife of 36 years. She had used his nickname. She was standing in the doorway, forcing a smile—a courageous smile.

Their's had been a relatively good marriage, he reflected—considering. He marveled at how she'd stood by him during those long, intense Cold War years. He'd left her alone so many times—often without the slightest warning. A phone call, day or night, and a few hours later, he was gone. Sometimes for weeks at a time, and most of that time she would never hear from him. She'd understood. She knew what his work was, and she'd never complained. Not outwardly. But the sadness in her eyes would always give her away. And while the years had taken a toll on their marriage—of that he was sure—there was still something there. And that something had grown and even flourished these past five years.

Even during his active years as an intelligence officer, they'd managed to bring up two children. One successfully; one.... he preferred not to think about that one. It pained him too deeply. It was easier to think about Sonia. Sonia was now married with her own children. Living in Petersburg. One of the highlights of these past five years had been seeing Sonia and her family. It was a treat he'd come to look forward to when Ludmila and he would take the night express train from Moscow to St. Petersburg to see Sonia and the grandchildren. Even Pyotr, her husband, had turned out to be better than expected. Their chess matches had evolved into a welcome ritual. In all, he was content with the way Sonia had turned out, though he wasn't sure he could take much credit for it.

Andre was another matter. He'd gotten into a bad element. A very bad element—the Russian Mafia. The Mafia, which some said controlled much of the Russian economy, had somehow lured his son into its web of crime and corruption. The boy had always been in love with money, maybe because the family had never had any to speak of. That was no excuse, though. Nobody in Soviet Russia had had big money. Some had privilege, but money. Hah! Vyugin and Andre had never been able to talk. Oh, they would exchange superficialities—athletics, the weather, even casual talk about women—but they never had been able to talk about themselves or about each other. There was always the barrier.

A smart, aggressive Mafia soldier was assured of financial success. But Vyugin knew Andre was in it for more than the money. The money was part of it, but it was also the thrill. Vyugin hated to admit it, but his son was just like him—a risk taker. It was a need to take risks, a getting off on thrills. Ironically, it was the need to flirt with death that made father and son feel most alive.

In light of what Vyugin was about to undertake, he could no longer pretend he didn't understand his son. He understood all too well. But he still didn't approve of the choice. The Mafia didn't care about Mother Russia. It didn't care about the people. How had Andre become so seduced by this evil force? So ironic, so tragic. It never occurred to Vyugin to view his own profession as having moral or ethical failings. The odious similarity of his son's work and his own totally escaped him.

His son was doing well, if you measured success in money, but the people he worked with... He threw up his hands as he thought about it. He shook his head in resignation. He saw no way out for his son. In the last two or three years they'd seen each other less and less, and their conversation had become increasingly strained on those infrequent times they did meet.

Vyugin looked up at his wife, who was still standing patiently in the doorway. Her still abundant blonde hair was coarser now and streaked with gray. She refused to color it. She'd always been proud of her hair. She'd filled out somewhat over the years—mostly in the hips and thighs, but actually all over. Still, he thought, the result was not so bad. When he'd first met her at that noisy party meeting so long ago in Petrograd, she'd been too thin. He remembered kidding her about it on their second meeting. She'd pretended that he was awfully familiar with someone he scarcely knew, but he'd known then that she was as attracted to him as he was to her.

Ludmila was not happy with his latest decision. For that matter, he wasn't completely reconciled himself.

"Of course I'm happy," he lied. "With a wife like you how could I not be happy?"

"You're going away in a few hours, Volodya. Be serious. I know whatever assignment they've given you is important. It must be important for them to drag a man of your years out of retirement." She sighed, the patient sigh of one who's seen it all, but would somehow still bear up under the *sturm und drang*. "Haven't you done your duty to Russia—many times over? Why can't they send a younger man?"

She was right, at least about his having done his duty. He *had* given the best years of his life to his country. Vyugin had justified it in his own mind because he knew that distasteful things sometimes needed doing in order to facilitate the greater good for one's country.

Throughout history unsung heroes had circumvented the laws of other countries so that rightful governments could survive. There were times when lawful procedures were too awkward, too cumbersome—sometimes just plain wrong. Evil forces took advantage of the law all too often. Russia was still going through a wrenching transition, the biggest transition since the Revolution in 1917, almost a century ago. The results of this current transition or revolution—whatever you chose to call it—were still very much in doubt. He was convinced that Kirov and the people who'd given him this assignment were the best bet for the future of his beloved country. True, there was no certainty they would succeed, but if they weren't given the opportunity, he believed that Russia might very well erupt into chaos, very possibly accompanied by a bloody purge of anyone remotely connected with efforts to convert Russia into a democratic state. These concerns, he knew, were not just his own. Russia's history was living testament to its ability to tear itself apart. It had happened before—too many times.

It had not taken him long to be convinced by Bulgakov that the unstable Kirov government was likely to be taken down by civil unrest if something wasn't done—and done soon. Bulgakov had told him that Prime Minister Malenkov, the number-two man in the government, had a plan that would help Kirov turn Russia into a Western-style nation, if only certain inimical foreign interests could be deflected. Vyugin had this nagging feeling that Malenkov's idea of a Western-style nation didn't exactly include Western-style democracy, but at present, he and Kirov were the nation's only chance. The numerous other political parties scrambling for control of the country tended to be controlled by the military, the extreme left, or the extreme right. For the near future, stability that was pointed in the direction of Western-style democracy seemed to be the safest course for Russia.

Vyugin was not completely comfortable with his decision. True, Malenkov was a strong leader, but maybe too strong. He had a lot of the old Russia in him. The Russia of intrigue. The Russia where men ruled—not by persuasion, but by fear. But if, as Malenkov claimed, he was a new Malenkov, whose only desire was to help his boss lead Russia into a new era, it was the best chance for a better Russia. Clearly, if Russia had any chance at all, it was with Malenkov and Kirov working in concert. Vyugin knew Bulgakov expected him to perform, and perform he would.

He had other reservations, too. Since his retirement he'd had time to think about the validity of what he'd done with the KGB. As a young man, patriotism had been enough to get him through the worst of the things he'd been called upon to do. We were good, and they were bad. A simple moral algorithm, but it sufficed. Recently, though, that thinking had not been sitting well with Vyugin. Ah, well, the sooner he got it over with, the better for all concerned. Well, not all, but certainly the vast majority of people on both sides of the Atlantic.

"Mila," he said softly, using the term of endearment he saved for such serious moments. "I wish I could explain to you why I must do this. I know you don't want me to, but whatever you feel, believe me when I tell you that it's not hormonal. It is not the man-child in me longing for one more adventure. I don't miss the work, Mila. Believe me, I don't. Not anymore.

"I admit that, for the first two or three years after I retired, I did miss working—at least certain aspects of my work." He had never enjoyed the killing. He had done it, but he had not enjoyed it the way some agents on both sides enjoyed it. He knew one man, and come to think of it, one woman, who actually looked forward to that part of their assignments. Intelligence work attracted a lot of sick people. They were accepted because they were focused and good at their work, and it was the kind of work that not everybody would or could be good at. He had never found the killing exciting. He had done it when it was necessary, the way a soldier kills on the battlefield because it is necessary. In point of fact, the majority of intelligence agents never killed anyone. But they were all trained to do it, and they were all supposed to be prepared to do it if necessary.

He looked out the window at the sullen sky. Did she understand that the executions had been necessary, had been the acts of a soldier killing to defend his country? To defend himself? Could she ever understand that? He studied her expression. Her eyes were sad, but loving. Did he deserve her love? Did he deserve anyone's love? No time for these thoughts now. His next words were barely above a whisper.

"Our time together these last five years has erased any longing I had for the work. No, I'm doing this now because this is a time of crisis for Russia. Russia needs me, and I must do what I can for her—one last time. And, besides," he smiled hopefully, "they've assured me that my pension will be guaranteed. Something nice to count on in these uncertain times."

"I suppose the pension part is nice," she replied sadly, "but what good is it if you get killed? You've served your country with distinction. That I know, Volodya—for nearly forty years. For nearly forty years you've survived in the most dangerous profession in the world. These past five years I've thanked God that you could enjoy the remaining years of your life. Why, now, do you have to push your luck, and mine, too? If you don't care about yourself, think of me. Think of the grandchildren. They want and need you. They don't want a dead hero for a grandfather."

"If I didn't think it was the most important mission of my life, *moya doroga*, I wouldn't do it. You must believe me, Mila." He smiled, reflecting on how many terms of endearment he had for her. "You know that I can't give you details. I would if I could. This, I promise you, though. It will be my last assignment."

Her voice rose desperately, "You say it's your last assignment, but can you promise me that you'll come back from this last assignment? I have a bad feeling about this assignment, Volodya."

* * *

Looking back over his career, Vyugin had to wonder how he'd ever gotten into intelligence work in the first place. He knew the specifics, of course—every last detail. He remembered vividly how he'd been recommended by his teachers when he was in his second-to-last year at the polytechnic institute. He remembered how his father's being a prominent and respected member of the party had given him that extra boost. He remembered how his intellect, his physical strength, his athletic ability, and his facility with languages had made him the ideal candidate. He allowed himself a moment of bittersweet satisfaction as he thought how he still had more of these qualities than people would expect in someone his age. He didn't look his age. Most people took him for a man at least ten years his junior.

To this day he wondered why he hadn't done something to get out of being sent to the KGB academy back in '61. At one point when he was under consideration he probably could have gotten out of it. Once the party picked you, of course, you had to go—unless they learned something about you that would have made you undesirable. Otherwise, it wasn't easy to avoid becoming a spy. Hell, most candidates would have killed to be accepted. He smiled wryly. Once a candidate was accepted he usually got the chance. But if you didn't want to become a spy, and they still wanted you, they usually got you. Defying the party was fraught with risk. Of course, being an agent for the KGB carried its own risks, but it also carried a certain amount of respect. Or was it submissiveness? People didn't mess with the KGB. Still, if you didn't want to be part of that murky world of espionage, there were ways to avoid serving. But you had to act fast and decisively as soon as you knew you were being considered.

You could say that you preferred the arts. You had to be good at something, of course. Just anybody couldn't say that. But he *had* been good at something. He still was, for that matter. By any standard he was an excellent violinist, perhaps good enough to have become a national phenomenon if he'd stayed with it back then. Maybe not, of course, but he'd certainly been good enough back then to have tried this approach. If you had no particular talent, you could feign illness, or claim an inability to kill even the smallest animal. And if you were really willing to risk your future in order to avoid a career in espionage, you could pretend you were a homosexual.

He had not opted for any of these escape routes. Honesty compelled him to admit to himself that, at the time, the romance of being a spy for Mother Russia loomed larger than what he had viewed as the sick side of spydom. Yes, he remembered having doubts, wondering how he'd perform when he had to make his first kill. Somehow, though, he'd rationalized all that, forced it into the back of his mind—partly because of the romance and partly because of patriotism. He had loved Russia back then. He still did. He'd had some reservations about the Soviet system, but he'd loved Russia, and since Russia was at the heart of the Soviet Union, he was even proud of being part of the great Soviet Union. The Soviet Union was one of the two greatest powers the world had ever known. People didn't always love you if you were from a superpower, but they did respect you. In some cases it was fear, but even that was better than being a third-rate nation on the dole.

Some of the qualities that had made him a good candidate for the KGB had also been the things that should have put him off such a vocation. He was intelligent. You could go either way with that, he realized. And he was sensitive, even caring, though he'd seldom let on to his colleagues or superiors. He was also introspective. He'd spent too much time thinking before every assignment he'd ever had—not just the mechanics and the logistics of the assignments, but how they affected the people involved. Of course, if he'd shared this with his superiors he would have been brought in from the field and given a harmless job pushing papers. Or worse.

In his heart he knew why he'd become a spy. It was the excitement, the matching of wits with the best operatives in the world. Every time he came out on top, he felt a rush of excitement. It was an addiction. Just as every other addiction was a sickness, he knew that this one was, too. And because it was an addiction, he couldn't shake it.

He was not a young man now. The last few years, he had to admit, had been pleasant. He had finally known contentment. He'd gotten to know his wife better than he had in the first thirty years of their marriage. He'd gotten to know his three grandchildren. Life had been sweet.

When Yuri Bulgakov had first approached him with his proposition, he'd said no. It hadn't been easy, for Bulgakov was an important man now, with important friends. And he sat at the very seat of power in Mother Russia. He'd told Bulgakov and Anatoly Sorokin that he appreciated being considered, but that he was out of shape and not as quick as he should be. And he was too old.

Bulgakov had not pressed. He'd been patient, like the fox he was. He'd said that he understood. Bulgakov was not known for his patience, either. Vyugin didn't know Sorokin. He'd heard of him, naturally. Who hadn't? But they'd never met. Besides, on this visit, Bulgakov did most of the talking. Sorokin, who worked for Bulgakov, deferred to him throughout most of the conversation. Still, Vyugin sensed that Sorokin had come along for a reason.

Bulgakov and Vyugin reminisced about old times. They'd both begun their careers in the KGB, though Bulgakov had gone on to bigger things. But there had been a time, when both of them were on the way up, that they had been friendly. Not close friends, but friendly enough to talk about family and about the rigors of travel and even to exchange an occasional joke. Then, just as Vyugin retired, Bulgakov had been promoted to the number-two job in the new FSB (Federal Security Service), the successor to the KGB. Things had happened fast after that.

A year after Bulgakov's promotion, Antonin Kirov became President. Kirov said that he intended to make changes, changes for the good. In order to save his government, though, Kirov had been forced to accept the Communist Mikhail Malenkov as his Prime Minister. After the collapse of the Soviet Union in 1991, the Communists had become unpopular and hardly a factor in government. Recently, though, they'd had a resurgence, mostly because Gorbachev, Yeltsin, and Putin had not been able to control a wild and reckless Russian form of capitalism. Putin, in a desperate and probably necessary move to build a coalition government, had invited the Communists in to share in that government. He'd recklessly moved to remilitarize the government by reinstating universal military training and commitment and by toughening up the country's policy toward those countries that differed with Russia. He'd made the Chechnyan conflict his *cause célèbre*. It was good politics because the Russian people were up in arms over the bombings in Moscow that were allegedly caused by Chechnyan rebels. But he'd made too many mistakes and the Russian voters had decided to give democracy one more chance. That's how Kirov had gotten elected.

But the Russian Mafia and other criminals had exerted more control over the economy than the government had, and the government's problem was exacerbated because it was unable to collect taxes as efficiently as other developed nations. Many simply did not pay what they owed, and the new bureaucracy was so overwhelmed by the sheer numbers of tax scofflaws that they had a hard time enforcing the collection of taxes. As a consequence, public services were failing because the government couldn't meet payrolls, and in turn, people couldn't buy goods and services, and even those who managed, often didn't pay their bills. The situation was grim, and many people were willing to try anything, including going back to Communism if it would bring some order out of the present chaos.

The Communists now made up a strong and growing minority in the Russian Parliament. One of Malenkov's first acts when he took office was to ask Bulgakov to become his Chief of Staff. It was a position of much power. Malenkov had, by dint of his personality and with the Communist Party behind him, become a force to be reckoned with in the political landscape of Russia. Bulgakov had hungered to be part of that change. He'd been ambitious, and he'd had aspirations to go higher in the government, though he knew he had limitations. He had come from a remote district of the Ukraine and to some Russians that made him less pure than a native-born Russian. He'd overcome those prejudices most of his life, but he knew there were limitations. So when he'd been asked into that rarified circle at the pinnacle of government it had exceeded his wildest dreams.

Bulgakov and Kirov had nothing in common—either ideologically or in their background. Kirov said he was a democrat and wanted to help create a Western-style economy in Russia. Even back in the old days, Kirov had never been a strong party man. He came from an elite old Moscow family, and that family never fully endorsed the party that had changed their lives so dramatically. Yet Kirov rejected his privileged aristocratic background, almost as much as he rejected Communism. He believed too much in the individual and in the rights of the individual. Yet, since Malenkov had become Prime Minister, he'd supported Kirov and worked with him to the surprise of Kirov supporters everywhere. It appeared that Malenkov had truly become a new man politically. Unless he was just biding his time.

Vyugin had always had reservations about Bulgakov's principles, but old ties were hard to break. Bulgakov had an infectious manner. He was very likeable. Before Bulgakov left Vyugin's modest dacha, they'd hugged warmly. It had been good to see each other after so many years. And it had been flattering to Vyugin to have the Prime Minister's most senior aide make the trip to him with this important proposition. Bulgakov had then gotten into his chauffeur-driven black Volga 3105 and returned to Moscow. But not before making one last low-key try. "Promise me, Vladimir, that you'll give it some thought. President Kirov and Prime Minister Malenkov are counting on you. Still," he paused pregnantly, "I'll respect your decision either way."

Funny, Vyugin reflected. That's all he'd done after Bulgakov had left—given it thought. He hadn't been able to get the assignment out of his head. Five days later he'd called Bulgakov and said that, while he was probably still not interested, he did have a few questions—just to be sure he understood what the proffered assignment consisted of. In retrospect, he realized, he'd already made up his mind before he made that call. When the two of them met again, in a final move to clinch the deal, Bulgakov said that he had been empowered to promise that the government would not only guarantee that his full pension would be paid for the rest of his years, but that they would build in cost-of-living adjustments to keep pace with Russia's serious inflation problem. The government would thus insure that he and Ludmilla could maintain their present standard of living. Pension stability was a major issue in Russia, for some people were no longer receiving even the smallest of pensions. Many others had had their monthly stipends reduced. With the ruble declining in value almost daily, a guaranteed pension that wouldn't lose its value was very tantalizing to someone his age.

But that wasn't what had decided it for him. It was what Bulgakov and Sorokin had told him was likely to happen in Russia if action wasn't taken.

Chapter 2

Vladimir Vyugin looked at the tall angular man next to him as the two of them made their way toward the South end of the huge indoor mall. Artur Shevsky was young, not more than 30 years old, but the hairline on his narrow head had already receded. It made him look older than his actual years—especially now, as he was clearly very tired. The lights from the mall reflected off his dome-like forehead. He was a nervous man, who kept brushing the few strands of hair that remained away from his eyes. If you didn't look closely, it looked as if he were brushing air. When Vyugin looked at him, he couldn't help but think of an undernourished turkey. A likeable turkey, though, thought Vyugin puckishly. Vyugin wondered if his younger colleague was as tired as he was.

As Vyugin reflected on it, he was amazed that he wasn't far more exhausted, considering how much walking they'd done. They'd devoted the entire day to walking the streets of Moscow, visiting shops and stopping to talk with ordinary citizens. After a brief lunch on the run, they had walked the length and breadth of this giant indoor shopping mall, interviewing shoppers and shopkeepers alike. Aside from the physical exhaustion from being on their feet all day, Vyugin and Shevsky both felt beaten down from the constantly recurring depressing message they were getting from virtually everyone they spoke with. Vyugin was now ready to call it a day, but Shevsky had just said in his youthful desire to impress that perhaps they should do one more interview. Vyugin, as the senior member of the team, couldn't very well say no — especially since they were doing this for his benefit.

In any event, it would be the last stop of their informal informational tour of GUM, Moscow's legendary indoor shopping mall. Today's GUM was a sparkling contrast to the GUM of the past. Now an elegant blend of the old with the expansive glass and gleaming brass of the typical upscale indoor mall in a Western country, today's GUM was a dazzlingly pretentious showplace for most of the big names in high-fashion retailing.

The building that housed the present mall had been built in 1890 as a central market for Moscow. In 1921 Lenin had nationalized the market, and in 1953 the building and the huge state-run store within it had been completely renovated. It became known as *Gosudarstvennyi Universalny Magazin* or simply GUM. After the break-up of the Soviet Union in 1991, GUM had become a privately operated indoor mall. The new management rented space to hundreds of shops and larger stores—many of them branches of world-famous boutiques from around the globe.

It was Vyugin's last day in Russia before leaving for his assignment in America, and Bulgakov had sent them out into the city to gather information. He was convinced that once Vyugin saw first hand how bad the economy was, he'd be firmly committed to his assignment. It was important that Vyugin be as emotionally and intellectually committed as possible, since everything hinged on his completing the assignment successfully. He couldn't order the man to do it now as he once could have, so pragmatist that he was, he had decided to resort to psychology. His version of brain washing. Actually it was Sorokin who'd given Vyugin and Shevsky the assignment, but he'd done it on behalf of Bulgakov. Bulgakov made the decisions, and Sorokin handled the details for him. GUM was the last stop on their fact-finding tour.

The two men now stood at the entrance to Il Veneto, the chic Moscow branch of the trendy Italian-based chain of men's clothing stores. Vyugin approached a hollow-cheeked, fashionably dressed male salesperson with the latest haircut from Milan. The modishly gaunt clerk eyed him suspiciously. Vyugin flashed his wallet open to his official Office of the Prime Minister ID card and asked if he could see the manager. The slender sales clerk lost a fraction of his self control and asked them to wait where they were for a moment as he went into the back of the store to notify his superior. A minute later he poked his head out and asked them to follow him into the back of the store.

Viktor Kashvili had started his retail career in Soviet Georgia over 20 years ago. Unlike so many of his fellow bureaucratic *apparatchiks* of the Soviet era, he'd been facile and quick to adapt to Western ways. After a stint with the Benetton chain, he'd joined the growing group of Il Veneto stores that had spread across much of Europe and effortlessly worked his way up the ladder. Until recently, the Moscow store had been one of the best producers in all of Europe. It had been made clear to him that if he pulled off the GUM venture, his next stop would be a key position in the front office in Milan. But then Russia's fragile new economy had gone on the skids.

Kashvili was large of frame, though not especially tall. His hair formed a bushy dark mass framing round, almost cherubic features. His nose was round, his cheeks were round, and his eyes nearly popped from his head. He had a personality to match.

"So, gentlemen, what can I do for the representatives of our great Prime Minister?"

"We actually report to the Prime Minister's Chief of Staff, Mr. Bulgakov," explained Vyugin as genially as he could muster this late in the day.

Kashvili rolled his eyes. "Same thing."

Vyugin nodded and said, "The President and the Prime Minister are deeply concerned with the present economic conditions in Mother Russia." Kashvili looked skeptical, but allowed Vyugin to go on. "He has sent Mr. Shevsky and myself on a fact-finding mission." (Actually, Sorokin had told him that Bulgakov wanted him to see for himself just how bad things had gotten in Mother Russia and had sent him out to become indoctrinated first hand. Shevsky had been sent along to make sure that he completed the assignment, as Vyugin had always been known for having a mind of his own and not always following orders to the letter.) "He wants to know specifically how citizens are being affected by this economy."

A wry smile broadened the already wide face of Viktor Kashvili. "You have come to the right person, my government friends. I will tell you how I am affected, though I doubt that you really want to hear the truth." Vyugin suspected that Kashvili smiled all the time, whether he was happy or angry. He sensed a keen intellect hidden by the jovial exterior. He would not underestimate this affable fellow.

"Oh but we do, citizen. We do. The Prime Minister is not happy with the way things are going, and he knows he and President Kirov cannot fix things until they fully understand what's wrong."

"You want to know what's wrong! I'll tell you what's wrong," bellowed the burly store manager, the smile never leaving his heavily jowled face. "Runaway inflation. The ruble loses value every day. People who shopped here three months ago can't afford to browse here now. I've tried to keep my prices down, but to do that I give away what little profit margin I have so that the sales I do make are breakeven at best. There's no profit in that. I won't be able to pay next month's rent at this rate. The few customers I still retain are the rich and the Mafia." He sniffed, "These days there's not much difference, is there?"

Vyugin knew there was much truth in what Kashvili said. The Russian Mafia had grown exponentially since the fall of the Soviet Union. By some estimates it influenced—in one way or another—well over 50 percent of the Russian economy.

"Believe me, Kashvili, we understand. It's a story we've heard over and over from many businessmen."

"*Da*, and what do the President and the Prime Minister intend to do about it, gentlemen?"

"I don't pretend to know, but I assure you they do not take these matters lightly. Already they have plans to deal with the Mafia."

"Bah! What can they do about those thieves? They own the government anyway." At this, Shevsky's mouth fell open. People didn't talk this way to representatives of the Prime Minister. Vyugin noticed Shevsky's reaction and held up his hand. He did not want to intimidate Kashvili. He wanted to hear what else the man had to say. He then responded to the store manager.

"There is some truth in what you say. I don't deny that they have paid off some government officials, but I urge you to believe me, Kashvili, when I tell you that the Prime Minister is not one of them. (Vyugin didn't know this, but wanted it to be true.) There are many in the government who are not in the pockets of the criminal element, many."

"But the number who are grows every day, admit it Mr. Government man."

"It's a problem. I don't deny it." Shevsky winced at this candor. Vyugin, ignoring Shevsky's discomfort, continued, "We are going through difficult times." Vyugin found it hard to argue the government's case, as he'd found himself feeling much the same feelings as Kashvili. Now, though, was not the time to complicate things. Candor was more likely to elicit candor from Kashvili. "I don't have to tell you that. It is difficult for Mr. Malenkov and Mr. Kirov. They do not always see eye to eye."

"It is well known," said Kashvili sardonically. "It is also well known that the Prime Minister would like Kirov's job—that he would like to see him fail. Who does the average person trust? No disrespect, Mr. Government man, but not many people have faith in the President or your boss—especially your boss." Shevsky's eyes bulged. He could hardly contain himself at such audacity.

"If they fail, we all suffer," said Vyugin gravely, ignoring the cheekiness. "I know that some say Malenkov would like to replace the President so that he could take the country back to the old ways—that if Mr. Kirov is replaced there will be no private business. That you could not drive your Mercedes and you would not have your six-room apartment."

"Seven."

"Whatever. I know you see my point." At this, Vyugin took a step forward and placed an arm around Kashvili's shoulder. "Look, Prime Minister Malenkov is on generally good terms with the President, despite certain philosophical differences. They are working together to take on the Mafia. I don't know if Malenkov wants Kirov's job. I do know that they are both good men working at difficult jobs." In all honesty, he knew nothing of the sort. He had suspicions about one and doubts about the other. "I don't know who will be successful. I would like to see them work together more, but I can't tell you that will happen. I can tell you that the two of them are going to turn Russia around, one way or the other." How easy it was to spout political babble when you wanted to believe it.

"But does Malenkov believe in private enterprise?" asked Kashvili, who continued unabashedly, "There is nothing in his record to indicate this. To the contrary, everything he's ever done indicates he's against it." Shevsky looked as if he were going to have apoplexy. He couldn't believe the impudence of this store manager.

"He believes," blurted Shevsky, unable to contain himself any longer, "in expanding the Russian economy so that Russia will rank among the great economies of the world." Vyugin did a double take. Shevsky was spouting the party line. Unfortunately, it sounded like the party line from the Cold War days. Could Shevsky be this naive?

"You say this," responded Kashvili, "but how do we know? The word of a politician. What is it worth?"

"I understand how you feel," said Vyugin calmly. "Only time will prove if we're telling you the truth. I don't know why we're saying this much to you anyway," he said in mild reproach, glancing at Shevsky. "We're the ones looking for information."

Kashvili grinned. "People love to talk to me."

Vyugin smiled back. "I can see that. I don't suppose you would tell me if the Mafia has you under its thumb?"

"You can't be serious asking me a question like that?"

"I'm dead serious."

Kashvili shook his head incredulously. "I thought you said you've been talking to my competition. If that's true, you already know the answer. Of course I pay tribute. Everyone here pays tribute to these thieves. The bigger the store, the more they pay. It's protection money. Hah! What a laugh. We pay to protect ourselves from the same ones who protect us."

"And if you don't pay — ?"

"If we don't pay, they send their thugs to rough us up." He paused, as if trying to decide how much he should reveal about this. After a few seconds, he turned his palms upward and continued, "At first we resisted. Not all of us, mind you. Not me. I'm no hero, but some of the people here, they resist—at first, that is. One, Avram Rusoff, the Jewish jeweler on the upper level, he ends up in the hospital with three broken ribs and a bruised kidney. When he gets out he pays. These Mafia guys are not gentlemen, believe me."

Kashvili pointed across the mall atrium to a small, but elegant boutique. "See that store across the way there. No, not that one, the next one down, on the other side." Vyugin and Shevsky nodded. "Yes, that one, Cité, the ladies boutique. French. Very classy. Out of Paris. Natasha, who runs it, lived in Paris since the collapse here back in '91. Last year she comes back as Managing Director of their Russian operations. Hah! So far she's Managing Director of one store. Still, that's not bad. See for yourself—a classy operation. So last year she comes back to Moscow from Paris thinking like a Frenchman, like a Westerner. A proud woman, Natasha. You think because she's a woman these animals treat her any differently? No way. These guys come in one day and give her their usual ultimatum. She's says 'get the hell out.' They don't get out. You want to know what do they do? They destroy her computer, smash three display cases, and break her nose. Now she pays. Now we all pay."

Shevsky said, "If the government gets this under control, can you as a businessman conduct business successfully?"

Kashvili rolled his eyes. "Good God, my young friend. Surely you have a better grasp of the situation than you let on. Russian business is fighting at least three different kinds of thieves. The Mafia is just the most obvious. But inflation is a bigger thief. And the government's failure to collect taxes from everyone is even bigger. When you people don't collect taxes, you can't pay government workers. If they don't get paid, they don't shop." He shook his head disconsolately. "I consider myself an optimist, but I'm pessimistic about the chances of this government or any government ever bringing these three thieves under control."

"I think you are too pessimistic," said Vyugin without much conviction.

"You think so, do you? Then why hasn't Mr. Kirov's government already done something about these problems? My opinion? The government is a big part of the problem. Let me tell you something mister presidential aide. You people in this government fail, and the Communists will regain power. Some of us think your Mr. Malenkov would like that." Shevsky cringed, and Vyugin bit his tongue. Kashvili continued—oblivious or uncaring, "The people will allow this to happen. Why, you ask? Because they value order and predictability more than they value the chance to earn a good living. You see, many Russians mistakenly equate free enterprise with dog-eat-dog conflict. At the very best they see it producing a huge disparity in incomes. The Russian people don't want that. We've been conditioned to be jealous of anyone who does better than we do. Better that all be poor, than some do well. Russians prefer order above all else." He shook his head in quiet disapproval. Then he sighed and added, "Today, my customers represent one percent of the population. The rest can't afford my store."

"So you're part of the problem, too."

"No, no, no, no. If you believe that, then you really don't understand what's going on here in this country. If you people would allow private enterprise to develop as it has in the West, most of the people in Russia would be able to afford goods. They wouldn't all shop here at my store, but there would be stores for all incomes. And even my store would sell to a bigger segment of the population. Bigger than the one percent I get now."

"You don't consider what we have now to be private enterprise?" asked Vyugin, anticipating the answer he was going to get. "Your store is not owned by the state. What do you call it then?"

"Chaos. Chaos exploited by the Mafia. Even I think we need more order than what we have now. The present chaos will have the people begging for Communism again. Look, in France, in Italy, in the U.S., the reason free enterprise works is because they understand the system, and everyone plays by the rules because they know that everyone comes out ahead when they do. Here we are new at this. As a result we are like a schizophrenic society. Half of us want to set out on our own in search of opportunity, but the other half resents those of us who are successful. They call us greedy and say this is why Communism existed—to prevent people from getting rich on the backs of the rest of society. It is understandable that we have this schizophrenia, but it is responsible for the success of the Mafia and the weakness of the government. Some people secretly are glad that the Mafia exploits business. They see this as a crude way of keeping business down, of robbing the rich like in the Robin Hood fable."

"You said this schizophrenia as you call it is also responsible for weak government. How so?" asked Vyugin.

"Government is a mirror of the greater society—the confusion in the greater society. Today, your government is a delicately balanced coalition of democrats, socialists, Communists, and anarchists. Everyone but the Communists wants a government that is different from those of the past—ideally a democracy, but since we've never had anything close to democracy, we have nothing to go back to. Most of us wouldn't recognize democracy if we fell over it.

"All of you in government have your own idea of what a democracy should be, but none is based on experience so you must learn by trial and error. Think for a moment. Compare Russia with other former Soviet countries. Hungary had a legacy of democracy. So did Czechoslovakia, and Poland. They weren't perfect democracies, but they worked. After they left the Soviet bloc there were people still alive in those countries who remembered how democracy worked. Russia doesn't have that advantage, and look at us. We are fumbling. And while we fumble, the gangsters exploit us."

"The Prime Minister intends to take action soon," said Vyugin, hopefully with some authority in his voice.

"He had better do so very soon. There is not much time left, believe me."

Tomorrow, thought Vyugin, with an involuntary shudder, I'll be off to America to do my part for the cause.

Chapter 3

Mark Dantry took a hurried last gulp of coffee before heading toward the door to the garage of his comfortable five-bedroom colonial. He bent down and gave his wife a quick kiss on the run.

"You look intense this morning," said Beth Dantry, a touch of concern in her voice. "You'll get there in time." she smiled, a smile of understanding. "They're not going to start without you."

He stopped and grinned. "I suppose not, but this is more than just another meeting. When it's over, we'll know whether we're likely to have enough votes to approve the loan or not. It's going to be very close, and we're all feeling it." He was referring to a $40 billion loan that the International Monetary Fund had been considering for Russia. By all accounts, without the loan, the present Western-leaning Kirov administration might not survive. The I.M.F. had been considering it for months, and today, finally, it was coming down to a vote. As an American and as Executive Director of the I.M.F., his thoughts on issues of this import carried considerable weight. He was the number-two person in the I.M.F., so naturally, people unfamiliar with the prestigious, but arcane, world of the international financial organization would expect his influence to be somewhat less than that of the top executive,

Managing Director Claude DeBuchet of France. But that's not the way it worked. The founders of the I.M.F. had come up with a system that allocated a total of nearly one-and-a-half million votes to the member countries. The U.S., as the major source of money for the organization's loans, was entitled to slightly more than 265,000 votes of the total—nearly three-and-a-half times as many votes as second-tier members such as France, Germany, and Japan. Third and fourth-tier countries—countries with even less to contribute—got still fewer votes.

Dantry cut an impressive figure. He was well above average in height, with dark, almost black wavy hair that set off the sculpted, angular features of his strong face. When he looked at you, his gaze was arresting. He looked the part of a heavy hitter in the world of international finance. He could easily have passed for a finance minister or even a head of state.

Dantry had his hand on the knob of the door to the garage when he remembered something. "If I have an hour free after the meeting this afternoon, I'll run into DC and take another look at that townhouse we saw last weekend. That is, if you're still interested." The fact was, she had never been as interested as he was. She'd been happily content living in the Virginia suburbs. But for the last two or three years he'd had his heart set on moving into Georgetown in the heart of Washington. Considering his schedule, it would be more convenient living in town, he said. She knew that convenience was only part of it. He'd always wanted to live in the city and had accommodated her interest in living in Falls Church because he knew living in the suburbs would make her happy. Then, three months ago, he'd brought the subject up again, and she'd reluctantly gone along with it.

She'd pretended to be enthusiastic, for she knew that if he suspected that her agreement were given with any hesitation, he never would have pursued it. It was always a source of amazement to her that her husband could have risen to such an important position in the world, given his personality. He wasn't self-absorbed. He simply didn't hunger for power the way 95 percent of the people in Washington did. He had the power, but he hadn't sought it, and he didn't seek more. She smiled inwardly at how lucky she was to be married to such a man.

"You know you like it, Mark," she said. "You don't have to look at it again if you really want it. You already said it's perfect." Then hoping it didn't sound like an afterthought, she added, "I think so, too. The only thing I wonder is can we afford it?"

"I think we can," he said, accepting her support at face value, and trying to suppress the excitement he felt at hearing her express that support. Then, to at least appear somewhat mature about it, he added, "But there are a few things I didn't look at very carefully the first time. I've made a list of things that I want to check out more carefully." He'd be going through the motions to make it look good, and they both knew it.

She smiled, "You're so methodical, my husband."

"Worked with you," he grinned, adding, "but, my checklist was a lot longer then."

"Get out of here. Now you will be late, mister international money man. No, wait. I almost forgot."

"What?"

"Have you done that bio for Princeton?"

He pursed his lips. "Damn! No, completely forgot. Remind me tonight, and I'll take care of it." The president of Princeton had called him recently saying that the university wanted to grant him an honorary doctorate at next year's graduation ceremony. Would he mind sending the university an up-to-date bio for the special booklet they prepared for the event. Also so the president could introduce him properly. He'd agreed, of course. It was flattering, but this Russian emergency had completed dominated his life in the last month. "God, I hope this meeting goes well so I can get back to living a semi-normal life."

Inwardly she laughed at the unlikelihood of that, but all he saw was a warm smile.

He kissed her again and was gone.

The Lexus purred to life, and he backed carefully out of the garage into the street. When he'd first bought the car a few months ago, it had been one of life's small pleasures. He remembered how he'd looked forward even to the short drives to his office. Now, though, his mind was so occupied with his work that he took the car for granted.

Dantry eased his foot onto the accelerator and started down the street. Before he let himself be caught up in the intensity of the upcoming day, he took one last moment to "smell the roses." It was spring—in his opinion, the best time of the year in Virginia. The upcoming summer would inevitably be oppressively hot and much too muggy. And winters in recent years had brought almost as much snow as he remembered from his childhood days in Upstate New York. But the spring in Virginia was delightful.

The streets in Dantry's upscale neighborhood wound gracefully through a verdant exurban topography of balsams, southern pines, silver maples, and plentiful magnolias. It was an area of two and four-acre zoning, and, he reflected wryly, correspondingly high taxes. Not that he was complaining. He and Beth both loved the area. His reason for wanting to move into the city was that for as long as he could remember he'd had this urge to be part of the energy that only a city could offer. He realized that he might discover that the city wasn't what he'd expected, but he had to give it a try. They could always come back to the burbs.

He took a right onto Cypress Drive. He always enjoyed driving on Cypress because of the way it gently coursed through the rolling hills that made this end of town so attractive. The finely manicured lawns, each vying with their neighbor, made him feel a bit guilty at being fortunate enough to live in such an area. His first-hand experience at seeing how much of the rest of world lived had only intensified such feelings. Over the past 20 years he'd visited underdeveloped countries in Africa, South America, and Asia. He'd seen how the other half lived, and it had touched him deeply. Up ahead Cypress took a fairly sharp drop. The first time he'd driven the street, shortly after they'd first moved here, he'd gone too fast and nearly ripped off the underside of a brand-new Acura. Since then he'd driven more carefully. The kid part of him couldn't help but think that this part of Cypress would be a great hill in the winter for sleigh riding. SLEDING.

As he headed down the steep incline, deliberately keeping his speed to a prudent 35 miles per hour, a spinning soccer ball spurted out from a lush green lawn on his right. Where there were soccer balls, there were surely kids not far behind. Dantry's reflexes were still sharp for a man in his mid-fifties, and he jammed his foot on the brake in a nanosecond.

Nothing happened, though. The Lexus kept going. A boy, who couldn't have been more than 11 or 12, darted into the street. Dantry jammed his foot on the brake again, this time harder than the first. Nothing. The pedal went all the way to the floor. The Lexus barely missed the startled and clearly frightened boy, who leapt out of the way with inches to spare. The car was gaining speed. Brake, dammit! Nothing.

He swerved and barely managed to avoid hitting another kid. But the swerve had taken him too far to his left, and the Lexus ricocheted off a small red car parked at the curb. Dantry heard screams from the car as he hurtled past it. Nothing he could do. The Lexus was now doing over 40. Dantry had all he could do to keep the car from hitting a white-haired woman leaning into the open door of a parked white sedan. The road wound to the right now, and the hill was steeper. Dantry felt panic as he realized that he had no control over his car's speed, and very little control over its direction. Without brakes, he would never negotiate the next turn. His only chance was to find an open field and hope that he could keep the car upright until it came to a stop.

Suddenly it dawned on him. The parking brake. He gave a tug. There was no resistance. It was as if the handle were not connected to the brakes. He tried again. Still nothing.

The only open area within sight was protected by a low metal guardrail. The guardrail was the least of his worries. Just beyond the rail the ground appeared to slope downward, though he couldn't tell how steeply, and there was no time to check. The speedometer said 55 now. He had no choice. Nether set of brakes responded. If he didn't go for the guardrail, he'd plunge directly into a large Colonial-style house. He yanked on the wheel and aimed the Lexus directly for the guardrail and prayed. As the front end of the car made screeching contact with the metal guardrail, he could now see that the drop-off was far more precipitous than it had first appeared from the street. Things had happened so fast that it never occurred to him to ram the car into low gear. That is, until now as the slope of the land fell away into a deep abyss of trees and granite outcroppings. Before Mark Dantry died, he had less than five seconds to consider how well hidden the small canyon was from the deceptively peaceful street he'd left behind him.

Chapter 4

President Kirov pushed back from his massive wooden desk—its first user had been Czar Nicholas in the late 19th Century. An ancient deep slash across one edge of the desk was said to have been made by the Czar with his dress sword in a fit of rage when told that a group of Bolsheviks was protesting his reign. A fiery intensity burned in Kirov's coal-black eyes. His slender appearance belied the latent strength of his wiry frame, a body that had helped his team prevail in two all-Soviet Union soccer cups when he was a much younger man. He stared at Gennadi Potemkin, the man sitting across the desk from him. Potemkin, the president's chief of staff, and normally a man of considerable self-possession, felt a churning in his stomach as he met the glare of his superior.

"It's too soon to know, Mr. President. It could have been an accident, but it does look suspicious. I had someone contact Lexus in Japan, and they claim that they have never had a car whose brakes failed."

Kirov nodded his acceptance. "It's a good car. For the present we'll believe what they say. I don't like this, Gennadi. You realize that if what we suspect is true, this could be disastrous for Russia."

Potemkin pursed his full lips and nodded grimly. "Yes sir. Things could go very badly indeed."

"What's the likelihood of this being orchestrated right here in Russia?"

"Malenkov?"

"Or Bulgakov?"

"I wouldn't put it past either of them, sir."

"Well, we may be getting ahead of ourselves. We have no proof yet that this was done deliberately."

"No, but it is strange that one of the key votes we need should die on the eve of the voting—and in a car that has never had a problem with failing brakes. Do you believe in coincidences like this, Mr. President?"

"No. I'm afraid that we need to assume the worst. If we're wrong, we can deal with that later."

"I just learned from our embassy people in Washington that the I.M.F., out of respect for Dantry, has postponed voting on the loan for at least a week. Even without his votes, we may still have enough."

Kirov leaned forward. "I hope so. We can't keep the army at bay much longer. And the miners. And, well, you know as well as I do."

Kirov was referring to the military that had gone without pay for weeks. Coal miners and other essential workers, too, were owed back pay. The troops were literally getting restless. The military had never trusted his inclination to improve Russia's relationship with the West anyway, and now, the saber rattling by the generals was serious. Russia desperately needed the I.M.F. loan to pay the soldiers, the sailors, the miners and a dozen other critical groups before all hell broke loose. The stability of the nation depended on that loan. Without it, Kirov feared a takeover by the military, whose leaders would like nothing better than a good excuse to "save" the nation from his ineffectual leadership. Kirov knew his promises were losing their credibility. Workers couldn't eat promises. With the loan, there was a better than even chance that he would have time to implement his plans to kick-start Russia's foundering economy. By eliminating much of the red tape that stood in the way of business, and by denationalizing more of the the former Soviet-era industry, he was sure he could prime the pump of the latent entreprenurial spirit in the nation that only needed encouragement and support. Whether this was going to happen now, he realized, looking up at his trusted aide, was iffy at best. He continued the gloomy discourse.

"If someone else doesn't die, too, maybe we'll get lucky. Let us think about this for a moment. Who would have the capability of bringing about a death like this?"

"A trained assassin. The KGB had plenty of them in the past. So did the CIA."

"Precisely. And most of them are probably bored out of their minds since the break-up, eh?"

Potemkin allowed himself a flicker of a smile. "No doubt, sir."

"If you were to guess, Gennadi, who would you bet on?"

"KGB old-timers. Bulgakov knew most of their former operatives. Hell, many of them worked for him at one time or other. He could bring one of these people back for a private mission. Most of them would do anything for him. And now he can pay them a lot better."

"Do you think Malenkov would even know about this?"

"He's the one who would benefit, and he is a Communist, sir."

"I was, too, but I wouldn't do this."

"I know, sir, but Malenkov is still a Communist at heart— an old-style Communist. He adored Stalin and was devoted to that bumpkin, Khrushchev."

"True, but I'm not sure he'd approve of something like this, unless I'm really wrong about him."

"He'd be taking a terrible risk."

"And what would he gain—chaos, open rebellion?"

"The voters would blame the disorder on you, sir. They'd say you couldn't govern, that you'd allowed the country to fall into anarchy."

Kirov leaned forward, rubbing his eyes slowly. Potemkin observed him carefully and couldn't help thinking that his boss seemed older lately. Potemkin had serious reservations about his boss's ability to handle the demands of his job. Kirov was too good a man to lead an undisciplined, confused nation to prosperity Gradually the President dropped his hands to his lap and spoke quietly to his chief of staff. "If it's Malenkov, he must not be allowed to do this, Gennadi. You and I both know what kind of government he would impose on Russia."

"I have a good idea, sir. He'd take us back to the Soviet era."

"He believes in a strong Russia."

"You do, too, sir."

"Yes, but he would achieve it by controlling the people. I know him, Gennadi. He believes that the people need to be told what's good for them. They need to be told what they can and cannot do. He believes that they want to be told—that they want order more than they want democracy. He's an authoritarian of the old school. He's not a Stalin or a Khrushchev, but he would do whatever it takes to create the kind of order he believes Russia needs."

"Maybe he would, sir."

"I just don't know if he'd go this far to gain control of the country."

"Someone is, Mr. President."

Chapter 5

Washington—The Oval Office

"You see this, Ron?" The President reached forward across his desk and handed his senior advisor the front section of the *Washington Post*. "Lower right hand corner, page three. Almost missed it. It's short. Go ahead and read it. Then we'll talk."

Ron DelCicchio read the brief item carefully. He'd learned from past experience not to scan things President Coleman asked him to read because Coleman often expected him to have full command of the details—even after a quick read. When he'd finished he looked up. "Jesus! He was here for lunch last week."

"Hell of a guy, too," said Coleman. "Knew him at Yale. Funny thing, I always thought that someday he could be President."

"This could have serious repercussions, sir."

"Russia you mean?"

"Yessir. His vote could very well have determined whether they got that loan that Kirov was counting on. Without his vote..." DelCicchio turned the palms of his hands upward and returned the President's intent gaze with a grimace of his own.

"I'm sure his number-two man, whoever that is, will vote the same way," said Coleman.

"From what I understand of the I.M.F., sir, that's not always the case."

"As an American, Dantry would have reflected American foreign policy. His back-up would certainly do the same thing. Why wouldn't he?"

"You'd think so, but most of these guys are pretty independent thinkers from what I've heard. They're all highly successful wealthy men. Most of them self-made. They like to think they've made up their own mind. What Dantry's back-up will no doubt do, is take some time to study the situation—even though you'd think, as Mark Dantry's number two man, he'd be up to speed. Apparently the organization culture in the I.M.F. is such that no one likes to be thought of as rubber stamping a country's policy, or for that matter a colleague's."

"That could make for some fairly bizarre voting," said the President. "Carry that to its logical end, and I could see someone voting against his own country's best interest—just to show how independent he is."

DelCicchio smiled. "Usually that doesn't happen. All I'm saying is that, on rare occasions, it has occurred. It probably won't this time. What's more likely to happen, though, is that the back-up guy may take several weeks to prepare himself before he's ready to cast his vote. The I.M.F. would humor him and delay the vote for him. I don't know if President Kirov has that much time, sir. He's under an awful lot of pressure."

"Yes, the clock is ticking on this one. Strange, most people reading the item in the *Post* will react to the fact of his death at the peak of his career, but they'll have no idea how grave the implications of his death are for international stability. This could mean the return to the Cold War."

"Or worse."

Chapter 6

Tony Dantry eased up on the throttle of the aging twin-screw 36-foot Chris Craft cabin cruiser. It was beginning to show its age—it was nearly 18 years old—but it was still in pretty good shape. Good enough for him. He couldn't have afforded a new one, anyway.

Much of April and May had been cool and damp in New York. Then June came in, and it felt as if Mother Nature had skipped spring and moved directly into summer. The heat in the city hung heavy, and the humidity made you feel like crap. This was one of the reasons last year he'd chosen to move to City Island, a small community literally on an island just off the coast of Bronx Borough. At least here you got some relief from the oppressive heat. What little breeze there was seemed stronger on City Island. And you could always take the boat out on the sound as he had today. Some residents liked to say that City Island was a little bit of New England right there in the Bronx. That might be stretching things a bit, thought Dantry. Still, it did have the feel of a small coastal town. The New England analogy wasn't all that far fetched. Well, maybe a little. Anyway, he liked it. Felt comfortable there.

He'd lived on the boat for awhile, partly because he loved the water and partly because it was relatively cheap. Not as cheap as his friends thought, but cheaper than a decent apartment. Of course you didn't have a lot of room on a 36 footer, but what there was was all his, and it was mobile. He could go anywhere with that boat.

Then he'd met Joanna. Two months after they met, he'd moved in with her. It was good, but there were times when he missed living on the boat. Still, that didn't keep him from using it. Her apartment was on City Island, so it took all of five minutes to walk to the dock and crank up the engines. He still went out on the sound. He did that as often as he could. This was one of those times.

He was now only a couple-hundred yards from shore. He throttled the two engines down to a throaty gurgling chug and slowly directed the boat toward the marina at the foot of Ditmars Street, where he rented a slip. It was approaching noon, and even though he was on the water, now that he'd slowed the boat down to a few knots, he could feel the oppressive weight of the midday heat, the hot summer sun reflecting back off the water nearly blinding him. He reached for his sunglasses, thinking it rather foolish that he'd waited till the end of his trip to do so. He waved to a man who looked to be close to seventy steering an old Boston whaler. The boat was less than a hundred feet to his port and was also returning from fishing.

"Any luck, Charlie?"

"A few blues, Tony. Pretty small, though. How about you?"

"Couple of flounder. That's all. Jeez, this heat."

"Yeah. Looks like we're in for one of those summers. Hey, you take care now, Tony." They waved to each other again and returned their concentration to their navigation.

As Dantry approached the weather-beaten dock he notice a familiar figure standing at the end. She wore khaki shorts with a white blouse. It was Joanna, and she looked great. As the boat eased closer to the pier he could see that she looked serious. Normally, when he came back to the dock and found her waiting there for him she'd be grinning—or at least smiling.

He smiled and waved. She waved back, but still no smile. The boat eased alongside the pier, bumping gently two or three times against the gray sunbleached wooden posts. With the touch of someone who'd done it many times before, Dantry reversed the two engines and brought the boat to a lumbering rest as it pitched and lurched in the choppy water. The Chris Craft rocked gently as Joanna helped him tie up and then jumped agilely into the boat onto the weathered wood-slatted rear deck. He killed the engines and made his way toward her, expecting a welcoming kiss, but getting only a quick perfunctory peck.

Something was wrong.

"What is it?" he asked, suddenly experiencing a sense of dark foreboding.

She looked away, avoiding his eyes. He grabbed her shoulders, forcing her to face him. "For Christ's sake, what is it?"

"It's your brother. He's been in an accident."

"And?"

"Oh God, Tony, he's—"

"He's dead. You're telling me he's dead? Oh Jesus! Oh Christ! What happened?"

"All I know is that he was driving—to work I think—and somehow he went off an embankment. I don't know the details."

"Who told you this?"

"A policeman, from Virginia. He wanted to talk to you, but I told him he could tell me whatever he had to say. Oh God, Tony, I'm so sorry." She hugged him and burst into tears. They stood there a few seconds rocking. Finally he broke away.

"You have the name of this cop? And a phone number?"

"Yes. I brought them with me."

He took a deep breath, and exhaled slowly. "Better give 'em to me."

With the information in hand, he disappeared briefly into the boat's cabin and returned with his cell phone. He was already dialing.

Barely twenty words had been exchanged between them since they'd been on the road. Twenty-four hours ago, he'd been in his boat heading up the coast in search of flounder. Today, he and Joanna were in his Jeep Cherokee heading south on I-95 to Virginia. He still couldn't believe it. Nothing in his life had prepared him for this. When his father died of liver cancer, it hit him hard, but it had been expected. He'd been sick for quite awhile. His dad hadn't been especially young—74 to be precise—so it wasn't exactly premature. But Mark, his big brother, was at the top of his game. He had what some people called presence. He had money. He rubbed shoulders with world figures. Everything he touched turned out perfectly. He'd never known failure in his life.

Strange, he thought, that his brother's death had hit him like an unexpected blow to gut. He was having a harder time dealing with it than he would have expected because the two of them had not been close while Mark was alive. Not close at all. Hell, they'd avoided each other except for the obligatory family get togethers. It wasn't just the age difference, either. Everything Mark had done had pleased their parents—not intentionally, but because that's just the way he was. He was a doer. He was good at everything he did. In some cases, very good. Things came easily to Mark, while Tony, the younger one, had failed to conform to what everyone expected from the first-born son. Tony'd never been conventional. He'd been a maverick from the start. And when he joined the CIA, his liberal, dovish parents didn't hide their disappointment.

Damn! Why was it all of a sudden so complicated now? For the past 52 years he'd been comfortable with his own interpretation of why his brother had been such a pain in the ass. Now the son-of-a-bitch hadn't even given him a chance to sort out his feelings. While Mark was alive, there had always been time to deal with it. In the back of his mind he'd always figured that he'd eventually stop and take the time. Now there was no time.

Chapter 7

Vyugin sipped from a steaming cup of coffee he'd prepared in the little coffee maker provided in the hotel bathroom. The coffee was actually better than he expected. Not weak like so much of the American coffee he'd had. He kept one eye on the TV where from Moscow a female CNN talking head was expounding on the political crisis that was building in the Russian capital city. Just yesterday Vyugin had arrived at the Marriott Courtyard Crystal City in Arlington, Virginia. He'd spent the previous nine days in DC at the Hilton on Connecticut Avenue under a different name. It was good to change hotels periodically. Longtime residents of hotels aroused suspicion. He'd chosen the Courtyard because it was adjacent to Washington's National Airport and only a short drive into DC.

Bulgakov had told him the job had to be done within a week, but he'd demanded a few more days. It was extremely important to immerse yourself in the intimate details of the target's daily routine. You needed enough time to allow an acceptable margin of safety. It was true that most targets followed a similar routine day in and day out. But there were too many exceptions. If the target was away from home on holiday or on business travel, he could easily vary from his usual routine. And even when the subject was at home, this kind of variance sometimes happened. Some targets deviated from their normal pattern every other week —or every Friday. A week of observation and planning wasn't good enough.

He'd been using his time in Washington to plan the operation. He gradually came to realize that he didn't need as much time as the two weeks he'd told Bulgakov he would need. After a few days in D.C., he knew that he was ready—that he had the operation pretty well scoped out. But he didn't tell Bulgakov or

Sorokin. Instead, he took his time—more time than necessary. In effect, he'd been foot dragging.

He tried to remember when the first doubts had set in—when he knew that he couldn't go ahead with the assignment. He hadn't been comfortable with the mission from the first time Bulgakov outlined it for him, but he hadn't until the last day or two been able to put his finger on why. He now realized that, when he accepted the assignment, he'd been thinking like an old-time Communist—as if the U.S. and Russia were still enemies. Something on the TV caught his eye.

The CNN woman was saying something now about how the Russian crisis had intensified virtually overnight as a direct result of yesterday's accidental death of I.M.F. Deputy Managing Director Mark Dantry. She went on to describe the car accident. Vyugin did a double take and leaned closer. Was he hearing right? Mark Dantry dead? What was going on here? He knew he hadn't done it, as he was still planning the operation. Admittedly, he'd been procrastinating. It wasn't all that difficult an execution. Or wouldn't have been. But now the TV was telling him Dantry had died, and in exactly the manner he'd discussed with Bulgakov. What the hell was going on here? It was too similar and too timely to be a coincidence. But who else would want Dantry dead? And even if there was someone, how likely was it that they would do it the way he'd been planning to do it?

The CNN segment broke away to some old footage of Mark Dantry. An accomplished man, thought, Vyugin appreciatively. More footage now showing a much younger Dantry in an American football uniform back in his Yale University days. Apparently Dantry had been a star athlete in his day. Now more footage showing him with his wife at his side, followed by another 15 seconds or so of him receiving some sort of award from President Clinton back in the late '90s.

Vyugin switched off the television. This sort of thing made him uncomfortable. It was always harder to eliminate someone who was obviously likeable and who was not himself an international foot soldier. Getting rid of Dantry had been necessary, he supposed, but it would not have been pleasant. Not the kind of kill you could easily reconcile with your soul. A religious term, but one he could understand. He slammed the palm of his hand against the door casement. Damn! The only way to justify this kind of job was to view it in relation to the greater good. Fortunately, he no longer had to rationalize this one because the man was already dead.

CNN had switched to the familiar visage of Preston Hartman in Washington, who was explaining that the death of Mark Dantry could have a direct bearing on the internal stability of Russia. Hartman proceeded to explain that Russia had applied for a huge loan from the International Monetary Fund, and now it was uncertain whether that loan would be approved. "President Kirov has been counting on this loan, rumored to be in excess of $40 billion," said Hartman. "The shocking death of Mark Dantry, an American and the man who controlled the largest number of votes at the I.M.F., could mean at worst that the loan will not be approved. Since the board member with the most votes is dead, out of respect for the United States, it's likely that the voting will be postponed for a week or more. At best, it means that Russia will have to wait a week or two to find out if the loan has been approved. This could be disastrous for the Kirov government." Archive footage of the Duma, the Russian Parliament's lower house, showed a member shaking his hand violently, obviously agitated about some legislative point he was trying to make. Hartman continued his commentary:

"There is no certainty that Kirov can hold off the wolves that long, for many believe that Mikhail Malenkov, the prime minister, has been clandestinely working to undermine his boss so that he can become President." More archive footage, this time, of an angry Malenkov with news people somewhere in Moscow. "In the eyes of the West, such an eventuality has to be viewed with grave concern, since Malenkov is an avowed Communist, who landed his present position as a compromise candidate foisted on Kirov by the rejuvenated and growing Communist Party. It is known that Malenkov dislikes the West and the U.S. in particular. He has become popular in Russia because of frequent speeches in favor of rebuilding Russia into the world power it once was when it was the dominant nation in the old Soviet Union. It is no secret that Malenkov believes the way to regain this power is through a renewed emphasis on the military. If Kirov's government fails to achieve the desperately needed loan, Malenkov and the Communists who back him will undoubtedly try to make a case for a no-confidence vote in the Duma, the lower house of the Russian national parliament, and force a new vote. The likely outcome of such a vote would be the election of Malenkov to the Presidency. Should he fail to be elected, it would not surprise this observer if the Communists were to actively foment civil unrest in order to wrest control of the country by *coup d'état*." Video footage changes to a scene somewhere in Beijing.

Vyugin sat back stunned. According to the TV, Dantry would probably have voted in favor of the loan. Bulgakov had said they expected him to vote against it. How could Kirov and Malenkov have been so wrong? And how could Bulgakov have been so wrong? Unless…..

The phone rang. It could only be Bulgakov or Sorokin.

Vyugin turned off the TV.

"Good morning, Vyugin." It was Sorokin. "Congratulations. You've done well."

Vyugin had been playing out this conversation in his head since he first heard about Dantry's death a few moments ago. Should he play along and take the credit? It would probably be easier. Less complicated. He'd be assured of his pension. In his own mind he'd know he hadn't done it, but it wouldn't matter. Bulgakov and Sorokin would be pleased, and he could go home to Mila. But then, what if by some chance Bulgakov and Sorokin did know. Perhaps they even knew who did it. It's amazing, he reflected, how much the brain can cover while watching a brief newscast.

"Vyugin? Are you there?"

"Yes, I'm here. Sorokin, I wish I could take the credit for this event, but I can't. I don't know who did it. Maybe it *was* an accident."

Vyugin heard a long breath being taken on the other end of the line. "It was no accident, my friend. Bulgakov sent a second team to Washington, and it looks as if they moved too fast. Though the results are good, of course."

Vyugin was furious. "And you're telling me this now! Good God, Sorokin, what the hell is going on? You're telling me that Bulgakov didn't trust me? That he sent someone else to do my job?"

"I know how you must feel. Believe me, I wouldn't have done it this way, but Bulgakov is a perfectionist. It's not that he doesn't trust you, it's just that he likes to build in assurance—to be sure a job gets done."

"You gave me the assignment. That should be all the assurance you need." In all his years with the KGB during the Cold War he had never been undermined like this. Never been subjected to this kind of insult. "As for the loan, I was told by Bulgakov that Dantry was going to vote against it. I hear now that it is very likely that he would have voted for it. I have to tell you that I find this very upsetting. Did your other team kill someone who would have helped our government, and if so, why? And if that is not the case, why was he killed?"

"It is a very complex issue, my friend. Do not concern yourself with the politics. It is enough that you remain committed to helping us save Russia."

"My God, man, you ask me to come to America and risk my life taking out another man—a good man I might add—and now it appears that it was all unnecessary, that I never had to take these risks."

"I appreciate what you're saying, but if you really care about Mother Russia, then you'll see that the greater good has been served. Besides, comrade, we…"

"Don't call me comrade," snapped Vyugin. "I am not your comrade." The holdover term from the Communist era annoyed the hell out of him—especially when used by the unctuous Sorokin.

"I did not mean to offend you. Please accept my apologies."

Vyugin was about to comment on the absurdity of his being the friend of such a weasel, but decided it wasn't worth it. Better to get the call over with. He sighed and tried to control his voice, "Accepted. Go ahead. You started to say something."

"It has been decided that Dantry's demise is good for our cause, but it's probably not going to be enough to insure that we achieve our goal. We've decided that at least one more member of the I.M.F. must have an untimely death in order to insure that we achieve our goal.

"You've what?"

"I think you heard me. We've decided another key I.M.F. figure must be eliminated. So you see, you still will get your chance to do your part for Mother Russia."

Vyugin couldn't believe his ears. "I have to tell you, Sorokin, that I'm beginning to have serious doubts about this whole scheme. First you people ask me to take out one man. Then I learn that someone else was sent to do the same job and that he was allowed, hell not allowed, encouraged to beat me to the job. Now you're asking me to take out another man—a man who I'm guessing would vote in favor of a $40 billion dollar loan for our country. I am no financier, but I think I'm missing something here. Anyway, assuming I don't fully understand this, and the mission has merit that somehow eludes my limited capacities, how do I know this other operative won't preempt me on this, too? Hell, how do I know we won't get in each other's way? By the way, who is this other man?"

"He's J. Martin Chandler, First Deputy Managing Director of the I.M.F., from the U.S." Vyugin didn't recognize the name.

A pregnant pause before Vyugin replies, "I see. Another American. Are they our only targets?"

"It has nothing to do with that. It's just that they have the power in the I.M.F."

"Incidentally, I was not asking about the intended target. I was asking about the other operative. Who else did you people send over here?"

"It….. it is not important that you know this."

"God damn it, Sorokin, who is it?"

"Very well. We sent two men: Oleg Pentovsky and Yevgeny Zhukov. You probably don't know them. They are er…..younger than you. Very good, though. They are there to assist you, if you need it."

"I don't need any help. Keep them out of my way."

"Bulgakov wants you to use them. They will arrange to meet you today. You work out the details of how the three of you do the job."

A sigh of resignation.

"All right. I'm in charge, though."

A pause. "Of course, you're in charge. By the way, Bulgakov is concerned that the death of a second I.M.F. official might arouse undue suspicion, so he has a plan he would like you to use when you eliminate Chandler."

Vyugin felt a tightening in his stomach. "Yes, what kind of plan does he have in mind?"

"In order to divert suspicion, he has directed me to have you take out Chandler when he's in a crowd or at least with several people." Vyugin felt his stomach tighten again. "Of course, that means that some of the these other people will have to be eliminated, too, I'm afraid." Sorokin paused to let this sink in. "You understand, Vyugin?"

"I understand—entirely too well. This is reckless and unjustifiable. I am not a terrorist, Sorokin, I'm a soldier."

"I understand, but I'm afraid there is no other way. Remember, it's important that these others have no relationship to the I.M.F. Do you read me?"

"I read you," barked Vyugin angrily. "For Christ's sake, do you know what you're asking me to do?"

"Yes, of course I do. It's a very unpleasant business. We know that. But this is for the greater good, the good of Mother Russia."

"These people, whoever they are, are completely innocent."

"Dantry was innocent, and so is Chandler, you have no qualms about them."

"That's where you're wrong, Sorokin. You think because I do this that I like it. Dantry and Chandler are central to solving our problem. Or so you tell me. With them it is unavoidable. But what you and Bulgakov are suggesting..."

"Not suggesting, my friend. This must be done."

Vyugin gritted his teeth. "I don't see why."

"In a sense they, too, are central to solving our problem. It is not pleasant, I grant you, but unfortunately it must be done. We cannot let Mother Russia be destroyed by West-leaning bankers and their circle of greedy capitalist friends, can we?"

"Those are tired old Communist words, Sorokin. Times have changed, or at least I thought they had."

"I don't like what you're saying. I thought you were committed to helping us save Russia?"

"That I am, Sorokin, but I'm beginning to wonder how I go about doing that. You're willingness to kill any number of innocent people in the name of a good cause sounds more like Stalin than it does Kirov or Malenkov. You and Bulgakov told me that we need to get rid of these I.M.F. bankers because they would vote against this huge loan for Mother Russia and that failure of the loan's passage would allow the country to slip into anarchy or chaos. Malenkov, you said, would help Kirov bring order and stability to the country without imposing the old Stalinist terror. Now, I'm beginning to wonder who the real threat to the country is." Vyugin couldn't believe that Kirov would let Bulgakov and Sorokin get involved with such directives. He even doubted that Malenkov would support such measures. Malenkov was known for his toughness, but as far as Vyugin knew, he had never ordered the death of people just because they got in his way. Vyugin was beginning to wonder who was behind these assassination missions.

"Calm down, my friend," said Sorokin. "You've got it all wrong. We told you the truth. I know your assignment is unpleasant, but this is a form of warfare, and I don't have to tell you that war is messy. There really is no other way. Just take care of it, and you can retire to your dacha in comfort."

Again the appeal to his material comforts. He now saw that this is what had persuaded him to accept the assignment in the first place—against his better judgment. This and the carefully orchestrated tour of Moscow businesses that Bulgakov must have believed would be the final clincher. As Vyugin reflected, he realized that he had overlooked the obvious signs from that little tour—that many business people were as distrustful of Malenkov and his followers as they were of Kirov. He'd overlooked it because there had been enough negativity to go around for all. He'd allowed personal gain to have the upper hand and had rationalized that he was serving his country.

Now he was caught in the middle. If he refused to carry out his assignment, there was a very good chance that Bulgakov would order his execution. For all he knew, that was the real reason he had sent Pentovsky and Zhukov. He, Vyugin, knew too much. The best thing he could do now was play for time and try to figure out how to get out of this mess before he allowed himself to become as evil as the people he was working for. So far, through an unexpected turn of events, he could still live with himself—that is, if Bulgakov and Sorokin would allow it.

"All right, all right," he said finally, "I was just spouting off. This change took me by surprise. So tell me about these people. I don't even know them."

"Bulgakov knows them. They used to work for him. He says they're the best—you excepted, of course."

"Of course. Look, I don't care how good they are. I don't need them. But if Bulgakov feels strongly about it, I'll work with them. How do I reach them?"

"They'll contact you within an hour of this call. Please make sure you're available for their contact."

Vyugin did not like being at the beck and call of two junior agents—agents he didn't want to work with in the first place. This whole assignment was becoming a nightmare. He hesitated only a few seconds before finally saying, "I give the orders, or I'm out of this."

"No problem. You give the orders."

Vyugin sighed and drew in a deep breath. "What you're talking about means using a bomb. Is this what you want?"

"There are other ways, I suppose, but a bomb would seem efficient and expeditious. But I'll leave the method to you. You're the professional. And don't forget, you have help now. Pentovsky and Zhukov will be at your side." He paused to let this sink in. "We have every confidence in you. Your country needs your help. Don't let us down."

"Sounds as if you people are starting to panic."

"That's ridiculous. We just need to be sure. We cannot afford to have that loan approved. Do you realize what that would mean?"

"I'm beginning to wonder. When Bulgakov first presented this to me, I seem to recall the concern was that the loan might not be approved. You seem to have completely reversed your position on this."

"I think you are mistaken, my friend. You must have misunderstood."

"Right."

Chapter 8

The Washington offices of the International Monetary Fund
Managing Director Claude Saint-Germain, of France removes his
reading glasses, rubs his tired eyes and slowly scans the concerned
faces around the 20-foot boardroom table. As the eyes of his
colleagues meet his, he begins the discussion he had dreaded. He
speaks in English, the lingua franca of international discourse.

"Gentlemen, if you're like me, you still have not quite
accepted the death of Mark Dantry." A couple of nods and a few
subdued comments of agreement greet him from each side of the
long table. Saint-Germain nods solemn confirmation and
continues. "We must, however, go on with our business. All of you
know, regardless of your position on the subject, just how
important our impending vote on the proposed Russian loan is. As
a result of Mark's death, Martin Chandler will cast the votes of the
United States." He looks down the table at Chandler. "Naturally,
Martin, we want to give you as much time as you need to prepare
for this vote, but it would help if you could give us some sense of
when you think you might be ready. As we all know, a lot rides on
the outcome of our decision, and the world is watching and
waiting."

As much time as I need, eh, thought Chandler as he returned Saint-
Germain's steady gaze with a wry smile. Ah well, it was true. The
world did await their decision. Still, he felt that he needed to
review some of the finer points, even though he was well informed
as to the essential facts of the loan application. Most importantly,
he needed to reassure himself as to the stability of the Kirov
government and the likelihood of their being able to repay the loan

on schedule. So many of these international loan recipients, for one reason or other, after being granted a loan said that they were unable to meet the original terms. The I.M.F. then found itself in the unenviable position of restructuring the debt, which was banking talk for granting a more generous repayment schedule. And in rare cases, the I.M.F. ended up forgiving the loan altogether. This one, however, would be too big to forgive or to reschedule, so the initial vote had to be the right one. Chandler felt fairly comfortable with the Kirov government, but now that it was his vote; not Dantry's, he wanted to take some time to consider these factors. He broadened his smile as he spoke to Saint-Germain.

"I'll try not to take more than a week, Claude. I know how important it is that we vote soon."

A former president of one of America's largest banks, less than three years ago Chandler had voluntarily retired at age 54 to spend more time traveling with his wife and to write mystery novels. At the time, industry officials expressed surprise at his decision, some openly wondering what was really behind such a startling move. Not many years earlier, Chandler had been considered by insiders to be the *wunderkind* of finance. It was hard for these observers to accept his abrupt termination of such a stellar banking career as being voluntary. There had to be something behind the move.

After Chandler left the bank, he remained active in charitable organizations and retained a few directorships in major companies, so it was less of a surprise when he was asked to join the I.M.F. as the number-two member of the U.S. contingent. Now, with Dantry dead, he was the de facto leader of the U.S. delegation, and odds-on favorite to be named U.S. Executive Director.

Chandler was generally believed to be in favor of helping Russia, so it was likely that he would vote in favor of the loan currently under consideration.

* * *

Sorokin's instructions, directly from Bulgakov, were to kill Chandler within one week. Vyugin had violently protested both the assignment and the accelerated timetable. To begin with, he was

against killing Chandler because he believed the deaths of two
I.M.F. officials within a period of two weeks would arouse too
much suspicion. This could not only make his own situation more
risky, but could increase the likelihood that the Americans would
learn that Russians were behind the executions. But Vyugin had
still another reason for wanting to reconsider the assignment,
though he didn't share it with Sorokin. Quite simply, it turned his
stomach. He had serious doubts as to whether he was working for
the right cause.

Sorokin had sensed Vyugin's reticence, but argued that it
was up to him, Vyugin, to make Chandler's death appear accidental
or natural. They'd gone back and forth longer than they should
have considering the risk of exposure during an international
phone call, even though it was encrypted. Vyugin had had no luck
arguing for more preparation time. Sorokin rung off after once
again stressing that time was of the essence and that the added risk
of less preparation time would have to be factored into the
equation. If Vyugin considered himself a true professional, said
Sorokin, this would be his finest hour.

Chapter 9

"I have a week to make up my mind," said Chandler. "Just a week," he gestured emphatically with the glass of Merlot in his right hand as he leaned back in his favorite chair on the sixth-floor balcony of his Watergate apartment. It was warm, but not as hot as you'd expect it to be this time of year in Washington. Much of the summer, up till now, he and his wife Corinne had found it too steamy to sit outside, despite the view. But not tonight. Tonight would have been perfect if it weren't for the decision he was wrestling with.

"Do you need that much time," she asked. "I mean, you've been living this loan in the shadows of Mark for so long, you must know all there is to know by now."

"I know the numbers part so well I could recite it in my sleep. It's not the numbers, though. It's the degree of comfort I feel —or don't feel— about granting one of the largest loans in the history of the world to the unstable government of a country that could blow up at any moment. A country that not too many years ago was the most fearsome nation on the face of the earth."

"I thought you respected President Kirov."

"I do. He's a moderate who's trying to help his country along. I honestly think he believes in democracy and free enterprise, but it's not that simple over there. With their totalitarian legacy and with their national paranoia, half the population considers someone like Kirov to be a traitor. Hell, it may be more than half." He paused to take a sip of wine.

"It's not that the Russians want to go back to the days of Khrushchev or Stalin—or even Brezhnev—because they don't. At least most of them don't. But many Russians are conditioned by their Soviet background to distrust free enterprise and even democracy. They really don't understand how either one of them works. They think democracy is a license to do whatever you want to do, and they think free enterprise is a code word for a wild and untamed dog-eat-dog economy. Not that there isn't some truth to this, but they have an exaggerated view. I suppose the American movies and TV reinforce this.

"Many Russians miss the structure of the Soviet days. They didn't have to rely on their own resources to get ahead. The state provided them a job—not always the job they would have chosen, but a job—and it virtually guaranteed them security. Granted, they were secure in knowing they would share a crowded apartment with one or two other families, but at least they had that. Many Russians are uncomfortable with having to plan their own lives. They have no experience in doing so, and nobody in their family does. Neither did their parents or grandparents."

"What about the new rich I've heard about over there?" asked Corinne. He smiled. His wife was well informed. Not that he was surprised. Summa cum laude from the University of Pennsylvania, and an accomplished journalist on the Metro beat with the *Washington Post*, she was naturally curious and knew how to get answers. She probably already knew the answer to this question, but wanted to know what he thought. She did that a lot. At first he'd found it annoying, but eventually he learned to view it as a challenging mental game, one that tested his ability to express thoughts that needed clear expression.

"There are some notable exceptions," he acknowledged. "There's a small, but active minority of Russians who've caught on to capitalism pretty fast. Aggressive, bright, and often ruthless, they epitomize the worst aspects of capitalism. While we're on the subject, there's also the Russian Mafia, which makes the Sicilian Mafia look like a bunch of choir boys. But the vast majority of Russians, while envying us our material wealth, can't help but mistrust anything Western. So when Kirov attempts to democratize Russia, he has to tread lightly, lest he appear to be a puppet of the West, especially America."

"Are you going to take your full week?"

"Probably, though you read me correctly. I've just about made up my mind. Still, a lot of people in the next week will try to persuade me to vote either for or against. I might as well hear what they have to say."

"But you don't want to take more than a week, do you?"

"No, I don't think I can afford to. Kirov's government is in precarious shape. If I'm going to vote for the loan, I'd better do it pretty soon, or it won't matter. It'll be too late."

"What's the worst that could happen? No, let me put it another way. I realize that not getting the loan could be destabilizing for Russia. But what does that mean, and how would it affect us?'

"It could mean that the Communists and splinter parties could demand a new election. Kirov could either stall and risk rioting or a *coup d'etat*, or call for the vote and be replaced by Malenkov, the Communist. Malenkov claims he's not a Stalinist or a Khrushchev-style Commie, but nobody really knows. Besides, Bulgakov, his Chief of Staff, is an old-style hard liner who hates the West and the U.S. in particular. It's feared that they would rebuild the military and begin reclaiming territory they lost in '91. At least some of these recently liberated countries would put up a fight. So we could have one or more wars, plus a resumption of the Cold War, for starters. Then there's the real possibility that Malenkov and his buddies would take out revenge on the Russian moderates." He took a long pull on his wine and sighed. "So I take my vote seriously. After that...?"

"Then we go to the mountains."

He grinned. They'd been trying to get away for a year now. Just a month ago, they'd made reservations at a lodge in the Adirondacks for the last two weeks of July. With the heat now in full force in the capital, the mountains sounded good. "If the world doesn't come apart after the vote."

"You're making yourself sound pretty important," she grinned mischievously as she said this. "Do you really think your vote could have that big an impact?"

"It might. Believe me, it's not me, it's the vote that's important. After we vote we'll have about ten days before we leave for the Adirondacks. We should have a good idea of which way the wind is blowing in Russia by then. Let's hope the lid hasn't blown off."

Chapter 10

Tony stopped halfway up the red-brick walk leading up to the front door and took in the scene. It was a house that in most towns would be considered palatial. Here in Falls Church, Virginia, in the suburbs of DC, it was just another upscale house. This was only the second time he'd been to his brother's house. He'd forgotten how big it was. He did some quick calculations as he tried to figure out how many boats the size of his Chris Craft would fit inside the house he was about to enter. He smiled at Joanna next to him and continued on up to the door.

Beth Dantry forced a tired smile as she greeted the two of them. To Tony, she still had that slightly intimidating patrician look. It was a look that had always kept him off balance—as if she were of royal blood and he were a commoner. But as soon as she spoke, the effect her appearance had on him was overshadowed by the warmth of her personality. He'd forgotten how much he liked her. He looked at her and shook his head, the intensity of his estranged relationship with his brother somehow conveyed by this gesture of futility and compassion.

"Jeez, Beth—"

She smiled understandingly. "I know." A few drawn-out seconds. "I'm glad you came, Tony."

"Oh, this is Joanna, a good friend."

"Nice to meet you, Joanna."

"I wish it were under better circumstances. Tony's told me a lot about you."

"I'm sure he has," said Beth with a knowing look.

Tony reddened. "It was good stuff, Beth. Believe me."

She smiled generously. "I do." This was not the time to go into ancient history. "It's been a long time, Tony."

He nodded. "Yeah. Can I do anything, Beth?"

"Just be a shoulder, okay?"

"Of course." He was taken back by her wanting his support. She'd always seemed so independent and self-assured—so much like his brother.

A half hour later, after quickly unpacking in the spacious guest room that Beth had taken them to, they were downstairs, sitting in the living room. Upstairs, when they'd been alone in the bedroom, Joanna had remarked to Tony that it looked as if Martha Stewart had decorated the house. Tony had grinned and told her she had. At least her employees had. Now, Beth and Joanna were sipping ice teas—Joanna with more enthusiasm than Beth. Tony had a cold bottle of Samuel Adams in front of him. Their choice of beers was one thing that he and his brother had agreed on.

Tony took a deep swig of beer and leaned forward.

"You up to talking about this, Beth?"

"You want to know what happened, I suppose?"

"All I know is what you told me on the phone—that the car's brakes failed, and he went off an embankment."

"That's all I know, really. That's what the police said."

"If I know my brother, the car was a recent model designer car."

"A Lexus. He just got it a few months ago. You disapprove?"

He held up a hand as he realized how close to the surface the old resentments lay. Most surprising, though was the discovery that the resentments apparently went both ways. Why in God's name had his brother, who'd had everything, resented him? This was not the time to pursue it. "No, no. That's not what I'm getting at, Beth. It's just that a car like that rarely has brake trouble. The police didn't say anything about foul play, did they?"

A stunned expression came over her face. "No. My God, Tony why would you even suggest such a thing?"

"I'm sorry. It's probably nothing. Just that it's so unusual for a car of this type to have this kind of problem. But I suppose stranger things have happened."

"But, I don't understand, Tony. Who would want to kill Mark?"

"Look, I'm probably overly suspicious. It's my background, Beth. I'm trained to be suspicious." When Tony Dantry left the agency ten years ago, it had not been the way he'd envisioned it when he signed up right out of college at the age of 22 as an eager adventure seeker out to defend his country from foreign bad guys.

But it could have been worse. He could be dead. He was fortunate that the Cold War was over or his exit might have been terminal. After the Cold War, when a CIA agent wanted to get out or they wanted to get you out, you could usually work out something less lethal. That's what he'd been able to do. Not that it had been a happy separation. Far from it. But at least he'd gotten out alive, or without having to change his identity and make a whole new life. He'd known people who'd just disappeared. He never knew what happened to them: whether they were given new identities or simply eliminated, but it had to have been one or the other. Neither solution had appealed to him. He'd been lucky.

His tour of duty with the agency hadn't been totally wasted. He'd learned a lot. Probably too much for his own good. Tony shook off his musings and returned to the present. His sister-in-law was waiting for what he had to say. He saw that he'd upset her.

"This is the last thing you want to concern yourself with now, I know that, Beth, but people with far less responsibility than Mark have had enemies. If, and I repeat, if, Mark had enemies, they could be big-time enemies. Face it, he was in the big leagues, dealing with people who wield a lot of power. I don't have to tell you that politicians and their aides can be ruthless. Can you think of anything he was involved with recently that people might kill for?"

He could tell that as well informed and sophisticated as Beth was, she had never dreamed of her husband being the target of a killer. She was thinking now, and it was obvious that what she was thinking was causing her distress. Finally, she spoke—in a controlled, deliberate manner. It took her a few minutes, but she slowly told them about the loan to Russia that Mark had been working on.

"So, yes, Tony, it was big," she said as she concluded. "Very big. Mark felt that the very stability of Russia could be at stake. But if you ask who would have killed Mark over this—I..., I have no idea. For one thing, other than President Kirov, I really don't know who the players are."

He smiled understandingly. "Yes, of course. But that doesn't mean that the players don't exist." He saw immediately how agitated these words had made her and added, "That's assuming that somebody deliberately did this to Mark and that it wasn't an accident. It certainly could have been an accident."

Beth drew in a deep breath. "Say you're right, and somebody did kill Mark. How do we confirm it, since even the police are saying it was an accident?"

He'd been expecting this question. On the trip down from New York, he'd been rehearsing in his mind what he might say to her. He finessed it by asking one of his own. "Can you give me the names of the policemen who first told you that Mark had been killed?"

"Yes. It was an officer Benitez and—wait, they left their cards. Hold on just a minute." She rose and left the room, more quickly than necessary, as if glad to have something to do." He turned to Joanna and pursed his lips, conveying how much he hated this whole scene. She nodded her understanding just as Beth Dantry returned and handed two business cards to Tony, saying, "Officers Benitez and Phillips. They were very nice—considering."

"Thanks," said Tony, feeling her anguish. Then, turning to Joanna, he said, "What was the name of the cop you spoke to?"

"Kennard, I think. Yes, I'm pretty sure it was Kennard."

"What do you intend to do?" asked Beth.

"I thought I might talk to these guys—Kennard, Benitez, or Phillips—as many as I can get to actually—and try to get a clear idea of how they saw the accident. Probably come to nothing, but it's worth a try. You mind if I do?"

"No, I suppose not, though Benitez and Phillips seemed pretty certain it was just an accident."

"Well, they're probably right. Still, I'd like to talk with them or Kennard."

When he called the station house a few minutes later, neither Kennard nor Phillips were there. Benitez, however, had just come in and agreed to meet with Tony if he got there in the next hour or so.

"You should probably go alone," said Joanna. "It's more professional than if I tag along. I'll stay here at the house and read."

He didn't disagree, though having Joanna along was never unpleasant. This time it worked to his advantage to go alone. If she came along it would be harder to establish that indefinable camaraderie that often existed between lawmen—though, he realized all too well that it didn't always exist between local cops and feds. Still, if he had any chance of getting these cops to open up with him at all, it was more likely if he was alone rather than with his girlfriend. For starters, though, he wouldn't mention that he'd been with the CIA. Hopefully, just being Mark's brother would get him a few answers.

Beth said she was sorry, but she was going to have to go out—arrangements to be made and details had to be attended to, she explained. She hoped they understood and that Joanna wouldn't mind being by herself for awhile. They'd all have dinner together later.

It wasn't hard to find the police station. Tony entered the contemporary one-story red-brick station and asked for Officer Benitez.

The sergeant on duty picked up the phone, and in less than a minute a uniformed officer came in from another room and shook Tony's hand. Well-muscled arms filled much of the tailored short-sleeves of his blue police shirt. Guy works out, thought Tony.

"Phil Benitez," said the cop, offering his hand with a wary expression on his cleanly shaven face. He looked more Anglo than

Tony had expected. They faced each other at eye level, which put Benitez at least as tall as his own six feet.

"Tony Dantry," he smiled. "Nice to meet you," he said as he shook the proffered hand.

"So, what can I do for you? Want to come in and sit down?" Tony could see that Benitez hoped he wouldn't accept. It would mean getting tied up longer than he wanted to.

"Sure, this won't take long."

"Follow me," sighed Benitez resignedly, leading him into an adjoining room—a room that looked as if it were probably used for interrogations. When they were seated, he said, "Sorry about your brother. From what I hear he was quite a guy."

"Yeah, he was that. So what can you tell me about what happened?"

"I don't know how much you already know."

"Just that he was in an accident. No other cars. That he went off some kind of embankment. That's all I know."

"It was more like a cliff. Good seventy-five to a hundred feet straight down. Or nearly straight down. From what we can determine, the car's brakes failed, and he started to pick up speed. Couldn't make the turn and went off the road continuing on off the cliff. Wasn't far from his house."

Tony could visualize the scene. He imagined what must have been going through his brother's mind those last few seconds.

"Late model Lexus, right?"

"Yeah, great car."

Tony snorted. "Not that great if the brakes failed. What's the chances of that with a new Lexus?"

"One in a million. To be honest with you I never heard of it happening. At least not till now. Real freak accident."

"I assume somebody checked the brakes to be sure no one tampered with them?"

A flash of annoyance showed in Benitez' eyes. "Of course. The line wasn't cut, if that's what you mean."

"Was it disconnected in any way?"

"Well, yeah, at one end. As if it hadn't been secured properly. Or hadn't been tightened. That could happen in a shop. More likely at the factory. I doubt if this car's been in a shop, it's so new. Funny thing, though. Both the foot brakes and the hand brakes were loose like that. No sign of being cut. Just loose."

"Pretty sloppy for a car of this caliber. You ever heard of that happening?"

"Hey, look Mr. Dantry, I know he was your brother, and I feel for your loss, but what're you looking for anyway? It was a terrible accident, but that's all it was. If you want to be suspicious you can read this as some sort of dark criminal act. However, more than likely, if they got sloppy with one set of brakes, it's probably no surprise that both sets would be loose. Just takes one careless worker."

Tony was having a hard time controlling his growing frustration. "Look, I'm not trying to tell you your business, but my brother was in the kind of work that could easily have made him enemies—enemies who would stop at nothing to prevent him from carrying out his job." Tony then quickly summarized Mark's position as the Executive Director of the I.M.F. and how the things he was involved in could sometimes have a direct influence on governments. He explained that this time he had been about to cast a key vote that could conceivably have changed the course of events in Russia. So, maybe, just maybe he wasn't out of line asking a few questions of the local police.

Benitez held up both hands in a calming gesture. "Okay, I understand. I really do." He drew a deep breath, choosing his words carefully. "But unless something else turns up, we're gonna have to treat this as an accident."

"Are you still looking?"

"No, we're not, for the reason I just stated. No reason to."

"But you'll grant that this was a pretty unusual accident, all things considered?"

"Yeah, I'll grant you that—especially in light of what you just told me." He paused for a minute before continuing. "Tell you what I'll do. I'll talk to the other guys, and I'll tell the Lieutenant what you just told me. If they want to dig further, I'll let you know."

Tony could see that that was about the best he was going to do as the bereaved brother, so he decided to risk bringing up his former CIA affiliation.

"Look, I wasn't going to mention it. Usually it hurts more than it helps when I do, but I used to work out of Langley, and—"

"You mean CIA."

"Yeah, and, as I was saying, what happened to my brother fits the MO of a few KGB operatives I used to chase. I can think of two in particular. Now I'm not saying that's what happened here, but you can understand why I'm not happy accepting this as an accident."

Benitez snorted. "I should'a known."

"As I said, I *used* to be with them. I'm not anymore."

"I thought once you guys signed up, you were in for life." He grinned sardonically. "Sorta like the Mafia."

Tony didn't return the grin. He was not in the mood.

"Not anymore. Not since the breakup of the Soviet Union. Actually that was never really true—unless you knew too much."

"And you didn't?"

"No, it's not that. It's just that after the Cold War ended, everybody wanted to make nice-nice. All was forgiven."

"Like it was all a game, huh?"

"No, but I guess you have to get on with your life. Things do change."

"But you're suggesting that some of these KGB guys may still be playing the game?"

"Maybe. Look, it's like police work. Some guys sign up because they like the power they have when they wear the uniform. Others believe in service to the community. Some just treat it as a job. A lot of guys go for the camaraderie. Hell, most of the time it's a combination of all of those reasons." Benitez nodded his general agreement. "It's the same with intelligence work. Some guys do it out of patriotism. Some do it because they like knowing things nobody else knows. Still others like killing, and here's a way to do it and do it with a clear conscience. Almost always guys do it because they like adventure. Anyway, since my brother was involved with a loan that could have made a difference in the politics of Russia, it's not too much of a stretch to imagine that some old hard-line KGB guys might be involved. Maybe they still see the U.S. as the enemy."

"Maybe they're still playing the game," said Benitez.

"Maybe they are."

"Like I said, I'll talk to the lieutenant and the other two guys. If you're right about this, we should be on top of it. Give me a number where I can reach you. I'll get back to you tomorrow, okay?"

"Yeah, thanks," said Dantry, far from convinced.

Chapter 11

Joanna was waiting for him when he got back from the police
station. In her hand she had a paperback Spenser mystery, which
she'd been reading. She was dressed in faded form-fitting jeans
with a loose-fitting gray New York Yankees T-shirt. She was
sipping from a chilled plastic bottle of Evian water. It was so
humid that the bottle was coated with beads of condensation.

"How'd you make out?" she asked, glad that he was back.

"I honestly don't know."

"What's that mean?"

"Well, the guy I spoke with said the department is treating
it as if it were an accident."

"Wasn't it? I know, I know. You said before that you had
suspicions. But my God, Tony—"

"Look, I'm not sure. It could have been, I suppose, but then
again—"

"What else could it have been, Tony?"

He explained what he'd told Officer Benitez, about how the
failed brakes matched the MO of certain KGB killing styles, and
about how, with his brother being involved with maybe the
deciding vote on a loan for Russia, he couldn't ignore the
possibility.

"Don't take this the wrong way," she said, running a hand
through her chestnut hair to get it off her face, and knowing as she
said it that those were the words that often triggered arguments,
"but is it possible that your CIA background makes you overly
suspicious in a situation like this?" She'd known Tony for just
under a year. When she first learned that he'd worked for the CIA,
she'd been both fascinated and turned off. The intrigue and the

mystery appealed to one part of her, but the fact that he might have killed people, albeit in the so-called line of duty, made her more than a little uncomfortable. It had made it hard to fall in love, but eventually, she now admitted to herself, she had done just that. The way he treated her and more importantly than that, she believed, the way he treated other people—people he wasn't trying to impress—convinced her that if he'd killed anyone in the past, it wasn't because he was at heart a killer. It was more like the way soldiers killed in times of war. They did it because they had to— because often it was kill or be killed.

Tony felt a surge of anger, but he didn't have time to debate this now. Every hour counted. Still, one of the reasons Joanna Barbeau was part of his life was that her interpretation of events often helped him see things more clearly. The other reasons included a certain something that made him feel more alive whenever he was in the same room with her, and a mind that often was able to penetrate his thoughts. Then, of course, there was her great body and the most inviting eyes he'd ever looked into. As an associate professor in Slavic studies at Hunter College, Joanna had an in-depth understanding of both Russian history and of human behavior. She also had a reasonably good, but rusty command of Russian. She didn't teach the language, but had had to learn it when she, herself, was a student.

Tony forced himself to calm down. As eager now as he was to take some action, not to talk, he realized he'd be a fool if he didn't stop and at least get her take on things. She stood there waiting for his response.

"Sure, it's very possible," he said. "But the circumstances are unusual enough that I'd be naïve not to at least look into it some more."

So logical, she thought. It was hard to argue with it. Even though she didn't feel it herself. Maybe if she'd done what he'd done for over 20 years she would feel it. She thought back to the time—about three months after they'd first met—when he'd told her why he left the CIA. He hadn't wanted to tell her. She'd pulled it out of him.

The assignment had been in London. His orders had been clear—eliminate four enemy agents. Only they weren't all agents.

At least there was no evidence that said they were. Two Russians
—Soviets in those days—and two Brits. One of the Russians was
known to have taken out an American operative in London, and in
a particularly gruesome way. This one Soviet also knew the
identities of at least two other American agents and at least one
British agent. These friendly agents were at great risk unless the
Soviet spy was taken out. Langley had learned all this from the
dying words of the American agent, but it was unclear whether the
other Russian or the two Brits had been involved in the killing.

The Soviet hit man had been brutal and ruthless. But he'd
been arrogant and careless, too. Tony always investigated before he
carried out an operation—especially when lives were on the line.
He learned that one, possibly two of the four he was being asked to
eliminate were probably completely innocent—friends that the
Soviet agent or agents made in London to maintain their own cover
as cultural attaches. The problem was, while they knew for certain
that one of the Soviets was guilty, they weren't sure which one.
Neither did they know if any of the others was even an agent. Tony
had balked at killing all four. He'd asked for more time to
investigate. He wasn't above taking out the guilty one, but he had
no stomach for killing a group of people just because one of them
was an enemy. They'd said sorry, but no. Time was of the essence,
and it was unfortunate, but necessary. You couldn't leave two or
three of our own guys out in the open like that. It was a classic case
of them or us. Tony'd argued that some of the people he'd be
killing could very well *be* our guys. Why couldn't Langley warn
our people who were at risk while they checked out the foursome
to see if they could determine which were the good guys and which
were the bad ones? In the end he'd lost the argument. They'd
called him in and sent someone else to do the job.

Naturally, they never told him who they sent. The less he
knew, the better—especially since he no longer could be relied
upon. He was persona non grata as far as Langley was concerned,
and he'd been surprised to find that he liked it that way. Most of
the time, anyway. That, of course, was why he became a freelance
investigator, living for a few years in the Flatiron District of
Manhattan, and then, just three years ago, moving to a boat on
Long Island Sound. The investigating work paid his bills—barely.

Enough to allow him to go fishing when he wanted to, which was several days a week, weather permitting.

She knew that he'd lost his taste for spy work—especially the killing. For that she was thankful. But she could tell he wasn't going to let this go. Not until he knew what really happened. She resigned herself to that. She also knew that he needed time to think, so she changed the subject.

"Are we going to eat with Beth tonight? Do you think she wants that, or is she just trying to be a good hostess? Maybe we should leave her alone and go out someplace and get something by ourselves."

He shook his head. "Wish I knew? I do know that we need something. I haven't eaten all day. I'll talk to her."

"Are you kidding," said Beth a few minutes later. "I need somebody around me. That is, if you two don't mind. I'm probably not very good company."

Three-quarters of an hour later they were sitting in the family room eating pizza with varying degrees of enthusiasm.

Beth looked up from a barely touched piece of Margherita-style pizza. "I appreciate your coming down, Tony. I know you and Mark weren't close."

"I wish we had been. Predictable isn't it? My brother's dead, and now I wish we'd been closer."

"I always felt it was such a waste. You both missed out on what could have been something special."

Tony dipped his head.

"He respected you, Tony. You know that, don't you?"

"This is probably not the time, Beth."

"Yes, it is the time. For God's sake he's dead. If this isn't the time, when is? I want you to know that he respected you. He felt he couldn't communicate with you, and he didn't know why. Sometimes he blamed himself. Other times—"

"He blamed me."

"No, he never did. He sometimes wondered whether two people can just be so different that they're on different wavelengths, that they just can't fully understand each other." She drew in a deep breath and let it out slowly. "It bothered him even more," here she allowed a smile, "because he was supposed to be such a good communicator, but he couldn't communicate with his own brother. No, I think he blamed himself more than anything."

* * *

"Well, that went well," said Tony when he and Joanna were back in their room. "I came down here feeling guilty, and now I've just had a refresher course that proves to me that I was right."

"She didn't mean it that way," said Joanna, her arm around his shoulder. "She was just trying to say how sorry she was that the two of you weren't closer. If anything, she thinks he put up the barriers."

"I didn't get that at all. Anyway, it's late. We should probably get some sleep."

"What'll you do tomorrow?"

"I'll help Beth, if she needs me. Otherwise, I plan to contact another one of those cops—see what I can learn—that is, if I don't hear from Benitez."

She sighed and said, "Okay. Tell Beth I'll be glad to help, if she wants. By the way, are there any kids involved? You never mentioned—"

"No, I guess they tried, but they never had any. Too bad. Especially now."

The next morning came fast. When Tony awoke, it seemed as if he'd just gone to sleep. He yawned and looked out the window. It was going to be another one of those steamy Washington summer days. The sun was already generating heat, forcing its way through the thick morning haze that portended a muggy, energy-draining day. He looked at the clock in the bedroom. Eight-fifteen. Damn! He never slept that late. He turned and looked over at Joanna—into her smiling face.

"Well, you must have been tired."

"Yeah, still am. But I've gotta get going," he said seriously. "Looks like I'm not going to hear from that cop."

"It's only quarter after eight, Tony. Give him a chance. If he said he'd get back to you, he will."

"Yeah. Christ, what's the matter with me? It's not like Mark meant so much to me when he was alive. Why does it mean so much to me now?"

"He obviously meant more to you than you thought. Unless this is just a challenge to your ego or something."

As soon as she said it she knew she shouldn't have. She saw the red rising on his neck. He was trying not to say something he'd regret.

"What the hell do you mean by that?"

"It's just that—oh I don't know what I meant, Tony. I guess I was just thinking that, even if you two weren't close, if his death wasn't an accident, maybe you saw it as a test of your professional ability. That you couldn't let his killer, whoever it is, get away with it because it would somehow mean you weren't capable of bringing him down. Weren't capable of avenging your brother. Forget it, I'm just rambling."

He frowned and looked out the window a moment. Then turned to her. "Sorry I jumped on you. To be honest, I've been wrestling with those same thoughts since I first heard how he died —when I had my first suspicions that it might not have been an accident. I don't know, Joanna. I've got a million thoughts rushing around in my brain. I honestly don't know what's motivating me. All I know is I've got to do something. Maybe it's because I didn't do enough when he was alive."

"Damn it, Tony. Don't get down on yourself. These things work both ways. Did he make a big effort with you?"

"I, I... aw hell, maybe not, but I know damn well I didn't do much from my end."

They heard the phone ring downstairs. Then sounds of footsteps on the staircase. It was Beth, halfway up the stairs, "Tony, officer Phillips is on the line. You can take it in your room, if you want."

"Thanks, Beth." He took three long strides across the room and picked up the receiver. "Yes?"

"Mr. Dantry, this is Officer Phillips. My partner, Phil Benitez said he talked with you about your brother's death. I'm really sorry about that, sir."

"Thanks, You uh...you have something you want to discuss? Something about the case?"

"Well, it's interesting that you should call it a case. Like it's a criminal investigation. I mean, we've been calling it an accidental death…"

Tony's heart sank. "So you don't think there's anything funny about this?"

"You didn't let me finish. Like I said, we've been calling it an accident, but we're beginning to wonder now. We had a nagging feeling about something not bein' just right. Then, what you said to Phil made us think some more. Frankly, we're not so sure now."

"Then you're continuing your investigation. You're treating it like a crime or at least a suspicious death?"

"That's why I called you. Yeah, we're still lookin' into it."

"Can I be of help? In any way?"

"You told Phil that the way your brother died reminded you of the MO of some guys in the KGB. Right?"

"Yeah."

"Well, maybe you could come down here tomorrow morning and talk with me and Phil." Then he added offhandedly, "Might be one or two detectives. The lieutenant might want to sit in, too." Tony found it encouraging that the lieutenant wanted to be involved, and obviously had made a decision to get some detectives involved—though he was sure that Phillips and Benitez weren't so thrilled.

"I'll be there. Name the time."

Chapter 12

Vyugin inserted the plastic card into the slot in the door to his room after returning from breakfast in the hotel coffee shop. He could hear the phone ringing inside the room. He knew who it was—who it had to be.

He took his time opening the door and entering the room. When he was inside, he let the phone ring one more time before picking up the receiver.

"Yes?"

"Vyugin?" It was a man's voice, speaking in Russian.

"Yes?"

"I've been ringing your room for almost an hour. You were supposed to be at your phone."

"Who is this?"

"Pentovsky. Oleg Pentovsky. Were you not expecting this call?"

Vyugin tried to contain his exasperation. "Yes, my young friend. I was told you would call within the hour. I had my breakfast. I rushed it as a matter of fact so that I could get back here to my room for your call. It is only 45 minutes since I spoke with Sorokin. Perhaps you can now tell me why it was so important that I wolf down my food?"

"It's important that we meet soon. We need to do some planning."

While Vyugin had already made up his mind that he didn't intend to carry out this mission, he knew that tipping his hand to the two operatives sent to ensure that the assignment got carried out was tantamount to signing his own death warrant. It could also mean exposing his wife, Ludmilla, to pressure, threats, or worse. Until he could figure out what he was going to do next, he had to play along with these two eager and lethal watchdogs.

"I assume, Pentovsky, that Sorokin made it clear to you who was in charge of this operation?"

"Yes, yes." His quick agreement sounded hollow to Vyugin. "Now where shall we meet?"

Vyugin wondered if Pentovsky was merely humoring him in order to move things along. He tried not to let his suspicions show in his voice when he replied. "Meet me at the Lincoln Memorial at 11 o'clock this morning. We can talk there without being overheard." The irony of three Russians plotting the extermination of U.S. citizens in such a bastion of American democracy did not escape him.

"That is acceptable."

"What the hell do you mean, acceptable? Don't forget who's running this operation."

"Of course, comrade, of course." Did Vyugin hear contempt in Pentovsky's quick agreement?

"How will I recognize you?"

"We will recognize you."

Vyugin had the feeling he was losing control of the situation. He felt a visceral churning. Was it the first sign of panic? An emotion he'd never felt in his 20-plus years as an intelligence operative. At his peak he'd known that he was one of the KGB's elite. Now, just because he was no longer active, he was not going to be outwitted by two greenhorns who were probably still in school when the Cold War ended. Still, he had to play along.

"I see," he said, as dispassionately as he could under the circumstances. "Sorokin showed you photos. I'm not so young now as in those pictures."

"We have up-to-date ones. We'll recognize you. At eleven. Dosveedanya, comrade."

"We're not comrades. Dosveedanya."

* * *

Vyugin realized that he had only an hour or so to decide what he was going to do. He had to have a plan when he met Pentovsky and Zhukov. He had deliberately set their meeting at the Lincoln

Memorial, not only so they could talk without being overheard by eavesdroppers, but because it had occurred to him that these two agents might have been ordered to eliminate him. After all, he realized, he'd balked at what Sorokin had assigned him. It wouldn't surprise him to learn that Sorokin and Bulgakov felt it would be safer to get rid of him knowing that he harbored these doubts. No telling what he might do if a sudden attack of conscience got the best of him. Yes, from their point of view he might very well be a liability they could ill afford to indulge. Vyugin knew Sorokin could give the order to eliminate him without the slightest hesitation. It might be harder for Bulgakov, but not that hard. He was known for his ruthlessness.

Vyugin was sitting on one of the steps leading up to the Lincoln Memorial when he heard the voice. It was the voice on the phone—Pentovsky.

"Mr. Vyugin?" The question was delivered the way someone would who was expecting to meet a person he'd never seen before. As if he were addressing someone who was expecting the meeting—businessman to businessman. A bystander would think nothing of it.

Vyugin looked up. "Pentovsky?"

"Da."

Pentovsky wasn't at all what he'd expected—a giant with a blond crew cut and a scar down his cheek. The man was much more urbane than that. The only similarity was his hair color— blond combed casually to both sides from a faint mid-part. While he was certainly no giant, he did look to be a well-sculpted six feet. Vyugin snorted to himself and thought "film actor." Pentovsky's smiling tanned chiseled features would no doubt appeal to women. Vyugin wondered if this contemporary version of a Russian spy could really be a threat to him? He forced a smile back at the fellow as he spoke:

"And your colleague here must be Zhukov?" The other man, who was perhaps an inch taller with nondescript brownish hair, and an apparent genetic inability to smile, nodded and permitted his face to crack in what Vyugin interpreted as his way of acknowledging another's presence.

"Yes. Shall we sit here and talk?" asked Pentovsky.

"All business, I see." Vyugin shrugged. "Very well, let us talk business. Yes, here is good. But first, let us try some American ice cream. I hear it can be quite good. Not as good as Russian ice cream, but then," and he turned to grin at his two companions, "we are not in Russia, are we?" He rose and headed toward a nearby pushcart.

The vendor smiled as Vyugin approached.

"What kind do you have?" asked Vyugin.

The vendor was a thin bald man who looked to be in his late 60s or early 70s, who enjoyed his work in the nation's capital. While not very rewarding financially, he met people from all over the world: tourists, diplomats, statesmen. To him it was stimulating. He enjoyed being ambassador of good will for America.

"I have chocolate, chocolate passion, and vanilla bean in cups. I have vanilla and chocolate ice cream bars, and lemon, orange, and cassis ice pops. I also have—"

Vyugin grinned and held up his hand. "You have already confused me, my friend. Since it so hot today, I will take one of your cassis ice pops. Cassis is not such a common flavor here. I'm pleasantly surprised."

"I learned the first year I got into this business that you Europeans go for cassis. You are from Europe, right?"

"You have a good ear. Yes, I am from the Czech Republic. As are my two friends." He turned to see Zhukov and Pentovsky hanging back, somewhat taken aback by his familiarity with the locals. He motioned for them to join him, saying, "And what will you have, gentlemen? Our friend here has a much bigger selection than we would ever find back in the Czech Republic." As he said this, the two smiled their understanding.

A few minutes later, back on the steps of the Memorial, Pentovsky said, "Are you ready to talk, business now?"

"Yes, Pentovsky, let's get down to business. I know you and Zhukov are eager to get to work."

"Sorokin said that you have reservations about doing the Chandler assignment? Is this true?"

"Of course it is true, anyone who has no reservations about an assassination is a fool or a knave." He paused to assess their reactions. Then, in deliberate fashion, he continued, "But it has to be done. This is how we shall proceed."

"Plastique, no?" It was Zhukov.

"Some sort of explosive. We must determine what is best."

"We don't have a lot of time," said Pentovsky.

"True, but we cannot do this until we familiarize ourselves with the man's routine. I'm sure Sorokin told you how important it is that Chandler's death appear to be an accident. If anyone here in this country suspects that he was the intended target, it could be disastrous for Malenkov and everyone working for him. It would be disastrous for Russia." Zhukov and Pentovsky exchanged glances.

"So how do we handle this, then?" asked Zhukov impatiently.

"We must observe his routine and look for those times when he is with other people. Unfortunately, in order to divert suspicion we must kill several people when we eliminate Chandler. That means no bomb in his car, or his house, or his office. This will not be easy, my friends."

"This is ridiculous," blurted Pentovsky. "It could take us weeks to find the right opportunity to take him out. We don't have that kind of time."

"You're right, of course. No, if we each follow him for three or four days, believe me, we'll find something that we can use. Perhaps it will be something he does on the weekend, something with his family or at his golf club. There will be something."

The two young agents looked at each other and slowly nodded their understanding. Zhukov then asked, "How do we proceed?"

"Chandler is an important man. His day will most likely be longer than the day of the average working man. Very likely he starts early and goes all day, with meetings into the night. I suggest we split up the day. I'll follow him from the time he arises in the morning until…let's say when he leaves work at the end of the day. We should stay in touch so that you can pick him up at that point and follow him until he returns home. We can do the same thing on the weekends. I know this is a longer day for you. You might want to divide your time up or one of you start later than the other and then overlap in the middle of the night. I leave that up to you. The two of you should overlap me. Join me towards the end of the work day—to be sure that we don't lose him. The important thing is for him not to see us. He cannot suspect a thing."

Pentovsky looked annoyed. "That goes without saying, comrade Vyugin. We are professionals."

"I told you on the phone, I am not your comrade. The Soviet Union is dead."

Pentovsky raised an eyebrow and looked over at Zhukov, who shrugged. "As you wish. Oh, incidentally, there is something you should know."

"What is that?" asked Vyugin suspiciously.

"This Dantry fellow, the one—"

"The one you already eliminated."

"Yes. Sorokin says that he learned from Bulgakov that this man's brother used to be CIA."

Vyugin appeared to be concentrating. He got up and took a few steps away from the Memorial, as if he were unaware of his two colleagues.

"Vyugin, did you hear what I said?" asked Pentovsky.

"Yes, I am not deaf." He turned back to face the two men still on the steps. "Are you sure about this?"

"According to Sorokin. He said that this other Dantry, an Anthony Dantry, operated in Europe, especially the Eastern States when they belonged to us. Even operated in Moscow on occasion, I believe. Why are you so curious?"

Vyugin sneered. "Sorokin wouldn't ask that question, my young friend—because he already knows the answer. You see, I remember this Dantry. Our paths crossed on more than one occasion. Damn!" He slammed a fist into his opened hand. "Damn!"

"I see," said Pentovsky. "You are worried that this man will try to avenge his brother? Is he formidable?"

"Yes, he is formidable. Am I worried? What you really mean, Pentovsky, is am I afraid of him?"

"Perhaps I should have asked why you are angry."

"I am not angry, you fool."

Pentovsky struggled to control his own hostility toward the older man. "I don't understand," he said deliberately.

Vyugin rolled his eyes, "Look, Pentovsky, don't you see. Bulgakov and Sorokin committed a grave error selecting this Mark Dantry for execution. I know why they picked him, but if they knew about his brother, they were just, as the Spanish say, throwing up a red flag. If this Anthony Dantry is still healthy, he can cause us and Mother Russia a great deal of trouble."

"Not if we get to him first," blurted Zhukov.

Vyugin shook his head impatiently. "And just how do you propose to do that? We don't even know where he is. And even if we did, do you think he's still there after hearing about what happened to his brother?"

"So you think he's already on to us?" said Pentovsky.

"If he's healthy, I'd bet on it."

"If he's not?"

"He's probably no threat to us—though it would depend on just how unhealthy he is. He could be physically disabled and still put some troubling ideas into the heads of the authorities. We shall have to find out where he lives and if he is there now. This is not easy to do when you're 5,000 miles from home. The first thing we need to do is contact Sorokin to find out if he has an address for Dantry. If he doesn't, we could waste a lot of time looking for him."

"This whole thing could be a waste of time," said Zhukov. "Why not just proceed with our plan and keep an eye out for Dantry, on the off chance that he might be here?"

"You're a real gambler, aren't you, my young friend? If this Dantry is here, the chances of our identifying him before he gets to us are nearly zero. You have no idea what he looks like. Are you willing to take that chance? No, don't answer that. You probably are, but I suspect your colleague here is not so eager to commit hari-kari. Nor am I."

An angry look transformed Zhukov's reddening face, but he held his tongue.

Pentovsky said, "Vyugin is right, Yevgeny. I don't like this delay either, but if this Dantry is on to us, or even suspects that his brother was killed by Russians, then the political implications could be critical for Malenkov." He glanced at Zhukov. "I admit, too, that I don't like the idea of some former CIA man following me around."

Vyugin allowed a trace of a smile, thinking that maybe this Pentovsky wasn't as dumb as he'd first thought.

"All right then," he said, "let's find a phone, and I'll contact Sorokin to see if he can tell us where Anthony Dantry lives. Once we know that, we can decide what our next move is. Hopefully we can get on this today and not waste time."

They took a taxi to the Hilton Hotel on Connecticut Avenue where Vyugin went immediately to a phone booth on the second-floor level near the meeting rooms. Not a good idea to make too many calls to Moscow from the Courtyard across the Potomac where he was currently staying. It took Vyugin nearly 40 minutes to get Sorokin on the phone. He had left his Kremlin office, and the call had to be patched into his home phone. Sorokin sounded slightly annoyed when he came on the line.

"Yes, Vyugin. What is this about?"

Vyugin shook his head at the irritation he sensed in the man's voice. Could the man not see that he, Vyugin, was the one who should be annoyed? He was sure that his feeling came across when he spoke: "I just learned that Mark Dantry has a brother—an Anthony Dantry, who just happens to be a former CIA man. A CIA man I have crossed paths with in the past. Why didn't you tell me about this before you sent me over here?"

"I didn't know at the time. I just found out the day that Pentovsky and Zhukov left for Washington. They were already in the air."

"Then you could have pulled them off the assignment, or changed the target. This is crazy."

"I'm afraid it had to be him, Vyugin. It was a risk we had to take."

"Does Bulgakov know of this?"

He could hear Sorokin expel air slowly, his anger rising at the audacity of this has-been operative who was second-guessing his decision. "Yes, he knows about it. In any event, the decision was made, and the execution took place. You should focus your attention on your next job, and forget about what is a *fait accompli*."

"You cold-hearted son-of-a-bitch! You send three people out to do a job when you know their lives are in jeopardy, and you don't give a damn about their safety." Vyugin threw up his hands and continued on, "All you have to say is get on with your next job." He then turned and looked out of the booth. He'd been so involved with the call that he'd forgotten his two companions standing just outside. He tried not to smile as he took in their shocked expressions. They'd obviously heard him unload on Sorokin, and couldn't believe their ears. He turned away again and resumed speaking into the phone:

"We're not proceeding with the next job until we find out where Dantry is and what he's doing. We can't afford to have him nosing into what we're doing."

"I thought you old spies were tough guys," sneered Sorokin. "You don't sound so tough if you're worried about a worn-out agent who's probably accepting his brother's death for what the police called it—an accident."

"You don't know that. You don't know what he's thinking or doing. And he may not be so worn out, either. If my memory serves me right, he'd be in his early fifties. Unless something unexpected struck him down, he may very well be a worthy threat to the success of the mission that is so dear to you. Do you have an address and phone number for him?"

"I don't have his file here at my home," said Sorokin unenthusiastically. "I'll find out and call you back. Where can I reach you?"

"We're in a phone booth in the Hilton Hotel on Connecticut Avenue." He gave him the number. "We'll wait here by the booth. Please make it as quickly as you can."

"It won't be long. I want to move this along as fast as possible. It's imperative that you get on with your mission."

"We understand that, so get us his address so we can get on with the mission."

It was only 19 minutes before the phone rang in the booth. Vyugin picked up the receiver.

"Yes?"

"Who am I speaking to?" asked Sorokin cautiously.

"It's me. Vyugin. You can proceed. What do you have for me?"

Sorokin gave him the phone number and added, "Apparently he lives in some kind of a boat up in New York. It's in a marina at the end of Ditmars Street on City Island. That's in Bronx borough."

"I've heard of City Island. Interesting choice of lodging for our Mr. Dantry."

"Are you and the other two going to visit him there? That's quite a distance from Washington."

"No, at first I'm going to place a phone call. Depending on that, we'll take it from there."

By now Sorokin was doing his best to be diplomatic. He had very little choice when the people he was depending on were so far away. At least for now. "Do you think this will take long?"

"I hope not. Anyway, the sooner we get on this, the sooner we can attend to the primary mission. None of this would be necessary if you hadn't chosen a target whose brother was CIA."

"As I said, it's unfortunate, but it had to be him."

"We could argue that a long time, but Pentovsky and Zhukov are chomping at the bit here, so I'll say good night."

Chapter 13

Immediately upon hanging up, Vyugin placed a call to the number for Tony Dantry that Sorokin had given him. He got a recorded answering machine message saying that Dantry would be out of town for a few days. Please leave a message, as he checked his messages on a regular basis. Vyugin related this to Pentovsky and Zhukov.

"So what do you propose we do?" asked Zhukov impatiently.

"My guess is that he's here in D.C. or, more accurately, in Virginia where his brother lived. Certainly I would think that he's made contact with the wife. Another phone call should tell us if we're right. I may as well try that now." Vyugin placed a call to Information and got the number of the house in Falls Church.

"Hello?" It was a woman's voice. Vyugin smiled. He was making progress.

"Is this the Dantry residence?" he inquired as unthreatenly as possible.

"Yes, this is Beth Dantry. Who's calling?"

"I realize this is not a good time to be calling, Mrs. Dantry, but I'm a former friend— No, that's not quite accurate. I'm a former acquaintance of your husband's brother, Anthony. My name is Jürgen Kiefer. I'm with Interpol in Brussels. I'm trying to reach Tony. I tried his home in New York. Then, when I heard about what happened to your husband—for that you have my deepest sympathies—it occurred to me that he might have gone down to Washington to be with you and the family." He felt fairly certain that an American would not detect the difference between a

German and a Russian accent—especially since he also spoke German and French and had been told that he had a vaguely, but indeterminate European accent. Most people would know that it was European, but would find it almost impossible to identify.

"Yes, he is here, though he's not in right now. Shall I have him call you, Mr. Kie— I'm sorry, I didn't quite catch your name?"

"Kiefer. Yes, you could have him call me here in Brussels at (02) 512-3567." Vyugin deliberately gave a wrong number. "And once again, Mrs. Dantry, please accept my deepest condolences." Surprisingly, he thought, he found himself really meaning it as he said these words.

Pentovsky couldn't resist smiling at the cleverness of the older man. "So, our man, he is here in Washington. What now, com — er colleague?"

"I need some time to think. We cannot afford to make a mistake here. Let us take a walk. Some fresh air will do us good."

Outside, they headed south on Connecticut Avenue. As soon as they exited the front of the crescent-shaped hotel, they were assaulted by a steamy blanket of heat. In less than ten minutes Vyugin stopped and pulled a handkerchief from his hip pocket, slowly wiping the perspiration from his brow. He grinned. "At times like this we miss Moscow, *da*?" Pentovsky conceded an obligatory smile. "There is no reason why we cannot proceed with part of our plan," continued Vyugin. "Why don't you two start monitoring this Chandler. Keep track of him until he goes home. He's probably in his office at the I.M.F. now. I'll pick up his trail from his house tomorrow morning. In the meantime, while you keep him under surveillance the remainder of today, I'll work out something for Mr. Anthony Dantry."

"Please explain," said Pentovsky suspiciously. "What do you mean, work out something?"

Vyugin thought fast. "I mean work out how to get him out of the way, how to eliminate him." He noticed a glimmer of a smile on Zhukov's face. Then he added, directing his words more to Pentovsky than Zhukov, "I'll leave a message at your hotel. Check every couple of hours. Once I have a plan worked out, we'll want to proceed without delay." As they parted, Vyugin wasn't sure they were completely happy with the plan, but at least they hadn't objected.

A half hour after Pentovsky and Zhukov left Vyugin, they were back at one of the phone booths in the Hilton.

"He is saying the right things," said Pentovsky, "but I sense something is not quite right."

"Be more specific," said Sorokin.

"Perhaps he is overcautious. Perhaps he is going out of his way to be sure we don't make a mistake."

"You think he should be careless?"

"No, it's not that, it's just...I cannot quite put my finger on it, but he seems to see problems that probably don't exist. I suppose what I'm saying is that I get the feeling he would drag this out forever if we didn't keep pushing. And I detect a softness that I wouldn't expect in a man with his reputation. I hope sentimentality isn't interfering with his judgment." He hesitated a moment before continuing. "I'm probably imagining all this, but I just wanted to get your read on it. You know him better than we do."

"Not exactly true. I only met him recently. But Bulgakov does know him well, and he has nothing but praise for the man. I must say, however, that I see him the way you do. I think that getting old has softened him. The man worries too much about people who mean nothing to us. Watch him carefully, and keep me informed. This is too important a mission to allow foolish emotions to get in the way."

Chapter 14

Vyugin had to think fast. Pentovsky and Zhukov were impatient. That was obvious. When he next contacted them, which would only be a matter of hours, it was entirely possible they would have a venue to suggest for Chandler's execution—an execution that would by design kill several people intentionally. Unless he, Vyugin, had a good argument against it, his two young colleagues —God how he hated thinking of them that way—would construe any hesitation on his part as foot dragging. And rightly so. He was pretty sure that they wouldn't hesitate to contact Sorokin to get his approval to do the job themselves. It was also possible that Sorokin would order them to take him out of the picture, as well. Vyugin fully realized that Sorokin was not likely to give him the benefit of the doubt if he had the slightest reason to think he might interfere with the elimination of Chandler.

It was 15 years since Vyugin had last been in the United States. He'd forgotten how easy it was to get around this country, how few questions were asked. Any questions that *were* asked were not intended to make you feel as if you'd done something wrong. When he stopped to think about it, it was amazing that he could purchase a ticket to San Francisco or Dallas or wherever in this rich country without getting approval from the government. Of course that was now true in Russia, but it hadn't been 15 years ago. And even now, travel in Russia was not easy, not pleasant.

He was here in the United States as a spy, yet he was almost certain that no one was watching him. How trusting these Americans were. Or was it naïve, foolish? Whatever. It was a refreshing change from what he had grown up with. How long would it take for someone with his background to grow accustomed to the strange ways of the Americans? Would you miss the security of a controlled state? Would so much freedom be uncomfortable, forcing you to make choices you'd rather not make?

No one was watching him, that is, unless it was another Russian sent by Sorokin. The irony of it didn't escape him.

It had been in the back of his mind for days now that he had it in his power to take back control of his life and at the same time do the right thing for Russia and for the U.S. Why had he been so slow to see this? Why had he agreed to this assignment in the first place? The answer, he realized, was all too simple. Old habits were hard to break. He had been conditioned for six decades to think of the U.S. as the enemy. And he had let himself be persuaded by Bulgakov and Sorokin that financial help from the U.S.-dominated I.M.F. would not be forthcoming if Mark Dantry was allowed to vote on the $40 billion that was desperately needed by Russia.

He had allowed Bulgakov and company to convince him that what Russia needed was Soviet-style toughness and control of the general society. Bulgakov had referred to it as order. He contrasted it with what he claimed was the disorder the country would get if Kirov continued in power.

Vyugin saw things more clearly now. Perhaps getting out of the country had enabled him to gain a better understanding of what Malenkov, Bulgakov, and Sorokin stood for. Now that he understood, he hoped he could do something about it.

The sudden clarity, the sudden surge of excitement—feelings that he'd lacked from the start of this assignment—were tempered by a realization that the course of action he was about to take was fraught with far more risks than was the original mission.

Having made the decision, Vyugin set off to find a phone booth. The sooner he made the call, the better.

Chapter 15

Dantry put the phone down slowly and deliberately. It had to have been the strangest phone call he'd ever received. Joanna studied him silently, concern on her face.

"What was that all about," she asked.

"I'm about to meet one of my former enemies."

They had agreed to meet in the bar at the Mayflower. "We might as well be comfortable," Vyugin had said.

It was five-thirty and the clubby, inviting hotel bar was abuzz with conversation. It was one of those European-style bars with small tables and comfortable chairs and sofas distributed at discreet distances around the large softly lit room. The clientele was an international mix of Washington figures. Most were unknown to Tony, but he did recognize a senator and two members of Congress. No doubt most of these people were here to facilitate a deal, whether by persuasion or arm twisting or blatant buy-off. The atmosphere, though, was one of warm collegiality. Tony scanned the room, looking for a face that he hadn't seen for at least a dozen years. How much would the man have changed over those years?

Tony recognized him immediately. Vyugin arose from a comfortable leather chair and stood so that Tony would see him. The thick black head of hair he remembered was now touched with more than a smattering of gray. His hairline had receded a bit, too. On balance, though, the man hadn't aged badly. He took a few strides forward to meet Tony. He still walked with assurance, a walk Tony had seldom seen in the men of Eastern Europe. But then, Vyugin had been KGB. They'd always carried themselves with authority. One of the characteristics that often gave them away.

Vyugin smiled as he held out his hand. Tony hesitated, if only for a moment. Did Vyugin catch the hesitation? So what, he would certainly understand.

Tony smiled back as he grabbed the older man's hand. "Vladimir, I'm not exaggerating when I say this *is* a surprise. I thought you'd retired to a dacha on the Black Sea."

"A small lake…two hours north of Moscow. Not so glamorous, but quite pleasant." He forced a smile. "And you, I want to hear about what you've been doing, but I suppose this is not such a good time. Your brother, I mean. Anyway, come join me at my table, and I shall tell you why I called."

An attractive waitress, who looked too young to be working in a bar, materialized within seconds. She smiled amiably and Dantry noticed that she wore a small nose ring—tasteful as nose rings went, he supposed—and had a small tattoo of a rose on her forearm. A few years ago Dantry would have done a double-take, but now he hardly gave it a thought. He ordered a Bass Ale. Vyugin touched his nearly empty glass indicating he wanted another vodka.

When the drinks came, Vyugin clinked glasses. Dantry nodded graciously and said, "You've got my attention, Vladimir. On the phone you said it had something to do with my brother."

For the better part of a half hour, Vyugin explained the assignment that had been given to him by Bulgakov and Sorokin. He eventually got around to his decision to back out of the assignment. He paused to nibble some Japanese rice snacks and sip from his vodka, eyeing Tony cautiously as he did so, trying to assess his reaction.

"You're saying that these two other guys, Pentovsky and Zhukov, killed my brother before you got to him?"

"I wasn't going to get to him, Tony. You need to believe that. If you don't believe it, I've taken an even greater risk by telling you this. I had come to the conclusion that this mission wasn't in the best interests of Russia. Yes, my first thoughts were of Russia, but I also realized that executing an innocent man, when it might actually make matters worse in my country, was simply perpetuating the insanity of the Cold War. I have discovered that I am what you might call a very reluctant assassin."

"You expect me to believe that you didn't realize this until you were already here in this country? What the hell made you change your mind?"

"I suppose it was perspective. Being here in America again —after so many years. Seeing how different things are here—from a new perspective. Call it perhaps an enlightened perspective. It all contrasts so dramatically with the suspicion and paranoia of the people who sent me. Don't misinterpret this, Tony. I'm still not comfortable with your openness here. It is…how shall I say it… difficult to take. To us Russians, too many choices make us feel ill at ease. It is a cultural thing that works both ways, no?"

"I suppose so," Dantry downed a healthy quaff of ale before continuing. "Christ, Vladimir, I should report you to the police and to the CIA. You know that, don't you?"

"Yes, it is a risk I am taking. I hope you don't do that. At least, not yet."

"You'll have to do better than you have, so far. I'm going to need something pretty damned convincing to persuade me why I shouldn't."

"Because my two young associates intend to execute another key I.M.F. executive, and, in the process, they plan to deliberately kill several other people. Innocent people."

"Jesus! Then I have to report them."

"No, wait. Hear me out. If you report them now and the police take them in, or Langley eliminates them, we'll have an international incident on our hands."

"Not we, Russia will."

"These things have a way of working both ways. Admittedly Russia will look worse, but it won't be good for the U.S., either."

"Those bastards killed my brother."

"I know, I know. There's a better way to get even—without destroying the delicate balance between our two countries. You know, we Russians are not all like these two. And even before, when you and I were enemies, all Russians were not KGB. If this becomes an international incident, which it could if the CIA gets involved, it will be a black eye for Russia." At this Tony started to say something and Vyugin raised his hand. "You may not care. I can understand that—your brother was killed by Russians, so bad publicity for Russia is probably the last thing you are concerned with. But I care. It is my country, and we are struggling to pull ourselves up from 75 years of Communist domination. I know, I was part of all that, but it is time to move beyond that ugly era. It is time to try democracy. Perhaps not your form of democracy, but a form that might work for Russia. The people who sent me, I am now convinced, would take us backward. On the other hand, I believe that President Kirov is a decent man. Not perfect for sure, but his heart is, as you Americans say, in the right place. He is trying to reform the system. The loan your brother hopefully would have approved would strengthen Kirov's position in Russia. A scandal such as this would scatter mud on everyone, including Kirov. I would like to undo Bulgakov and Sorokin without taking Kirov down or diminishing him in the world community. Will you help me? At least listen to what I propose?"

"You're asking a lot. Even if I like what you propose, you're asking me to take the law into my own hands. I could go to prison for that—if they don't shoot me first."

"Before I tell you, I should mention that there is one other reason for not bringing in Langley."

"I can't wait to hear what this is."

"This is closer to home. It has to do with my wife. Bulgakov and Sorokin are sure to use her—she is, of course, still in Russia—to try to force me to cooperate. Who knows what they would demand, but—"

"I understand," sighed Dantry. "Okay, what are you proposing?"

"What I'm proposing is that you and I work together first to insure that Pentovsky and Zhukov fail, and then to bring down Bulgakov and Sorokin."

"Is that all?"

"I know, I know. It will not be easy, but I think it can be done."

"What about Malenkov? You didn't mention him."

"He is an anachronism, but I don't think he has authorized these killings. If we can get rid of Bulgakov and Sorokin, that should be sufficient. It can be leaked to Malenkov that the game is up—that should he persist in trying to overthrow Kirov, we would reveal what his people have already done and what they were planning to do."

Tony drained the last of his ale, and, catching the eye of the waitress, motioned for another.

"If Malenkov is not behind this, are you saying that it's Bulgakov himself, or do you think someone is giving him orders?"

"I don't know. It may very well be Bulgakov. The man is ambitious. But I'm not sure. In any event, we have to stop him."

"Whew! Us work together."

"Yes, is it so inconceivable?"

"How do I know—?"

"How do you know that I am not taking you in with some clever scheme?"

"Yeah."

"Why would I do that? Why would I risk telling you what I've already told you, when you could take it to your people and at the very least embarrass the hell out of my government? Something we Russians don't need right now. And, of course, you could have me locked up for the rest of my life. You must see that you are in control here, Tony. If you don't believe me or don't agree with my plan, you can still report me and have me arrested."

"Yes, I could. Okay, I have to admit you've aroused my curiosity. How are you going to stop this Pentovsky and….what's the other one's name?"

"Zhukov."

"Zhukov. Listen, Vladimir. I don't know what you've got planned, but I hope it's good. These bastards may not be anything to you but ideological adversaries, but to me they're the sons o' bitches who killed my brother."

"It's good," said Vyugin with a hint of irony in his face. "Tell, me, Tony. You were close to your brother?"

"I resented the hell out of him, if you must know."

"Yet you need to take revenge. Is this revenge for your brother or for yourself?"

"Christ, I thought you were a spy; not a shrink. First you have a political change of heart, and now you want to counsel an old enemy. You've gone soft, Vlady, m'boy."

"I suppose you're right. It's a wonder I've lasted as long as I have. I suppose I've lived this long because this softness only came upon me recently."

"Well, if you want to survive another month, you'd better reclaim a little of that Russky toughness that got you this far." Tony downed the rest of his ale, wiped his lips with the back of his hand and said, "Okay, tell me what you have in mind."

"As I've already explained, my two young colleagues expect that the three of us—they and I—will take out Chandler with a bomb when he is in the midst of a crowd or small group. The idea is to make it look like an act of random terrorism. Obviously, the last thing Bulgakov wants is for it to appear that I.M.F. people are being targeted. Pentovsky and Zhukov are at this very moment monitoring Chandler's every move, hoping to come up with a behavior pattern that puts him in a group of people— hopefully unrelated to the I.M.F.—so we can execute him the next time he is in such a group."

"Go on, I'm with you so far."

"I'm supposed to be doing my share, too. When they rest, I take over, monitoring Chandler. It could take a few days before we can identify the kind of group situation that recurs on regular basis, or it might take only a few hours."

"I understand."

"So you and I must be ready to act."

"You still haven't told me what you have in mind."

"I wanted to be sure you had a clear picture of what is happening."

"Only too clear. What's the plan?"

"Regardless of the location, the plan is to use plastic explosive with a sophisticated timing device attached. Probably C-4. Now while the location doesn't affect our choice of explosive device, it does make a difference in how we proceed. If it's an outdoor gathering—such as an alfresco concert or food cart on the street—where it would be difficult to determine in advance exactly where Chandler will be located, one of us is to take the bomb and as discreetly as possible drop it in the midst of the group and then calmly walk away. The bomb will be concealed in some kind of harmless looking package so people will not immediately recoil or scream. They'll probably ignore it, figuring the person who dropped it will pick it up."

As Vyugin related this, Dantry listened in shock at the grotesque audacity of the plan. He'd seen a lot in his time, but Russia and the U.S. were supposedly on friendly terms. It wasn't that he was naïve, but the total disregard for bystanders. He drew in a deep breath and slowly shook his head as Vyugin continued.

"On the other hand, if it's an indoor location—such as his usual seat in a restaurant or his regular seat on the Metro, one of us is to plant the bomb a few minutes before he arrives. In this case the timer would be set to account for a reasonable delay in his arrival."

Dantry was leaning forward, his hands in his face as he took all this in. As Vyugin finished, Tony drew in a deep breath and sat up, dropping his hands as he did so. "Okay, that's the plan the three of you worked out. What's your plan for preventing this disaster?"

"This is where the police come in."

"I thought you said—"

"I said no police now, and no Langley now. The police are actually critical to the plan, but they have to be notified at the exact right time. I'd rather that the CIA not be involved at all, but I see no way to avoid it eventually. Still, if we do this right, even their involvement can work for us; not against us."

"I'm listening."

"One of us has to place a call to the police and tell them that two international terrorists are in Washington. That they are staying at the Hilton on Connecticut Avenue. That, if they check out their rooms they'll find bomb material and no doubt other incriminating evidence. If the terrorists are not in their rooms, they simply have to keep an eye on them until the two men return."

"You know their room numbers?"

"Yes, we exchanged room numbers so we could reach each other at any time."

"Aren't you afraid they'll implicate you when they get caught?"

"They very well may, though by training they are not supposed to. Besides, they will not know for sure that it's me. When we call the police—I will do it I suppose, since I have a foreign accent," he allowed himself a half smile. "I will, of course, not identify myself. I will say that I had learned through sources—I shall be vague about what these are—that these two men are involved in some sort of anti-American terrorist group. I will, of course, not mention anyone in the Russian government. Even if Pentovsky and Zhukov do implicate me, the police will still have to find me. It is a risk I'll have to take."

"Once the police take these two in, they'll eventually find out that they're Russian. You realize that, I'm sure."

"Yes, but I'm counting on their keeping quiet about the real purpose of their mission. Or at worst, that they'll be seen as radical-fringe terrorists who will quickly be condemned by the Kirov government. There's no way that Malenkov or Bulgakov are going to claim them."

"Okay, then. We…. or rather…you notify the police. Then what?"

"Once those two are in custody we fly to Moscow for the second half of the plan."

"This ought to be good. Go ahead. I'm listening."

Twenty minutes later, Tony leaned back into the embrace of his expansive club chair. He threw his arms over the back of the chair and stared at Vyugin. "You've got balls, my friend. I'll give you that."

"I knew you'd approve."

Vyugin said that he'd like to meet Tony again tomorrow. By then, he'd have more specifics on Pentovsky and Zhukov, maybe even what sort of plan they were hatching.

"Shall we meet here again?" he asked. "Say 4:30?"

Chapter 16

Dantry was already seated the next day when Vyugin entered the bar. He was in no mood to exchange pleasantries with his former enemy. For all he knew, Vyugin was still his enemy, and was now pulling some elaborate mind game calculated to involve him in some sort of international scheme. He didn't think so, but his guard was up.

"Bring me up to date," he said seriously as the Russian took a seat to his left.

Vyugin sensed Tony's suspicions and responded as directly as he could. "They believe they have already detected a behavior pattern that will allow them—us—to proceed soon. They feel that they need only one or two more days to confirm that they're correct, and then we'll be ready to—"

"Kill a bunch of innocent people."

"Yes."

"So when do you make the call to the D.C. police?"

"Now is as good a time as any. First I'll call the room to see how my colleagues are doing. If they're in the room, the police will kill...how do you say it?"

"Two birds with one stone?"

"Yes, two birds with one stone. That would be good, wouldn't it?"

It was a different, more somber Vyugin who returned to the bar 15 minutes later. Something had happened. Tony recognized the signs—signs that an operation had gone sour. He'd witnessed these signs in the faces of his own partners on more than one occasion back when he'd been working for the Company.

The confidence had drained from Vyugin's face. His pale Slavic features were whiter than usual. The deep-set intelligent eyes radiated concern.

Tony broke the spell, "What happened?"

"Bastards! Chandler uses the Metro; he'll take it home tonight. They want to move now. I tried to stop them, to stall for time. I said we need time to plan the execution in detail. These guys...they have no patience. They're going to move tonight. He takes the train sometime between six and six-thirty. They expect me to meet them there before six. We must hurry."

"How did they learn—? Never mind, it's not important. We've got to do something."

"We can still stop them, Tony, but I'll need your help."

Dantry felt a rush of the old excitement. "Name it."

"They say they want me to double check the explosive device." He flashed a helpless look at Tony and raised his eyebrows a fraction. "I have a dubious reputation for knowing about bombs. But this will work to our advantage. It will give me the opportunity to insure that there's enough time on the timing device for you to make a mad dash for the bomb, defuse it, and get it out of the crowd before it goes off. As far as Pentovsky and Zhukov are concerned, you're just a public-spirited citizen who's interfered with their plan."

A look of astonishment spread over Tony's face. He held up his hand in protest. "Hold it, hold it. How did I get the job of retrieving a live bomb?"

"It has to be you, Tony. They would recognize me. Look, I know how you feel, but it sounds more dangerous than it is. You'll have plenty of time—if you move fast." He saw the look of disbelief on Dantry's face, but persisted anyway. It was now or never. "Just hear me out, please."

Dantry shrugged. "What the hell, why not."

At this hour of the day, it took a few minutes to get a cab, but once they did, the ride from the Mayflower up Connecticut Avenue to the DuPont Circle Metro Station took less than 15 minutes. The station was filling up with commuters, as one would expect at the close of the work day in the nation's capital. Vyugin and Dantry moved as fast as their aging legs would carry them, dodging and occasionally bumping into harried, sweating commuters—all intent on getting to a train. The two men pushed frantically past one irritated commuter after another they, finding themselves on the receiving end of more than one angry look. Vyugin and Dantry were in too much of a hurry to stop and explain, finding it easier to ignore the glares and the occasional shouted invective.

As they entered the station, a train was just leaving the station, headed for the suburbs. While watching it pull out, Vyugin took the opportunity to tell Tony that Chandler took the Red Line out to Bethesda, and he always rode on the second car from the rear. Well, maybe not always, said Vyugin, but that's where he'd ridden the past two days. Apparently he and a friend made it a point to ride home together. That's where Pentovsky or Zhukov intended to place the bomb. They would wait until Chandler got on the car. "Then one of them will sit down, nonchalantly place the device under his seat, and get up and casually move to one of the cars closer to the front of the train. He'll then get off at the next station. As soon as Pentovsky or Zhukov leaves his seat to go forward, you have to move in, get the device, dart from the car, and toss it onto the tracks. All of this has to be done in less than a minute, or the train will be out of the station. And remember, this will be in the second car from the end, so you'll have to run to the rear on the platform and toss it behind the last car." He forced a half grin. "How are your legs?"

Tony shrugged helplessly. "They'll do."

"Keep your eye out for Chandler, and I'll look for my two associates. We can't be sure which train they'll place the device on."

"Won't they wait for you before they act?" asked Tony. "Otherwise, how will I know what they look like?"

"They're supposed to, but I wouldn't put it past them to take matters into their own hands. They've already preempted me on when to strike. Don't count on anything. When I see them I'll point them out to you, but I won't speak so as not to call attention to myself. The other one is likely to remain on the platform near me."

Dantry rolled his eyes. "Fuckin—" The enormity of what was about to happen was sinking in. He had seen photos of Chandler, but wasn't sure he could identify him in a crowd. And he had no idea what the two loose killers from Russia looked like. He'd have to leave that to Vyugin and hope for the best.

It was now 5:55. Hopefully Chandler hadn't gotten on an earlier train. For all he knew, the train he'd seen pulling out a couple of minutes ago already had Chandler and the bomb on it. He prayed that that wasn't the case and that they were in time to intercept the killers. At this hour of the day, the next train could be expected to arrive within another ten or twelve minutes. He felt his heart pounding as they waited. He half expected someone next to him to comment on how loud it was. Each minute seemed like an hour.

People were pouring onto the platform now like ants finding a scrap of food at a picnic. He craned his neck to see if maybe he'd missed Chandler further up the platform—or somewhere behind him. There were so many commuters now that he wasn't at all certain he'd pick Chandler out of the crowd—even if he were there. He was beginning to regret that he hadn't reported this to both the police and to Langley as soon as he'd had that first conversation with Vyugin. The FBI, too, for that matter. He'd allowed the Russian to talk him into something that he wasn't equipped—either legally or physically—to take on. Of course they'd intended to call the police to raid Pentovsky and Zhukov's rooms, but that hadn't happened. What the hell had he gotten himself into?

A comforting flood of images conspired to force the ugly present situation from his mind. He was alone on his boat somewhere east of City Island making his way towards open sea somewhere beyond the tip of Long Island. The images struggled to force Vyugin and his plan into the background. He needed to get them out of his mind entirely. Maybe he should just abandon the whole thing. Out on the sound he was master of his own briny realm. A misty morning, the imperious calls of gulls swooping curiously over his boat, waiting for him to drop something of interest overboard. The friendly hellos from other boat people—some familiar and some total strangers. As the morning wore on and when the sun was directly overhead, he'd reach into the cooler and pop open a frosty can of beer. "The bawdy hand of the dial is now upon the prick of noon." He forced a smile at the recollection of his favorite Shakespearean passage. He never touched beer before noon—a rule he'd stuck to all his life.

This Russian intrusion into his life wasn't his responsibility, anyway. But then he thought of his brother and how these bastards had killed him without a second thought. And now there was Chandler, just as innocent as Mark. Not to mention the others on the train.

He felt a nudge on his right elbow. "They're coming," said Vyugin barely audibly, not looking at him. He continued to look towards the tracks—like any other commuter. "To your right. Stand away, but close enough to get a good look at them and, remember, as soon as I've handed the device back to them one of them will take it onto the train. That's where you come in. Now don't say anything."

Tony saw them immediately. He'd never laid eyes on them before, but he'd bet his boat that these were the two. One was a hard-looking sandy-haired steely-eyed type, probably in his late twenties; the other, a younger, slightly taller dark-haired thuggish type. The blond guy looked as if he was the decision maker. The two men stopped and stood motionless, scanning the busy platform for Vyugin. Tony could see the light of recognition in the blond guy's eyes as he zeroed in on Vyugin. The young man scanned the platform and then motioned to the other guy, and they began threading their way through the mass of bodies on the platform, trying to move quickly, but without attracting undo attention to themselves. The idea was to be virtually invisible, in order to pull off the operation without a hitch.

As they emerged from the crowd and joined Vyugin, Zhukov spat out something in Russian and pointed towards a man approaching the track side edge of the platform. It was Chandler. Suddenly Tony heard the soft hiss of an approaching train. The

Washington Metro was so much quieter than the subway in New York. At almost the exact same time that he heard the train, Tony felt the push of air as the head car neared the platform. Chandler stood there, unaware, waiting for the train to come to a stop. Things would move fast now.

Chapter 17

Joanna was sitting restlessly in the spacious Dantry living room,
discarded sections of the *Washington Post* strewn next to her on the
massive fawn-colored sofa. Normally a voracious reader, she'd
gone through the paper listlessly, more to pass the time than out of
any desire to catch up on the news. She couldn't concentrate now
on anything but Tony. She was alone in the big house with nothing
else to do but wait for his return. Beth Dantry was out attending to
details at the funeral parlor.

Joanna was beginning to worry. She hadn't heard from
Tony in hours. She probably shouldn't worry. But Joanna had no
idea where Tony was or even if he was alive. Knowing how much
of a hands-on kind of guy he was, she was convinced that her
concern about his mortality was warranted.

Tony was a big boy—more than fifteen years her senior.
He'd said that he was going to be away from the house for a few
hours—that if he was late, not to worry. Said he was meeting
someone who might have some information about his brother. Just
go to bed without him. That had not made her a happy camper.

She'd cut him some slack because his brother had been
killed, and that was all he could think about now. He was obsessed.
Focused like a laser. So she'd cut him that slack, but when she saw
him next, they were going to have to work something out. She
understood his need to get to the bottom of his brother's death, but
she wasn't going to just sit on the sideline until he'd done whatever
it was that he was going to do. She knew, that with his background,
he was going to do more than just bug the police for answers. Tony

was anything but passive. That's one of the things that had
attracted her to him in the first place. He wasn't afraid of
responsibility or of meeting problems head on.("A hands on kind of
guy," he'd said on more than one occasion when they were making
love.) *that is not relevant, surely.*

Joanna was not content to be treated as some dumb babe
who was satisfied to watch her guy from the sidelines. Not that that
was Tony's style. When Tony shed his residual CIA macho, which
he'd worked hard to do, he not only recognized, but appealed to
her intellect. In many ways her knowledge of European history had
helped him better understand the world that he'd coped with most
of his adult life. The perspective she gave him on history made him
wonder why grown men in the twentieth century did some of the
things they did. One decade countries were enemies; the next
decade they were allies. But to arrive at this rapprochement a few
thousand or even million innocent people usually had to give up
their lives.

She wanted to help Tony now. Wanted to be involved. Just
sitting around the big house waiting was beginning to get to her.
Beth Dantry had left her alone. She had her own problems. But
being left alone meant that she had nothing to do but wait. And she
couldn't take much more of it.

Tony didn't deliberately keep things from her. It's just that,
as he'd told her once, he was kind of a loner when it came to his
work. She guessed it must have gone with the territory—given the
kind of work he used to do. If you were a spy, the more people
who knew what you were doing, the more chance somebody would
leak something that could end up being fatal for someone.

She still wasn't sure why they were attracted to each other.
Based on the raw facts, he was a bad risk. They were really quite
different in so many ways. She was not a gambler. Was not prone
to take chances. She certainly didn't get a rush from risking her life
—from doing dangerous things such as sky diving, rock climbing,
or flying an airplane. She could be quite content reading a book,
sipping an iced tea, going to a good movie, teaching a great lesson.
She loved doing research, discovering new information. Life was
its best when things were orderly and predictable. Her idea of

adventure was to travel and stay in comfortable hotels and eat in great restaurants.

Tony, she knew, had grown restless in recent years. He secretly missed doing intelligence work. He'd never admitted it, but she could tell. True, he liked going out on his boat, which was certainly not high adventure, but she could tell that he was spending too much time on the water. It may have been mellowing him, but it was aging him, too—at least his attitudes. He was beginning to accept an easy, slow-going lifestyle, but it was making him think like an older man. She could have lived with this, if it weren't draining the very soul from him.

She could tell in little ways that he missed the excitement of the hunt, of putting himself at risk. How he could miss that, was beyond her. She could only imagine it the way you imagine excitement when you're watching a movie. For her comfort and security were too important to put these commodities at risk deliberately.

It wasn't as if he were hyperactive or unable to deal with the things that mattered to her. He read a lot—mostly fiction—but also biography and even a little philosophy. But that wasn't him. It was part of him, but the bigger part of him, his inner core was the man of action. And until his brother's death, this part had been denied him—mostly because of circumstances—primarily because of the collapse of the Soviet Union and the end of the Cold War.

Tony was a person who cared deeply about causes and about people. About right and wrong.

She sighed and started to get up to go for more coffee. She'd been sitting there so long the residue of the rich dark blend had dried in the bottom of the cup. As she tossed the section with the crossword to the side, she heard footsteps approaching from the rear of the house.

"Hi, been here long?" It was Beth, back from her depressing errand. She sounded better than she must have felt.

"Couple of hours, I suppose. Everything taken care of?"

"That it is. That it is," she said resignedly, nodding her head as she spoke. "Mind if I join you? I haven't sat down since—" she hesitate. "Since the accident."

"Of course not. I welcome the company. You still believe it was an accident?"

Beth looked away for a moment; then turned back and faced Joanna. "I wish I knew. I know Tony has his suspicions, and I trust him on that. But we don't really know, do we?"

"I suppose not. But you do trust Tony? I...I got the impression that you and your husband and Tony haven't been that close over the years."

"Did Tony tell you that?"

"No. Well, that's not entirely true. He said when we were driving down here that the two of them had drawn apart over the years. You heard him yourself—the night we arrived. From what I gather they were just two very different people."

A wry smile appeared on Beth's face ever so briefly. "You can say that again. Mark was the consummate organization man, and Tony—"

"The CIA is certainly an organization," interjected Joanna.

"Yeah, I know, but that organization attracts a lot of loners and rebellious types. A lot of these guys operate almost as if they were freelancers. I think that's what Tony liked about it, because, from what I've heard—mostly from Mark—he was always his own man." She said it almost as if she admired her husband's brother.

"You see Tony as a rebel or loner?"

"Mark did. In a way, I think he envied Tony. It was something he could never do, but I think a part of him admired the free-spirit in Tony. Mark was an achiever, but he did it by playing by the rules. Some times I think he felt constricted by it. I suppose there's a little of that in all of us. I'll bet even now, you'd be hard pressed to pin down Tony's motives for pursuing this the way he is."

"I think you're right about that," said Joanna.

"Where is he right now?"

"All I know is he said he was meeting this guy who might have some information."

"Did he tell you who it was?"

Joanna frowned. "All he told me was it was a former enemy—someone he'd dealt with when he was working with the agency. A Russian, I guess." She sighed. "Tony's not a big talker."

"Yes, I know. Are you worried?"

"Oh God, yes. I could feel something when we were driving down here. Like he was dying to get back into action. Then, when he got that call from this guy yesterday, he seemed even more focused on this whole business."

"And, I take it, he seemed less communicative with you?"

"More remote, like he was now in his own world and with me he was just going through the motions."

Beth Dantry looked away and said, "Funny, Mark was like that at times, too. Must be a family trait. Anyway, you have no idea where Tony is now or what he's doing. Joanna, I'm sorry. I, I can imagine how you must feel. You seem to really care about Tony."

"Damn! Yes, I care about Tony. He doesn't make it easy, though. But thanks, Beth. You're amazing. You've just lost your husband, and you're concerned with my feelings."

"I've been through what you're going through, Joanna, more or less that is. The Dantry boys have never been easy. They've always been risk takers."

Chapter 18

Vyugin barked a command in Russian. He wanted to check the device before they planted it.

"There's no time," yelled Pentovsky. "Go Yevgeny. Hurry."

Vyugin shouted at Zhukov, who was already heading for the train: "Wait, give me the device, you fool."

Zhukov ignored Vyugin, as if he'd never intended to pay any attention to him in the first place. Tony, seeing this, realized that there might not be enough time on the bomb's timing mechanism to allow the Russian to place the device first before retrieving it. Instead of holding back until Zhukov was already on the train and in the process of placing the device, he decided to move immediately.

The car that Chandler was on was no more than 60 feet away, and Zhukov was already halfway there, pushing his way through the dense mass of commuters, themselves trying to get on the car. Tony was hoping to intercept Zhukov before he reached the car. Once the Russian was on the car with the device, it might be too late. Not only Chandler, but dozens more could be killed when the blast went off.

Zhukov was now no more than a dozen feet from the train and Tony was gaining on him fast. He was only a few feet behind the Russian. At this rate, he'd be able to grab Zhukov before he reached the door. As he was about to pounce on the Russian, Zhukov elbowed his way past a large overweight man. The big man's eyes blazed with anger. Seeing that the offender was already past him, he did the thing that any enraged citizen would do after a hard day at the office: he went after the nearest person he could get. Seeing that Tony was right behind the Zhukov, he decided to step in front of Tony. It was enough to allow the Russian to make it onto the train. Tony side-stepped around the irate passenger and pursued Zhukov onto the car. The car was filling rapidly, now, as the crowd on the platform pressed inward, hoping to make it aboard before the doors closed.

Zhukov was unaware that Tony had been chasing him. He knew that he'd annoyed numerous commuters on his reckless dash for the train, but he hadn't noticed that he was being chased. Once on the train, he proceeded as planned, casually sitting down as close to Chandler as he could get. The seats on either side of Chandler were already occupied so Zhukov ended up two seats away. Close enough, though. Once seated, he simply leaned down —as if he'd dropped something—and pushed the device under his own seat. The car was so crowded that his action went unnoticed— except by Tony, who'd just entered the car halfway down the aisle.

The doors started to close as Tony pushed his way past one annoyed passenger after another. He was now only a few feet from the seat under which the Zhukov had placed the device, but it looked now as if he wouldn't make it—that he'd probably die along with Chandler and most of the passengers on the car. The doors were almost closed now. Then they reopened because a passenger had forced herself halfway into the car. Tony knew, though, that they'd close again—this time for good. It was only a matter of seconds.

Zhukov was up now, making his way toward the door at the far end of the car. The doors began to close again. Tony was now at the seat that Zhukov had just vacated. His facial muscles were distorted, his eyes crazed with a singular obsession: to get to the explosive device. Chandler gave him a puzzled look—as if he were one more example of the Capitol's many nut cases. Tony lunged for the seat, groping underneath just as another passenger made a stab at being the last one to get on the car, forcing the doors open once more. Tony caught this with his peripheral vision and wondered how much longer his luck could hold out.

There! He could feel the device with his fingertips. Damn! It slipped out of his grasp. There. He had it. He rose and made for the nearest of the two side doors. The persistent commuter had finally given up and pulled his arm out. The doors hesitated in indecisiveness, shuddering dramatically as they readied themselves to close once again. A standing passenger yelled "Hey," as Tony shouldered his way past and gained the door as it was starting to close. He lunged forward, worming his way through the slowly narrowing opening as the insistent door finally closed behind him.

Tony was on the platform now. It was still teeming with commuters. He couldn't get rid of the bomb here. He had to get to the end of the train, only a car-and-a-half away, but slow going in this densely packed mass of sweating bodies. He had no choice but to forcefully bull his way through the crowd of annoyed commuters—people totally unaware of his mission and of the jeopardy they were in by just being in proximity to him. He glanced at the device. Maybe there was something as simple as an On/Off switch. No such luck. Just buttons and electrical contacts. They meant nothing to him, and there was no time to try to figure them out.

The end of the train was now in sight, barely half a car away. Could his luck hold much longer? As he pushed and shoved his way through the crowd, his crazed behavior attracted the attention of many of the hot, tired commuters waiting on the platform. Rather than confront him or obstruct him, they parted, giving him a clear pathway to the end of the platform. Realizing that he was literally living on borrowed time, Tony wasn't about to wait until he reached the end of the train. Instead, he flung the device as far as he could out onto the tracks behind the last car.

The bomb never hit the tracks. It exploded in mid-air, sending shards of glass from the two rear windows of the car onto the platform and inward into the back end of the car. The deafening explosion was made even more earsplitting by the confined area of the subway station.

At first Tony felt nothing but the sensation of being unable to breath as he was catapulted backward by the force of the blast. He felt a terrible pain in his ears. Stunned and confused, he gradually became aware that he was lying on his back in the midst of a screaming, writhing mass of humanity. Slowly and painfully he pulled himself up on his elbows, noticing people in pain to his left and to his right, many of them also lying stunned on the unyielding concrete platform. He was aware now of moaning and crying from every direction. To his left an older man was bleeding from the head. A young woman just in front of him was screaming, "I can't see! I can't see!"

Cautiously and slowly Tony got to his feet. He felt dizzy and nearly fell down. Now that he was on his feet he had a better view of the scene around him. Several people were down. Some were not moving. He couldn't tell if they were alive or not. There was blood everywhere. He turned and yelled, "Is there a doctor here? Is there a doctor here?" A white-haired man raised his hand. "I'm a doctor." He then made his way uncertainly into the middle of the downed bomb victims.

Tony shook his head a few times. He was beginning to get his balance. The pain in his ears was acute. He may have suffered a broken eardrum, but otherwise, he was fairly certain that he was okay.

He peered down the platform, hoping to see help on the way. Two policeman were running toward him. He had to decide how to play it and he had to decide fast. Clearly he'd saved Chandler's life, plus those of countless others, but he had no desire to claim credit for what he'd done. It would only raise questions about himself and how he happened to be near the bomb in the first place. He'd done what he'd done, and now he just wanted to get out of here without attracting attention. He hoped Vyugin could manage, too.

He looked around for Vyugin and the other Russians. Vyugin hadn't gone far. He was a few feet away, lying prone and motionless. He'd obviously been stunned. He moved slightly. He shook his head. He was just now coming out of it. Then Tony saw Pentovsky. He was on his feet walking briskly in the direction of the policemen. He was careful not to run and call attention to himself. Further down the platform, almost even with the cops, stood Zhukov waiting, a smirk on his face. The cops were past him now and Zhukov grinned arrogantly as Pentovsky joined him. Feeling safe, they were in no hurry to get away, evidently preferring to stand on the sidelines and enjoy the scene of mass terror they'd just created.

The two cops pushed their way into the center of the crowd. "Stay where you are everybody," bellowed the one who seemed to be in charge. "Just stay put, please." He waited until the buzz receded somewhat before continuing. "Can someone tell us what happened here?" he demanded to no one in particular.

A yuppie whose stylish black hair remained amazingly in place despite what he'd just been through, emerged groggily from the train. The cop repeated his question: "Can someone tell us what the hell happened here?" The young businessman pointed to Dantry and said, "This guy saved our asses. I don't know who he is, but someone planted a bomb on the train, and this guy grabbed it and got it out of the car before it exploded. It went off right here."

A blonde woman, attractive despite a face smeared with sweat and soot, blurted out, "No, I was here on the platform. He threw it onto the tracks, back there." She pointed to the dark area behind the last car. As she said this, Vyugin slowly got up and eased back into the gathering crowd, which now consisted not only of the injured, stunned, and confused, but curiosity seekers from farther down the platform.

"Anybody see who planted the bomb?" barked the second cop. No one answered. Dantry was faced with a decision. He wanted to maintain his own anonymity; yet the thought that his brother's killer was going to get away was impossible to accept. It was an easy decision. He pointed down the platform in the direction of the two Russians.

"Those two guys down there," he yelled to the cops. "The one on the left placed the bomb. I saw it."

By now more cops were rushing to the scene. They approached the confused scene from the opposite end of the station —behind the two Russians. One of the two cops already at the bomb scene yelled to the oncoming cops, motioning for them to hold the two Russians. The smug looks on Pentovsky and Zhukov's faces faded as they realized that they were no longer invisible.

The Russians had the advantage in that they could tell who the cops were, while the police hesitated for a few seconds, not sure who the cop at the scene meant for them to go after. It wasn't much of a delay—not more than five or six seconds—but it was enough for the two terrorist agents to elude their pursuers and disappear out through one of the station exits. Three cops continued in pursuit for a few minutes, but it was rush-hour, and it was easy for the Russians to lose themselves in the crowds of pedestrians on busy Connecticut Avenue.

Meanwhile, inside the station on the platform, the police were busy establishing crowd control and getting names of people at the scene. They'd already called for ambulances and EMS, and sirens could be heard in the distance. It was apparent now that at least one and maybe two people had been killed by the blast. Tony had seen one blood-smeared commuter he was sure had to be dead. He felt a sickly feeling in the pit of his stomach. He blamed himself for not having thrown the bomb far enough away from the train. If he'd only run another two or three yards, the dead victim might still be alive. Suddenly he was feeling woozy. A nearby cop grabbed him and kept him from falling. "Hold on pal. You wanna sit down for a minute?"

The cop's voice echoed in his ears. Was it his hearing or his balance that wasn't right? Or both?

"No, I'll be all right," he said, almost yelling to compensate for his own hearing deficiency. "Thanks."

"Sure?"

"Yeah, I'm okay now. A little woozy, but okay. Thanks."

The cop studied him for a moment and then moved off to do what he could for other passengers and victims. As Tony regained his balance, he scanned the scene for Vyugin and the Russians. Then he remembered that Pentovsky and Zhukov had fled from the station. He should have gone after them, but he'd been in such a fog that he couldn't have. And now it was too late.

But where was Vyugin? Then it came back to him. He vaguely remembered seeing his former enemy and now collaborator stealing off in the confusion. Good. At least he hoped so. He prayed that the trust he'd placed in this man was not misplaced and that he'd not been victimized by some sort of Machiavellian conspiracy dreamed up in Moscow.

In any event, he knew he had to get away from the scene as quickly as he could. He'd done what he could, and still someone had died. For this, he felt terrible, though he convinced himself that had he not gotten to the bomb, things could have been a lot worse. What he didn't want to do now was answer a lot of questions. He hoped he could just walk away from the scene and find Vyugin.

He drew in a deep breath as he turned to leave, as inconspicuously as possible under the circumstances, and started to walk away in the direction of the exit at the other end of the station. He'd gone less than ten steps when he felt a hand on his shoulder. A loud voice boomed in his ear:

"And where might you be goin' me lad?"

"I was leaving. Why?"

"The detectives have got a few questions for you—at the station." Then, realizing where he was, the cop added, "the police station, that is."

Chapter 19

He looked up at the clock on the wall in the drab interrogation room. Twenty after seven. It was still light out outside in the capital city, but you couldn't tell it in here. Joanna would be worrying by now. He'd wanted to call her when he arrived at the police station half an hour ago, but he'd hoped that he'd get lucky and they'd just put him through routine questioning—that he'd be released fairly quickly. That way he would have been able to call her after he was released. If he called her from the police station, he knew she'd worry even more, wondering *when* and *if* he was going to be released.

He'd been brought to the station with half a dozen others from the scene. Vyugin and the Russians were not among them. No surprise there. He and the other six had been kept apart from each other, and just now he'd been brought into this empty, green-walled room by two detectives. One was a slight, wiry fellow who was below average in height with closely cut sandy hair that was thinning in the front. The other, a light-skinned black man, was slightly above average in height, maybe five-ten, as closely as Dantry could judge. He was well-built with tightly cropped black hair. He had a round, friendly looking face, and it was clear from his muscular arms that he was in good shape. Probably worked out in the police weight room.

The skinny detective spoke first.

"I'm Detective Markowitz, and this is Detective Williams. Sit down, Mr. Dantry. Make yourself comfortable." He motioned to a chair on the far side of the chipped, gray-metal table in the middle of the cramped room. The two detectives then sat down on the opposite side, facing Dantry.

Dantry knew the drill. He'd used it on many occasions himself when he was with the company. The big difference was that the CIA wasn't always this polite.

"What do you want to know?" he asked flatly.

"We just wanted to congratulate you, Mr. Dantry." It was Williams who responded. "From what we hear, you're a hero. You ran onto that train, grabbed the bomb, and got it out of there before it killed half the people on the car. You're a hell of a guy. Hell of a guy."

Tony didn't respond. He thought he knew where this was going.

The two detectives stared at him a few seconds before Markowitz resumed where Williams had left off.

"Yeah, hell of a guy. What bothers us, though, Mr. Dantry, is how you happened to know this guy was gonna put a bomb on the train. The answer to that would be real interesting."

"I didn't know. Not for sure, anyway. I better back up. I used to work for Langley, and—"

"You were a spook?"

"I worked for the CIA, yes."

"Looks to me like you still do," said Williams.

"No, I'm retired now. I just happened to notice something that got me curious. I suppose it's the training. I'm sure most people wouldn't have given it a second thought."

"Like what did you notice?" asked Markowitz. "Tell us exactly what you noticed that made you curious."

Dantry tried not to show the frustration he was feeling. "I was standing on the platform, waiting for the train, when I noticed this guy standing in front of me pull something out of his briefcase. I'd seen things like this before. It looked an awful lot like an explosive device. I immediately passed it off as a figment of my imagination or a flash of paranoia from my past." He stopped and looked at his two inquisitors. He couldn't tell much from the deadpan expression on Markowitz's face, but Williams returned his glance with a look of disbelief.

"So what made you take it seriously?" asked Williams.

"A couple of things. First, I noticed that the briefcase looked really cheap. Next thing I know, he's dropped the briefcase on the platform and tucked the device under his arm, as if to hide it, but still keep it easily accessible. And it looked like he'd abandoned the briefcase. Pretty strange behavior."

"All of this went through your mind in a few seconds?" said Markowitz, sounding skeptical.

"Yeah. I've been trained to note these kinds of details. I spent twenty years paying attention to such things. In my line of work your life often depends on it."

Yeah," interjected Markowitz, "but if I remember my psychology courses, people tend to perceive what they're conditioned to expect. I can't imagine why you'd be expecting a bomb in a subway station in Washington, DC, on this particular day."

Okay, thought Dantry, so you're educated. I won't underestimate you. "I wasn't expecting a bomb that day. It's just that I'm conditioned to be suspicious when things look er... suspicious. And as I'm sure you know, the threat of terrorism was never limited to the Soviet Union. And I'm sure you also know that it's been more than just a threat. How can you forget 9/11? And the Federal Building in Oklahoma City, or—"

"Okay, okay. I get the point. Still, I find it hard to believe you noticed this in a busy Metro station. What else did you happen to notice?"

"Because he already had my attention, I followed him onto the subway car. I wasn't going to get on that car myself, but since he'd aroused my curiosity, I did. I watched him sit down toward the middle of the car and immediately reach under his seat with the device. Other passengers probably didn't notice this at all, or, if they did, thought that he'd dropped something or found something. But I was already suspicious, so when he got up immediately after leaving the mysterious object under his seat, I had a feeling this might be serious. That's when I made the dash for the seat and you know the rest."

Markowitz shook his head slowly. "That's some story. So tell me, Mr. Dantry, you live in New York City. What brings you to DC?

"I'm here for my brother's funeral."

William pursed his lips and nodded—as if maybe Dantry just might be telling the truth. "Sorry to hear about that. You realize that we'll have to check on that?" he said.

"Of course. Falls Church." He gave them the house address, as well as that of the funeral home.

"What do you do in New York, now that you're retired?" asked Markowitz.

"I have a boat on Long Island Sound. Do a little fishing. A little charter work."

"Charter work?"

"Yeah, people hear that I have a boat and want to charter it for a day to go fishing. I do it once in awhile, just for something different. You meet nice people that way—most of the time."

"You don't do any freelance spy work, do you?" queried Williams.

"No. That would be getting involved in foreign policy matters. It's against the law."

"And you'd never break the law?"

"Not intentionally."

"Do any freelance investigative work, or domestic spy work?" asked Williams.

"I've done a little investigative work—domestically. Nothing big."

"Think if we sat you down with a police artist you could describe this guy?"

"I'll give it a shot."

"Good. Shouldn't take long."

The process didn't take too long, once it got underway. It took 25 minutes to round up the artist. He wasn't really an artist, though. He was actually a cop trained to use a computer program where, with Tony's help, he kept trying different facial characteristics until they built a reasonable good likeness of Zhukov. When Markowitz took a look at what they came up with, he thanked Dantry and looked at Williams. In that unspoken way that cops communicate they made a decision.

"Okay, Mr. Dantry, we have your address in New York and Falls Church. Thanks for your time and thanks for saving a lot of people. You can go."

"Nobody's told me anything about the victims. Anybody die?"

"Yeah. A young woman, and a middle-age gentleman. But it woulda been a lot worse if you hadn't done what you did," said Markowitz.

"You get the guy and his buddy?"

"Not yet. We'll get 'em."

"I hope so." Dantry started to leave. His hand was on the doorknob when Williams said, "Oh, Mr. Dantry."

"Yeah?"

"Did you know the guy who planted the bomb?"

"No." Nice try, he thought. "Is that it?"

"Yeah," said Williams. "Oh, I do have one more question. What did your brother die from?"

"What does that have to do with all this?"

"Probably nothing, but I'd still like an answer," said Williams.

"It was an auto accident. He went off the road."

"Anybody else involved?"

"No, he just went off the road."

"Just went off the road. Hmm. Okay, Mr. Dantry. You can go. But don't leave this area without notifying us. We may want to talk to you again."

Chapter 20

"This better be good," roared Sorokin, sleep still in his voice. "It couldn't have waited a few more hours?"

"We felt you should know right away," said Pentovsky into the phone. Sorokin sounded as if he were next door. Fortunately, he wasn't. "We missed Chandler."

"What do you mean, you missed him? How do you miss someone with a bomb?"

"Yevgeny placed the device on the train, and as soon as he left the seat where he placed it, some guy grabbed it and ran off the train. He threw it onto the tracks, and it exploded. I think one or two people on the platform may have been killed. A lot were injured, but we missed Chandler because he was on the car."

"This is a colossal fuck-up. Can't you two do anything right? Where's Vyugin, by the way?"

"We don't know. He was with us on the platform, but he wanted to interfere so we moved without him. Maybe the police have him."

Pentovsky could feel the surge of anger from the other end of the line. Finally Sorokin said, "You don't know. This is a goddam nightmare. What do you mean, Vyugin tried to interfere?"

"He wanted to check the bomb before we used it. Yevgeny told him we didn't have enough time for that so we—"

"So you went ahead half-cocked and screwed up the whole operation. Not only that, the authorities could be interrogating Vyugin as we speak. Vyugin, by the way, may be a difficult son-of-a-bitch, but at least he's a pro. He doesn't fuck up operations. Now we don't even know where he is. And worse, you guys have been seen by the police, and Chandler may still be alive."

"We'll get him if he is," said Pentovsky confidently.

"If he is." Sorokin sneered in disgust. "First find out."

"We will. And then we'll take care of him."

"Find out, but don't do anything else until I tell you. Do you hear me?"

"Yes, but—"

"Just do as I say. Am I clear?"

"Yes, but—"

"By the way, who was this guy who grabbed the device?"

"We don't know, but we'll find out, if you think it's important."

"If I think it's important!" The anger was palpable in Sorokin's voice. "We don't know if it's important, do we? We need to know more about this man. Then we can decide if it's important. Find out what you can and be ready with the information when I call you back."

"But how do we—?"

"In the name of Lenin, man. Use your head. Check your television. It'll probably be on the news. If not, you'll think of something. Listen, I want to talk to you in a few hours. Stay at your hotel so I can reach you. If you hear from Vyugin, let me know immediately. And don't, I repeat, don't do anything else till you hear from me again."

Chapter 21

It was past ten when he finally pulled into the driveway of the Falls
Church house. It had just gotten dark out, and a single light shown *SHONE?* *SHOWED?*
warmly from the living room window.

Tony had called Joanna from his cell phone as soon as he'd
left the police station. He'd heard the anxiety in her voice, and told
her he'd explain when he got to the house. Little did he know when
he opened the front door of the sprawling house that she'd already
know what he'd gone through.

"Thank God," she said, throwing her arms around his
shoulders. "Oh God, Tony, I saw it on the news. You could have
been killed." As he greedily returned her embrace, his cheek felt
the mascara-smeared wetness under her eyes. She pushed the door
closed with one hand, continuing to cling to him with the other
arm. At this moment she felt closer and more intimate with him
than in all their previous love-making. Perhaps it was the way he
held her, the way he responded to her tenderness.

Across the dark suburban street an outstretched arm pulled
a sensitive pencil-like microphone back through the open driver's
side window of the parked rental car. The man placed the
expensive piece of equipment on the seat and turned to his
associate in the seat next to him. They both smiled.

Inside the big house, Joanna pulled away a few inches and
looked up at his tired eyes. "Are you hungry?"

"Right now I could go a beer."

"C'mon. Sit down and relax. I'll get you a beer."

Ten minutes later, shoes off and comfortably settled in the massive sofa, he sighed exhaustedly. He tossed down half a glass of beer in one long swallow and then slowly leaned back in the enveloping embrace of the couch.

"Are you all right?" she asked. He still hadn't spoken, except to ask for the beer. She knew enough not to ask him too much as soon as he got in. She'd learned the hard way that he needed unwinding time. The problem was, she was never sure how long that was.

"I saw the son-of-a-bitch, Joanna."

"The guy who planted the bomb?"

"Yes, the one who planted the bomb. He's the one who killed Mark, too. I was that close to getting him."

"How do you know he killed your brother?"

"Vyugin. The guy who called yesterday. He told me."

"And you trust this man?"

"Yeah, I think so. What'd they show on TV?"

"The inside of the DuPont Circle Metro station. God, there were people sprawled all over the place. It looked really bad, Tony. They said at least two people were dead—that someone had put a bomb on the train and that you'd run into the car and gotten the bomb and thrown it out. The news guy said that if you hadn't gotten to the bomb dozens of people might have died."

"They used my name?"

"Yes, they said you were a visitor down from New York. That it was unclear so far how you happened to notice the bomb and that the police were investigating. God, Tony, who was this guy who planted that bomb?"

He took another drink of beer. "It's complicated. International politics. Probably better I don't fill you in. Better you don't know."

"Why not?"

"If it's the people I think it is, the less you know about them the better."

"Whether I know who this killer is or not isn't going to change things. He's not this Vyugin guy, the guy who called you here yesterday?"

"No, Vyugin's one of the good guys. At least I think he is."

"Where's he?"

"He was with me when all this went down. He disappeared after the blast."

She snorted. "And he's a good guy?"

"I think I know why he disappeared. If I'm right, it's good that he did. But I need to see him, and I don't—"

"You don't know where he is. If he's a good guy, he'll get in touch with you, right?"

"Yeah, he will. Has anybody called for me tonight?"

"No. You really think this guy will call you? Are you sure you can trust him?"

"Right now I'm not sure of anything, but I think I can. Though I'd feel a lot better if I heard from him."

She pursed her lips, not sure how he'd react to what she was going to say next. She had to say it, though.

"Tony, what's going on? I mean, you're in the middle of some kind of terrorist bomb attack, and you get this call yesterday from some old KGB enemy, who's somehow disappeared, and I don't know what's going on."

"Joanna, I'd like to tell you, believe me. I don't like not having someone to bounce ideas off, but the less you know, the better. For your sake."

"If we're an item, Tony, and not just wasting our time with each other, I want to be a part of this. I'm not going to sit around here all day just waiting to find out if you're dead or alive. You've gotta let me in."

"When I first told you what I used to do for a living, I was glad that all that was in the past, because on more than one occasion I've seen the other side use people to get at agents. People you care about become your Achilles heel." He grinned, "Don't take that the wrong way, but you know what I mean. And, damn it, now I'm in the kind of situation where these guys, if they know about you, could try to get at you to control me."

"If they're as smart as you think they are, they probably already know about me."

He nodded resignedly. "It's possible."

"In that case, I might as well try to be of help. Maybe two heads can—"

"I get the idea." He exhaled audibly. "Okay, if you're game. Christ, what have I gotten you into?"

"If this all stems from your brother's mysterious death, then you haven't gotten me into anything. It's the bad guys who've done that. Now what's our next move?"

Chapter 22

"You still don't know where Vyugin is." It was a statement; not a question. In the intervening hours Sorokin had done his homework. "And it looks as if the police don't have him. Unless you know something more current than my information."

"No, I think your information is correct, sir. We do know who interfered with the mission, though. He's—"

"Anthony Dantry."

"Yes," said Pentovsky, unable to hide the surprise in his voice. He's the one you told us might get involved. The brother of —"

"Yes, you fool. I know who he is. He's the brother of the man you killed in the Lexus. This complicates things badly. You'll have to eliminate him before he messes up our whole operation."

"He's not going to be the easy target his brother was. He's obviously on to us, and he can identify Yevgeny—maybe me, too."

"Why the hell do you think I said he needs to be eliminated? Because he can identify you two." Sorokin then changed to a more moderate tone. These two were no geniuses, but he had to work with them. He didn't have time to replace them. Since the collapse of the Soviet Union and the end of the KGB, it was hard to get top people for intelligence work. Especially hard if you wanted them for work that wasn't strictly government work. "And, yes, you will have to be careful. This man is dangerous, and smart." He left unsaid *"unlike you two."*

"You want it to look like an accident?" asked Pentovsky.

"Don't worry about making it look like an accident. Just make sure no one sees you do it. Let them think what they want, so long as they have no proof. The important thing is to get the job done as quickly as possible, so you can get on with taking Chandler out of the picture. Have I made myself clear?"

"Yes. We understand. What about this Dantry's girlfriend?"

"What about her?"

"Shall we take her out, too?"

"I don't care what you do with her. Has she seen you?"

"No."

"Then there's no need to eliminate her is there? Our goal here is not to attract attention. If she gets in the way, that's different. Otherwise focus your efforts on Dantry—and then Chandler. Have you got that?"

"Yessir."

"*Khorasho*. Good. Let me know when Dantry is taken care of." He hung up.

Chapter 23

It rained the day of the funeral. The sky, overcast and gloomy, seemed to merge in Monet-like haziness with the trees in the background. A perfect day for a funeral, thought Tony Dantry as he looked out over the gravesite. The dark figures of mourners standing in rows two and three deep, holding dripping black umbrellas, recalled images from a Hitchcock movie.

He was surprised that his feelings ran so deep as he stood there within six feet of the grave, listening to the minister say prayers for his brother. His senses, deadened of late from the boredom and hollowness of his retirement years, were super sensitive this morning. It's not as if he'd ever given the mortality of his brother much thought before. The likelihood that Mark would one day die, like the ultimate end of everyone else he knew, was a given, but his brother had been such a vital—if ofttimes resented—force in his life that he'd never conjured up images for a day like this.

He couldn't remember when he'd been this confused. He felt something wet on his cheek, and he knew it wasn't just from the rain. His feelings reached out to Beth, who he knew had adored Mark as Mark had her. They'd been one of those perfect couples. That's probably one of the reasons he'd resented Mark. Until Joanna, he, Tony, had not come close to the sort of happiness with a woman that Mark had enjoyed with Beth. And why not? From everything he could tell, Beth was a terrific person.

His mind wandered now. With all that was going on, it was hard to stay with one thought very long. Before they left the house for the cemetery, he'd received a call from Vyugin, who'd said that he was safe and that he needed to talk with Dantry as soon as possible. Vyugin said that as long as Pentovsky and Zhukov were on the loose they were not only a threat to Chandler, but to Tony as well, since they knew he could identify them. They'd agreed to meet in a parking lot of a shopping mall in Tysons Corner after the funeral.

The minister was finished now. The immediate family and a few close friends were moving slowly past the casket now, each placing a single flower on the casket. Some paused to kiss the casket. Others, who must have been Catholics, thought Dantry, crossed themselves as they laid their lonely blossom on the growing pile of flowers on the coffin. It was almost over. Soon, he and Joanna would be saying their good-byes to Beth and be on their way. Or that's what Joanna was expecting. He had a few items to attend to before they left Virginia and started preparing for the mission they'd set out for themselves.

The first was to warn Chandler that his life was in danger. He still had to figure out how to do this without revealing to the police that he knew about the plans of the two assassins. Somehow he had to get word to Chandler without Chandler knowing who he was. This would be relatively easy, except for one thing. By maintaining his anonymity he also reduced his credibility. He could be a crank as far as Chandler knew. Then it came to him—a way to have Chandler take seriously his warning without the need to reveal his identity. He'd have to act fast, though.

In the pines that formed a somber backdrop a hundred feet away two men without umbrellas, but with coat collars drawn up around their necks, surveyed the assemblage of mourners as it started to break up.

Tony felt Joanna's presence next to him. He looked down into her eyes and smiled that sad smile that people muster only at sad events. He gave her side a quick squeeze and turned to leave.

"Let's go."

The three of them rode home together in the funeral car. When they arrived at the Dantry home, at Beth's invitation they took the time to have a final cup of coffee before getting on the road. An hour later, Tony and Joanna said their good-byes, vowing to do whatever they could for Beth. All she had to do was call. She said she'd be fine, but thanks for just being there the past few days.

Tony's emotions were very real at this moment. He was surprised to discover that he thought he knew what Beth would be going through in the coming weeks. His guilt at not making more of an effort to heal the breach between himself and Mark was close to the surface, and he wondered when, if ever, it would recede into the more remote recesses of his mind.

"You okay?" asked Joanna as they settled into the seats of the Cherokee. "Want me to drive?"

"No, I'll be okay. Just thinking." He smiled at her. "I'll get my mind on the road."

As the Jeep pulled away from the echoing rooms of the nearly empty Dantry home, a Ford Taurus, which had pulled over a few hundred yards behind them, started up and pulled into the quiet street, and followed discreetly.

Fifteen minutes later, the Cherokee entered the sprawling commercial area of Tysons Corner and Tony pulled into the parking lot of a huge regional shopping mall. He parked the car as far from the heavy concentration of other cars as he could.

"We have to wait in here for a little while," he said. "First, I've gotta make a call. I didn't want to do it in front of Beth's house. She has enough on her mind. Last thing she needs now is something else to worry about." He then proceeded to explain the reason for the call and what was going to happen after that.

She didn't interrupt him, as much as she wanted to. She had a lot of questions. By the time he'd finished, most of her questions had been answered. He was pleased that she agreed with the plan. If she hadn't, it would have made things more complicated. Still, her agreement meant her participation, and for her sake he wasn't too enthusiastic about that. It wasn't that she couldn't contribute. He was sure she could. It's just that he didn't like putting her at risk. He explained that, too, and she assured him that she knew what she was doing. He sincerely hoped so.

He wasn't so sure that she could know, since he wasn't convinced that he, himself, knew what they were getting into. For better or for worse, they were now partners in something neither of them had anticipated when they first started seeing each other. If they came through this intact, they'd both be different people.

It took two phone calls to reach the person he wanted. Twenty minutes later, he pushed the End button on his cell phone and smiled.

"I feel better now that that's done. Now we just have to wait here until Vyugin contacts us. Shouldn't be long. You want something while we wait? Coffee, a Coke, anything?"

"How long will we be here?"

"Not long, I hope. I know, this kind of thing isn't nearly as glamorous as they make it look in the movies."

"No, that's not what I meant. I just didn't know. That's all."

"He should be here pretty soon. He has to be sure he's not being followed by those other Russian clowns. By now they've probably got orders to kill him."

She gasped involuntarily. "God, Tony, you mean it?"

"It's a good bet. And Vyugin knows the score. Once he shakes those guys he'll be here. You sure you don't want something. There's a McDonald's over there. One of us could grab something and bring it back."

"No, that's okay. You should be here to make sure this Vyugin doesn't miss you. And I'm not thirsty…unless you are?"

"No. So let's talk. We haven't had much chance lately."

Chapter 24

Chandler's corner office at the I.M.F. was an imposing one. Easily the equal of that of a senior vice president in a major corporation. Pendleton was still standing, waiting for Chandler to get off the phone. He looked out on 19th Street, alive with a swarm of pedestrian and vehicular traffic. To his right he could just make out the Washington Monument.

He heard the click of the receiver as Chandler hung up. He was a tall man. Pendleton guessed six-four or five. He carried himself well, thought Pendleton. The perfectly cut dark blue suit was most certainly custom made. He wouldn't have been the least bit surprised to learn that it came from some legendary bespoke Savile Row tailor. Chandler would cut an impressive figure in any world gathering.

"Please sit down, Mr. Pendleton. Can I offer you some coffee?"

"No, no. I'm fine. Thanks," he said as he sank down into the black-leather couch seemingly half a football field away from Chandler's desk.

Chandler chose a matching black-leather chair at right angles to the couch.

"You made this sound serious on the phone, Mr. Pendleton. To be candid, the only reason I'm seeing you is your reputation at the Post, and, quite frankly, my own high opinion of the way you cover international affairs. I'm an admirer of your writing. I'm not sure I'd've made the time on such short notice, otherwise."

"Thank you, sir. I appreciate that coming from you."

"So what can I do for you, Mr. Pendleton?"

"Tom. It's what I can do for you, sir. This friend er… acquaintance has asked me to warn you of possible danger to yourself."

"Are you telling me that a 'friend' of yours is threatening me?"

"No, no, no. That's not what I'm telling you at all. What I'm telling you is that he has knowledge of a terrorist threat that could put you in real danger."

"And why doesn't he just deliver this message to me in person?"

"Because, sir, he's an intelligence operative, and he can't afford to disclose his cover—even to friendlies." Pendleton neglected to mention that his friend was no longer an intelligence operative. That would have made the conversation even more difficult than it already was. He was beginning to wonder why he'd agreed to help Tony out.

Chandler pursed his lips grimly as he considered what his visitor had said. "Okay, let's hear it."

"Apparently there are two Russian terrorists here in the DC area who want to prevent you from voting on the I.M.F. loan to Russia. In terrorist and intelligence terms that translates into assassinate." Pendleton watched Chandler's face for a reaction. Nothing. Cool customer. "This person—my intelligence source— says that these two guys work for someone connected with Malenkov and….now here's where it gets confusing. One version is that Malenkov would love to have his boss Kirov fail so he could take over. If this big I.M.F. loan doesn't get approved, Kirov…."

"Yes, I see it. Brilliant in a diabolical sort of way." He rose and took a couple of paces; then turned and faced Pendleton. "If they're after me, that probably means they had Mark Dantry killed."

"You could be right. The police are calling it an accident, but these guys are pros. Who knows what really went down. Anyway, the other version is that Malenkov is working to help Kirov maintain his power, and to do that, he needs to be sure that the loan is approved."

Chandler appeared dumbstruck. "But that makes no sense at all. Why would they kill the people who would vote to approve the loan?"

"As I said, sir, this is where it gets confusing. My source thinks it's the former—that Malenkov wants to undermine Kirov by having him fail to get the loan. The reason for the confusion is that he's getting conflicting information. It may be that these Russian agents have themselves been misled as to what the real reason is for the attacks on Mr. Dantry and you. My source will eventually find out, but as of now, it doesn't matter as far as you're concerned. Either way, you seem to be a target."

"I see," said Chandler pensively, though Pendleton wasn't at all sure that he did see. How could he? "This has to be handled carefully. I can't believe Kirov knows anything about this. I'm even surprised a little that Malenkov is involved. He's a Commie through and through, but I wouldn't have thought it was his style. God knows, we don't need an international incident."

"You'll pardon my saying so, sir, but it already is. More importantly, I think you have to start thinking about yourself. You're going to need to take some precautions. These guys are not gentlemen. They could strike at any time and anywhere."

"Yes, of course. I'm sure you're right," he said quietly with scarcely any emotion. Pendleton still couldn't tell if the man appreciated the danger he was facing.

"Sir?"

"Yes?"

"Weren't you on that Metro car that nearly got blown up?"

"Good God! Don't tell me....?"

"Yes. That was the first attempt. As you can see, these guys don't care who they kill so long as they get you. You've gotta take this seriously or your wife'll be a widow."

Chapter 25

He hoped Vyugin would make his appearance soon. He needed to relieve his bladder in the worst way. Good thing they hadn't gotten anything to drink.

"Having a good time?" he grinned. He reached over and gave her a tender peck on the cheek.

"It's okay—as long as I know he's coming. Don't you hate to wait for someone who doesn't show up because they got side-tracked for some reason? When you see them next time they say, 'Didn't you get my message?' or 'I wanted to reach you but I didn't know how?'"

"I'll be very surprised if he doesn't show up. By the way, good thing we didn't get something to drink. I've gotta go like crazy."

"You men are so weak."

"Can't argue with you there."

"Why don't you walk over to that McDonald's? If he comes I'll entertain him." She grinned wickedly. "Will he recognize the Jeep?"

"That's the problem. There's so many of these things on the road these days, he could easily check out a dozen just in this parking lot. And I wouldn't be in any of 'em. I better wait."

"Here comes someone." She pointed to a slowly approaching sedan.

"Let's hope it's him." He peered out the driver's-side window, trying to get a view of the person behind the wheel of the approaching car, hoping it was Vyugin so that one, he could relieve himself, and two, they could plan their next move. The glare from a nearby light atop a tall stanchion reflected off the windshield of the oncoming car making it impossible to see who was in the vehicle. The car was closer now and the reflection not so bad.

What the hell! Something was blinding him, something from the window of the approaching car. A red pinpoint of light—a laser-guided gun sight.

"Duck!" yelled Dantry, pulling her downward as he dove toward the floor. Joanna swallowed the beginning of a scream. The sound of shattering glass reverberated in their ears as a thousand shards assaulted them like airborne jetsam in an oncoming hurricane. It was more than one shot. A burst, probably a dozen or more rounds from some kind of automatic weapon.

Then it was quiet, but only for a second. Suddenly a squeal of tires and two more bursts of gunfire. No more glass, probably because it had already been shot out by the first assault. Now the rapid staccato of footsteps approaching the Jeep. Whoever it is, they were coming to finish the job. His mind raced. He had no doubt who it was—the two Russian killers. They'd already got his brother. Now they'd get Joanna and him. He was unarmed. Without so much as a whimper it would be over in seconds. He held his breath and waited.

Someone was pounding on the car door. Tony turned to look, knowing he could be greeted by a face full of lead. A dark, shadowy face peered cautiously into the car through the jagged space where the window glass had been less than thirty seconds earlier. It was Vyugin. So, his new associate had turned on him and was about administer to Joanna and himself the *coup de grace*.

"Anthony? It's me, Vladimir. Are you okay?"

"Yeah. What the hell happened?"

"Pentovsky and Zhukov."

"Dead?"

"Quite. The police will come any minute. We don't have much time. We must leave. Can you meet me….say, in the parking lot of the Courtyard Hotel in Crystal City?"

"Yes, what are you driving?"

"Over there, a green Pontiac. Rental car. Don't drive fast. We don't want to attract attention."

"Vladimir, please. You forget who you're talking to."

"Of course, forgive me. See you at the Courtyard."

"Vladimir."

"Yes?"

"Thanks."

Chapter 26

"You're bleeding," said Joanna, dabbing gingerly at his forehead with her handkerchief as the Cherokee pulled to a stop at a light. "You could have been killed."

"You are absolutely amazing, you know that?" said Tony. "I drag you down here and get you involved in this goddam mess, and all you worry about is me." This tendency of hers, Tony acknowledged to himself in his more reflective moments, was one of the qualities that had endeared her to him in the first place. Not that she was self-sacrificing to the point of self denial. Far from it. Joanna Barbeau had a well-defined, highly evolved sense of who she was and what she expected from life and those around her. It's just that she saw Tony Dantry as more than just a guy she could be comfortable with. Despite, or maybe because of, his own sense of security with who he was, she saw in him both an integrity and an intensity that she'd seen in no other man. He didn't seek or need the things most men sought or needed. Money to Dantry was important only for maintaining his independence; not for keeping score. Fame was to be avoided. If people liked him, he wanted it to be for who he was; not for who he appeared to be.

She looked at him now with those green eyes. They weren't really green, he realized. Closer to blue with flecks of amber.

"Once again I remind you," she said easily, "that you didn't drag me anywhere. I wanted to come." A look of contentment suffused her features. "I'm glad I did. Wouldn't have missed this for the world." Then she paused, as if realizing what she'd said. "I don't mean the funeral, Tony. I—"

"He smiled understandingly. "I know what you mean. What you're telling me is that you're a thrill junky."

"Always have been. Though this is a little more than I'm used to," she said, rolling her eyes. "At least in rock climbing people don't shoot at you."

"I've never gotten used to being shot at." He said, leaning closer to her. "Jesus, you don't have a scratch on you. You must have nine lives."

"Consider me your good luck charm, macho man."

"This is just a lark to you, isn't it? You know how close you came to being killed? Both of us for that matter."

She turned serious. "No, I don't think this is a lark. It's just that suddenly, coming this close to death, I feel more alive than I have in years. You know, being a professor of Slavic studies is interesting, but it's not exciting. Intellectually yes, but this is....I can't explain it."

"I repeat, you're a thrill junky." The light turned green and he eased the Jeep forward.

"I suppose in a way, I am. But it's not because I have some sort of death wish. On the contrary. I very much want to live— especially with you."

"I'll drink to that," he said and then fell silent. They drove silently through the busy suburban traffic, both of them coming to grips in their own way with their narrow escape from the jaws of death.

After a few minutes she said, "Do you think anyone saw the Jeep back there? The shots— I mean, could the police find us?"

"Depends. If someone in the parking lot saw what happened. Or heard it, they probably called the cops. But we were quite a ways from the busy part of the parking lot. These things can be weird. You never know. If the cops do trace us, it won't be easy explaining what we were doing there. Keep your fingers crossed."

Up ahead now they could see the sign for the hotel. As Dantry pulled the Cherokee into the parking area he scanned the lot for Vyugin or a police cruiser. The lot looked clear of both, so he pulled in and found a slot as far from the entrance to the hotel as possible. As soon as he came to a stop, Vyugin walked up to his window, or what was left of it. Dantry wondered how he missed Vyugin's car.

"Get in," said Dantry.

Vyugin opened the back door and got in. Tony was amazed at how unruffled the Russian looked, considering what they'd all been through, and considering that the man was no spring chicken.

Vyugin looked at Joanna and smiled graciously. "I don't believe we've met. I'm Vladimir Vyugin." He pronounced the Vladimir in that way that only Europeans can, but otherwise he could have been educated at Michigan State. Dantry, whose own language skills were considerable, couldn't help but be amazed at the Russian's linguistic adroitness.

"Joanna, Joanna Barbeau. I've heard a great deal about you, sir."

"Is that so?" A bemused look came over his face. He turned his attention to Dantry. "And what have you told this young lady about me?"

"That you're a smart old fox."

Vyugin feigned a frown. "Old fox, eh." He then turned serious. "We had better get down to business. Did anyone see you back there at the shopping mall?"

"I don't think so, but who knows? I didn't know those two clowns had followed us, either."

"They won't follow you again," said Vyugin with finality.

"I guess not. So what are you going to do now?"

"I'm going back to Russia." He glanced at Joanna before continuing cautiously. "Can we talk now?"

"You mean with Joanna here? Yeah. It's okay. What's on your mind?"

"Your, how do you say it here in America….your score is settled now. Or partially anyway. The guys who killed your brother are dead." Tony nodded slowly, a sober expression on his face. Joanna inhaled deeply as the enormity of Vyugin's words hit her. "But only partially settled, right?"

"Yes, only partially," agreed Dantry. "Whoever sent them over here is still alive in Moscow."

"Exactly. Bulgakov and Sorokin are still alive."

"And Malenkov."

"Yes, Malenkov, too. But I think I told you that, as much as I think he is bad for Russia, I'm not sure he was behind this."

"You're not sure he wasn't, either."

"True." Vyugin's manner changed, and he leaned forward, peering first into Joanna's eyes; then Dantry's. His manner became more deliberate. Joanna and Tony had no doubt that he was deadly serious.

"Do you want to finish the job?" asked Vyugin.

"Vladimir, as much as I hate those bastards, I don't need to taste more blood. You've done enough for me and my brother. For that, I thank you. You've put your own neck on the line. I can never repay you for doing what you've done, and the risks you've taken, but I don't need to have more people killed—even though they deserve it, for God's sake."

"You are sorry that Pentovsky and Zhukov are dead?"

"No, I suppose not, to be honest. But I think that's enough."

"Are you forgetting that there will be replacements and that their assignment almost certainly will be to finish the job. Killing Chandler will be their top priority. And are you forgetting that, in addition to killing your brother, the people behind this are responsible for killing two people in the Metro station? This is not over. It may be over for you, but it is not over. More people will die unless we do something about it."

Dantry frowned as he listened to Vyugin. As pedestrian as his retirement had seemed at times, he now realized that he'd come to enjoy the lack of responsibility that went with it. What Vyugin was suggesting was that he take on a lot more responsibility and assume a lot more risk than he'd been used to the last few years. But it wasn't in his nature to avoid responsibility. Not indefinitely.

"What's this 'We' shit?" he said, finally.

"If you will help me, we may be able to put an end to the killing, and at the same time bring stability and democracy to my country—something that you in this country should have an interest in. Worthwhile goals, wouldn't you say?"

Tony laughed. "You should have been a politician instead of a spy, Vladimir. You sure have a gift for sweet talk."

Vyugin shrugged, trying not to let his feeling of satisfaction show on his face. "I am just presenting the facts. If you help me, we can do good. Maybe more real good than we ever did when we were adversaries. Will you at least listen to what I have to say?"

"Okay, I'll listen. What's the deal?"

"I want you to come to Moscow with me."

A look of open-mouthed incredulity transfigured Joanna's face. Tony shook his head in disbelief. "You're serious, aren't you?"

"Yes, Tony, I'm quite serious."

Dantry folded his arms over his chest and leaned back. "Explain."

"Whether he's behind this or not, we must embarrass Malenkov by disclosing—or threatening to disclose—what his lieutenants have done. We discussed this in the hotel, remember?"

"Yes," said Dantry, without enthusiasm.

"Of course. What I want to do is force him to resign. If he doesn't resign, we must inform Kirov, who will sack him. This all sounds simple, but I assure you, it won't be easy."

"It doesn't sound simple at all. Do you really think you can do this?"

"With your help we have a chance. It will take a few days to get you a visa. In the meantime, we can use the time to plan. Are you with me?"

"You're only asking me to violate the laws of Russia and those of my own country as well."

"If we succeed, you will have the satisfaction of knowing that you saved Russia from another era of dictatorship."

"If we fail, I'll have the satisfaction of knowing I died in a good cause. Besides, I'm an American."

Vyugin smiled understandingly. "Yes, what you say is true. But if we succeed, you will also prevent Russia from becoming your country's enemy again. You tell me if that's worth the risk?"

"Why me?"

"You have the experience and the ability that is needed. I can't do this alone. And you speak Russian fluently. I remember that from the old days." He fell silent for a few seconds before adding, "Besides, I trust you. Ironic, isn't it?"

Dantry exhaled nervously. "Yeah, it sure is. What makes you think you can trust me?"

"You have a very personal reason for wanting to punish the people who are doing this. This is not merely ideological; it's...." He searched for the word, "it's visceral with you. Am I not right?"

"No, you're right," Dantry conceded.

"You're seriously thinking of doing this, aren't you?" asked Joanna.

"You think I'm a lunatic, right?"

"A few days ago, when we were still in New York, if you'd said you were considering this, my answer would have been yes, you're a freakin' lunatic. Now...."

Vyugin said, "You see, Tony, she agrees that you should do this."

On several levels, Dantry knew that he wanted to do it. It occurred to him that the only reason he even appeared to be hesitating was that he wanted to at least appear rational.

Tony looked at Joanna, and, when he spoke, his voice was barely above a whisper, "Do you mind? It shouldn't be long." He glanced at Vyugin, and added, "It better not be."

Vyugin replied soberly, "It should be over within a week or ten days. Hopefully sooner. Though we can't leave for Russia till Tony has his visa."

Joanna said, "I'm going with you."

"No, no chance," Tony exploded. "This is too—"

"Too risky?"

"It's.....just that..." he fumbled for words.

"It's what?"

"It is risky, and there's no way I'm going to expose you to this. Look, you heard Vladimir. I'll only be gone a week or so. I have to do this, Joanna."

"I understand that you feel you have to do it. But think about it, if I travel with you, you'll attract less attention over there. You'll appear to be just another American tourist traveling with his girlfriend. But if you travel alone, you'll invite scrutiny. And you certainly can't travel with Vladimir. They know who he is, and you're being with him would...."

He frowned. "Yeah, that's probably true, but this really could be dangerous, Joanna. Besides, what would you do over there when Vladimir and I are out doing our thing?"

"I might just be able to help you, you know. I don't speak Russian fluently, but I took a few years of it. I do speak French and German, though. You never know when they'll come in handy. And I happen to be a pretty good researcher, if I do say so. You might be able to use another brain. You obviously have enough brawn for the job."

"Ouch!" said Dantry. Vyugin winced and then smiled. He was enjoying this.

"So I'm coming. Right?"

Tony closed his eyes and tried to think of what he could say next to dissuade her.

She grinned and said, "Deal?"

He threw up his hands in mock defeat. "Deal. I hope the hell you know what you're doing."

"I hope *you* know what you're doing, spy boy."

Chapter 27

President Kirov took off his stylish new glasses with their thin matte-finished wire frames—the ones he'd gotten in the trendy optical shop on one of his infrequent sorties into GUM before he became President. He rubbed his eyes and sighed. The job wasn't as exhilarating as he'd thought it would be.

Kirov was an aficionado of American Western films. He'd had them smuggled into Russia even during the height of the Cold War. In his mind he often found himself comparing the unruly conditions of Russia with the conditions of the American West of the 19th Century. It must, he thought, be rather nice to be chief of state of one of the Western nations. Oh, he knew they had their problems, too. But essentially they were governable. He sometimes wondered if Russia would ever be governable.

Potemkin was standing in front of his desk, waiting patiently. Potemkin was so damned disciplined. He'd buzzed Kirov from his office to say that he had something of interest, something he should probably be aware of as soon as it was convenient for the President. Potemkin was so damned proper and deferential it sometimes drove Kirov crazy. He supposed he should just accept it as one of the few perquisites of high office. If only Malenkov and some of the members of the Duma were half as respectful. Fortunately, he didn't have to worry so much about the Federation Council, the upper house of parliament. Those members had been appointed since Putin had overhauled the system in 2000.

"I am not Stalin, Gennadi. I won't bite your head off. You will not be executed if I don't like the message."

"Yes sir. I know, sir. I mean, you're right, sir."

"At least a few things have changed in Russia."

Potemkin forced a weak smile before continuing. "I thought you'd want to know this. I was just informed that another attack was made on an I.M.F. member in Washington."

"Who?"

"A J. Martin Chandler, First Deputy Managing Director and the person designated to vote in place of Mark Dantry, the man who was killed a few days ago."

"Where did you get this information?"

"Our news agency in Washington told our embassy."

"And?"

"And what, sir?"

"Was he killed….this Chandler fellow….was he killed?"

"No, the attempt failed, but two innocent bystanders were unfortunately killed."

The President sighed, leaning back in his comfortable chair. Suddenly he felt very tired. "What happened?"

"A bomb was placed in a train in a Washington Metro station. Chandler was on the train, but escaped injury because some guy apparently dashed into the train, retrieved the bomb, and threw it onto the tracks. Only it didn't make it to the tracks. People on the platform were injured. Two were killed."

Kirov leaned forward, elbows on his knees. He covered his face with his hands. Potemkin waited patiently. Finally, the President sat back and said, "The next time they'll succeed."

"Very likely, sir."

"It must be Malenkov. I didn't want to believe it, but who else? Who else would have anything to gain from this?"

"No one that I can see. He seems like the most logical candidate. What are you going to do, sir?"

"If I had any evidence, any at all I'd let Malenkov know that I was on to him, that this had better end it or I'd unmask him to the public." As much as he knew the prime minister would deserve it, he didn't want to arrest the man and have a public trial. It would be one more embarrassment that Russia could ill afford. If a trial turned out to be the only alternative he'd do it, but he hoped he could end this evil without one.

"You're pretty sure now, Mr. President."

"Yes, but not that sure. The President of Russia doesn't go accusing his Prime Minister of murder unless he can back up his charge."

"And yet...."

"And yet, if I do nothing another man will be killed, and so will our loan. And with the loss of the loan goes the credibility of this government and Russia's hope for democracy."

"You could call a special meeting of your Inner Council."

"And not invite Malenkov? How do I explain that? No, I have to decide this by myself."

"If I'm out of line, sir, let me know, but it would seem to me that if you are going to take some action, you will want to do it fairly quickly, otherwise it will be too late."

"I'm well aware of that, Gennadi," snapped Kirov. "My options would appear to be all bad. If I do nothing, at least one more innocent American will die. Maybe more. The loan will go down to defeat, and Russia will have a new president—one who does not look kindly on democracy. In other words, Mother Russia will take a giant step backward toward totalitarianism." Potemkin solemnly nodded his affirmation. "On the other hand," Kirov went on, "if I publicly accuse Malenkov of being behind this, he'll turn around and accuse me of what the Americans call mud slinging. He'll deny it and make good use of my accusation to ingratiate himself with the Duma and with the voters. He'll come off as the victim. Which brings us back to where I'd be if I did nothing, only this way it will happen sooner." A bitter smile flickered across his face.

"Perhaps, sir, there's a third option."

"I'm listening."

"Perhaps I could, unofficially, of course, make contact with Bulgakov and let him know that you have your suspicions and that you are watching closely. That if anything else happens, you'll launch a full scale investigation and so on. That if nothing further happens, you will say and do nothing about this matter so far as Malenkov is concerned."

"Hmmm. It could work. This way, everybody saves face if they're innocent. If they're not, the last thing they'll want is to draw attention to themselves for something like this. Still, it's a longshot because you can never predict what Bulgakov or Malenkov will do. Hell, they could continue the killing and claim that they weren't involved—the assumption being that if they did stop the killing, it would prove to us that they'd been behind it all along, and only stopped because they were now under our scrutiny. Hah, our scrutiny. Who would I use to check on these guys anyhow? Most of the current FSB and former KGB people are in Malenkov and Bulgakov's camp. I seriously doubt if I could count on them."

"They can't be sure of that, sir. For all they know, you have a group of loyal operatives that you can count on. No, I think that you may be able to call their bluffs. Don't forget, you are the President."

"Yes, but what if we're wrong? What if Malenkov and Bulgakov are not behind this?"

"Who else could it be, sir?"

"I don't know, but I don't think we can discount some of our former Soviet republics. Belarus, for example, would love to see us weak. Even Tajikistan. Or how about the CIA? It's always in their best interests to keep us weak and off balance."

"But would we be weak if Malenkov ran the government? Wouldn't he rebuild the military?"

Kirov frowned. "Yes, he would do that. All right, it is almost certainly Malenkov and his supporters. I have to assume that. But on the off chance we're wrong, it's best that we do as you suggested. He has to be warned that this cannot be allowed to continue. You talk with Bulgakov off the record. It will give us wiggle room, if we're wrong."

Chapter 28

Bulgakov was in a foul mood. He pretended to concentrate on the document in front of him. Finally, he picked up his pen and scrawled his initials on the paper and set it aside. He looked up and glared across his desk at Sorokin, who'd been sitting there impatiently for nearly a minute. Bulgakov could see that Sorokin was becoming annoyed at being made to wait without so much as an acknowledgment of his presence.

As soon as Bulgakov had gotten the call from Sorokin telling him about the failed attempt on Chandler's life, he'd ordered his lieutenant to come to his office. Things were not going the way they'd planned them, and time was not on their side. The vote on the I.M.F. loan was only days away.

Making Sorokin wait was Bulgakov's way of showing him who was in charge. It was important to do this once in awhile because Sorokin had a big head and was ambitious. He sometimes thought he was in charge. Give him the slightest opening and he would be. Bulgakov knew that the younger man wanted his job and would grasp at the slightest miscue on his, Bulgakov's, part to show that he deserved it. The man was a snake, but, if controlled, a most useful snake.

Bulgakov set his pen down deliberately and glared at Sorokin.

"So, Anatoly, I assume you can explain the series of blunders in Washington?"

Sorokin's face turned scarlet. He fought to control himself to keep from blurting out some invective at the senior man. Instead he said, "These FSB men are not as well trained as the agents of the KGB were. Peacetime makes for complacency and sloppiness, I'm afraid."

"Yes, but my old friend Vyugin is not FSB. He was a decorated operative in the KGB. I can't imagine that he has been, as you say, sloppy."

Sorokin sneered. "No, I don't think he was sloppy. Whatever he did, I doubt it was sloppy. As a matter of fact, I don't know yet what role he played here, but I'll find out. That I assure you. Frankly, I have my suspicions. I told you from the start I had no faith in this man. Old age has made him soft." He paused to see how Bulgakov was taking this. He wasn't that much younger than Vyugin. There was no discernible reaction, so he continued, emboldened. "Your old friend," said Sorokin deliberately and with a hint of sarcasm, "has disappeared. No trace. No contact. Funny, don't you think, that the old man who expressed doubts about the operation from the start should disappear right after our two young FSB operatives are shot down in cold blood by some mysterious assailant?"

Bulgakov, who was as ruthless as Sorokin, nevertheless found this last comment as amusing as it was distressing. "Anatoly, let us not assume the mantle of moral indignation."

Sorokin appeared puzzled. "I don't follow you."

"Shot down in cold blood. Our operatives are not exactly on a mission of mercy, are they?"

"No, but...."

"I know, I know. I'm not happy with the result either, but the way you put it. Let's just stick to the facts, shall we." Sorokin was about to say something, but Bulgakov held up his hand. "No, let me finish. I'll let the reference to Vyugin's age pass—he and I have been on this Earth for about the same number of years—for I'm sure you don't consider me an old man." Sorokin avoided his glare. "We have a job to finish. That is all that matters now. We will deal with Vyugin when we have more time."

Sorokin couldn't resist interrupting this time. "Unless he continues to sabotage our plans."

"If that is what he's been doing, that could be a problem. But we don't know that do we?"

"No, but...."

"And why don't we? How did you lose control of this mission?"

"You can't hang that on me. These people had their assignments and someone got wind of it. As I see it, there are four possibilities. One, it could have been CIA or FBI who shot our men down in that parking lot. Two, and I consider this very unlikely, it could have been random criminals who mistook our men for someone else. Maybe drug pushers cutting into their territory or something like that. You know how crime-ridden Washington is. But, as I say, it's a stretch. The third possibility is Dantry, I suppose, and the fourth is Vyugin himself. I honestly believe he's the one. Believe, me, I know he's your friend, and I don't enjoy saying this." *I'll bet you don't*, thought Bulgakov.

Sorokin proceeded to explain his thinking. "The CIA or FBI seem least likely because they didn't identify themselves. The shooter or shooters fled the scene. The CIA or FBI would have no reason to leave the scene. They'd want credit for stopping the international terrorists and solving the crimes."

"Not the CIA. They're not supposed to use operatives domestically. But it is conceivable that the FBI might overcome their normal penchant for headline grabbing, and try to keep this as quiet as possible so as to force us into a careless move." Bulgakov smiled. "But that's probably giving them too much credit. I think I agree with your assessment. All right, continue with what you were saying."

"The second possibility is that our men were shot down by local criminals. They could've been Colombian drug dealers—not so local, actually—eliminating other dealers they thought were cutting into their territory, or they might have been local toughs high on crack or alcohol shooting at random. You know how rash these Americans are." Bulgakov nodded and indicated that Sorokin should continue. "But as I said, I think this second possibility is highly unlikely because I'm sure our men did nothing to attract attention to themselves, nothing that would even suggest they might deal in drugs. And as for a possible random act of violence, I understand that Pentovsky and Zhukov were the only ones targeted. No one else was shot at. So, that leads me to Vyugin."

Bulgakov pursed his lips and folded his arms over his chest. "All right, go on."

"You know, sir, how he had reservations about this assignment from the start."

"It was not the assignment per se, Anatoly, it was the whole idea of coming out of retirement. It took some adjustment, but once he made the decision he was committed. Of that, I am certain."

"I'm afraid that commitment didn't come through to me. But, anyway, let me continue. Later on, when he was in the States, in Washington, he had moments of doubt on the phone with me."

"Well, I'll have to trust you on that. You spoke with him, I didn't. Anyway, go on."

"Then, when Pentovsky and Zhukov brought the explosive device to the Metro station, they told me later that Vyugin wanted to waste time by examining the device—that if they'd allowed him to do that, it would have held up the operation. They said that, as it was, they almost didn't get the device onto the train."

"As it was, getting it on the train didn't seem to matter, did it? This mysterious good Samaritan came out of nowhere to save Chandler and to complicate things for us."

Sorokin frowned. "Yes, but that has nothing to do with Vyugin's unpatriotic actions. Pentovsky and Zhukov told me that it seemed to them that he was deliberately interfering with what they were doing."

"He was in charge, Anatoly. And let us not use words like unpatriotic. How do you think the supporters of President Kirov would view our efforts?"

"What we're doing we're doing for Mother Russia. What could be more patriotic?"

"Don't be an idiot."

It was all Sorokin could do to contain himself. He would kill Bulgakov if he thought he could get away with it. Someday he would get rid of the bastard. He took a deep breath before he spoke.

"All right. We all know why we're doing this. Still, we can't tolerate one of our operatives working against us. We agree on that I hope."

"Of course. If what you suspect of Vyugin is true, we shall deal with him. Right now, our priority is to eliminate this Chandler before he casts his vote. The latest word out of Washington is that the I.M.F. intends to put off the vote for another week. Maybe ten days. So we have time. How quickly can you get someone over there to replace Pentovsky and Zhukov?"

"Four, maybe five days."

"Make it sooner."

"You know I would if it were possible. It will take discreet discussions with the right people. Then we have to meet the candidates to be sure we trust them. They need to be briefed. And don't forget, when they get to Washington they need a couple of days to get their feet on the ground and scout out the territory."

"Get fast workers, Anatoly. This is your number-one priority. This is your only priority. We must finish Chandler off before that vote."

"On this, we are agreed."

"Oh, and Anatoly."

"Yes?"

"We must make certain this doesn't point to us. If this can't look like an accident, then it must look like some kind of Middle Eastern terrorist act. A bomb is probably still the best way to do this. Only let's be sure the bomb is big enough to include our intended victim. I know it's messy, but we can't afford to miss this time."

Chapter 29

Tony propped himself up on his elbows and looked down at
Joanna's smiling face. The boat was rocking gently in a light chop,
and Joanna felt at peace. They'd left City Island early that morning
and set a course east-by-northeast. When they were just east of
New Rochelle, he'd dropped anchor and they'd had breakfast.
Nothing fancy, just coffee, juice and bagels with cream cheese.
After breakfast, instead of fishing, they'd headed inside the cabin
and made love.

It was a hot day, and a trail of perspiration had formed
between her breasts. He dipped his head down and kissed her first
on the lips and then on each breast. They were lying on one of the
four narrow berths on his boat. Boats weren't made for sleeping in
comfort, but it didn't matter. That's not what they were doing. It
was the first time they'd done it since his brother's death, and he'd
felt a pang of guilt. She'd sensed from his first tender overture that
he wasn't really "ready," but she'd gone through with it—partly
because she thought he would enjoy it and partly because she knew
she would.

"What's troubling you?"

"I don't know. Guess it's just this thing in Russia. A lot
could go wrong. You could get hurt. I could get hurt."

"That doesn't sound like you. Sure it isn't guilt?"

"Why should I feel guilty?

"You know, your brother dies, and here you are in the
comfort of your boat screwing your brains out."

He exhaled a quick sigh and smiled. "Maybe. My mind is churning. I suppose I'm sort of confused by everything that's happened and is still happening. But, yeah, I suppose I do feel funny about our enjoying ourselves so soon after Mark's been killed. I know one thing shouldn't have anything to do with the other, but I guess it's in the back of my mind."

"Or the front."

He grinned. "Or the front."

Later, dressed in shorts, and lounging in the sun up on deck in the faded-blue canvas deck chairs, he broke that special spell that comes to those on boats while they're cruising peaceful sun-washed waters. The only sounds came from screeching gulls as they soared overhead, making occasional curious sorties over the deck, and from the throaty chug of other boats off in the distance.

"Our visas came," he said matter-of-factly.

"When'd they come?"

"They were at the post office yesterday afternoon." They got their mail at the City Island post office box, as did many local residents.

"When were you going to tell me?" The annoyance in her voice was palpable.

"Today. I didn't feel like getting into it last night."

"Don't you think that's a bit strange? I mean these visas are what we've been waiting for, and you put off discussing them until now?"

He frowned; then laughed. "I can be weird. I told you that a long time ago."

"Yeah, but I didn't believe you until now." She pursed her lips disapprovingly.

"I'm sorry. Look, I wanted to have one more so-called normal day with you on the Sound before we took off for Moscow. We could leave as early as tomorrow, you know. I'm gonna call Vyugin when we get close enough to shore and tell him we're ready."

"It's really going to happen, isn't it?"

"Yes, it's really going to happen. Still want to go?"

She drew in a deep breath and slowly exhaled. Sort of like before taking a game-winning foul shot or attempting an important putt.

"Yes."

"Okay, after I call Vyugin, we'll know what's what. We need to know what kind of plan Vyugin has come up with. He's not going to tell me that on the phone, though."

An hour later, as the boat approached City Island, Dantry placed the call to Vyugin. Tony told him that he and Joanna had their visas and that they were ready to travel. He and Vyugin agreed that they should first meet to go over their plans. Tony suggested the Staten Island Ferry so that they could talk freely. While neither of them thought that they were being followed, it wasn't entirely out of the question. And if they both met on Dantry's boat, it would look more than a little suspicious. Neither Dantry nor Vyugin knew for sure that the people in Moscow behind the assassinations didn't have someone else already in the States maintaining surveillance on Vyugin, especially since Vyugin had been out of touch with Moscow for several days. They had to wonder whether Vyugin was dead, on the run, or deliberately avoiding contact with them. The worst possible scenario Dantry and Vyugin imagined was that Moscow did know and had been following Vyugin ever since he'd killed Pentovsky and Zhukov back in that mall in Virginia.

Tony didn't completely discount the possibility of his being watched by the Washington police, either. When they'd released him after questioning him, he'd had a nagging feeling that they suspected him of more involvement than he'd admitted to.

The Staten Island Ferry wasn't a perfect meeting place. What was? But it was better than a lot of possible places. In their former lives, both Dantry and Vyugin had had plenty of experience taking evasive action, so their chances of avoiding surveillance, should there be any, were a lot better on the ferry.

When Tony told him that Joanna would be joining them, the Russian had sounded surprised, even though he'd been present when she'd first said she was going. It was hard for a Russian to accept this kind of involvement in such things on the part of a woman. Tony said he'd explain when they met. Not to worry. The meeting was set for three o'clock that afternoon when the ferry wouldn't be too crowded and they'd be able to find a corner of the deck where they could talk without being overheard.

The heat had been building all day and was now over 90. Tony wished that he and Joanna were back on his boat in the Sound. At least there'd be some sort of breeze. As the ferry left the Manhattan Battery pier, the air was suffocatingly still and weighed heavily on them.

They hadn't seen Vyugin yet. Joanna wondered to herself if he'd made it—a thought that never occurred to Tony, who figured that the Russian would make his appearance when he was good and ready. He was certain Vyugin would find them. As the ferry eased out into the harbor, Tony felt a welcome breeze. He hadn't been on the Staten Island Ferry in years, and had forgotten how enjoyable the trip was. He was surprised to learn that, now, if you boarded as a pedestrian, it was free. One of the last great bargains left in Gotham. Any other time he would enjoy this short voyage. Today all he could think about was the mission that lay ahead of them half way around the world.

Less than a minute into the trip they saw Vyugin approaching them from across the deck. He smiled as they met.

"A good place to be on such a hot day, no?"

"I'd enjoy it more if I didn't have Moscow on my mind," declared Dantry.

"I, too, my friend. I, too. He hesitated briefly and directed his attention to Joanna, "So you will be joining us, Miss Barbeau." He turned to Dantry and added, "Is this wise?"

"I think so, Vladimir. While Joanna doesn't speak much Russian, she does read it moderately well and she speaks French and German fluently. And she happens to be a professional researcher."

"Not any more," corrected Joanna, "but it's still a big part of my work. And, when I can find the time, I shoot traps, so I'm a better-than-average shot with a rifle." Vyugin raised his eyebrows.

"She's an excellent shot," said Tony, adding, "Besides, we could use another person we can trust."

Vyugin looked pensive as he considered this. "So be it," he said finally, breaking into a smile. 'I trust your judgment, Tony. How soon can you leave?"

"Tomorrow night, if we can get a flight."

"I'm sure you can. Wednesday flights to Moscow are not usually fully booked. That's good. We will need some things when we get there—things such as weapons and hi-tech equipment. I can take care of that when I arrive in Moscow. We should not risk traveling with anything suspicious. And, of course, we should travel on different flights."

"I agree." At that moment a man in a business suit walked by. He glanced briefly at the threesome and continued on, finally standing at the rail perhaps fifty feet closer to the stern of the boat. Tony turned and looked out at the slowly shrinking Manhattan skyline until the man was past. Was the man just a commuter going home to Staten Island earlier than usual, or did he have a different reason for being on the ferry?

Dantry looked at Vyugin. "Recognize him?" he asked in a low voice.

"No, but let us make note of where he goes when the boat gets to Staten Island."

"Yes," said Dantry, frowning. "Okay, where do we meet in Moscow?"

"You know Gorky Park?"

Tony smiled. "I read the book. Yes, I know it."

"During the summer months a circus performs there. Let us meet near the entrance to the circus. The weather for Moscow should be good for the next few days, so we don't have to concern ourselves about rain. You should fly Delta tomorrow night at 6 p.m. and arrive at Sheremetyevo-2 Airport around 11:30 a.m. Thursday. Check into your hotel first; then we shall meet. Say five p.m. Thursday."

"We'll be there."

"By the way, bring with you an attaché case or something of the sort with appropriate construction. I hope to have something for you then."

Dantry knew that he meant an attaché case with a false bottom for storing a gun and any other equipment that might be needed for the job they would be doing.

He nodded his assent. "Will do. What flight will you be taking?"

There's an Aeroflot out of J.F.K. at 3 o'clock tomorrow afternoon. I'll arrive in Moscow a few hours earlier than you. It will give me time to take care of a few things."

"And if there's a problem?" asked Joanna.

Vyugin smiled. "Yes, we should have a Plan B. Since my home is north of Moscow—too far away for me to stay there—I'll be staying in a small hotel off the tourist circuit. There is only one phone—at the desk. The desk will give me the message. They can be trusted. Not with too much, but with information on where you can be reached. I'll be using the name Igor Antonovich." He gave them the number of the hotel. I suggest you stay at the Cosmos. It is not wonderful, but it is large and easy to get lost in. And relatively inexpensive compared with the newer hotels there, which can run you $400 a night. You can probably use your real names." Dantry and Joanna took all this in. Then Dantry spoke.

"Vladimir?"

"Yes, Tony."

"Do you think your wife is okay?"

"She should be now. As a precaution I've called her and told her she should go visit our daughter and son-in-law in St. Petersburg for awhile—until she hears from me that it is safe to return to our home. So I think that she is safe. But thank you for asking. It is certainly another reason for settling this matter as soon as possible. I suppose it is not beyond the capability of Bulgakov and Sorokin to track her down if they decide to use her. Then I will have put not only my wife in jeopardy, but the lives of my daughter, my son-in-law and my grandchildren. You can see that it is imperative from my perspective at least that we act quickly."

The ferry landed at the St. George pier on Staten Island, and Joanna and Tony got off. They bought a Coke, walked around for a few minutes and boarded the return ferry for Manhattan. Vyugin, they assumed, had also gotten off and would take a later ferry back to New York.

Halfway into the 25-minute return trip, Dantry swore he saw the man who'd walked by them on the trip over, but he wasn't certain. It was only a glimpse and it was from half the boat's length away. He was about to mention it to Joanna, but decided against it. Why worry her, especially since he wasn't sure.

Chapter 30

The **Cosmos Hotel overlooked Prospekt Mira on the northeastern edge of Moscow. It had been built in 1979** as an Intourist hotel by the Soviet government to house Olympic athletes, tourists, and government visitors as well. To this day, many, if not most, of the hotel's visitors arrive by bus as members of group tours. Prior to 1991 the only way for a foreign tourist to arrive was by Intourist group. With over 1700 rooms, the Cosmos was the second largest hotel in the Soviet Union after the Rossya. It was a huge, crescent shaped building built with the clean, sterile lines of the dominant Soviet architectural style of the '50s and '60s. At the time it was the Soviet Union's proud symbol of modernity, though it never compared favorably with even the most mediocre of western chain hotels. When it opened in 1979, it was relatively efficient by Soviet standards. It rapidly fell into the more standard and typical Soviet inefficiency through poor management and bureaucratic neglect. Since the fall of the Soviet Union, the hotel's physical structure had undergone renovation, and the service was somewhat improved. They'd even added a casino. The hotel was still below the standards of the West, but they seemed to be trying. And due to its sheer size it was still an impressive edifice as you approached it from the street.

"On our next visit to Moscow," said Dantry, "we'll stay at one of the new hotels. They're run by western hotel companies, and the amenities, service, and food are better. Still, Vyugin's probably right. This time we're better off at the Cosmos. Besides, I'm not really in the mood to enjoy Moscow."

"I know what you mean," said Joanna. "This is my first time in Russia. It would have been nice to have seen it as a tourist."

"Well, Vyugin was right about the weather. You'd never guess it could be thirty below here in January, would you?"

"No, this is beautiful. Nice weather for spying and clandestine activities."

"Jeez, don't even kid about that here. It's like kidding about bombs when you're flying. They take those things seriously here."

They'd arrived at Sheremetyevo-2 Airport about a half hour later than the 11:30 a.m. scheduled arrival time. By the time they'd gotten their luggage and gone through customs they'd used up another hour. Now, it was almost two p.m. and they were scheduled to meet Vyugin at five.

"Well, what d'you think of the Cosmos?" asked Tony as they settled into their room on the 11th floor.

"It sort of reminds me of the first time I was in a Holiday Inn," she grinned, adding, "though not as elegant."

"First time I've been here since 1989, I think. Hasn't changed all that much, though the people behind the desk appear to have aged badly."

At first she wasn't sure whether he was kidding. Then she said, "Right, but are they any more helpful?"

"Marginally, I suppose, but not as much as I would have hoped. Old habits are hard to break."

"Not if your manager rewards you for giving good service and fires you if you don't."

"Don't forget, most of these managers are left over from the old days. They think the same way the other employees do. The newer hotels in Moscow—the ones owned by western hotel chains —are better because they brought in managers from outside Russia —people who understand the concept of service. Gradually they've passed that along to the locals who work in the hotels, and it shows. This country has a long way to go, but Russians are a smart, well-educated people. If they can shake off the old ways, I think they'll make it."

"Yes, but apparently the old ways still have a strong grip on the way many Russians think."

"It's true. It won't be easy to break the cycle."

After a late lunch in the hotel coffee shop, Joanna and Tony went outside for a walk. It was the first time since they left J.F.K. that they'd had a chance to stretch their legs.

"What I'd like to do now is take a nap," said Dantry. "Most people feel that way after an all-night flight, unless they're among that lucky minority who can sleep well on an airplane. It's better, though, to stay up and get to sleep at a decent hour tonight. Tomorrow we'll feel better. If we napped now, we might not get up, or if we did, we'd have a hard time sleeping tonight."

"I'm in your experienced hands. You're the expert. But do you think we *will* get to sleep at a decent hour tonight? Do you have any idea what Vyugin has in mind for today, or more properly, for tonight?"

"No, but you're right, he may have something in mind for tonight. I know he wants to get on this as soon as possible. Just between us, I wouldn't mind waiting till tomorrow. A good night's sleep is beginning to look pretty good right now."

"I have this funny feeling we're not going to get it."

At four forty-five they got out of a taxi on the Leninsky Prospect and walked toward Gorky Park. The taxi ride was less than four miles, but because of the traffic, something that was never a problem on Dantry's previous visits to Moscow, it took 45 minutes. Part of Gorky Park over the years had become an amusement park, and it was not unattractive as amusement parks went. Much of Gorky Park's roughly half-square mile of land, which was nestled between the Moscow River on the west and Leninsky Prospect on the east, was still devoted to traditional green space. There was even a pond at the southern end. In all, it was a pleasant place for Muscovites and visitors alike to spend a day or portion of a day.

As they strolled the few hundred yards from Leninsky Prospect to the section of the park where the circus had become a permanent fixture, Dantry turned to Joanna and smiled as if to say what a great day this was turning out to be. She returned his smile. "My first time in Moscow and so far I love it."

"Hope you feel that way when we leave."

"I know, I wish we could be tourists and…."

"Me, too, but I'm afraid that's not in the cards."

She slowed to a stop and faced Dantry.

"Tony, so many reasons have been given for coming here, I'm not sure which one is really motivating you."

"Which one do *you* think motivates me? I'll tell you what I think, but I just want to hear how you see it."

"I suppose it's getting even with the people who killed your brother, though, knowing you, it's probably not that simple. I assume you care, at least somewhat, what happens in Russia, especially as it could affect the U.S., so you probably would like to see Malenkov embarrassed or unseated." She paused, and asked, "How'm I doing?"

"You're right on. You really do know me. Christ! It's frightening how well you know me. The only thing I'd modify is the last part of what you said. After seeing what Vyugin has done and how he's put his life on the line to do what he now sees as right, I guess I've been sort of shamed into doing something for my country. Hell, my brother's already dead, so any revenge I get is for me more than it is for him, I suppose. But if Vyugin and I— and you, my God, I can't forget you—if the three of us can do something to improve the chances for peace between our countries, I want to do it. Man, does that sound sappy or what? This is a new me, believe me."

"Maybe it's a you that's just been lying dormant for a few years. I mean you did risk your life for your country for more than 20 years."

"I don't know. To be honest, I think I did it for myself as much as for my country. It was a good reason for having a life of adventure. Sort of like the French Foreign Legion. Those guys want the adventure. They don't care if they're on the right side or not."

"When you were with the company were you that cynical?"

"Probably not. I did think we were the good guys, though I have to say, there were times when I wondered if some of things I was asked to do were necessary or even right. But I did them anyway. Christ, I sound like some fuckin' Nazi at Nuremberg."

"No! Not in the least. You didn't authorize mass killings. You didn't supervise the annihilation of innocent men, women, and children. And I'm sure that, if you did have to kill anyone, it was an enemy agent or someone connected with the enemy cause." As the last of these words escaped her mouth, it suddenly occurred to Joanna that, if she were wrong, her feelings toward this man—this wonderful man she thought she knew so well—could not help but be altered forever. She looked at him, pleadingly, praying that his next words not deal her a crushing blow.

The color had drained from his face. He hadn't done these Nuremberg-scale things. Not mass killings, not the slaughter or supervision of the slaughter of innocent people. But he had killed. Even at the time, when he'd been in the flush with enthusiasm for his career, he'd been uncomfortable with killing. The first time he'd lain awake the entire night preceding the assignment. Not the second time, though. It was true that it got easier. But not that easy.

Looking back, when he'd permitted himself to reflect on it, he realized that he'd comforted himself (if you could call it comfort) with the belief that they'd been 'good kills'—the term they used in the intelligence field. Meaning the victims deserved it. They were not like his brother, who just happened to be in the way, who created a problem of inconvenience for some shadowy politicians in Moscow. No, his kills had been good ones. One victim had killed a fellow American agent. The other had information that would have resulted in the deaths of several American and British agents, had he been able to get that information to Moscow. By the ethical standards of intelligence work, they'd been good kills. But by the moral standards of Western society, he wondered. He'd been looking at his feet as he was reflecting on this. Now he looked at Joanna, whose eyes hadn't left him.

"I've dealt with this every day of my life since the first time I had to eliminate someone. I almost quit on the spot when I got that first assignment," he paused a few seconds, then heard himself say, "but I didn't. I don't know what that says about me. I'm probably not as good as you think I am, but for the sake of my own sanity I've convinced myself that I'm not as bad as I could have been. I never went looking for that kind of assignment."

"And that last time in London, you drew the line there."

He sighed. "Yeah, I drew the line there."

He directed his attention to the circus off in the distance. "We'd better get moving. Vyugin'll wonder what happened to us."

She forced a wan smile and entwined her arm with his as they resumed walking. Nearing the circus, they could see people milling around the entrance. Dantry squinted vainly trying to catch sight of Vyugin. Joanna saw him first and waved.

"I see you made it," beamed Vyugin vigorously. "Good, let us find a bench and talk."

A few minutes later, Vyugin and Joanna were seated on a park bench as Dantry leaned casually against a tree. Vyugin spoke first.

"I would like to commence our activities tomorrow. I realize that jet lag can take its toll and that you may not be at your best tonight."

"If you want to proceed tonight," grinned Joanna, "we can do it." She glanced up at Tony for confirmation. He grinned back, dipping his head a half inch.

"You mean if this old man can do it, you can do it," said Vyugin wryly. Joanna blushed and Tony chuckled. "Of course you could do it," continued Vyugin, "but I have seen too many missions go afoul because of fatigue. It is not a question of willingness, so much as asking too much of the body. I think it is best that we all be refreshed for what lies ahead of us."

As willing as they were to get started right away, neither Tony nor Joanna offered any objection to Vyugin's decision. Suddenly they felt the heavy weight of fatigue setting in, and a good night's sleep sounded pretty attractive. They agreed to meet the following morning at 9:20 a.m.

Chapter 31

Alexei Borodin became a KGB agent in 1980. To all who came in contact with him during the rigorous training that the KGB imposed on its candidates, he was transparently ambitious. He was also good at what he did—smart and physically superior to most of his fellow agents-in-training, and good with languages. He'd come out of KGB training fluent in American English. So fluent was he that he could fool most Americans. His youthful good looks and his easy grasp of American culture, body language, and slang would have gained him acceptance on any American college campus.

His first assignment back in late 1980 had taken him to Garmisch-Partenkirchen, Germany, so that he could mingle with the soldiers and officers at the nearby U.S. Army base. It was not a true intelligence assignment, but rather a test of his ability to pass himself off as a private citizen amongst foreigners. He would also be able to hone his linguistic and cultural skills in order to make him completely conversant with the latest idioms and cultural fads in the West. It would prepare him for more serious work later on.

Borodin had loved the Garmisch assignment. He was a moderately good skier and he was able to sharpen his skill on the nearby Alpine slopes, all in the name of becoming more proficient at his job.

When the Soviet Union broke up in '91, and the Cold War ended, Borodin was devastated. He'd had his heart set on making a career in intelligence work, hoping someday to rise to be head of the KGB. He had little doubt but that he would make it. Borodin was not lacking in self-confidence. But the break-up changed everything.

Being the consummate pragmatist, Borodin looked for something else in government. Something that would put him near the seat of power. Something that would provide him with the opportunity to meet the right people so that he might acquire some of that power. He could, of course, have stayed in intelligence work and become a part of the FSB, the KGB's successor organization, but in his mind it wasn't quite the same. People didn't respect, nor to be honest, fear the FSB the way they had the KGB.

In his few short years with the KGB, he'd made a name for himself as a rising star with a future. The names of the institutions may have changed with the collapse of the Soviet Union, but many of the players in the new government were the same people. Some adopted the democratic ideology of the new Russia, and some only pretended to. Borodin's reputation as a talented operative brought him to the attention of important people and ultimately landed him the job as Malenkov's personal aide. Being the personal assistant to Prime Minister Malenkov was nearly as influential as being his Chief of Staff.

But Borodin almost didn't make it, for one night in the winter of 1980-81, when he was much younger, when he was on that first KGB assignment in Garmisch-Partenkirchen, he got himself into a situation that could have brought his career to a screeching halt. It happened in a ski lodge that three American girls had rented. In truth, it was more of an alpenhaus or mountain house than lodge. Borodin, the three girls, and some of his American and German male acquaintances, had been skiing all day, and drinking all night. Atypically, Borodin had eaten practically nothing that night and was feeling his drinks.

Around midnight, the American girls brought out marijuana and they started smoking. Borodin had never smoked cannabis before, and the combination with alcohol made him giddy. He soon lost control of his normal inhibitions and found himself participating in what could only be described as an orgy. Around three in the morning, in the heat of this ongoing Saturnalia, one of the young Germans brought out a camera and began snapping shots of the debauchery. A couple of the girls and one guy objected, but they were all in such a dazed state that their protests were weak and soon forgotten in the lustful heat of the moment. As the German clicked away with his Leica, Alexei Borodin was in a most compromising position, providing pleasure to one of the girls —a particularly well-developed, nubile blonde, while at the same time receiving pleasure from one of the other German males—a rather insignificant wisp of a young man.

Borodin's on-site supervisor at the time was Vladimir Vyugin. Vyugin had been given the assignment as a sort of perk. He'd just come out of an undercover assignment in Berlin, where he'd barely escaped with his life. Supervising a young neophyte operative in Garmisch-Partenkirchen was a pleasant contrast to what he'd been through. Vyugin was at least 15 years Borodin's senior, so he rarely attempted to keep the bar-hopping pace of his younger colleague.

Tonight, however, he'd had a funny feeling. He'd had dinner alone in one of the town's restaurants that catered to the skiing crowd. Just by coincidence he noticed Borodin at the restaurant's bar surrounded by a bunch of new-found acquaintances. Vyugin had never seen his young colleague drink so much, nor behave so recklessly. After retiring to his room for the night, Vyugin got to worrying. Being out of control was a definite no-no in the intelligence trade. He did not want one of his charges to get in trouble—especially when he was supposed to be training him. He decided he'd better go check on Borodin.

He went back to the restaurant, only to find that Borodin and his friends were no longer there. Gisela, the barmaid, told him that she'd overheard one of the three American girls mention that they were staying in an A-frame on Kirchstrasse. He'd told her his young colleague had an appointment in the morning that he didn't know about. He smiled as he told her that he was sure his friend would want to curtail his evening once he knew about the meeting. She smiled back knowingly and described the place she thought it was. Vyugin thanked her and went off to find Borodin.

As Vyugin approached the house, he noticed there was no light coming from the windows. Could it be the wrong house? Slowly he walked around the building, peering into each window as he came to it. As he approached the back of the house, he noticed a patch of pale yellow light on the snow-covered ground. It came from a rear window. Cautiously he edged closer. Sounds of laughing, punctuated by squeals and amatory screams came from within. A diaphanous curtain was drawn over the window, but it was mostly cosmetic. Ninety percent of the light in the room passed through it, and it was not difficult for Vyugin to see what was going on inside.

While no prude, Vyugin stood in open-mouthed amazement at the sight that met his eyes. He'd never participated in, nor even seen a bacchanal, orgy, whatever one cared to call it. As he stared through the porous curtain, he was embarrassed to find himself being aroused by what was going on before him. He turned away for a moment—to regain a modicum of composure and presentability. The shock of what he'd seen had prevented him from noting details the way he was trained to record them. Christ, he'd make a lousy witness tonight, wouldn't he.

He listened carefully for a full minute to be sure no one saw him or was nearby. Then he went back to the window and peered in again—this time with a purpose. Yes, damn! It was Borodin, as he feared. Stupid bastard.

Vyugin stepped back to give himself a chance to think. His mind was in a turmoil, and his hormones were raging. He was in conflict with himself. Finally, his mind won out. He had to protect the integrity of the KGB. He couldn't allow his young charge to destroy himself (not that the stupid shit didn't deserve it) and embarrass the organization. This wasn't going to be easy or pleasant, but he was going to have to go in there and drag Borodin out. He took one last look inside. Damn! He wouldn't have believed the situation could get worse, but it just did. Some tall, skinny guy was standing there stark naked with a camera taking pictures as fast as he could click the shutter. Vyugin knew he had to act now.

He ran around to the front of the ski lodge and tried the door. It offered no resistance and opened on his first try. Stupid fools, didn't even lock the door. Once inside, it was easy to tell from the noise where the party was taking place. He checked to make sure that no one was wandering around the first floor or hiding in one of the other rooms. Nobody. He was alone. Obviously no one wanted to be left out of the festivities in the room at the rear of the house. Vyugin headed in the direction of the revelry. The door to the orgy room was closed, though he doubted that it was locked.

He took a deep breath and threw open the door. At first, no one noticed him. A momentary advantage, and he seized it. The skinny guy with the camera was still clicking away with his back to Vyugin when the Russian went for him, coming up from behind and deftly yanking the camera from the naked kid's hand before he knew what happened. Vyugin opened the camera, pulled the film cartridge out, and jammed it into his pants pocket.

The youth's reflexes were dulled by the substances he'd been ingesting most of the evening. He turned and stared at Vyugin with incomprehension at what had just happened. Vyugin didn't wait to explain; he'd already taken two strides toward the *ménage-à-trois* on the floor—a ménage in which Borodin appeared to taking an active part.

Vyugin hoped that Borodin hadn't compounded his foolishness by using his real name with this crew, so he didn't use it either. Instead, he barked, "Get up and grab your cloths. Fast!" Borodin, who moments earlier had been lively and agile in his movements, suddenly appeared catatonic as he pulled himself slowly to a sitting position. His thought processes seemed to have slowed to a glacial pace, no doubt induced by drugs and alcohol and exacerbated by the shock of being yelled at by an angry, sober Vyugin. Slowly he focused on the source of the voice he'd just heard.

"Vladimir? What are you doing here?"

Vyugin rolled his eyes. "Just get your clothes. I won't even ask you what you're doing here. I can see for myself."

"Leave him alone," muttered one of the young Germans halfheartedly.

"Yes," chimed in one of the young women, "leave him alone."

Vyugin scanned the room. In their condition, no one seemed capable of offering serious interference, but you never knew. Any one of them could have a weapon and might use it. Barring that, someone could pick up a lamp or something and bring it crashing down on his head. Or if they all ganged up on him, it could also get ugly. He had to get Borodin out of there fast.

He bent down and pulled Borodin up by the armpits. God, he was slippery with sweat and who knew what else. Vyugin had to get a better grasp, which wasn't inviting, but this was no time to be finicky. Borodin offered little resistance other than that of the dead weight of his limp, slippery body.

Vyugin felt someone's hand on his shoulder. He swung around knocking the hand away, at the same time barking, "Back off!" A short, thickset young man, slick with perspiration, stepped backward, not wanting to test the will of the intruder further.

Quickly Vyugin regrasped the sinking sweaty body of Borodin as it started to slide limply to the floor. "Damn you, Bor —" He caught himself just in time. "Damn you, if I get you out of here…." He left the rest unsaid.

"You can't do this," protested Borodin feebly.

"The hell I can't. Where the hell are your clothes?"

Borodin pointed a wavering finger toward a pair of jeans and a yellow T-shirt lying in a heap on an overstuffed chair. "There."

Vyugin grabbed the clothes and handed him the jeans. "Here. Put these on," he snapped.

Meanwhile, the remaining duo of Borodin's ménage à trois, had resumed their torrid activities, occasionally glancing up at Vyugin and Borodin for no apparent reason other than curiosity. Another couple, who'd been gripped in their own little world of erotic bliss, seemed paralyzed by what had been going on since Vyugin arrived on the scene. They'd barely moved in the past few minutes. The rest of the undraped sweaty assemblage stood or sat in various parts of the room, apparently waiting out the unpleasantness. They seemed to have decided that whoever it was who'd invaded their party was not to be trifled with. No doubt, being completely nude reinforced their decision. It's a lot harder to engage in heroic efforts when you have nothing on your body.

Finally, through persuasion, threats, and a little tugging and shoving, Borodin was dressed in jeans, shirt and shoes. He didn't seem sure that they were his shoes, but it was enough to satisfy Vyugin, who guided him out of the room to the sound of jeers and catcalls behind them. As they approached the front door, Borodin whined something about it being cold out and not having a coat. Vyugin had no patience for this and pushed him out the front door sending the younger man sprawling in the snow.

Ten minutes later, Vyugin got Borodin into his room and placed him on his bed. When he woke up, he'd have a headache that would last for days. Good, thought Vyugin, as he left, wondering how he'd handle this the next day when they saw each other. Right then he was leaning toward reporting the son-of-a-bitch to Moscow.

The next morning, Vyugin was sitting by himself, reading a newspaper in the place he usually ate breakfast in Garmisch. It was a *bier stube* by night and a café serving breakfast and lunch during the day. Because of the late night, he was taking breakfast around eight o'clock, about an hour later than usual for him. As he was halfway through his meal, his young colleague walked in and came up to his table.

"Mind if I join you?" he asked sheepishly. Vyugin motioned for him to sit down across the table from him. His face showed nothing as he continued reading a few seconds more.

"Go ahead and order. I'm not finished," said Vyugin indifferently. "You look like you could use some coffee."

"You could say that." Borodin forced a weak smile; then waited for the waitress to come over. When she came, he quickly ordered. Vyugin took a sip of coffee and went back to his paper. The silent treatment was driving Borodin crazy. "Look, about last night....."

Vyugin put his paper to one side. "Yes?"

"I've never done that before. You probably don't believe me, but I've never even tried any kind of dope before. Alcohol, yes, but not dope."

"The combination almost got you killed. I should report you."

Borodin dipped his head. "I know."

"So?"

"I don't know what you mean."

"So can you think of a reason why I shouldn't report you?"

"My career would be ruined."

"You should have thought of that."

"I know. Look, I've always been a serious student. I've never fucked up before. It's crazy. This isn't me. Believe me. It will never happen again." Vyugin had read Borodin's personnel file. It was true. He'd been an exemplary candidate and an exemplary trainee. Not a trace of dereliction or craziness. When he spoke next, he stared Borodin in the eyes.

"The KGB doesn't generally give second chances. Not when the offender brought it on himself."

"You can make an exception. Please."

"You screw up again, and it's *my* head for trusting you. Then it's my career. I wouldn't look kindly on that. I would take it personally."

"I understand. Please, Vladimir, do this for me, and I will be in your debt for life. I will not forget this."

"You realize, Alexei, that if you'd been on a sensitive mission, you could have compromised everything last night? You could have gotten yourself, me, or someone else killed. Not to mention putting national security at risk."

"Yes, I was an ass. A fool. But, I swear to you, it was not the real me. Give me this chance, and you won't regret it."

"If I regret it, Alexei, you will regret it. You do understand that?"

"Yes."

"Then it is behind us. To be remembered, but not discussed."

Chapter 32

The Russian "white house," the home of Parliament, overlooked the *Moskva* River, about a mile-and-a-half from the Kremlin. It was also where the office of the Prime Minister Malenkov was located. He maintained another office, primarily for ceremonial functions, in the Kremlin.

The Russian "white house" gained notoriety in the West in September of 1993, when President Boris Yeltsin, in the midst of a heated power struggle with parliament, suspended the legislative body and the constitution for three months. Parliament mutinied, barricading itself in the building. On October 4th, after violence broke out in the streets, Yeltsin ordered the military to take back the building. Army tanks shelled the "white house" into submission until several hundred members of parliament and their supporters surrendered. The damage to the building was eventually repaired and parliament later resumed deliberations in the building. In many ways, what happened at the Russian "white house" was a microcosmic snapshot of the country's violent history.

Today, though, as Dantry, Vyugin, and Joanna Barbeau emerged from the Ukraine hotel across the river from the "white house," the huge government building loomed majestically as it reflected the bright morning sunlight. It was easy to see why it was called the white house. The white stone surface was dazzlingly brilliant in the mid-morning sun. Outwardly, the building revealed nothing of its violent past.

They'd used the Ukraine as a meeting place. On emerging from the Cosmos Hotel after eating breakfast, Tony and Joanna had taken the Metro from Prospekt Mira Station into central Moscow, where they'd changed lines. From central Moscow, the ride to Smolenskaya Station had taken no more than ten minutes. The Moscow Metro had been one of the most efficiently run operations in all of Russia from the day it went into service. Throughout different regimes and contrasting ideologies, it somehow managed to remain efficient. From Smolenskaya Station, they'd then walked the short distance to the Ukraine Hotel. Now, the three of them were walking across the bridge that would bring them to within a few hundred yards of their destination.

"Now comes the first test, my friends," said Vyugin. "Since those bombings by the Chechnyan rebels, or whoever it was, they've tightened up security in major buildings. Especially government buildings. It's worse now than it was under the Soviet Union. In those days, nobody dared to penetrate a government building without proper authority. Since the break-up in '91, not as many people fear the government. There is no respect anymore." He said this somewhat nostalgically, thought Dantry.

"How will you get us in? We have no government documents. This could be a problem. Come to think of it, if you do get us in, how will you get us out?"

Vyugin chuckled out loud. "You raise a good question, Tony. Two good questions." Then he turned serious. "However, if we don't get in, your second question becomes academic, yes?"

They were off the bridge now and approaching the entrance to the huge office building. Joanna said, "Before we go in, tell us what we need to know, Vladimir. We'll let you do the talking naturally, but what if we're spoken to? What do we say we're doing there?"

"There is no reason for concern, Miss Barbeau. We will not lie. We may not reveal all, but there is no need to lie. Since I shall announce our intentions, I shall assume most of the questions will be directed at me. Oh, by the way, if we are searched or even strip-searched, do not let this bother you. They are a bit nervous these days. It is nothing personal, I'm sure."

Tony then asked, "You never did tell me why you're so confident we'll get in to see him. All you said was that you thought there was a good chance that we would."

"It so happens that his personal assistant is a former colleague of mine. During his training for the KGB, I was, for a time, his supervisor."

"Okay, so you know him. Still doesn't sound like a guarantee that we'll get in to see his boss."

Vyugin smiled. "You didn't let me finish. I was about to say that I did him a favor once. He owes me one."

"You're sure he's here today?"

"I called before I left. We should have no trouble."

Tony rolled his eyes and glanced at Joanna. "Jesus, Vladimir, don't say that."

Vyugin grinned. "You think it's bad luck to be so confident. That is such an American reaction."

"Well...."

"We'll get in. Don't worry."

There were two armed military guards at the front entrance to the building. Vyugin flashed his identification, and motioning to Tony and Joanna, said in Russian, "They're with me."

One of the guards nodded and waved them into the building. Inside, Vyugin walked directly to the reception desk and addressed an officious-looking woman in civilian clothes who put down the paperback novel she was reading. She appeared mildly annoyed at the interruption.

"We are here to see Alexei Borodin," said Vyugin.

The trim-looking young woman, whose hair was cut in the latest fashion, couldn't have been over 25, but she was all business.

"Is he expecting you?"

"He is. Tell him Vladimir Vyugin and two associates are here to see him."

The woman picked up the phone, punched in a number, and spoke briefly into the receiver. Moments later she hung up and smiled indifferently.

"You may go up. Seventh floor, room 7008." As the last few words left her mouth, she had already returned to her book.

As they approached the bank of elevators, a guard waved them over and gave them all a quick frisking. Joanna noticed that no effort was made to use female guards to frisk female visitors. The guard then asked for identification, and Vyugin flashed his ID once more. They were then allowed to board the first empty car. Two minutes later they emerged from the elevator on the seventh floor, and, after walking what seemed like a hundred yards, came to a door that said, Office of the Prime Minister — Room 7008. Vyugin paused, glanced first at Tony and then Joanna as if to say, 'Are you with me?' and turned the knob of the heavy door.

The room they entered was large, formal, and comfortably appointed with rich woods and softly stated fabrics; the furniture from some historic period Tony was unable to identify. It reminded him of the reception room of a large, well-heeled law firm in New York. A number of people occupied chairs placed casually around the room. Apparently they were waiting to see the Prime Minister or one of his aides. Vyugin headed for the reception desk. A woman in her middle years looked up and smiled. She seemed to mean it, which was a pleasant surprise, thought Tony, whose experience with Russians behind desks and counters had been more like their encounter with the young woman in the lobby downstairs. Russians had the reputation of not being overly interested in providing service. It was a holdover from the Communist era—a holdover that seemed to be giving way only grudgingly.

"Yes, what can I do for you?"

"My name is Vyugin, Vladimir Vyugin. We are here to see Alexei Borodin. I believe he is expecting us." Dantry couldn't help but be impressed with his Russian colleague's urbanity.

The woman punched in a four-digit number and spoke quickly into the receiver. She replaced it and said pleasantly, "Please take a seat. He'll be with you shortly."

They'd barely seated themselves when a tall, athletic-looking man with sharp, angular features walked into the room through a door on the side of the room. The man smiled as he saw Vyugin. While he was strikingly handsome with his blue eyes and carelessly tousled blond hair, Joanna found herself drawing back ever so slightly. There was something about those blue eyes that seemed distant, icy.

"Vladimir." The man drew out the 'mir' affectionately in the way that only non-English speakers can do—a way that seems to Americans wondrously foreign sounding and exotic. "It's been a long time. What a surprise."

Vyugin, too, was surprised. The green, impulsive youth he'd pulled out of that Alpine orgy two decades ago had transformed himself into a polished, high-level, middle-aged bureaucrat. He held out his arms and the two men embraced in the typical Russian fashion.

"Alexei. The years have been good to you."

"You, too, my old friend. You, too."

Vyugin laughed it off nonchalantly. "I'm not so sure about that. But thank you, anyway. Here, let me introduce you to my American friends." He quickly introduced them by name without revealing what they did or had done for a living.

"So, come into my office. We can have coffee or tea. Or something with a little more kick, eh?" As he said this it must have reminded him of that time 20 years earlier when Vyugin had saved him from things with 'kick,' for he trailed off and changed the subject back to something that he thought would be safer. "Come into my office, and tell me what's on your mind."

Borodin's office was comfortable, but far from luxurious. Perhaps 12 feet by 12, it was functional and strewn with stacks of papers. He rushed about the room clearing off chairs so that his guests could sit.

"Now, how about something to drink?"

"I'm sure you're busy, Alexei. There is no need for coffee. Perhaps I should come right to the point." Borodin stiffened at the change in tone from his former supervisor.

"As you wish. How can I be of help?"

"We would like to see the Prime Minister. Not for long, but it is important that we see him."

"I'm sure you realize that he's a very busy man. I, I think maybe you should be talking with Mr. Bulgakov." Borodin knew that Bulgakov would not take kindly to having a former KGB agent go around him to see the prime minister—and with his, Borodin's help.

"Alexei, this is a matter of urgency for the state. I'm sure he will want to see us when he finds out what this is about. We do not want to talk to Mr. Bulgakov."

Borodin sighed. "And what is this matter of urgency?"

"I'm sorry, Alexei, but I cannot reveal that to anyone but Mr. Malenkov himself."

"You must give me something, Vladimir. The Prime Minister is not going to see you, if he doesn't know what this is about."

Vyugin could see that he would have to divulge a little in order to get what he wanted. "Tell him we have information about the murder of the American I.M.F. banker that ties his death to Russia—in a way that could prove embarrassing to the Prime Minister and to Russia."

"You mean Mark Dantry?"

"Yes."

Borodin appeared puzzled. "He was not murdered. It was unfortunate, but his death was accidental, I believe."

"You believe wrong, Alexei. It was murder, and we know who did it. Now do you see why it's so important that we speak to Mr. Malenkov?"

Borodin shook his head in frustration. "He is with the finance committee this morning—until noon. Then he greets a delegation from Kazakhstan at a luncheon. He meets with the Kazakh president after lunch. After that he is meeting with the mayor of Moscow on the crime issue. Honestly, Vladimir, I don't see how I can get you in today. I think I can sneak you in first thing in the morning. Say nine o'clock."

"This is definite?"

"Fifteen minutes. Know what you want to say and get to it quickly. He has little patience for verbal foreplay."

"And I have little patience with people who promise something and don't deliver. Remember, Alexei, you owe me one."

Borodin reddened. He had worked hard to put that incident in Germany behind him. He almost convinced himself that Vyugin had, too. Vyugin had made him uncomfortable, and he didn't like that at all.

Chapter 33

They had agreed, at Vyugin's suggestion, that they not eat together that evening. "The three of us together is just a little too suspicious, no?" Dantry wasn't convinced that it mattered, now that they'd played their first hand at the ministry, and Borodin already knew that the three of them were in Russia together. Still, he figured Vyugin knew his country better than he did, so he went along with the suggestion.

They'd left it that they would meet the next morning in the Ukraine lobby, as they had today. If they met at 8:15 it would leave them more than enough time to keep their appointment with Malenkov. It was imperative, however, that they not be even one minute late. They didn't want to give Borodin the slightest excuse for canceling their meeting.

The concierge at the Cosmos suggested *Parziale*, a new Italian restaurant that he guaranteed would remind them of Florence. The place was small with excellent service. It was one of those places where the owner comes out to meet the patrons. Giuseppe had taken the bold step of moving to Moscow from Italy. He knew it would not be easy, but the potential of being one of the first Italian restaurants in Moscow that was actually run by an Italian brought out the adventurer in him. From the very beginning he took a liking to Joanna and Tony and made their meal a delight. The food was as good as they'd had anywhere. But they had a few laughs over the concierge's description of *Parziale*, because it reminded them more of Naples than of Florence. The menu was comprised almost exclusively of Southern Italian fare. But it was good. A far cry, said Tony, from the kind of food you got in Moscow back in the '70s and '80s.

"I can't exaggerate how bad the food was back then. With the exception of two or three off-limits places that catered to the Party apparatchiks, the food was uninspired, limited, and mysterious."

"Mysterious?" asked Joanna, not comprehending.

"It was impossible to tell what it was."

"Didn't you ask?"

"Yeah, you'd ask, and they'd say something like 'It's meat' or 'It's fish.' As hard as you pressed your waiter you'd never find out what kind of meat or fish. Even in the very few places that served fairly decent meals, it was virtually impossible to get the kind of food we're used to in the West. Some of the best food served in those days was Georgian or Central Asian. Anyway, Russia may have a long way to go in some ways, but if this place is any indication, they're finally getting their culinary act together."

They washed their meal down with an expensive but decent Barolo. "I should've tried one of the Georgian wines," said Tony. "They used to be pretty good. And they're a hell of a lot cheaper."

"This one seems pretty good," said Joanna innocently.

"It should be. It's one of the best Italian wines you can buy."

"Believe it or not, I knew that."

"Sorry," he said puckishly. "I thought only men were capable of understanding wine."

"Right."

The restaurant, the meal, and the evening were all a success. It was really the first time Tony'd been able to unwind since his brother's death. Tonight, though, there was nothing they could do, and knowing that soon they would be doing something, allowed him to relax. He always felt better when he knew something had at least been set in motion. Tonight, they'd relax, tomorrow they'd go to work.

At about 10:30 they asked Giuseppe to call them a taxi. The ride back to the Cosmos took less than 20 minutes. Before going up to their room, Tony checked in the lobby to see if there were any messages for them. As it turned out, there was one. He read the brief message aloud so Joanna could hear. "PLEASE MEET ME IN THE LOBBY NEAR THE CASINO ENTRANCE BEFORE YOU RETIRE. A. BORODIN"

Joanna returned his puzzled look with a baffled one of her own.

"What the....?"

"My sentiments, too. What the hell is Borodin doing here?"

"Only one way to find out."

Dantry frowned. "Something weird here."

"I agree, but let's go see what's what. The sooner we see him, the sooner the mystery will be solved."

"Yeah, let's go." He still didn't look comfortable to Joanna as they went looking for the casino entrance. It wasn't easy to find on the spacious lobby floor. Finally, after asking a woman at the reception desk, they were headed in the right direction.

"I don't see him," said Joanna.

"I don't either. Lot of people around this casino entrance, though. Maybe we've missed him. Keep looking. There, over there by that exit door. That big guy holding a sign that says DANTRY."

"That's not Borodin. He looks more like a professional wrestler." She laughed under her breath. "Igor the Giant."

"I know. Well let's go see what this is all about." He started off in the direction of the man with the sign, Joanna keeping pace at his side.

The man smiled as he saw them approach.

"You looking for me?" asked Tony.

"You are?"

"Name's Dantry."

"Mr. Anthony Dantry?"

"Yes, now what's this all about?"

"This is Miss Barbeau, no?"

"Yes," said Joanna. "Why?"

"Mr. Borodin wants to see you. Please come with me."

Tony hesitated. Something didn't ring true. "Wait a minute. I thought Borodin was meeting us here in the lobby."

"He is outside. In his car. He will explain. Please. Come."

"His note said he'd meet us here. We're here. Tell him that if he wants to see us, we're here."

"If you wish to meet with Mr. Malenkov, I suggest that you not insult Mr. Borodin. It is your choice."

While Tony wasn't comfortable with the situation, it appeared that this Russian equivalent of a World Wrestling Federation reject held all the aces.

"All right. Lead the way."

Chapter 34

As they stepped through the door into the chill outside darkness, they could see the vague outline of the black Volga limousine standing with its engine running not 20 feet away. An evening summer fog had crept into the Moscow night turning the alleyway into a murky, forbidding netherworld.

"Please get inside," said the large man, sounding more refined to Tony and Joanna than they'd expected from someone with such a thuggish appearance. Joanna and Tony leaned close to the car, trying to peer into the side windows, but the glass was smoked, making it impossible to see inside, especially at this time of night.

"How do I know that Borodin's in there?" asked Dantry.

"He is. Now please to get in."

"Tell him to show his face first. Then we get in."

"I'm afraid you'll get in now, Mr. Dantry. If you value your life." Tony turned and noticed something in the hand of the giant that he hadn't seen before—a matte finished nine-millimeter semi-automatic. It looked like a toy in the huge hand, but Dantry knew it was far more lethal than a toy.

"Better play along for now. —C'mon, let's get in."

As Joanna reached for the door handle, the huge Russian beamed a satisfied smile. "You are using good judgment."

"Too bad I can't say the same for you," said a voice from the shadows. It was Vyugin, with a 9mm Ruger aimed directly at the big Russian.

The huge man whirled to see who it was. As he did so, Dantry lunged for his gun, at the same time bringing his knee up into the man's groin with all the force he could muster. It happened so fast and with such intensity that the man grunted, loosening his grip on the weapon enough to enable Dantry to prise it from his grip in one deft motion. It was one of the things he'd trained for decades ago. In all his years in the CIA he'd never had to do it until now. The giant, clearly in pain, glared at Dantry, reaching forward awkwardly to get his gun back.

Tony sidestepped him easily. "Not so fast, Igor. Step back if you don't want a taste of this lead."

"Well done," said Vyugin emerging from the shadows.

"How the—?"

"I'll tell you later. First, let us see who is in the limousine." Vyugin reached for the door handle, all the while keeping his eyes on their captive. He flung the door open and peered inside. "No one! You are alone. Who do you work for?" Vyugin spat it out in a staccato voice.

Without his gun the large man had lost his confidence. "I told your friend here, Borodin."

Tony said, "He told me that Borodin was in the car."

"Did Borodin speak to you directly?" asked Vyugin, "or did you receive your orders from someone else?"

"It was Stepanik. He works for Borodin in the Ministry. He is in charge of the underground garage in the White House. He told me Borodin wanted me to bring you to him."

"In his office?"

"No, when I got back to the garage I was to tell Stepanik. I supposed that he would call Borodin and let him know you were there. To be honest, I didn't give it a lot of thought. My job was to get you and bring you there."

"Borodin is working late," said Dantry in Russian. "Does he normally work this late?"

If the big man noticed that Dantry spoke with an accent, he didn't show it. He'd apparently decided that his best chance to escape this situation alive was to cooperate and not to ask questions. "Not usually, but these people work crazy hours. You never know."

"What do you normally do?" asked Vyugin.

"I don't understand."

"For a living. Do you work at the Ministry?"

"I work in the garage."

"Do you get assignments like this very often?"

"Not often."

"But sometimes, yes?" asked Dantry.

"Once in awhile, for Borodin and...."

"And? Who else?"

"Bulgakov. See, when I'm not parking cars, I sometimes drive for some of the ministers and their staff."

"This was not a normal driving job, Igor," said Dantry.

The large man was about to object to being called by the wrong name, but decided it was probably not a good idea.

Vyugin, while not a small man, was several inches shorter and easily 50 pound lighter than the other Russian. He moved to within inches of the big man and grabbed him by the chin, his steely stare boring into the other man's now frightened eyes. "What is your name?"

"Ivan."

"Listen carefully Ivan, if you want to live to park another car. You are going to drive us to the White House garage, and we will keep our meeting with Mr. Borodin. Do you understand?"

"Yes."

"Now is there anything else you should tell us? We do not want any surprises when we get there. Do you understand."

"No, I have nothing else to tell you." The big man looked defeated, no doubt dreading the humiliation he would face when he got back to the garage.

"Good, then let us be off. We wouldn't want to disappoint Mr. Borodin."

Forty-five minutes later the limo bumped and jolted over the ramp as it pulled slowly into the underground parking garage of the huge government building.

At the gate, Ivan flashed a card and was permitted to go ahead. He eased the car to a stop in front of glass-paneled garage office. Joanna thought she saw a face behind one of the panels, and then it was gone. Ivan stopped the car and got out. "I'll be right out. Stay in the car."

"Where is this Stepanik?" asked Vyugin. "Shouldn't he be here?"

"He should be. Maybe he's in the back room, or maybe he's taking a leak. I'll find him."

"I'll go with you, Ivan. Remember, I have a gun—and my friend has your gun. They also have the car if you try any funny business."

Dantry couldn't remember seeing a man this big show this much fear. He was trembling visibly, his eyes the eyes of a cornered animal expecting to be pounced on by an even bigger animal. He turned and slowly made his way in the direction of the glass-enclosed office. Vyugin, one step behind him, turned in the direction of Joanna and Tony in the limo, and, keeping his voice from carrying, said, "If you hear shots, get the hell out of here." Before Tony could object, Vyugin and Ivan had disappeared inside the office.

The glass office was empty and Ivan looked puzzled. "Usually there are two or three people here. Stepanik is the boss, but he is not alone here. Follow me. They must be in the back room." He pushed the door and it flew open as if it weighed nothing.

"Ivan. Didn't know you were working tonight." It was a short, middle-aged man in a khaki jumpsuit that looked as if he had been wearing it for a week. The smile on his face made you forget what he was wearing. Vyugin took an instant liking to him.

"Yuri," said Ivan nervously. "Have you seen Stepanik?"

"He is in the toilet. Sit down and take a load off your feet." Then, acknowledging Vyugin's presence, "You, too, *tovarishch.*" You, too, *comrade.*

A car pulled into the garage, and Yuri went outside to meet it. A moment later Vyugin heard a flushing sound, and a stocky man of average height whom he estimated to be in his mid-thirties came into the office from an adjoining room. A mass of straight, jet-black hair kept falling over his right eye, and he repeatedly tossed his head to get it away from his line of sight. Vyugin wondered why he didn't cut his hair shorter. The man eyed Vyugin suspiciously. "You looking for someone?"

"You Stepanik?"

"Who wants to know?"

"I'll ask the questions. You sent big Ivan here for two of my friends. Why?"

Stepanik blinked, but showed no emotion. "Who are you?"

Vyugin pulled out his gun. "I said I'll ask the questions. You're about 30 seconds away from losing a kneecap. Now, once again, why did you send for my friends?"

"One of the deputy ministers asked me to send for them."

"His name?"

Stepanik took a deep breath. "Bulgakov. He's under Malenkov."

Vyugin scowled as he considered this new development. Borodin must have told Bulgakov about their visit.

"I know who he is. Only he's not a deputy minister. He's chief of staff." Stepanik shrugged. Vyugin continued. "Where was Ivan supposed to take my friends?"

"Here."

"And?"

"And what?"

Vyugin fired off a round within inches of the man's leg.

"Don't waste my time!" He barked. "Tell me what was going to happen when they got here? Next time it will be your knee."

Stepanik clearly thought he was dealing with either a crazy man or a terrorist. Either way, he didn't like his odds. "I was to call Bulgakov's office and let him know they were here."

"Then go make your call. I'll be next to you, listening. Don't try to get clever."

Shaking visibly, Stepanik walked over to a phone on a battered gray metal desk and began to dial. He held the receiver to his ear. "Stepanik. They're here. Yes. All right." He dropped the receiver in its cradle and turned to Vyugin. "He's coming down. Said for me to hold them till he gets here."

"We'll wait out there by the car," said Vyugin, jabbing the man in the back with his gun. "Move. You, too, Ivan."

As the three men approached the car, Vyugin leaned close to the driver's window and said, "It was Bulgakov who gave the order; not Borodin. He's coming down. Tony, be ready for anything. He probably won't come alone. You have Ivan's gun, right?"

"Yeah. Joanna, be ready to dive for the floor."

"And Tony, pull the car close to the door—facing out—so that, if we have to, we can make a fast exit. And keep the car running."

After five minutes of waiting—five minutes that seemed like ten-times that—Vyugin was even more convinced that Bulgakov would not come alone. He was probably rounding up his flunkies right now.

Bulgakov had been expecting the call. He'd alerted two of his most trusted aides, both former KGB people, to be ready when he called. The three of them were now riding an elevator down to the basement garage. Bulgakov was more than a little suspicious of Vyugin's motives. The ex-agent was supposed to be in America; yet he wasn't. He'd disappeared after the latest fiasco, and now he was here in Moscow. And he hadn't told Bulgakov or Sorokin. Instead, he'd just materialized out of the blue and presented himself, along with this Anthony Dantry and some woman, to Borodin, saying that he wanted to see Malenkov. Fortunately, Borodin was loyal, or at least had the good sense to cover his ass and tell him about the visit. Now he could head that treacherous bastard Vyugin off and do a little damage control. The last thing he needed was for this aging operative and his American friends to meet with the Prime Minister. He smiled grimly. That, he promised himself, was not going to happen.

Chapter 35

Inside the limo, Tony and Joanna waited patiently.

"When that gun went off," said Joanna in a low voice, "I thought you'd drive us out of here. Then I realized that it must have been Vyugin who'd done the shooting."

"Yeah, to get the guy's attention. Looks like it worked. If it was one of them who did the shooting, they'd already be here after us. There may be some more shooting, though, so be ready to get down as low as possible. I doubt if this Bulgakov will want to let us get away. Sorry to get you into this mess."

"I told you before, I got myself into it. I wanted to come with you."

"Not for this you didn't. This could get pretty hairy."

"Don't worry about me. Just use that gun if you have to. And if we get out of this in one piece—"

Vyugin had emerged from inside the glass-panelled garage office. Joanna left the rest of her words unsaid. Standing barely fifty feet from the limousine, Vyugin became alert. He made eye contact with Dantry and Joanna, mouthing soundlessly to them to get ready and for Tony to keep his gun drawn. Then he motioned for them to stay down.

Vyugin knew that, this time, his new friends might get their chance to save *him*. He stood with his back against a cold concrete wall facing the elevator, his eye was on the elevator door. It was the most likely way Bulgakov would make his appearance. But he wasn't taking any chances. He kept glancing to his left and then to his right, just in case the crafty chief of staff and his henchmen made a surprise entrance.

Vyugin had guessed right. The doors of the elevator opened and Bulgakov, looking tired, but alert, stepped cautiously out of the car, followed by two humorless, hard-looking men in their late twenties or early thirties. The chief of staff scanned the parking garage, trying to get an instant picture of the situation. When his eyes lit upon Vyugin, he smiled, a wicked smile of satisfaction, like the smile he imagined a lion would form when it finally cornered its defenseless prey.

"Vladimir, what a surprise. I thought you were in America on a patriotic assignment for Russia. Since you are back, I must assume that you have completed your assignment successfully." As he said this he motioned for his two armed men to spread out so as to form—with himself in the middle—a crude crescent surrounding Vyugin. "Tell me all the good news." He crossed his arms and grinned.

"How did you learn that I was back in Russia?"

"As soon as you left his office, Borodin told me. He is obviously much more loyal than you are, Vladimir. You disappoint me."

"Perhaps he values his skin more than I do."

"Perhaps that is true. That is something I do not have time to explore. My concern now is why this treachery from you and what shall I do about it?"

"The treachery, I have come to realize, is by you, Yuri. Unfortunately, I learned all too late that you are working to undermine President Kirov and the democratic process. You are willing to create new chaos in order to put your own man in power. And you don't mind who you kill to accomplish this."

"Good God, Vladimir, you sound like some naïve schoolboy. This is Russia, for God's sake. You don't accomplish the kind of change that's needed here with some sentimental version of what they do in America. Try democracy in Russia, and you'll end up with a multiracial mess like they have over there. Every minority group will be wanting to dictate national policy, and we Russians will end up with nothing but a rabble of Central Asians who will eventually overwhelm us by their sheer numbers. Can't you see that Russia needs strong medicine now? Can't you see it's disintegrating in front of your very eyes?"

"When was the last time you were in the United States?"

"That doesn't matter. You just came back. You saw it with your own eyes."

"Yes, and it wasn't so bad. We could learn a lot from them about getting along with each other."

"I can't believe what I'm hearing. You are a fucking traitor. There's no other word for it."

"The last time I looked, Yuri, we were not at war with the United States. How do I become a traitor by saying something good about them, if they're not our enemy?"

"This is unbelievable. If you don't think we're at war with the United States, then you've been living in another world. Just because that other traitor Gorbachev destroyed our great Soviet nation, doesn't mean that the treacherous Americans suddenly became virtuous. Hell, by spending so much on the military, Reagan and his bunch of capitalist cronies made it easy for Gorbachev to turn on his own country." It suddenly occurred to Bulgakov that he was getting carried away by ideological dialectic at a most inopportune time. He had a problem that had to be solved. The more he let Vyugin engage him in conversation, the less likely he was to solve his problem. "Vladimir, either you've always been a capitalist, or you've gone soft in the head."

"I never was a capitalist, and I doubt if I'm one now, but I do see that Americans, while far from perfect and far too materialistic for my taste, at least know how to get along with each other. Hate is not uppermost in their sociological vocabulary. One is not a traitor just because he sees good features in another society."

"Well, I don't have time to debate you on this. By the way, where are your two American friends?"

"Why do you want to know?"

"If they have something to tell Mr. Malenkov, they can tell me. I'll make sure he gets the message."

"I rather think they'd like to tell him in person."

"I don't think that's going to happen. Besides, what does it matter? They tell me, him, it's all the same."

"Is it? Does Malenkov know what you've been doing?"

"I'm the one asking the questions. If your friends are not here with you, my people will pick them up at their hotel. They are not going to see Mr. Malenkov."

"And what are you going to do with me?"

"You and I, and my two associates here, are going to take a little ride and discuss this further, Vladimir."

"I don't think so. I'm not going anywhere with you. You think I'm crazy? Don't answer that. You've already given me your opinion. So I will leave now."

"No, I'm afraid I can't allow that, old friend." He then turned to one of the two expressionless goons he'd deployed on either side of him. "Ilya, please escort Mr. Vyugin to our car." At this, Vyugin turned and defiantly started to walk away.

"I wouldn't do that if I were you, Vladimir," said Bulgakov. Ilya has orders to use his gun if you resist. It is getting late, and no one will see him shoot you if that becomes necessary." Vyugin knew he wasn't kidding. Vyugin pulled his handgun from his pocket and turned to face Ilya.

"It would appear that shooting me has its risks, Ilya. Why don't you put that in your pocket and walk away."

"I can't do that, sir. Besides, my partner over there has his gun trained on you, too. You really don't have a chance. Why don't you come with me quietly."

"Not so fast!" It was Dantry slowly emerging from the front seat of the black limousine. The gun he'd taken from Ivan was aimed directly at Ilya's colleague. "It would appear that we have a stand-off gentlemen. In fact, the odds may favor us, since both Vladimir and I are excellent shots. If I were you guys, I wouldn't take the chance. Why don't you both just drop your guns, and we'll be on our way. Nobody'll get hurt."

Ilya and his nameless buddy appeared to be paralyzed. They obviously didn't like playing with guns when the odds weren't in their favor. This was not their cause. They were hired hands for Bulgakov. Sure, they wanted his approval, but not as martyrs.

Bulgakov immediately sized up the situation and decided to act. He pulled a handgun from inside his coat and released two rounds in the direction of Vyugin. Vyugin returned the fire, hitting Bulgakov in the shoulder and spinning him around. Ilya then discovered his backbone and took aim to fire at Vyugin. A shot from Dantry's recently acquired gun dropped him in his tracks. The nameless goon on the other side of Bulgakov unleashed three quick shots in the direction of Dantry. Vyugin hit the man with one perfectly placed shot to the heart and turned his gun on Ilya who was slowly trying to get to his feet while feeling around the wetness in his mid-section trying to determine how badly he'd been hit. "Don't shoot," he said in a trembling voice. "Please."

"Let's get the hell out of here," said Vyugin. "I'll drive. I know Moscow better than you do. You two okay?"

Joanna pulled herself up from the floor in the rear. "I'm fine. How about you guys?"

"I don't think they hit me," said Vyugin. "Tony?"

"I think I have a scratch on my thigh. No problem. Vladimir, we can't go far in this limo. It's kinda easy to spot."

"And I don't think we can go back to the hotel," said Joanna.

"Let's just get away from here," said Vyugin as he eased the car out of the garage. "We'll think of something as we drive. Do you have anything you need at your hotel? If we get there fast, you can pick it up, and we can find you a bed somewhere else."

"We better stop there," said Dantry. "We'll make it fast."

Vyugin forced himself not to drive too fast through the city streets. They didn't want to call attention to themselves. Fortunately the traffic wasn't too bad, and they got to the Cosmos in fairly good time. Tony and Joanna ran up to the room as quickly as they could.

"Look," said Tony, when the two of them were in the room. "Take only half of what you brought. We want to leave the room looking as if we're coming back. It'll buy us a little time. I know it's tough to leave good stuff, but it's important. You with me?"

She gave him a weak smile. "Yeah. I understand."

"Leave some of your toiletries—your toothbrush—and probably your more dressy stuff. Doesn't look as if we'll be needing it anyway. Let's do this fast. We'll only take one bag, too."

They were in and out of the room in seven minutes. They did not check out. Tony figured that, if they made it back to the States, he'd check out by phone. It would cost a little more, but it was better than losing your life.

"What took you so long?" asked Vyugin as they got back into the limousine with their single stuffed bag.

Dantry ignored the question. "Anybody hassle you while we were up there?"

"No, but let's get going. Bulgakov will have his centurions here within minutes. I've decided that you'd better stay at my hotel."

"You sure we can get in at this late hour?"

Vyugin smiled. "You two may have to share a room, but I suspect that won't be a problem for you."

"What makes you think they haven't tracked you down to where you're staying?"

"The people I deal with at the hotel still think I'm KGB— or FSB. They wouldn't dare reveal that I'm staying there. Besides, I pay them far more than the room is worth. They'll have something for you two, and they're lips will be sealed. But we can't drive up in this limousine. That would be pushing our luck too much. We'll park this behind a building near the Krasnopresnenskaya Metro station and, just to be doubly safe, take the subway to some distant station—say the Kuznetsky Most station. By then, if anyone has been on our trail, we should have lost them. Then we'll take a train back to the Arbatskaya station. The hotel is just off the Arbat. The station is within walking distance of the hotel. This will take a good hour or more, but better to live in safety than to die in regret. I think you have some such saying, Da?"

"Close enough, Vladimir. Close enough."

"So," said Joanna, "how did you happen to be there when we needed you? I thought you'd gone back to your hotel."

"Yeah," said Tony. "That's the second time you've saved our bacon."

Vyugin looked puzzled for a moment, then smiled. "You Americans use such colorful expressions. If I must satisfy your curiosity, I will." He was enjoying this. "I had a feeling that something might happen after we'd made our call on Borodin. I never trusted that son-of-a-bitch. He was an ass twenty years ago, and he's still an ass. Naturally, if anyone was going to make a move on you, it would be at your hotel. And since you weren't there in the early portion of the evening, I assumed you'd gone out to eat. But that meant you'd be back at a fairly early hour. You had the appointment with the prime minister in the morning. Anyway, if anyone was going to make a move, the most likely time would be when you returned to the hotel. I waited in the lobby for you to return from *Parziale*."

"You knew we went there?" Joanna said, in amazement.

"He greased the palm of the concierge," said Tony.

"Yes, it was a simple matter. And in a lobby this large it was easy to see you without you noticing me. When you got your message, I followed you, and the rest, as they say, is history."

"How far before we get rid of this boat, Vladimir?"

"Five minutes, no more. We are close to Krasnopresnenskaya Metro station." They drove on through the busy Moscow streets, far busier than Dantry remembered them from his last time in the Russian capital. The car slowed and Vyugin pointed to a six-story building that looked as if it had been built in the twenties or thirties. "There, that apartment building is perfect. We pull behind it like this." He eased the long car into an alleyway between the apartment building and a medical office building. In the rear there were a few empty parking spaces, and he pulled into one that could not be seen from the street. He turned to his two passengers and beamed. "How is that?"

"Should buy us some time."

"Exactly. Now, let's get moving, we have a long night ahead of us. First, though, let me walk up to the edge of the building and check the street to be sure no one followed us." He hugged the side of the apartment building and inched to the corner of the building where the side met the front. He peered both ways and scanned the opposite side of the street. Then he motioned to the other two that it was all clear and that they should join him. "The Metro station is down the street two blocks and one over. We should be there in minutes. Let's go."

Chapter 36

Bulgakov grimaced as he held his hand to his bleeding shoulder, trying to stanch the flow. "You idiot," he roared, "you let two over-the-hill ex-agents make fools of you; not to mention losing Ilya and getting me shot.

"They were too fast for us, sir," whined Ivan. The nameless bodyguard remained silent, looking and feeling helpless. "You'd never expect someone as old as they are to—"

"Oh never mind." He looked at his ailing shoulder. "I've got to have this taken care of before I lose too much blood. I know a doctor who will do it without asking questions. Now see if you can handle this situation without botching it up. I don't want anyone, anyone you hear, knowing what happened here tonight."

"We can't just pretend it didn't happen," said Ivan. "Your shoulder…"

"In the morning, no one will know anything about my shoulder. I'll get it patched up tonight and nobody will be the wiser. It's up to you two to make sure this doesn't get out. I'll speak to Stepanik to make sure he doesn't talk."

"But what about Ilya out there on the garage floor?"

"Another victim of Moscow crime. Go get his wallet. Take whatever money he has and split it between you. Then toss the wallet on top of his body. Be sure you wear gloves. Remember, you're doing this for a better Russia. Sometimes things get messy along the way, but when we succeed in making Russia great once again, think of how proud you'll feel that you did your part."

"Yessir. What about Vyugin and the two Americans? They can still cause problems."

"Yes, I know. They have to be dealt with."

Chapter 37

It was a few minutes after one o'clock in the morning. Joanna, Vyugin, and Dantry, having negotiated a circuitous route above and below the streets of the great metropolis, were finally unwinding in sheer exhaustion in a cramped hotel room on the second floor of Vyugin's small, unpretentious hotel just off the Arbat.

Thirty minutes earlier, they'd entered the austere, but essentially clean hostelry and approached the glass-covered front desk. Beneath the glass were yellowed notices, ads for nearby restaurants, and business cards of neighborhood shops and services. A fiftyish man behind the counter was sound asleep in a battered cane-back chair. Hearing Vyugin and his companions enter, he'd slowly risen from his slumber, stubbing out the end of what appeared to be the latest of a dozen or so cigarettes that he must have smoked earlier in the evening.

Despite her own exhaustion, Joanna had noticed that the man needed a shave, a decent wardrobe, and a comb. And it was obvious that he didn't welcome the intrusion. He was about to say something about it being too late to get a room when, as wakefulness replaced sleep, he recognized Vyugin and instantly became alert and attentive.

On their round-about way to the hotel, Dantry had thought on at least two occasions that he'd seen suspicious-looking characters eyeing them. Vyugin had pooh-poohed Tony's sightings as nothing more than typical examples of some of the more questionable denizens of the Moscow night. Vyugin was certain that they'd safely negotiated their way to the hotel without being followed, and Dantry said no more about it.

The man in the lobby had managed to scrounge up a bottle of vodka and three glasses, and now, with Vyugin joining them in their room, a room that smelled of stale smoke, they toasted each other and smiled the satisfied smile of fatigue well earned.

As Joanna lowered her glass Tony noticed that her body seemed to sag ever so slightly, as if she were giving in to exhaustion or despair.

"You all right?" asked Tony.

"Yes, I'll be okay. It's just that—"

"What?"

Her eyes reddened, becoming full with emotion. "It's just that I've never seen a gun fired at people before." She shuddered and leaned into Tony's chest. He put his arm around her and kissed the top of her head. "God it was so close—any one of us could have been killed in an instant. And one of them was, for God's sake." She brought her hands up to her face and took a deep breath.

"These things are not easy to deal with," said Vyugin compassionately. "Tony and I have been trained for this kind of work, and still it is not pleasant. For you, it must be very difficult to take. Perhaps…"

She forced a weak smile. "I'll be all right. As you say, I'm not trained for this. Just give me some time." Tony pulled her closer and held her. After a minute or so she pulled away. "I'm okay. Really."

"You want to go back to New York?" asked Dantry. "I'll understand."

Her cheeks turned red. "Jesus, Tony, don't get macho on me. Girls can play in the big world, too."

"I, …I didn't mean—"

"I know, I know. I'll be okay. Just don't patronize me like I'm some helpless female, okay?"

He raised his eyebrows. "Okay."

"It's not that I can't deal with it. It's just new. Takes a little getting used to."

"You never completely get used to it. If you do, you're not human."

"Yes," said Vyugin. "Take that young man that I shot. He may have been a basically decent young man, who got his orders and didn't understand fully what he was doing or why. He was a soldier who got hit in a battle he shouldn't have been in. It was him or us. I had no choice."

"Good God, I wasn't judging you, Vladimir," blurted Joanna. "It's just that I'm not used to actual physical conflict. Funny, I teach about it to my students. I'm an expert on Medieval and Renaissance wars, but when you actually experience a battle, where flesh and blood are involved, it's something else again." As she slowly regained her composure, she looked at Vyugin and a quizzical expression formed on her tired, but still attractive features. "I was just thinking. This has to be as hard on you as it is on Tony. I mean, you have to deal with your own countrymen who are now trying to kill you. And then there's your wife…My God, you left a comfortable retirement, and now this."

Vyugin sighed and put his hand to his forehead. "Yes, I have gotten myself into a fine mess."

Tony asked, "Have you communicated with your wife since you've been back?"

"I haven't dared. If by any chance they've traced her to St. Petersburg, they'll have put a tap on the phone there. They wouldn't do anything to her or anyone else there—what would that accomplish—but they would listen in to see if they could find out where I was calling from. It's unlikely that they've found her, but not impossible. I can't take the chance. And I know she must be worried." He rested his forehead in his hand and sighed.

"So what's our next move, Vladimir?"

"We need to talk about it." He pointed to the half-empty bottle next to Dantry. "I'll have some more of that, if you don't mind." Tony poured another two ounces of the clear liquid and added some to Joanna's glass and to his own. "We know that Bulgakov will be looking for us. He'll be relentless now—especially since we've wounded him and embarrassed him in front of his lackeys. He'll add revenge to his original reason for wanting us brought in. We also know that Borodin can't be trusted. He still may be useful to us, though. We have to think about that. What we don't know, is whether Malenkov is behind all this."

"If he's not, who is?" asked Joanna. "Bulgakov himself?"

Vyugin, who occupied the single chair in the room, leaned back, forming a peak with the fingers of his two hands. "Let's consider that. Whoever it is wants to embarrass President Kirov, either by making him fail in his bid to win the I.M.F. loan, or by having the attacks on I.M.F. officials made public."

Tony leaned forward and spoke. "Be more specific, Vladimir. If he fails to get the loan, how does that hurt him? I know, Russia needs the loan, but failure to get it reflects more on the I.M.F. than it does on him—doesn't it?"

"You mean it makes the I.M.F. look mean, spiteful, and petty?"

"All of that, plus shortsighted. They can't afford to have Russia go down the tubes."

Vyugin grimaced. "That is true, but, since Russia is the supplicant here, and since Kirov is the one directing its government, failure to get the loan will be perceived as his failure. His and his government's. It will be looked upon as a failure to correct Russia's floundering economy. If the economy is not set on the correct path, the world economic community will fear that any loan to Russia will simply disappear down a black hole. And that would set the stage for a palace coup, or at the very least, a new election."

"Then that would rule out Kirov," said Joanna. "I know, that seems pretty obvious, but if we can rule out certain people, it will help us zero in on the more likely candidates."

"I agree. Yes, of course you are right. Kirov has everything to lose and nothing to gain here."

"I take it Malenkov would have a good chance to succeed Kirov, if Kirov fails?" said Tony.

"Unfortunately, I'm afraid that is true. In the old days, he was a hard-line Communist. Today he remains a Communist, though outwardly he softens his image a bit. Not much, though. He believes in a strong central government. He, along with a large percentage of the population, believes that stability is more of a virtue than democracy. He and his supporters believe that democracy means letting the rabble in the street dictate national policy. I know, I know, they don't understand democracy. We debate this all the time in Russia. But this is how many people feel. And, in all fairness, you must realize that it works best in your country because you have been doing it so long. It is not a way of life that you learn overnight."

"Then," said Joanna, "are you saying that you think Malenkov is behind all this?"

"I'm not sure. Let us go back to our original premise: Who would benefit if Russia fails to get the loan? Malenkov, for sure, but others as well. If Malenkov did become president, Bulgakov, as his number-two man would also move up in power. I sometimes think power is more important to him than position. Bulgakov, would essentially be the number-two person in Russian, and depending on how much influence he has on Malenkov, he could have a great deal to say about how the country is run. Sorokin is just as ambitious as Bulgakov. It is not inconceivable that he would work behind the scenes to give himself more power."

"These two men are that ruthless?" asked Tony.

"Believe me, they are."

"Who else?"

"The generals. The military in general. They're already backing him, you can bet on that. People like Marshal Suchinov, the former head of the Soviet Army. And, of course, the top people in the FSB."

"In other words, people of influence. People who would gain power, influence, or wealth."

"Generally speaking, that's true, but not anyone in a position of influence. Not so much those who seek wealth. For instance, not not Andrei Primov, the Russian Bill Gates. Seems like he controls half the business in Russia. He does better under someone like Kirov who understands Capitalism. Or at least doesn't despise it the way Malenkov and Bulgakov do." He thought for a second, then added, "And not Anatoli Yakov, the leader of the Mafia. Unfortunately, he, too, would do better in a free market economy."

Vyugin paused a few seconds before continuing. "I take it back. I suppose there are not a lot of serious contenders, but those two, the two I just mentioned, have to be possibilities. And, I suppose the Communist Party. They would love to see Malenkov in power. It would elevate their influence ten-fold. Even though Malenkov might not go so far as to bring Russia back to its former Communist ways, he could be the interim step, paving the way for an eventual return to a Soviet-style government."

"Anyone else?'

"How do you know? Our best bet is to get to Borodin or Bulgakov and put pressure on them to reveal who's behind this. Right now, they must fear us as much as we do them."

"I would think so," agreed Joanna. "If we go public with what we have, we could mess up their plan—badly."

"Yes, we could go to the press or TV now, I suppose, and embarrass them somewhat. But I don't think it would be enough to accomplish what we're trying to do."

"Which is?"

"Which is to force them to back off entirely. If we went to the press now, it would be embarrassing, yes, assuming we could persuade the media that what we claim is true. I suppose even if they weren't totally convinced, it would make a good news story, so they might run it. But without proof, the conspirators would still be in business. No, we need either proof, or some leverage that we can use with the conspirators. Do you agree?"

Dantry nodded his assent slowly. "Yes, I think you're right, Vladimir. We've taken too many risks already to do this thing half way. So what do you suggest our next step be?" He allowed himself to smile.

Joanna looked surprised. "You look pretty content for someone who almost got killed tonight. Since your brother was killed a few weeks ago, the news has not been good. Earlier tonight, the bad guys were shooting at us. Seems like we've been up forever. We're exhausted, and when we do sleep, it will be in a room that reeks of stale smoke. Why so happy?"

"I don't know. Well, maybe I do, but am just a bit embarrassed to say."

"Now you've aroused my—"

Tony smiled. "Mmmm! Aroused your what?"

"My curiosity." She returned his lecherous smile with a smug look of her own. "Well? Why so happy?"

"I'm afraid the answer makes me look pretty immature."

"It's the little boy in you that attracted me to you in the first place."

"It's just that, since we've been involved in all of this, I've felt about twenty years younger. At the same time I feel sorta guilty, too. Christ, it takes my brother's death to make me feel alive." At this, the sparkle went out of Joanna's eyes. Dantry caught it and immediately realized what he'd said. "Oh shit, I didn't mean it that way. Since you came into my life, I've looked forward to waking up every morning because I knew you'd be in my life that day. It's just that, I guess it's that I left the 'company' when I was too young. My pension and savings were enough to live comfortably, and I confused that with living with a purpose. All I had to occupy my time was recreation—boating, fishing, taking it easy. Believe it or not, it's not enough. Duh." He grinned weakly. "Not when you have nothing else to do with your time and your mind. Now, I feel as if my life has the full range of dimensions it should have. A woman I love dearly and a mission worth accomplishing. A purpose."

Her expression warmed, and she gave him a hug. "I think I understand. But, you realize, that if we make it through this successfully, though, you'll be back to having no purpose. How will you deal with that?"

"I'm too tired to worry about that now, though I know I'm going to have to find something to do, at least two or three days a week. If this has taught me anything, it's that you can have too much of a good thing." He grinned at Joanna and quickly added, "I'm talking about leisure and recreation, not you."

Vyugin cleared his throat. "This has all been quite inspirational, but I need my sleep. I think I'll retire to my room and leave you two young lovebirds alone."

"G'night, Vladimir," said Joanna. "By the way, when you were retired, did you ever feel restless and lacking in purpose like Tony?"

He nodded. "Yes, of course. You don't do what we did for twenty or more years and suddenly do nothing without missing the action. It is, I suppose, like you said about Tony. It's the little boy in me."

"Or the warrior?"

He frowned. "Perhaps some of that, too. Good night, my friends."

"Wait!" said Tony. "You haven't answered my question. What's our next step?"

"I think we need to get their attention."

"Like their shooting at us means they don't know we exist."

As tired as he was, Vyugin couldn't help but laugh. "No, but it's going to be difficult to get close to these bastards now. We can't go to the 'white house,' and if we set up a meet, they'll swarm all over us. No, we have to make them come to us. That way, we'll at least have some control over the situation."

"And how do we achieve this?" asked Dantry.

"We go to the media and tell them what we have."

"We just said we can't do that. We don't have enough evidence."

"Yes, I know, but the more I think about it, the more I believe we have to go to the press. If we do this right, they— whoever they are—won't know how much evidence we have. Then they'll talk with us. Then they'll deal. They'll have to."

"Okay, let's say they do come to us. What if they send enough men and enough fire power to blow us out of the water. They won't have to deal. They'll just get rid of us."

"Not if we control the situation. Not if we keep an ace in the hole."

"But we don't have an ace in the hole, Vlady." Vyugin winced. He hated that nickname that Americans liked to use.

"I think we do. The more I think about, the more I realize that we do have enough to make these guys squirm. I was going to save this for morning, but if you prefer I can explain now what I have in mind. Now?"

Both and Dantry and Joanna nodded. "Now. Let's hear it."

Chapter 38

By mutual agreement, they'd slept late. They all needed it if they were to function efficiently. They'd left the dreary little hotel at eight thirty and walked a few blocks until they'd found a nondescript coffee shop on the Arbat. There, they'd taken a quick breakfast and solidified their plans.

Vyugin had then called the *Moscow Times*, one of the more respected English-Language dailies and found an editor who was intrigued enough to see them. They'd chosen an English-language paper over a Russian-language newspaper like *Isvestya* or *Pravda* because they felt that there was less chance that the editor would be in the hip pocket of Malenkov or someone close to him. Vyugin was fairly certain that these two old, established papers were fairly independent now, but he didn't want to take any chances. He'd deliberately kept names out of his conversation with the editor, just in case the man felt obliged to contact someone in the government to alert them about his meeting. All Vyugin had told the man was that he was a former KGB man and that he had a blockbuster story about how someone high up in government had ordered the assassination of two Americans.

The editor had been cautious, but his curiosity had gotten the best of him. He couldn't afford to pass up an exclusive on such a story if there was any chance that it was true. He agreed to meet with his caller.

They were now sitting in a small conference room. The editor, a man named Alexei Lubov, was just under six feet. He was of indeterminate age, probably somewhere between fifty and sixty, thought Dantry. His graying hair was longish and wavy, combed back in a mane with the sides combed over his ears and reaching down over his collar. He'd brought one of his associate editors with him. He was a younger man, slightly taller than his boss and with shorter, but darker hair.

"Tea....or coffee?" asked Lubov. "I have an old samovar going. It goes back to the time of Peter the Great. Still makes excellent tea."

Vyugin was about to refuse, but thought better of it. "Yes, thank you," he Vyugin, looking first at Joanna and then Dantry as if to confirm that his acceptance included them, too.

"So you have evidence of an assassination attempt, eh? Americans, right?"

"One was an attempt; the other a *fait accompli*," said Vyugin soberly.

The younger editor raised his eyebrows, but said nothing. Lubov's expression barely changed. He'd heard a lot of so-called blockbuster stories in his time. Most of them had been slightly less than spectacular when he'd gotten the real facts. He would reserve judgment about this until he heard more.

"All right, Mr. Vyugin, why don't you tell me what you have."

"A man by the name of Mark Dantry was killed in the suburbs of Washington several weeks ago. This is Mr. Dantry's brother—Anthony Dantry." He pointed to Tony. "Mr. Dantry here is retired from the CIA. We are now working together. As the Americans say, strange bedfellows, eh. But back to Mr. Dantry. His brother, as you may already know, was a major figure with the International Monetary Fund in Washington."

"Yes, I do know," said Lubov flatly. "Please continue."

"We believe that his death, which was made to look like an accident, was an execution ordered by senior officials in the Russian government."

"Can you prove it?"

"Yes, I was one of the people sent to America to do the job." The younger editor's eyes bulged. Lubov, for the first time, allowed his emotions to show on his normally deadpan face. His next question revealed his confusion.

"I....don't understand. Why would you tell me this? Why would you implicate yourself?"

"I said that I was one of those sent to America. I didn't go through with it, though. Let's just say I had a change of heart. Two of my associates did carry out the assignment. They later carried out a second attempt on a man by the name of J. Martin Chandler." Vyugin proceeded to describe the bomb attempt in the Washington Metro station.

"I remember the bombing incident," said the younger editor. "Don't remember anything about this Chandler, though."

"You wouldn't," said Dantry. "He wasn't injured. Wasn't even mentioned in most of the news accounts over there. Two people were killed, though."

"I should tell you," interjected Vyugin, "that Mr. Dantry, here, through an act of heroism, saved many more people from being killed and injured in that bombing attack." The two journalists appeared surprised at this. Then Lubov turned grave.

"You'll forgive me, gentlemen, if I seem hesitant about your motives. On the one hand you tell us that you were sent to execute two Americans—" At this, Vyugin interrupted.

"No, I said that I had been sent to do an execution. Mr. Dantry only became involved when he learned that his brother had been killed."

"All right, only you, then. Then, on the other hand, you tell us that one of you has been an heroic good Samaritan, and that both of you wish to tell us of this government plot—a plot that you, Mr. Vyugin, until recently, were a part of."

"That is essentially it, yes," said Vyugin. "If you will permit me to continue, I think you will understand."

"Proceed."

Twenty minutes later, Vyugin, leaned back in his seat. "That about sums it up." He turned to Dantry and Joanna. "Did I leave anything out?"

"You covered it," confirmed Tony.

Lubov rose and walked to the window. It looked out on the street below. After a few seconds he turned and faced the table.

"Supposing I say I believe you. Do you realize the risk we take if we print this, even if it is true."

"It is."

"What do you think, Antonin?" It was the first time he'd addressed the younger man.

"It's one hell of a story. A scoop for us. I say we run with it."

"But if the facts are not exactly as Mr. Vyugin says they are." He raised his hand to Vyugin. "Please, I know you say they are, but we don't know you, sir. You must understand the situation in which you have placed us."

"We do," said Dantry. Vyugin nodded.

"And you have not identified the people behind this. You say that Bulgakov, Sorokin, this Borodin—they are all involved. And you've suggested that Malenkov may be behind it all, but you are not sure of him, right?"

"Right."

Lubov looked at his colleague; then back to Vyugin and the others. "I'm uncomfortable just now with what you have told us. I believe you, but if we publish this now, without further information, I think it could be trouble for the paper—and for Antonin and myself." A trace of a smile crossed his face. "On the other hand, I do believe something is going on, perhaps even more than you are aware of. It could be a much bigger story." He hesitated for a moment, as if not certain of how far to go. "There is something of which we have recently become aware that I believe you will find interesting. Antonin, I think it is worth the risk. We should share our information with our guests here."

Antonin frowned. "I'm not sure it's necessary. We really—"

Lubov cut him off. "Yes, I think it's worth the risk." Antonin raised his eybrows, but said nothing further.

Lubov turned back to face his three visitors. He walked to the window and began speaking, as if to no one in particular. "All I ask is that, if something develops from this, you might let us know so that we can be the first to tell the story." He then turned and met the eyes of his visitors, challenging them for their answer.

Vyugin turned first to Dantry; then to Joanna. They both nodded their agreement. Vyugin then nodded yes, and Lubov proceeded.

"Over the past few months we've been getting reports of a place outside of Moscow where a number of senior government officials have been seen coming and going."

"What sort of a place?" asked Dantry.

"Not a government office or other legitimate government installation so far as we can determine. A small sign on the building says that it is a warehouse. There are no windows. But it is not located in an industrial or commercial section. It is isolated in the woods not far from Noginsk and just outside a small nearby village. Certainly an odd place for people like Bulgakov and Sorokin to be visiting, wouldn't you say?" Dantry's brow furrowed and Vyugin squinted, as if trying to imagine what sort of business such people could be conducting in a warehouse.

"Have trucks been seen carrying goods in and out of the building?" asked Joanna.

"A few, but in our opinion, not enough for an active warehouse."

"I suppose it depends on what kind of products are being warehoused there," said Tony.

"I suppose so," said Lubov. "Another thing, though. Armed guards patrol the premises. Armed with automatic rifles. Not the kind of weapons you'd expect if they were storing consumer goods."

"Again," said Tony, "it might depend on what kind of consumer goods, But you're probably right. How far out of Moscow is this building?"

"About 50 kilometers. No more than that."

"What do you suspect?" asked Vyugin.

"It is easy to let your mind jump to conclusions," said Lubov, "especially in this country with its history of intrigue, cabals, and *coups d'état*. Perhaps it is a group of disgruntled government men who plot the overthrow of the Kirov administration. Then again, it may be a social club. It is possible that it is nothing." He expelled a long breath, then said, "But in light of what you have just told us, it looks extremely suspicious."

"You say that you have seen these people coming and going," said Vyugin. "Have you not gotten close enough to find out what is going on inside?"

"You must understand, that this is a newspaper. Right now we are barely surviving. We don't have the personnel to maintain ongoing surveillance. Nor do we have the money. We have a paper to get out. Someone reported to us that there was this suspicious place near Noginsk. I sent a reporter out there to observe the place. He was there three days, but now he is back. I have told you virtually all we know."

It occurred to Dantry that if the paper gambled and assigned one or two people to dig deeper, the story they might get could be well worth the time and money spent. But, since he, Vyugin, and Joanna were looking for help, he decided to ignore that issue and press on. It was not their job to second-guess the editorial judgment of *The Moscow Times*. "I see," he said. "Can you tell us the names of the people you have seen coming or going from that building?"

"Bulgakov, Sorokin, Borodin, Chechnyoff, Lubin." Tony whistled and looked at Vyugin and Joanna, who raised their eyebrows and nodded. "These are the ones we can identify," continued Lubov. "There have been others including several army officers." Dantry raised his eyebrows and looked at Vyugin and Joanna.

"Military, eh?" said Dantry. "Who is Chechnyoff, by the way?"

"A deputy defense minister. Lubin is also in the defense ministry. Yes, the presence of these army people is very disturbing."

Joanna cleared her throat. All eyes turned in her direction. "This is probably a giant leap, but it appears as if we might be looking at a group that's plotting to overthrow the Kirov government. The execution of Tony's brother and the attempt on Chandler's life may have been part of some complex Machiavellian plan."

"Or this could just be a coincidence and the warehouse might actually be a warehouse," said Antonin.

"I don't think any of us really believes that," said Dantry.

Chapter 39

It was eleven by the time they left the newspaper office. They'd
proceeded to rent a car—a fairly recent-model black Lada. Vyugin
had used a false ID and a false license so if Bulgakov or his
buddies were trying to find them, they'd be thrown off the track.
The three of them had then gone back to Vyugin's hotel, where
he'd picked up a few items he said they might need. "High-tech
stuff," he explained with a grin. "I'll tell you about them as we
drive." Dantry recognized some of the things that were now
sharing the back seat with Joanna. He'd used similar items himself
in the past.

The directions Lubov had given them were perfect. Their
destination was just outside Noginsk, a city of 125,000, on the road
to Vladimir, which was perhaps another 100 kilometers further
east. Until 1930, explained Vyugin, Noginsk had been called
Bogorodsk. It had been, and still was, he said, an important textile
center.

Dantry couldn't help but notice that the roads, once you got
ten miles outside of Moscow, were as bad as ever. They'd been bad
when he'd been here last, but as far as he could see, they hadn't
gotten any better in the last ten years. Virtually all the construction
and all the work on new infrastructure had been in Moscow, the
showcase city of the "new" Russia. What this meant in terms of
travel was that, it took longer to get from point A to point B in
Russia than it did in other Western countries. The trip they were
taking—50 kilometers or 30 miles—would take a little over half an

hour on America's Interstate highway system. Here in Russia, if all went well, it would take more than an hour.

They'd been tempted to take the train, always the preferred method of travel in Russia. The Vladimir Division of the Gorky Railroad commuter line stopped in Noginsk. The extensive Noginsk tram system could have gotten them virtually anywhere in that industrial city, but unfortunately, their destination was ten kilometers outside of Noginsk, so they'd needed a car.

Vyugin was at the wheel. It was just after noon, and they were about 16 kilometers outside of Moscow, passing through the suburb of Balashikha. The traffic was light. Most of the cars and other vehicles were heading toward Moscow at this time of day. Vyugin turned to Dantry and smiled.

"We should probably go over those items that Joanna is protecting back there. You probably recognize the dish, Tony. It's a parabolic microphone."

Dantry grinned. "Yes, I've used them on you guys."

"I'm sure. They've improved, though. This one can hear a conversation 400 feet away. There's another mike there that will pick up conversations through windows, and sometimes even walls. You didn't have those back when we were active." He paused for a moment. "Or did you?"

"No, nothing quite that good. If we wanted to hear something inside a building we had to plant bugs. And in those days, the bugs were not as small or as good as the movies make them out to be."

"Isn't that the truth," chuckled Vyugin. "Joanna, you see that device that looks something like a video camera?"

"This?" She held up what looked like a scope of some kind.

"Yes, that's a night vision scope. It's amazing. There's also a couple of modern bugs and even what is called a keyhole camera. So you see, we are well equipped. We probably won't need all this stuff, but we have it just in case."

"What kind of firepower do you have?" asked Dantry.

"A Kalishnikov and two Uzi's. The Kalishnikov has a little more range, but the Uzi's are more compact—easier to carry. Are you up to this, Miss Barbeau?"

She hesitated, but only for a split second. "I can handle it."

"Let us hope we won't need to use them, but I can't promise that we won't. These people are not going to, as you say, roll over."

"Are you planning to just attack them by surprise?" she asked. "I'm willing to do whatever is necessary, but it would seem to me that the odds don't favor a bold frontal attack. Not when we don't even know what we're up against."

Vyugin tried not to let his annoyance show. It was as if a master craftsman were being challenged about a matter of technique by a student. He turned to Dantry. "Explain to her, Tony, that we don't just barge in with guns blazing."

Dantry saw the annoyance on Vyugin's face and resented it. "She's not a fucking idiot, Vladimir. How the hell would she know what we're going to do. Hell, you haven't even shared your plan with me."

"That's because I don't have one yet," grinned Vyugin in a skillful attempt at defusing the tension. "I was hoping the three of us would come up with something when we saw the place. I'm sorry Miss Barbeau if I sound condescending. Certainly people in our trade have no reason to feel superior. Please forgive me."

"There's nothing to forgive, but please call me Joanna."

"To answer your question, I think we should do some surveillance first. Then we can decide what our next move should be. Is that agreeable to you two?"

"Sounds right to me," said Dantry. Joanna nodded. "By the way, Vladimir, where the hell did you keep this stuff at the hotel? I mean you can't just leave it around the way you do your shaving stuff or a change of clothes."

"I was wondering when you'd ask. A little history first. I used to stay in that hotel back in the '80s when I was in Moscow. My superiors would have authorized something better, but I liked it because it was easier to monitor who was coming and going. And it was easier to avoid being watched myself. On my very first stay in the hotel, I discovered a loose floorboard under the rug. I made it a point to pick that room on subsequent visits. I often used the space beneath the floorboard to hide my gun and any other items I didn't want to flash around. This time, though, before I got to the hotel, I realized that my little hideaway wasn't big enough to stash all this stuff." He threw his right arm over the seat back and pointed toward the high-tech surveillance equipment in the back seat. "I came prepared, though. I brought with me a—I believe you call it—a claw hammer. I loosened an adjacent board and expanded my hiding place so that it could accommodate all of what you see there. Imagine that, more than a decade has passed, and they never fixed that original floorboard."

"Maybe," said Dantry, "they know about the floorboard and check beneath it whenever a guest leaves the room."

Vyugin looked startled, then shook it off. "I don't think so." He went silent for a moment, then added, "Let's hope not, eh."

Tony said, "Why do I always feel paranoid when I'm in Russia?"

They were entering Noginsk, and Joanna was overwhelmed by a sense of melancholy, a feeling that this city had not changed since the Soviet break-up. Certainly not the way Moscow had. She'd never been here before, but she would have wagered a new Volga that it looked much the same ten years ago, and probably twenty and even thirty years ago. It was a drab gray city from the past, with tired-looking men and babushka'd women dragging their way through the streets as if getting to their destination was not the least bit important. In some ways Noginsk reminded her of pictures she'd seen of American Midwestern industrial cities during the Great Depression. Noginsk was a busy city in that a lot of people populated its streets, but it was not a bustling city. There was none of the energy she'd seen in countless American and European cities. Tony was thinking much the same thing as Vyugin skillfully negotiated Noginsk's streets. As far as Tony could tell, it was still in every outward way a Soviet city.

Fifteen minutes later, they took a left turn. Soon, they were leaving Noginsk behind them and heading northward out of town. The road they were on now was even more pockmarked than the previous road that had taken them to Noginsk from Moscow. They were in open country now, occasionally they passed neglected ramshackle farm buildings. Cows and goats could be seen in nearby pastures. Even the animals looked neglected and underfed, thought Joanna.

Vyugin handed Dantry a map that the editor Lubov had sketched for them. "I will need your help now. Tony."

"We're heading toward Jamkino. You know it?"

"Yes, it's not much. But we don't go into Jamkino, right?"

"Right. Jamkino looks to be about eight kilometers from Noginsk. According to this, we go about five and then turn off to the right. Jesus, this road is bad."

"Unfortunately, such roads are far too common. Many are much worse. How will we know where to turn off?"

Tony laughed quietly. "According to this, there's no street or road sign. It's just an unmarked dirt road. Lubov has a little note here saying the turnoff is just before a small stone church building. I remember when we were in his conference room he said that the little church had been used as a local *oblast* or autonomous provincial office building until a few years ago, when the Orthodox Church took it over again—after almost 70 years." Tony chuckled, "Unfortunately, we won't be able to see the church from where we're supposed to turn off, so we'll have to drive until we come to it, and then turn around and come back to the road we're looking for." Vyugin nodded, not seeing the humor in the situation, no doubt because he was used to such directions.

"Should be coming up soon," said Joanna. "God, it's amazing how desolate it gets here only a few miles outside of a town. We could be in the middle of nowhere."

"You're not too far from the truth, Miss Barbeau."

"Joanna."

"Joanna. Look!" Vyugin pointed to the right. "I'll wager that that's our road. Watch out for the church."

He was right. Less than a third of a mile further on they came to the stone church. "If I remember correctly, we go about three quarters of a kilometer on this road."

"Good memory, Vlad," said Dantry lightheartedly. "That's what the map says. Then there's another road, also to the right. Christ, by the time we find this place, we could be in Siberia."

"I've been in many places in Siberia that are more civilized than this," smiled Vyugin. "By the way, I'm getting hungry. I took the liberty of bringing some bread, cheese, and bottled water. I would have preferred wine, but we need clear heads, Da?"

"Da," said Tony. "Damn it Vladimir, you think of everything. Now that you bring it up, I could eat something, too."

"My God, you guys!" blurted Joanna. "We're about to risk our necks spying on some bad guys, and all you think about is your stomach!"

"If we're going to fight for right, we need fuel for these bodies," grinned Tony. "You can only go so far on adrenaline. Why don't you open up those bags, and pull out the food so we can eat something before we get there."

They'd eaten quickly and were polishing off the last pieces of cheese and ends of bread as they made the final turn into the secret compound. In the distance, they could just make out a portion of the building. It appeared to be of wood-frame construction. Vyugin slowed the Lada to a crawl. The road had narrowed so that only one vehicle could pass. About three hundred meters from the building, they could see a cut-off, where the road expanded for a few meters on the right side—just enough to allow another vehicle to pass if one pulled off to the side. About a 150 meters from where they were now, they could see that the building was a one-story structure surrounded by a chain-link fence topped with barbed wire. Vyugin eased the car forward a few more feet and stopped. "Could you give me those binoculars, please, Joanna?"

She fumbled among the numerous items on the seat next to her and passed him the glasses. Vyugin rolled down his window and leaned out, directing the binoculars toward the gate of the compound.

"There's at least one guard."

"I don't see anyone," said Joanna.

"You're not supposed to. He's just inside the gate, sitting behind a shield of some sort. Most likely they don't want the guards to be too obvious. They don't want to attract attention to this facility. If you tried to enter, however, I'm sure they'd make their presence known. He seems to be napping now. In any event, his mind is not on us—fortunately. I imagine guards get quite bored here. It's, as the three of us know all too well, out of the way, and they probably don't get many strangers wandering up to the gate. We can use that to our advantage."

"Let's do a little surveillance first to see what we're up against," said Dantry.

"Exactly what I was thinking. I'm going to back this thing up as quietly as I can and see if we can't get it off the road, where it won't be seen. While I back up, you two keep an eye on the gate. If you see anyone, that means they see us, and we need to change to Plan B."

"What's Plan B?" asked Joanna.

Vyugin leaned over the top of the seat to look backward as he put the car in reverse. "Tony will think of something."

After backing up a little over a hundred meters, Vyugin and Dantry saw the turnoff. It was an overgrown dirt road, obviously seldom used—more path than road because of the disuse.

"Anyone see the guard?" asked Vyugin.

"No, he didn't come out," said Joanna, who hadn't taken her eyes off the gate. She breathed a sigh and now directed her attention to the side road they'd discovered. The entrance to the glorified path was almost invisible because of dense underbrush and low-hanging birch branches. Vyugin slowly backed the car past it; then put the Lada in first gear and quietly pulled into the welcoming darkness of the narrow sanctuary.

"We're going to have to approach the place on foot through the woods," said Dantry. "It'll be slow going, but we have to stay off the road. Those guys have to look this way once in awhile."

"Yes," agreed Vyugin. "We can each take some of that stuff in the back seat. And make sure the weapons are loaded. Have you fired one of those, Joanna?" He pointed to the Kalishnikov and the two Uzis.

"No, a target rifle is about my speed. Just show me what to do, though, and I'll be okay."

"I'm sure you will. Tony, I think she might prefer one of the Uzis. What do you think?"

"I agree. They're a little easier to handle." He then turned to Joanna. "C'mon, let's get out the car, and I'll show you how to handle this little baby."

"There are three backpacks on the floor," said Vyugin. "We can divide up the hardware and carry it on our backs. Just so long as we hold onto the weapons."

Five minutes later they were making their way through the dense birch forest in the direction of the compound. Joanna couldn't remember ever seeing so many birch trees in her life. Back in the eastern part of the U.S. where she'd grown up, people had treasured birch trees because of their beauty and relative scarcity, but here, they were everywhere. The trees grew so densely that the bright sunny day they'd left moments ago was now a distant memory. The beauty of the cool, dark forest was not lost on her, despite the precariousness of their situation.

They were now on a diagonal about a hundred meters to the right of the front gate. The chain-link fence was directly ahead— perhaps 25 meters. Vyugin, who was leading the little expeditionary force, held up his hand for them to halt. He turned and whispered to his companions. "The trees are not as dense here. I can see the gate, and it looks as if there are two guards. They seem to be talking. Let's see what that parabolic microphone is capable of. Tony had been carrying the bulky dish on his back and now carefully detached it and gave it to the Russian. Vyugin connected it to its powerpack and placed the compact headphones on his head, motioning for silence as he listened. He frowned in concentration.

After a minute or so, Joanna silently mouthed, "Anything interesting?"

Vyugin pulled one side of the headphones away from his ear and smiled. "These have improved dramatically. It's as if they're right next to you. Of course you hear peripheral sounds like birds and even insects." He could see that his friends were impatient for something more substantive than his assessment of the current state of technology. "They're talking about a meeting that's going to take place here tomorrow. One of the names they mentioned was Bulgakov. That's the only name I recognized, though. Apparently a number of important people are expected." Vyugin removed the headphones. "Tony?" Dantry shook his head.

"No, your Russian is better than mine."

A couple of minutes later, Vyugin removed the headset. "End of conversation. One of the guards has gone into the building. At least I got the time for the meeting. One o'clock tomorrow. We should be here. Let us go back to Moscow now and formulate our plans."

"Er….maybe we should stay in Noginsk?" suggested Joanna. She was not lacking in confidence, but she was well aware of cultural differences and did not want to appear to be overstepping her bounds. After all, she was in Vyugin's country. Nevertheless her life and Tony's were just as much on the line as his. Besides, what good was she on this trip if she didn't contribute? "Less likely that they'll track us down there," she added by way of explanation. "And it's a shorter trip."

Vyugin pursed his lips and nodded approvingly. Tony said, "Good idea. You know any hotels in Noginsk, Vladimir?"

"There used to be a down-at-the heel place called the Internationale. We could try that."

Chapter 40

The recently renovated three-story brownstone building on Octyabreskaya Naberezhnaya overlooked the grand Alexander Nevskovo canal in St. Petersburg. Inside, Ludmilla Vyugin smiled as she balanced Mischa, her two-year old grandson.

"How long can you keep smiling, Mother?" asked the blue-eyed toddler's mother, her concern written all over her face. "You haven't heard from him in days. I thought he was through with all this spy business."

"Your father didn't seek this out, Sonia. The government came to him. Bulgakov, himself." She beamed with pride. "They passed over the young men and picked your father. It's a great honor."

"What is there to spy on now? Not the Americans. Not the British. Who, the Chechens? What could he possibly be involved in, Mother? Good God, you two deserve to enjoy your retirement. I just don't understand why he's out risking his life at his age."

Her mother sighed. "Nor do I, I have to admit. It must be important, or they wouldn't have asked him out of retirement."

"I don't like this Bulgakov—the little I've heard about him. I think he wants to take us back to the days of Stalin. Why would Papa get involved with a man like him?"

"He's the prime minister's chief aide. I'm sure whatever he's asked your father to do is for Mr. Malenkov, not for himself.

"Malenkov's not much better than Bulgakov in my opinion."

"What do we know of the problems these men in Moscow face. I'm sure it's not easy running the government—especially the government of Russia with so many problems. It's easy to criticize these people, Sonia. Maybe you should be a little more tolerant. We have no idea what they have to go through."

It was Saturday, and Sonia's husband Pyotr, who was reading the paper across the room smiled at this. He shook his head at what he viewed as the incredibly naïve, old-fashioned thinking of his warm-hearted mother-in-law. He went back to his paper as Sonia spoke.

"God, Mother, you're so gullible. Most of what they go through is of their own making. You don't think that the people made Stalin, do you? Or Khrushchev, or any of the rest of them? Good God, they did what they did to the people. Not the other way around."

"You're so young, my daughter. What do you remember of those difficult times?"

"I know because I have been out of the country. I've read about it. And I know what it did to you and Papa."

Ludmilla looked hurt. "And just what did it do to your parents that was so bad?"

"It made you insular, provincial, and chauvinistic. You saw Russia only from the Russian perspective." She was caught up in something now that she'd never given word to before, but she could see that her words were painful to her mother. "It wasn't your fault Mama. You weren't permitted to see anything else. Don't you see, that's the evil of what you and Papa lived through."

"It wasn't easy—not as easy as for you younger people. If things come too easily, it's not good. You and Pyotr both have good jobs. You take them for granted."

"No, that's not true, Mother. We know how fortunate we are."

"Do you realize how lucky you are that you could choose the kind of work you do? I never had that choice. Your father....well, your father had some choice. He went with the KGB. I know what you think, but it was patriotic, and it paid better than most. And, you were wrong about us not getting out of

Russia. At least wrong about your father. He went to England, Germany, France, even America."

"Yes, but he was a spy. And he probably killed people. Did he, Mother? Did he kill people?"

Her mother put her hand over her eyes. Sonia could hear her sniffling. "You never asked me that before. Why?"

"I never wanted to know the answer. I suppose I still don't, but I need to. I need to know who my father is."

"You know who your father is. You and he have always been close. He loves you very much."

"We've been close on one level, but—what is it, Pyotr?"

"There's a strange car parked across the street," said her husband soberly. "It's been there all morning, maybe longer."

"So, cars park on the street all the time."

"Yes, but there are two men in this one, and they keep looking this way."

"What are you saying?" asked Ludmilla cautiously.

"I think we're being watched. More precisely, Mother, I think you're being watched."

"You think it's the people Papa sent Mother up here to get away from?" asked Sonia.

"Don't you?"

"Oh dear God. I never dreamed....."

"Look, there's no reason to panic. They're not going to do anything unless—"

"Unless what?" blurted Ludmilla nervously.

"They're probably just watching the house to see if Vladimir comes here." Ludmilla gasped, and Pyotr hesitated a few seconds before continuing. "Look, I'm sure they have no problem with any of us—whatever their problem is. And they probably just want to talk to Vladimir. In any event, Vladimir won't come here without calling first. He'll know what to do."

Ludmilla was trembling. Her daughter went over and put her arm around her. They hugged for a long moment, and then Sonia said, "Mama, this will work out. We just have to wait until we hear from him. I'm sure Pyotr is right. They just want to talk to him."

Vladamir superspy!

Chapter 41

As it turned out, the Internationale was still in business. "That's the good news," said Vyugin. "The bad news is that it has not changed. Still, I think it is a good choice. But just to be doubly safe, I shall register about a half hour after you do—in case someone inquires about a threesome registering there today. And I think it is a good idea to use the false IDs that I've provided for all of us. We don't want to underestimate the people we are up against."

Joanna was impressed by this man, a man who a decade earlier was their mortal enemy. Events and the years had changed all that, but Vyugin must always have been different from most men. She hoped Mrs. Vyugin realized how fortunate she was to be married to this man of so many surprising dimensions. Joanna was no naif; she knew that he had killed. She'd seen him do it back in Moscow in that underground garage. But it was clear that he took no pleasure from this. She chose to believe that he would much prefer to solve problems in other ways. His pure intellect together with what she could only describe as a casual sensitivity were hard for her to ignore. And with all of this, he possessed an indefinable charm that made him stand out among men she had known. As she thought about this, she couldn't help but compare him with Dantry. She smiled at the comparison. Aside from age and physical appearance, they were surprisingly alike. She wondered if either of them would welcome this comparison.

They encountered no problems checking into the hotel. The rooms, while far from elegant, turned out to be clean, though easily as drab as Vyugin had predicted. They dined—Vyugin had questioned the appropriateness of the term 'dined' in light of the

But why register separately if you're going to dine together

depressingly uninspired menu and suggested 'ate'—in the hotel dining room, where they sketched out their plans for the following day. *and chat all evening?*

"Remember," said Vyugin. "our goal is to gain intelligence. We are not storming the castle. We don't have the manpower. The object is to get as close as we can without being detected, and to collect as much data as we can. Whenever possible, we should take photos or record what we find. If that's not possible, be sure that what you see or hear is noted on paper. We want to go away from there with as much persuasive information as possible."

"But in order to maximize our efforts," asked Joanna, "we'll be separating so that we can triple our chances of acquiring data by collecting from three different vantage points—correct?"

"Yes," said Dantry. "You never know where you're going to get something useful. The only exception to this is if we determine that every last one of them is in one room."

"Right," said Vyugin. "Our chances of getting useful data are improved this way, but bear in mind, there are risks either way. If we're together, it's easier to cover for each other. Separately, it's less likely that, if they get one of us, they get all of us. So, while we'll be separated, we must stay in touch with each other. Use the walkie-talkies I gave you, but be sure to use the earphones. And be sure to turn your back to the building and speak in a low tone when you talk into them. Remember, we are not dealing with stupid people. Each of us becomes vulnerable and without immediate back-up. We need to plan for that, too."

"Just to be sure we're all on the same page as to what our goal is," said Dantry, "we're after some kind of evidence or proof that people in high office in the Russian government are plotting to overthrow the Kirov government. Or at the very least, undermine it by embarrassing it and weakening it so that Malenkov can replace Kirov. If and when we get this evidence or proof, we'll take it to The *Moscow Times* or Kirov in order to prevent such a government overthrow. Are we generally in agreement on that?"

"Yes, I think that is a good summation of what our goal is. The only thing I believe we should leave open is to whom we deliver our information. It may be that the most effective way to undo this coup attempt—assuming that's what it is—is to deliver our evidence to Malenkov himself."

They all understood this. It depended on the evidence they came up with and whether they determined that Malenkov was involved. Their objective was to take their evidence to whomever could do the most with it.

"I gather there's no need to rise early tomorrow morning," said Dantry. "This doesn't go down until one in the afternoon."

"No, it's a good chance to catch up on our sleep. I'll be rising early, because at my age, it comes naturally. However, we will want to get there about two hours early, so I wouldn't sleep too late. We'll need to select the best observation points, and we'd better be there well before the others start arriving or someone is bound to notice us. We should be there, hide the car and set up our equipment before they'd even think to look for anyone lurking in the woods." He looked at the others for their reaction to what he'd been saying. Nothing. Good. He continued with the plan. "So we'll want to bring some food and plan on settling in around eleven o'clock. Figure on leaving here about 10:00. Okay?"

At this, Joanna looked somewhat surprised, but nodded agreement as the logic of the Russian's words sank in. Dantry said, "Yeah, fine."

Back in their room, as they were getting ready for bed, Joanna pulled Dantry down beside her on the bed. She felt the soft mattress give under their combined weight. Probably the original mattress, she thought with a smile.

"Am I being propositioned?" asked Tony.

"Not now, you're not. I want to put something to you. And don't make salacious comments."

"Serious, huh?"

"Yeah, serious."

"Okay, if I have to go through serious to get to salacious, let's get on with it."

"No, really. I am serious."

He wiped the grin off his face. "Okay, what's on your mind?"

"Are you sure you want to continue with this?"

"This conversation?"

"I said I was serious. Can you be serious for a minute, please?"

"I'm sorry. Go on."

"Are you sure that you want to continue helping Vyugin? I know it's in a good cause—at least for Russia—but I'm not so sure there's an up side for you, or me for that matter. We can get ourselves killed. It sounds as if there's a better-than-even chance of that. If we don't get killed, maybe, just maybe we can convince whoever needs convincing that there's a conspiracy to undo the Kirov government. But from my perspective, there's no guarantee we'll succeed. Then what? Do we continue trying until we do get ourselves killed? I know it sounds defeatist or maybe even cowardly, but we are facing pretty big odds.
I mean, the three of us against Russian heavyweights—with their resources and on their turf." She looked at him expectantly. "Am I being so awful even asking this?"

"You are serious. No, you're not so awful. Remember, I tried to talk you out of this back in the States."

"This isn't about me, dammit. It's about you *and* me. Us. As I said, I think the cause is a good one, but is it our cause? After all, the guys who killed your brother are dead. Doesn't that even the score?"

"I hear you, and I suppose many people, many sane, logical people, would agree with you. The score, as far as I'm concerned, is not yet even. Those two guys who killed my brother did it because they were ordered to do it. They were merely the instruments of someone higher up. Malenkov, Bulgakov, whoever. That's who I want to get."

"You won't be happy until you kill someone else?"

"I never set out to kill those guys. All I wanted was to bring them in and make them answer to the law. That's what I still want. I want to make whoever is behind all this face the consequences of their actions. I'll be happy to let the authorities decide what to do with them." She softened as he said this. It was something, at least, that he had no desire to kill. Deep down, her fear that he wanted to kill the people responsible had bothered her deeply. She wasn't sure she could live with someone who had the need to kill, no matter how justified he made it sound.

"Besides," continued Tony, aware that he somehow needed to convince Joanna that as obsessed as he was, his preoccupation was at least pure, "if I can do something to keep these guys from toppling the Kirov government, I want to do it." He could see the sadness in her eyes, and it moved him. He felt helpless. He knew he was obsessed, and he couldn't help himself. "I know, it's obsessive and excessive, but something is driving me to see this out. Still, there's no reason you should share my obsession. I want you to go home, Joanna. Christ, you've got to. I don't want you involved in this anymore."

"I am involved, dammit. Do you think I can leave you here, knowing that you'll be taking your life in your hands—literally. Don't you see, Tony, that I want to live, but with you. You've become part of my life. For the hundredth time, this is about us; not you. Not me. So, whether you want it or not, I am involved."

"Don't you see, if this doesn't work out and something happens to you I'll never forgive myself."

"Well, then you damn well better make it work out. You and your Russian chum."

"You think I'm off the wall, don't you?"

"This is all so surreal, I don't know what to think. My God, a few weeks ago I was just another frazzled New Yorker, trying to keep up with my bills and wondering where my life was leading me. This wonderfully sweet, intelligent man had become a part of my life. To be honest, I was sort of amazed at how someone that bright and that virile could be satisfied with a life of noncompetitive ease. It was nice after being a part of the busy New York whirl, but it was strange. I couldn't figure you out. I knew there was something deep down inside burning to get out. I knew you couldn't just go fishing on the Sound and take it easy forever, or you'd go nuts. But I never dreamed it would take something like this to ignite your flame. No, I don't think you're off the wall. I suppose I understand. I think I'm now witnessing the person you probably were before I met you, when you were with the agency. Or maybe there's two of you. All I know is my mind is a blur now." The tautness in her face relaxed and she added, "And I know that I love you, and I know we're in this together."

Chapter 42

It was unusually hot for this part of Russia, even for July. There was no air conditioning in the Lada, so they drove with the windows open. They neared the compound now, and Vyugin slowed the car as they approached the hidden lane where they planned to hide the car. Then something made him think twice about it.

"I don't think we should put the car here. Too close. For a meeting of this importance, they may very well check the surrounding perimeter. I think we should park the car farther away, perhaps half a mile or so. What do you think?"

Dantry nodded his head. "Yeah, you're probably right. If we're going to work up a sweat, it might as well be a good one." He turned to Joanna. "Okay?"

"Yes, I'm sure you're right."

Vyugin turned the vehicle around and headed back the way they'd come. About a half mile back, they came upon a narrow dirt road on the left. He turned in, found an opening in the underbrush about a hundred feet in and hid the vehicle as well as possible. They then set out on foot for the compound. They were carrying considerable hi-tech equipment, so the hike wasn't easy. Ten minutes later they were back at the point where they'd secreted the car on their first visit.

"See anyone?" asked Vyugin. "Check the sides of the road as well as the gate."

"Nothing. No different than last time," said Joanna. "At least it appears to be the same."

"Tony?"

"No, nothing. Still, let's be careful. They could have people stationed in the woods. Let's stash some of this stuff here, so we can get to it if we need it. We'll only take with us what we're likely to need. Now before we head in the direction of the building, I'll use the listening device and see if I hear anything." He placed the headphones for the parabolic microphone on his head and motioned with his hand for the others to stand silent. After a full minute, he took the headphones off and said, "Nothing. Seems okay. Still, let's be careful."

"Before we proceed," said Vyugin in a voice just above a whisper, "let's distribute our gear. If anyone is hungry, you should take something now. We may not get a chance for awhile." Tony and Joanna nodded and proceeded to wolf down some of the food they'd brought along. As they finished, they buried the wrappings so as not to leave any evidence that they'd been there.

"Ready?" asked Dantry.

"Yes," said Vyugin. Joanna nodded.

"Good. Remember, if you get caught, you're part of a joint U.N-Interpol group investigating a reported plot against President Kirov. Kirov doesn't know that, but these people may buy it, and let you go. If they're smart they'll pretend they know nothing about it and by letting you go lend support for their innocence. Don't count on it, though. And one thing you don't want to say is that you're here alone. They wouldn't believe you anyway—especially when you're carrying a walkie-talkie."

"All right," said Vyugin, "I'll approach toward the gate at first. I'll stay in that position until the "guests" have arrived. I want to see who they are and how many I recognize. Then I'll move to the right and cover that side of the building. Tony, you and Joanna go around the back and get as close as you can that way."

Joanna's eyes blazed. "No, I'll go around to the left side of the building. That way we have three sides covered, and our chances of learning something improve by fifty percent."

Dantry was about to object when he saw by the steely look in her eyes that he'd be wasting his breath. "Okay, but we stay in touch. You'll have to go the long way around the back of the building. Too risky to cross the road, even though it would be more direct." He inhaled deeply, resigned to, but still not in favor of, Joanna going off on her own. "Every few minutes either make contact by walkie-talkie or visually. If you use the walkie-talkie, keep it to one or two words—and keep it low. They may be able to pick up our transmissions, and the longer they last, the more likely they'll be able to. Oh, when you see that their meeting is about to break up, get the hell out of there. Recede into the woods."

"Yes," put in Vyugin. "We'll meet at the agreed spot within 45 minutes of when we notice that the meeting is about to break up. If you get held up, or if you have to take a more circuitous route, use the walkie-talkie, and use the agreed code. We have no idea how long this meeting will be—though I doubt it will be less than an hour. They wouldn't come all the way out here for a short meeting. This could go on for several hours, so be prepared and be patient." He paused dramatically. "And be alert. Remember, no heroics. Good luck. Oh, don't forget these wire cutters. If you think you can get closer to the building, you can cut through the fence. Just leave them after you've used them. No point in carrying any more than you have to."

Dantry stared at him. "There are three pairs. Yet you just spoke of Joanna and me as if we'd be working as a unit. What—?"

Joanna grinned, "Why Vladimir, I underestimated your sensitivity."

"I've learned never to underestimate a woman."

As they spread out through the woods, trying not to step on dried twigs or anything that was likely to make unnecessary noise, the distance between the three of them grew larger.

Since Joanna had the farthest to go, she was in the lead. She'd sounded confident when she'd demanded that she cover a third side of the building, but as she got closer to the fence along the right side of the compound, she couldn't help but look back to see how close Dantry and Vyugin were. She could still see both of them, and took some comfort in that.

She was now within 25 feet of the chain-link fence. She would maintain that distance as she made her way around the perimeter of the fence, using the heavy underbrush as a buffer so that she wouldn't be seen from the building, should someone be looking. The distance between the building and the fence appeared to be about 150 feet. In building the compound they'd obviously felt the need to leave considerable space between the building and the fence so that anyone who was able to make it over or through the chain-link barrier would still be vulnerable before reaching the building. She reached the corner of the fence where the section on the right met the back section. So far, she hadn't seen a soul. So far, so good. She turned the corner and worked her way along the rear fence section and was now heading toward the left side. If she could just make it without being seen, she could then size up the situation and decide whether it was possible or not to cut through the fence and get close to the building. She knew it was physically possible. That wasn't the issue. What she didn't yet know was whether she could do it without being seen.

She was perspiring badly. She'd never figured on heat being a problem in Russia. At least not in this part of the huge country. She reached up to swat a bug that had landed on her neck. A mosquito. New York never looked so good. She was glad she wasn't saddled with the bulky parabolic microphone. The cigar-sized omni-directional mike Vyugin had given her should do fine, if she got the chance to use it.

Chapter 43

Vyugin was now within a hundred feet of the front entrance. He hung well back in the woods so he couldn't be seen from the front gate. There was a guard sitting just inside of the gate. It looked like the same one they'd seen yesterday. He seemed to be preoccupied with a book that he was reading. A man in a suit came out of the building now and yelled something at the guard. The man looked familiar to Vyugin, but he was partially hidden by trees and foliage, so it was hard to be certain. The guard dropped his book and jumped to his feet.

"Yessir," he blurted, the fear evident in his voice even from where Vyugin stood.

"You're supposed to be alert. Pay attention or you'll be back digging ditches in Moscow."

"With all due respect, sir. It's quiet. There's nothing around, but birds and squirrels."

The man in the suit shook his head in disgust. "You idiot. Do you think someone's going to announce themselves? Now pay attention. You can read when you're off duty." The man turned abruptly and walked back into the building.

Yes. It was Sorokin. And if Sorokin was here, Bulgakov would be here, too. Who else? That was the question Vyugin hoped to find an answer to before this day was over.

* * *

Dantry had reached the rear section of the fence. He'd watched Joanna as she'd rounded the far corner and made her way along the left or north side. She was out of sight now. He couldn't help but worry about her. It wasn't that, as a woman, he felt she wasn't up to the task. He'd seen how well she handled herself in her *tae kwan do* class. He remembered the one time he'd surprised her by picking her up there. She'd never wanted him to see her in class, and she'd been royally pissed when he'd shown up. Still, he'd seen how talented she was before she'd realized that he was there observing. The instructor had leaned over and whispered to him that she was his best student ever.

No, it wasn't that she couldn't take care of herself in a fair fight. But he knew from personal experience that cornered rats don't fight fair. Besides, he worried about her a lot. She'd become more to him than he'd realized before all this business had started. She'd become a part of him. He'd have to tell her that sometime.

He looked back. He didn't expect Vyugin to position himself along the south side of the fence until after the meeting attendees had arrived. He'd have to assume that an old hand like Vyugin would know what to do.

Dantry positioned himself about halfway down the length of the rear section of the fence. He found a spot that had enough branches in front of him to obscure him from all-but-the-most-careful scrutiny. He had to leave a few openings so that he could see the building.

* * *

Inside the low-slung building, in a small windowless room that reeked of tobacco smoke, a middle-aged man with a florid complexion passed a hand nervously over his clean-shaven head. The expression on his ruddy face turned serious as he took the half-smoked cigarette from his mouth and sat bolt upright, staring at the monitor in front of him. He slowly expelled a lungful of smoke. A few feet away, a younger man, whose hair was already going gray, looked up from his monitor and noticed the sudden change in his colleague.

"What is it, Boris?"

"There's something out there. Beyond the outer perimeter."

"Something?"

"Someone. He's in the woods on the north side of the entry road. He's watching the gate. Here, look."

The man with the graying hair got out of his chair and came over. He leaned over Boris' shoulder, peering at the screen. "I don't see anything."

"Right there." Boris pointed to a point several feet beyond the fence.   "See. There's someone there. Look, he moved."

"Yes!" exclaimed the other man. "Looks like he's alone."

"What the hell's he doing out there? Now he's squatting or sitting down. Are those binoculars?"

"Maybe. Whatever they are, he seems to be settling in. You think he's alone?"

"Makes you wonder, doesn't it? Could be a sniper. Let's take a closer look at the rear and the north and south sides of the fence. We've got to deal with this before they start arriving."

Chapter 44

Dantry heard a car in the distance. It was approaching fast. Then it slowed, and he heard it pull up in front of the building and come to a screeching stop. Tony hoped that Vyugin was on top of this, because he certainly couldn't get back to the front of the building in time to see what was going on. The sounds of car doors slamming, voices yelling. Something was going on.

Dantry was frustrated because nothing was happening where he was, and clearly something was going on near the front of the building. He'd been watching the only window on his side of the building since he'd gotten into position half an hour ago, and there'd been nothing to see. The window had been dark from the start and remained dark. Tony was beginning to wonder if he wouldn't be making better use of his time by joining Vyugin or Joanna. There was bound to be more action in the front of the building. Or there might be more to see from Joanna's vantage point. He shook his head at his impatience, and repositioned himself. Might as well give it a few more minutes. He shook his head and grimaced. Waiting had never been his strong point. Not a good quality in a spy. He smiled. At least he knew himself.

The light went on in the room. Dantry rummaged in his backpack and found what he was looking for—the high-powered monocular viewer he'd gotten from Vyugin. He trained it on the window. Someone was being pushed into the room. A man. Yes, he was definitely being pushed with his hands tied behind his back.

Now he was forced into a straight-backed wooden chair. There were two captors. Dantry didn't recognize either of them. Why would he? But he did recognize the captive. Son of a bitch! It was Lubov, the newspaper editor. The car he'd just heard pull up must have brought him and these other two characters directly from Moscow. Tony's mind was racing now. What the hell was going on here?

They were tying Lubov to the chair. Dantry put aside his monocular and picked up a small mono-directional microphone that was capable of magnifying sound up to 75 times if there was a clear line of sight to what you were trying to hear. But it was also capable of picking up the sound vibrations from window glass and converting them back to recognizable voice sound. This was a perfect time to put it to the test.

As he adjusted the controls on the mike, he was able to make out a voice. While Dantry's Russian was fairly good, he knew he'd gotten a bit rusty. And he knew he could sometimes have trouble with dialects, so he was hoping that he wouldn't miss too much of what was being said. There, it was fairly clear now. He frowned as he concentrated on the voice he was hearing.

"You people are crazy. You can't get away with this, you know." It was Lubov. There was fear in his voice.

"I'm afraid, Mr. Lubov, we can. I wouldn't waste my time worrying about us, if I were you. You're the one with the problem."

"What do you mean? What do you want from me anyway? What are you going to do with me?"

"Enough questions, Mr. Lubov. Besides, I'm surprised that you don't get the picture. You have become a thorn in our side. We are at a crucial point in our plans, and we cannot afford to have you or anyone else interfere with them."

"Listen, Mr. Sorokin, your scheme is madness. It's been tried many times before in Russia—"

"Yes, and it has succeeded on more than one occasion," leered Sorokin. "Remember 1917?"

Dantry bit his lower lip. *So that's Sorokin. Not at all like I pictured him. Other than being a bastard, that is.*

"I repeat," said Lubov, "what do you want from me?" Tony knew that what Lubov really wanted to know was *Are you going to kill me?* You don't ask that, though. Don't want to plant any ideas in their heads—as if it would make any difference.

"For the present, we shall keep you here as insurance in case Vyugin and his American friends decide to do something foolish. Don't feign ignorance, my friend. We know all about how you told them about this place and how you spread vicious rumors about myself and Mr. Bulgakov and others in the government."

"That fucking Antonin! I knew I couldn't trust him."

"Don't talk to me about trust. You have turned your back on some of Russia's great patriots. These are people who risk all for Mother Russia. We do not appreciate, nor will we tolerate, such traitorous behavior from you or from anyone else. You had better hope that Vyugin and his American meddlers mind their own business. We are too close now to achieving our objective to let you or anyone else get in our way."

"You say 'for the present.' What do you mean by that, and what do you intend to do after 'the present?'"

"The present," sneered Sorokin, "is what I say it is. Probably until this meeting is over. After that—"

"After that, what?"

"We shall see. I must go now. I have visitors to greet." Sorokin then chuckled, "I hope you are comfortable." He walked out of the room, turning the light out as he left.

Dantry put the microphone back in his pack and reflected on what he'd just witnessed. So that weasel Antonin was somehow in cahoots with these conspirators, and Lubov had been right about all of this. It was pretty clear now that this compound was the headquarters for some sort of cabal against the Kirov government. What still wasn't clear was who the main guy behind it all was, and whether these people were true ideologues or just power seekers. As far as Kirov and Russia were concerned, it mattered little. If they were successful, the result would be the same—a democratically elected government would be overthrown by a group of secret plotters, who wanted to impose their version of the right government on a people who would have no say in it.

He was concerned about Lubov now. Sorokin sounded like the kind of person who wouldn't hesitate to eliminate someone who got in the way. He'd as much as said that himself. Tony decided to risk a short message to Vyugin on the walkie-talkie. They needed to decide whether they wanted to try to get Lubov out or wait until Vyugin had seen all of the attendees for the meeting that was now less than 45 minutes away. Going in, with the odds so much against them, had not been in their plans. Still, Lubov had helped them and it looked like he now needed their help. Already, Dantry could hear other cars drive up to the front of the building, so some of the attendees were already in the building. He grabbed the transceiver and said in a low voice, "Lubov held captive in building. Sorokin knows he talked to us. Shall we go in now, or wait until the meeting assembles?" He clicked off and waited for a response.

Within seconds he heard Vyugin's voice. "I know. I saw him come in. Let's wait until they're all here. Then I'll join you and we can figure out what to do. Out." Made sense. They wouldn't do anything to Lubov now. He was still useful to them. Once the group of conspirators was assembled, they could decide what to do next. At least they'd have all the bad guys in one place, and they'd have the luxury—admittedly a small one—of being able to make the first move. Still, they were outnumbered badly, so they'd have to consider carefully any action they took. And he'd have to let Joanna know, too. Christ, he didn't want to leave her outside on her own, but bringing her inside was even riskier.

Since they'd landed at Sheremetyevo Airport, Dantry had repeatedly been haunted by thoughts about Joanna. Not the amorous thoughts that he'd enjoyed so many times since their relationship had begun, but thoughts about why he'd ever agreed to let Joanna come to Russia with him in the first place. He knew, of course, that she'd wanted to come with him, but the more he thought about the risks he was exposing her to, the more it bothered him. He knew all the intellectual reasons why he shouldn't feel guilty. For one thing, she went into it with her eyes open. For another, she was far better equipped than most women to take care of herself, And, finally, he believed she loved him and wanted to help him and share EVERYTHING with him. But it still wasn't her battle to fight. He sighed, realizing that it was too late now to do anything but lament, and if he spent too much time lamenting, they both could get killed. Right now he needed to pay attention. Their lives depended on it.

Lubov's capture had complicated things. If they went into the building in an attempt to free the newspaperman, the risk factor escalated tenfold. And Dantry saw no alternative. They had to try to save Lubov. There was no point in sending for help, either. Who'd believe that some of the most highly respected figures in Russia's government were holding a journalist captive and would very likely kill him? Besides, it was entirely possible that the local police were collaborating with the cabal.

Another half hour passed, during which time Dantry heard at least six more cars pull up to the front of the building. But he hadn't heard any in the last seven or eight minutes. Maybe they were finally all here. God, he hated not knowing what was going on. And it was driving him crazy that Joanna was out of sight— 180 degrees away on the other side of the compound. He comforted himself from the assumption that she was probably all right. If they'd captured her, they most likely would have brought her into that room with Lubov.....unless...., unless they had her but deliberately kept their two captives apart.

Dantry smacked his open palm against his forehead. Why would they have her? They obviously had no clue that he and Vyugin were out there. So why would they be aware of only the north side where Joanna was positioned? Hell, if they did know she was there, they would've checked the other sides of the compound and by now he'd have been aware that they were checking.

He heard a twig snap to his left. It was Vyugin heading through the underbrush in his direction. Their eyes met as they silently acknowledged each other. It was so hot now that Vyugin wiped the sweat from his brow as he joined Dantry.

"Looks like they're all here now. What do you think, Tony? Should we go in and fetch our journalist friend? I hate to ask this....I know you and Joanna didn't bargain for this."

Dantry forced a smile. "We have to, and you know it. Got a plan?"

Vyugin grinned back in that way that only men who have taken mortal risks can. "I suppose we should try to accomplish as much as we can while we're here, so I think we should see if we can eavesdrop on the meeting, before we attempt any rescue. Let's get as much intelligence as possible before we make our move. We probably won't get another chance. Do you agree?"

Dantry pushed his lower lip up over his upper lip and nodded. "Yeah. Let's give it a shot."

Chapter 45

From the front of the building, Joanna could hear cars pulling up and doors slamming. The meeting participants were arriving. On Joanna's side of the building there were two windows and a solid metal door. Both windows were dark. It seemed to her that, if she were going to learn anything from the meeting that was about to get underway, she'd have to get closer to the building. She grabbed the heavy duty wire cutters and proceeded to snip away at the chain link fence. It wasn't easy, as the gauge of the fencing was much heavier than most types of wire. Even so, within minutes she'd cut herself a rectangular opening about 20 inches wide and almost that high. She cautiously wriggled her way through, taking care not to let her clothing snag on the sharp ends of the wire she'd just cut. Once she was inside the fence, she reached back through for her backpack. She left the wire cutters behind. Shouldn't be needing them again.

Joanna scanned the area, making sure that no one was watching. All clear. She switched on the walkie-talkie and quickly, but quietly said, "going through fence and up to wall of building. Out." She grabbed the backpack, her Uzi and dashed across the open compound area toward the building. She reached the wall of the building and hugged it while she caught her breath and checked to make sure no that one had seen her. Her heart was pounding now. For one illogical moment, she feared that the conspirators inside the building might hear it. She knew that on the other side of the wall there were men who wouldn't hesitate to kill her if they knew she was out here. She took a long deep breath and slowly exhaled. Calm down. You're in control, she told herself. As long as you know where they are and they don't know that you're here, you have the upper hand. Why, then, didn't she feel more confident? God, if her heart would only calm down.

Okay, she told herself. You're a big girl. Time to worry about it later. Now get with it. She moved cautiously in the direction of the first window. Reaching it, she found that she wasn't tall enough to see in, so she looked around for something to stand on. About twenty feet away, she saw a stack of empty wooden crates. She scanned the area and made a quick dash over to the stack. They were heavier than they looked. She found one that was smaller than the rest and started to carry it back to the window.

As she placed the crate on the ground below the window something warm and damp clamped onto her face. It was a large hand and it covered her mouth so that she was unable to make a sound. It happened so suddenly, she felt her heart stop beating. When it resumed, she had trouble catching her breath since she couldn't get air through her mouth. At the same time, her Uzi was yanked off her shoulder. A harsh voice barked something in Russian. The words were spoken too fast for her to understand precisely what was said—especially since she rarely conversed in the language now and only used it in Russian history classes to illustrate points—but she got the gist of it and could tell that it wasn't a friendly welcome. In one continuous motion, she dropped the crate and landed an elbow in the midsection of her captor. She heard a grunt and whirled to see a stocky man who looked like an overage skinhead. His face was contorted with rage. Then she noticed that there was another, younger, man, too.

Seeing that his older comrade was not doing so well with a mere woman, the younger man moved in to help control this hellcat. Her peripheral vision caught his move, and she turned, whirling in one of her most effective martial arts moves, catching him on the chin with her booted foot. The impact sent him reeling into the side of the building. Recovering slowly, he pulled a gun from a hip holster and was about to fire when the first man grabbed his arm.

"Felix! No! We don't want our guests to know we have a problem here. No noise." Then he smiled wickedly at Joanna. "Not unless it's necessary. If this young lady continues to resist, we'll have no alternative."

From her expression he could tell that she didn't understand what he was saying. "So, you don't speak Russian. Let's try English. Do you speak English?"

She hesitated for a moment, wondering if pleading ignorance of English could work to her advantage and concluded that it wouldn't. But she wouldn't admit to knowing the little Russian that she did know. One never knew if that might come in handy.

"Yes."

"So you speak English. I wonder what a good-looking English-speaking woman is doing spying on us here in the wilds of Russia. Don't you wonder, Felix?"

Felix was still rubbing his bruised chin. He was torn between wanting to kill this foreign woman and controlling his raging hormones. The woman was magnificent, even in fatigues. He could imagine what she'd be like in bed.

"Felix?"

The younger man shook himself out of his lustful reverie. "Yes, Boris. You have to wonder, don't you?"

"Let's get her inside and find out," said Boris. "You can walk, young lady, or we can drag you. Your choice." Joanna's eyes bore in on him like daggers.

"I'll walk. You can't get away with this, you know."

"Where did you hear that line?" asked Boris, feeling full of himself for landing his fine catch. "In the cinema?"

Boris pulled a ring of keys from his pocket and unlocked the side door. He pushed her in ahead of him. Felix followed close behind, not wanting to let this nubile number out of his sight. He was hoping that Boris would leave him alone with her for awhile so that he might personally 'interrogate' her. They moved quickly down a hall until they came to a darkened room. Boris opened the door and gave Joanna a nudge into the room as he flipped on the light switch. "Close the door, Felix, and lock it."

"We should tell Sorokin."

"In due course. First let's see what and who we're dealing with." Then, addressing Joanna, he said, "Please sit down my dear." He pulled up a chair in front of her and sat down facing her. "Felix, please pull up a chair and join us." He held up a hand and added, "First, why don't you bring us some tea. Our guest here looks thirsty. On second thought, since you're obviously not Russian, perhaps you'd prefer coffee?"

"I'd prefer to leave and get my own beverages."

"A feisty one, isn't she, Felix?"

"Yes, why don't you leave her with me for awhile." He leaned in front of her face and leered. "I'll take the insolence out of her."

"I'm afraid there's no time for your approach, now, Felix. We need information. Perhaps you can spend some time with her later, after we know who we're dealing with." The puerile Felix frowned, but said nothing. Joanna's expression gave away nothing. She tried to ignore him rather than give him the satisfaction of knowing he'd gotten to her. Boris continued: "Now then, Miss, why don't you tell us who you are and why you were outside our building spying on us."

"I wasn't spying. I was curious and interested in what was going on in here."

"Come now, this is no time to split hairs. Please don't try my patience. I'm sure you know that there are ways to persuade you to talk. It would be nicer for all of us, though, if you were candid without our needing to resort to such extreme methods. Let's avoid all that unpleasantness. Now once again, who are you?"

"You're right, I'm not a Russian. I'm an American. I'm working with the U.N. and Interpol on special assignment in cooperation with the Russian government. That's all I can tell you."

"Perhaps you could tell us your name and who in the Russian government you're working for?"

"I'm sorry. I can't tell you anything else, other than that you could be in a lot of trouble for abducting me like this. Now release me this instant."

"I'm afraid I can't do that."

"Release me, and I'll consider it nothing more than a misunderstanding. If you don't—"

He smiled disdainfully, "If I don't, what will you do, Miss?"

"My colleagues will find me and report you to the proper authorities in the government."

"I'm afraid you'll have to do better than that. I don't believe you're working with the government. I think you're freelance. What do you think about that?"

"I think you're making a grave miscalculation." She hoped she sounded more confident than she felt.

Boris scratched his chin as he considered the situation. Then his expression changed, as if something had struck him. "Felix, I think our lady guest here should meet our other guest. What do you think?"

Clearly Felix hadn't a clue as to why, but he tended to defer, albeit reluctantly, to his senior colleague, and gave a grudging, "Yes, why not."

Boris led the way down the hall and around the bend to the other room. "Open it," he order Felix. Boris gave Joanna a nudge and she tentatively entered the room, wondering who she was about to meet. Then she saw someone across the room. He was tied to a chair with his head slumped forward. Was he dead, or just asleep? His back was to her and she hesitated, not wanting to go forward. Boris nudged her ahead. "Go, I want the two of you to see each other."

So he was alive. Who could it be? Oh, dear God, don't let it be Tony. "Why do you want us to meet?"

"Just go over there where he can see you, and you can see him. Felix, come here." He whispered something into the younger man's ear and then returned his attention to Joanna and the chair-bound Lubov. Felix dashed from the room.

Joanna approached tentatively, not sure what to expect. Lubov turned his head and recognized her instantly. Boris caught this and said to Joanna, "You know each other, don't you?"

"I—"

"Don't pretend otherwise. Mr. Lubov knows you, don't you, sir?"

"No."

"You do, sir. I saw the light of recognition in your eyes when she came into the room." Lubov, clearly exhausted and almost beyond the limits of what he could endure, dropped his head in submission. "You see, Miss, you might as well admit it. You know each other. Perhaps you are collaborators, eh?" As he said this, Felix came running into the room, carrying something in a canvas bag.

"Got it."

"Excellent. I think this might be a good time for a little demonstration of just how serious we are. Why don't you show us what you have there, Felix."

Felix reached into the bag and pulled out the wire cutters Joanna had used to cut through the chain link fence. Joanna's already racing pulse accelerated.

"They should be perfect for the job. Before we proceed, check to be sure the door is closed. I don't want to disturb others in the building. Then, tie this young lady up and be sure that she faces Mr. Lubov." Felix quickly checked the door, tied Joanna to a chair, and returned to await his instructions. Boris proceeded, a gleam in his eyes that seemed to come from somewhere dark and malevolent. "Now here's what I want you to do, Felix. You should enjoy this. I want you to remove the pinky from Mr. Lubov's left hand." Joanna gasped.

"Noooo!," roared Lubov, filling the room with an ear-piercing scream—audible testimony to the palpable evil in the grim chamber.

"You can't do this," screamed Joanna. "It's inhuman. What kind of monsters are you?"

"Do it quickly, Felix. I'll hold his arm." He grasped the left arm of the weakened Lubov and held it steady with a vise-like grip. Enjoying his task, Felix grinned as he fumbled, trying awkwardly to place the ill-fated finger between the blades of the powerful wire cutters. Though Lubov was weak from sleep deprivation and lack of food, he wasn't about to succumb without a struggle. He thrashed about, screaming in an other-worldly voice. He formed a fist so as to make it difficult for Felix to get the finger between the jaws of the cutters. Realizing that this wasn't going to work, Boris took his gun and hit Lubov over the head with the butt, knocking him unconscious. "Now, Felix. Get it over with."

The crunching sound as Felix applied pressure to the cutters was sickening. Blood spurted onto Lubov, Felix, and the floor as if someone had punctured a balloon filled with ketchup. Joanna felt nausea grip her, and was unable to hold her meal down. Boris looked at her with disgust. Felix slapped Lubov's face. The editor remained unconscious.

"We need him awake," said Boris, as he grabbed a paper cup from a nearby bench. It contained the dregs of an insipid lemon-based Russian beverage he'd been drinking not long before. With a flick of the wrist, he dashed the sticky liquid onto the face of his insentient victim. Lubov's head jerked in reaction. He moaned as he slowly regained consciousness.

Felix, clearly enjoying this, stooped down and picked the bloody finger from the floor. He held it in front of Lubov's still blinking eyes.

"Here's your finger, you bastard," said the grinning sadist. "Say goodbye to it." With that, he flicked it away as if it were a spent cigarette. The finger landed in a dusty part of the floor, skidding to a stop on the concrete floor twenty feet from its former owner. "If this were a hospital," said Felix, "a good surgeon might be able to reattach it. Oh well, guess you're out of luck," he added gleefully.

Smiling approvingly at his colleague's naughtiness, Boris took charge.

"Now, Miss…."

"You monsters! You evil monsters."

"Yes, well there's no time for that. The point I was about to make is that I think you can see that we mean business. I know that you are not alone. I am going to give you a chance to address your accomplices and tell them to give themselves up. Otherwise, we shall not hesitate to remove other fingers from this miserable traitor." He turned to Felix and barked a quick, staccato order. "Find a handkerchief or towel for this man's finger and then help me take our guest here to our surveillance room. She's going to make a statement over the loudspeaker system."

"You sure you shouldn't tell Sorokin about this?"

"Yes, I'll speak to him in a minute. First get something to help Lubov stop his bleeding. He's making a mess on the floor. I'll wait until you come back. Now go." Felix dashed from the room. He was back in less than a minute with what appeared to be a dirty rag. He tossed it on Lubov's lap and awaited the next instructions from Boris. Lubov was awake now and moaning. The moaning was intermittently interrupted by eerie wailing that gave Joanna the shivers. She was sickened as she realized that the man, whose arms were tied, couldn't even stanch the flow of blood because he couldn't grasp the rag to cover the bloody stump where his finger had been minutes before. Boris and Felix seemed unconcerned.

"Good," said Boris. "Now take our lady friend here to the surveillance room, and watch her. I'll be with you in a minute."

Sorokin was not in his office, and Boris realized that he must be with the others in the meeting room. The meeting had probably already gotten underway. Boris didn't relish getting the surly Sorokin out of the meeting, but he had no choice. Minutes later, Sorokin was standing impatiently in the hall with Boris, who no longer had the composure he'd manifested in his role of bully and torturer.

"So what is so important that you must interrupt the meeting to get my attention?" asked Sorokin, not hiding his annoyance.

"We've captured someone spying outside the building."

"What'd you do with him?"

"Her. It's a woman."

"A woman? I—"

"She says she's on assignment for Interpol and the government. I don't believe her, but frankly I don't know what to make of it."

"Well, find out, and get me again when you know something. Is she alone?"

"No, she claims to be working with some Russians. Wouldn't give any names."

"Working with Russians. Then she's not Russian?"

"American."

"Hmmm. Interesting. I have a feeling I know who one of the Russians is. Just a feeling, but...."

More of a technician who took pride in his work, Boris wasn't curious about who might be out there. Whoever it was, he was a threat and needed to be reeled in. "I brought her in to meet Lubov."

"And?"

"There was a glimmer of recognition on his face. She wasn't so obvious."

"Could you tell if she knew him?"

"As I said, he gave himself away. But you couldn't tell from her. She's pretty cool, and she knows how to take care of herself." Boris hesitated, trying to decide how much to tell Sorokin. "I did something that should bring her collaborators out of the woods, if they're out there. It should work."

Sorokin's eyebrows went up a quarter of an inch. "Yes, go on."

"I....uh. I cut off one of his fingers. Or rather Felix did—as a demonstration of our seriousness." Sorokin nodded his approval.

"That should do it. If they're out there, that should bring them in."

"The only thing is, she's going to have to get on the PA and call them in. It could disturb the meeting?"

"I see your point. If they thought that someone was spying on us, they might get nervous and panic. We can't afford that now —especially at this most critical time. We don't want weakening of commitment now." He put his hand to his chin and reflected a moment. "All right, I have it. Tell me when she's going to make the announcement, and I'll close all doors and run our little a/v presentation in the meeting room while she's on the PA. Keep it short, though. I can't control these people very long. When you know something more, come get me." He walked away.

Chapter 46

Dantry was worried about how Joanna was doing. It was hell, her being on the other side of the building, completely out of sight. He had no idea if she was quietly observing something going on in the building, steadily gathering data or what? He kept his voice low as he spoke to Vyugin.

"I'm going to check on Joanna. I won't risk using the radio again. I'll stick to the woods—going deep enough so as not to attract attention. I'll tell her about Lubov and that, later, we're going to have to go in, that we'll meet at the rear side of the fence in half an hour. In the meantime, she should get as much info as she can." Vyugin nodded, then thought of something.

"Make it 45 minutes. I think the meeting will go on for some time. Let's get as much recorded as we can before we make our move."

"Okay. Be back in five minutes." He moved away. For some reason, he felt the heat more than he'd thought he would. Maybe it really was hotter than he could recall it ever being in Russia, or maybe it was because he was so concerned about Joanna that, right now, everything bothered him. He wiped sweat out of his eyes and pressed on through the brush. A branch caught him on the side of the face, and he swore under his breath. He couldn't wait to get Joanna, Vyugin, and Lubov, and get the hell away from this place. Then he heard a crackling sound coming from the building. It was the kind of sound associated with old-fashioned PA system—the sound you hear just before someone speaks.

"This is Joanna Barbeau. I'm being held captive inside the building. They want my colleagues to come and join me. Believe me, I didn't want to do this, but they're holding Alexei Lubov in here with me." There was a pause, followed by a catch in her breath. "They've cut off one of his fingers to show that they're serious."

Then a male voice came on. "We will give you two minutes to comply, or we will remove one of Miss Barbeau's fingers. Your two minutes begin NOW. Enter on the north side of the building. Repeat, the north side. That is all."

Vyugin spoke into his walkie-talkie: "Tony, in about a minute-and-a-half, you go in. Tell them I'm farther away, but you're sure I'll come in. Between you and me, I need to do something first; then I'll join you. When we're inside, follow my lead. Now you'd better go." For just a moment, Dantry hesitated. After all, this man had been his enemy not many years ago. Was he pulling a fast one now? But there wasn't time to deliberate, and he had to trust to the instincts that had brought him this far. He nodded his agreement and moved toward the north side of the fence.   Would he and Joanna ever see Long Island Sound again?

Chapter 47

Boris was relieved when he saw the man squirm through the hole in the fence and make his way toward the building. While Boris was reasonably certain that the American woman's associates would come in after hearing her appeal over the public address system, he wasn't a hundred percent sure. Professional agents did not always allow sentiment or the plight of others to interfere with their plans. Certainly Russian agents didn't. That she was a woman —an American woman at that—inclined him to think that whomever he was dealing with, would be inclined to give in to Western sentimentality and respond to her appeal. He'd been right. He moved away from the window and walked to the door. He wanted to personally welcome his new visitor.

"*Strasvweetya, tovarishch*," said Boris as he trained his automatic handgun on Tony.

"Hello, yourself. And I'm not a comrade. Where's the lady?"

"Ah, so you're not Russian, but you understand it. English maybe? No, from the accent, I'd say American."

"Where the hell is the woman?"

"I'll ask the questions, Mr.—"

"Dantry. What've you done with her?"

"Come, you shall see for yourself."

Boris brought Dantry into the room in which Lubov was being held. The editor appeared to have passed out. Or was he just asleep? Hell, if they cut off his finger, he could have passed out from lack of blood. Then he saw Joanna, herself bound to a chair not ten feet from the Lubov.

"Joanna, are you all right?"

"I'm fine. But Lubov's not. I think he's lost too much blood. These bastards—" She left the rest unsaid. "How about you, Tony? Did they do anything to you?"

"I'm okay. What the hell's going on here?"

"I'm afraid you're going to have to sit down….er, Tony, is it? Is that Anthony Dantry?"

Dantry glowered at him.

"Never mind. Felix, tie him up in that chair. Now, while my associate is making sure that you are immobilized, I'll explain what's going to happen. When the third member of your little party joins us, you're all going to tell us what you've been doing here. We don't appreciate being spied upon."

"Are you so ashamed of what you're doing that you don't want the rest of the world to know about it? Is that it?"

"This is a private organization. We are entitled to our privacy." Boris sneered. "But why am I bothering to explain this to you? You won't be around much longer anyway."

"Fine, then we'll be leaving," said Dantry. "Just get these ropes off us, and we'll see ourselves out."

"American humor, yes? Well, we shall see who's laughing in a little while. By the way, where is your friend? If he's not here in a minute, we shall remove another finger. Perhaps one from Miss Barbeau's lovely hand." He smiled wickedly at the horror he'd planted in their minds, and, too, at the real possibility that he might actually carry out the amputation. Why should Felix have all the fun? But first things first.

"Felix, get on the PA and give our man thirty seconds to get in here."

"Never mind," said Felix, who was peering out the window. "I see him now. He's coming."

during commie days
there were prominent women in
all places

Chapter 48

As the group assembled around the big conference table, the buzz
of muted conversation in the room was electric. In keeping with
Russian tradition, all of the people in attendance were men. Few
women had yet broken through Russia's glass ceiling—and
certainly not in extra-legal groups such as this one. Many of the
men seated around the table were military or former military. Most
notable was the former chief of the Soviet Army, Marshall
Suchinov. Seated next to him was ex-commissar Zlotov, chief of
military affairs during the last days of the Soviet Union. Also
present were several high-ranking current members of the Russian
military and of the national intelligence service, the FSB.

The conversation was cautiously guarded. Friends and
acquaintances exchanged brief, superficial greetings and
occasional banalities, but no one touched on the subject of the
meeting itself—though that was clearly uppermost in their
collective minds. They had come, in some cases, considerable
distances to get here. They could be patient a few more minutes.
Once the meeting began they'd find out just how well their
audacious plan was progressing. They'd been waiting over three
months for this briefing. It was the most important of all the
meetings, so they were hoping the news would be as good as it had
been during the two-and-a-half years they'd been planning their
bold strategy.

The door opened and Yuri Bulgakov entered the room. He strode briskly to his place at the head of the long table. As he sat, he indicated with his hands that the others should follow suit. When they were all seated and the last chair had shifted noisily into its position, an expectant hush came over the sterile, windowless room. Bulgakov cleared his throat and got right to the point.

"Our plan is moving ahead on schedule. Our goal is to replace Kirov with Mr. Malenkov within the next two-to-three months. I expect that the I.M.F. is going to turn down Kirov's request for the loan. We have taken steps to insure that will happen. When the loan fails to come through, our cadres of activists will go into action. First, there will be protests in Moscow, St. Petersburg, and Novosibirsk. These will escalate within days to riots. Cars overturned, shop windows broken, work stoppages in the Metros and other public transportation." Bulgakov paused to take a sip of water. He wiped his lips and surveyed his audience. They were following his every move. He looked down at his notes and continued.

"Key newspapers and TV stations under our control will call for a government that can bring back the glory and respect that prevailed during the Soviet era. They will couch it carefully so as to imply that it would not be a replica of the Soviet Union with its flaws, but a new Russia—one with the power of that bygone Soviet era, but not the repression. Our media will be sure to suggest that the new Russia would empower the people as well as the nation. This will be necessary to gain popular support, but we all know what kind of Russia that would be." Nervous laughter. "All of us here understand how important it is that we create a Russia that the world does not look down upon. Better to be feared than ridiculed. Better to be a superpower and rattle a few swords than to be a third-rate nation at the teat of Western philanthropical largesse. Cooperate with the West and the West will pull the strings. That is not for us." Applause burst from the assembled delegates. He waited for the room to quiet down before he continued.

"The papers we control will write about how once again Russia must control the inferior ethnic minorities of Central Asia and the Balkans. Just since 1991 it's become clear that, if you leave these tribes to their own devices, they create all kinds of social and political mischief. It is better that we control them and use their labor to further the ends of a new Russia." A fresh burst of applause, interspersed with *bravos!* and *das*! Bulgakov allowed this to go on for almost a full minute before resuming. He had no desire to squelch their enthusiasm. Their reaction thus far had exceeded even his own optimistic expectations, so he decided to hit them with one of the long-range goals he'd planned on revealing after he was finally in power. But he was already heady with power, and couldn't contain himself any longer.

"Once we have rebuilt our new Sov— er our new Union of Mother Russia, the Central Asian Countries, and several Balkan states, there is no reason why we should not build on that. This cannot be done overnight, but it need not take long. Within a few years we should be able to incorporate additional countries from Southeast Asia and even begin to move into Europe." A low rumble ran through the room as delegates exchanged startled expressions of surprise at this amazingly ambitious plan. Suddenly the room exploded in a roar of approval. The applause went on for several minutes. Bulgakov beamed with pride. His confidence rose to new heights. They were with him. They shared his vision of a Russian-dominated world. At that very moment, he realized that he could do anything. He looked expansively over his supporters. Finally, with both hands extended outward, palms down, he urged them to let him continue. When he could again be heard, he went on.

"A great nation cannot stand still. With your help, we will build a new, even greater Russia." Several in the audience noted that Bulgakov was no longer mentioning Malenkov, but they really didn't care. If this was the man to lead them to glory and power, so be it.

"And at just the right moment," continued Bulgakov, "the media under our control will call for Kirov and his miserably ineffective government to hold elections immediately, or, better yet, to simply step down. The papers and television will praise Mr. Malenkov as the only one who can bring stability and order to Russia. Within forty-five days, Malenkov will be president, and I will be prime minister. If Malenkov proves to be as sympathetic to our plan for Russia as we hope he will be, we shall all be able to build a Russia that the world will once again respect and fear." He paused for dramatic effect. "Or perhaps I should say fear and respect."

A voice boomed from halfway down the left side of the table. It was Marshall Suchinov. "And if Malenkov fails to be sympathetic to our views?"

"Then I shall wrest the presidency from him. With your help, of course." Suchinov and most of the others silently nodded their approval. One way or the other, the world would once again fear the Russian bear.

Bulgakov cleared his throat and waited until he had their attention again. "There is one small problem, however."

Suchinov's brow knitted as he considered what Bulgakov had just said. If Bulgakov was the leader of their ambitious scheme, Suchinov was generally acknowledged to be the one other person in the group that the others looked to for guidance. He was a revered figure, and his word carried more weight than most. He listened carefully now for Bulgakov's next words.

"We have learned that an editor at the *The Moscow Times* has been encouraging certain parties unfriendly to our cause. I don't mean just editorially in the paper, but by providing information directly to these people. The editor's name is Lubov, and he somehow became aware of our retreat here in the country. He apparently passed along his suspicions to a former KGB operative who—don't ask me why—is trying to undermine our efforts."

At the other end of the table, a small man, yet one with a commanding presence, volunteered, "Lubov fancies himself some sort of campaigner for Western-style democracy. He's always been a pain."

"I agree," said commissar Zlotov. "I hope we're going to deal with him. He cannot be allowed to continue."

"We've already taken action," smiled Bulgakov with satisfaction. "He's in our hands as we speak—here, in this building." Muted applause at this.

"Good," said the man at the opposite end of the table. "Let's learn what we can from him and then dispose of him."

"That's the intention," said Bulgakov smugly. Then, less arrogantly, "There is one more thing."

All eyes focused on the Bulgakov, who again cleared his throat before proceeding. "Sorokin's people have just brought in a woman who was seen spying on us outside the building."

"Have you interrogated her?" asked a raspy voice from the right side of the table.

"Not yet. She is apparently not working alone. We think there are at least two others—"

"What!" bellowed Suchinov. "You seem to be losing control. Do you realize what it could mean if these others get away?" The room erupted as the members of the cabal realized with alarm what exposure could mean to them. Just then, there was a knock on the door and Boris peered in, looking for Sorokin. When he made eye contact, Sorokin nodded, rose, and quickly made his way to the door. He listened for a moment to what Boris had to say and then leaned over and said something in Bulgakov's ear. Bulgakov smiled and pounded the table with his huge fist, startling the other conspirators. They began to settle down, but a low murmur continued. Bulgakov brought his fist down again, this time harder than the first.

"Enough! The situation is under control. We have just captured a second interloper, and expect to have a third shortly."

"Who is the second spy?" demanded Suchinov.

"A man. Apparently, he, too, is an American. That's all we know at present. I'm sure that Sorokin's men will know everything soon."

"Are they connected with this Lubov?" asked someone at the far end of the table. "Or with this former KGB person?"

"I told you, we don't know yet. We have just now brought these people in. Believe me, with the combined skills and years of experience under Sorokin's command—not to mention my own experience—we'll have our answers. And soon."

Sorokin rose. "I think my talents are needed elsewhere gentlemen. If you'll excuse me."

Chapter 49

When Boris reentered the room where Joanna, Tony, and Lubov were being held, he went over to where Felix was peering out the window.

Felix smiled. This was almost too easy.

"Looks like there's a third one coming in." He pointed to Vyugin, who was slowly heading toward the building.

"Can these people be this sentimental over the fate of one of their own, Felix? Two men come in because we threaten to hurt one of their colleagues. Still, they are American, and they're hard to understand. Whatever, we have two of them, and it looks as if we'll have another. I think I'll go and personally welcome this gentleman. Keep an eye on our guests."

Boris opened the door to the outside just as Vyugin reached the building. "And you are an American, too, I presume?"

"Russky. *Kak pozheevayetya*? How goes it?"

"*Khorasho, spaseba*. Fine, thank you." Boris tried hard not to laugh. It was truly a topsy-turvy world. He'd assumed the first two prisoners were Russian, and they'd turned out to be American. It was not illogical to assume that the next one to surrender would also be American, but that had turned out to be an incorrect assumption. Ah, well, all the more interesting. It wouldn't be long before he had all the answers he needed.

"Come, my Russian friend, and join the others." Boris trained his gun on Vyugin and nudged him forward. On entering the room where the other prisoners were held, Vyugin showed no emotion. Lubov, Tony, and Joanna revealed nothing, either. Vyugin was curious to see what his captors had in mind and how much they would reveal.

"Where's Sorokin?"

Boris smiled. What harm in telling him. None of these people were going to leave the building alive anyway. "He'll be here later. He's in a meeting. You know each other?"

"We've met."

"Well, you shall meet again, but later. The meeting will go all day. After that, I am sure you will meet. So, you must be the former KGB agent. I'm curious as to why you'd want to undermine our efforts, since one would think that our interests would be quite similar."

"You make quite a lot of assumptions. What makes you think that I want to undermine your operations?"

"Why else would you be spying on us?"

"Perhaps we're just curious."

"Then come to the front door and satisfy your curiosity."

"Your guards with the Kalishnikovs don't seem too welcoming."

Boris smiled again, this time more malevolently. "Ah, well, one can't be too careful these days. You never know who might drop in." He drew himself up and pointed to Tony and Joanna. "I assume you'd like to be with your friends here. I'm afraid they're tied up right now." He chuckled, as much for his own benefit as for Vyugin's.

"Get Sorokin. I want to see him."

"I'll give the orders around here. But don't worry, Sorokin will join us in a few hours. I'm sure he'll be delighted that you're here. In the meantime, I shall leave you. I'll be back later."

The time passed slowly, each of the prisoners exchanging words intended to show their optimism that all would end well. They all knew that there was no guarantee of this, however. They had no way of telling the time except from looking out the window, where the bright sunny day had now faded to a late afternoon grayish pink. Soon, the sun would drop past the horizon, and the only light would be the artificial light of the two bare bulbs hanging from the ceiling above.

The door to the room opened with a metallic bang, and Boris entered, followed by Felix.

"Felix," said Boris, "why don't you go tell Sorokin that an old acquaintance of his is here waiting for him. I can't wait to see how delighted he'll be to see that his friend is here."

When Sorokin entered the room he quickly surveyed the situation. When his eyes fell upon Vyugin, who was now securely tied to a chair, he beamed. "I had a feeling it was you, Vyugin." He lowered his head. "I must say, I'm disappointed."

"Not as disappointed as I am in you and your boss."

"That's a good one. You, a traitor, disappointed in us."

"I am not the one plotting against my own government."

"Vyugin, shame on you. You have lived longer than I. Surely you know that overthrowing unwanted governments is a time-honored tradition in Russia."

"When the unwanted governments are tyrannical. You cannot say that about the Kirov government."

"It is worse than tyrannical. It is weak and inefficient. Which would you rather have, Vyugin, a government that gets things done and commands respect, or one that is democratic and a laughingstock?"

"These are not the only choices. But it is interesting that you would choose totalitarianism over democracy. Clearly you and Bulgakov remain inflexibly Communistic."

"Your opinion of my political philosophy is of little consequence to me, Vyugin. I never liked you, and I suspect you felt the same way about me. Why should I value your opinion?"

"I wouldn't expect a Neanderthal to understand modern thinking. It is comforting, though, to know that my original opinion of you was right."

With a self-satisfied smirk, Sorokin ignored the taunts and proceeded with business. "The question before us is what shall we do with you and your friends? You know we can't let you leave here alive. I suppose the most I can offer you is a trade for a merciful demise if you provide us with the information we're looking for. Otherwise, I'll let Boris and his oversexed assistant have his way with this young lady. When he's finished, I'm sure he'll enjoy coming up with creative ways to dispatch the four of you."

"Anatoly, let's not talk about dispatching people just yet." The door had opened and Bulgakov had entered without the others noticing.

"Ah, who have we here? No, it can't be," declared Bulgakov, feigning shock. "Vladimir, is it you? It is. You don't know how much I've waited for this opportunity. My shoulder still throbs. And I suppose I don't need to tell you how embarrassing it was for me to see a doctor after you shot me. I couldn't go to one of the doctors that serve the ministry. Too many questions, and the answers would have led to things I didn't want generally known. No, I had to go to some hack and threaten him to keep his mouth shut. So you see, Vladimir, you not only wounded my shoulder, you wounded my pride, too. Not to mention the inconvenience."

"I'm beginning to think my mistake was in only wounding you," said Vyugin. "If I had any doubt at all about you before, you've succeeded in totally erasing it. You're easily as ruthless and cold-blooded as people say you are. Now, your thugs have taken us prisoner. They've brutally dismembered Lubov over there—and enjoyed doing it. What kind of a man are you, Yuri, to endorse this kind of thing? I knew you were a hard-liner, but this."

"I'm a patriot. I thought you were, too. What happened to you?"

"You know damned well what happened. I came to my senses. Unfortunately, not before some innocent people had to die."

"Vladimir." He pronounced the name with the emphasis on the *dim*. "I did not lie to you. You knew what the mission was from the start. You knew that some Americans would have to die so that Russia could rid itself of that pathetic excuse for a president, Kirov. It was unfortunate, but the necessary casualties of war."

"The last I heard, we were not at war with the United States."

"Such a naïve statement from a man of your experience. What do you call this invasion of McDonald's and Hiltons, if it is not economic war?"

"I'd call it an infusion of economic vigor. We need more such help from the West. Oh, you can argue the merits of a given fast-food restaurant. Some have questionable culinary merit, but you can't argue the business lessons we can learn from people who've done a lot better job than we have."

"So that's it, is it? You've fallen for the dazzle of Western capitalism."

"I've come to appreciate parts of Western culture, yes. Not all of it, certainly, but some of it. But that's not really why I pulled out of the mission, Yuri. The reason for that has more to do with you, than with McDonald's and Pepsi Cola."

"Really?"

"Yes, really. I had my first doubts when I learned that you had lied to me about Mark Dantry. He wasn't going to vote against the I.M.F. loan, and you knew that. You deliberately misled me. Then, I began to think for myself about what kind of government Malenkov would bring us as opposed to the one we have now under Kirov. I know Kirov is far from perfect, but at least he's going in the right direction. And I believe he's a decent man. Then I look at Malenkov. He'd take us back to the days of Khrushchev." He frowned and added, "And if you had your way, I believe it would be back to the days of Stalin."

"I'm not sure we need to do as much housecleaning as Comrade Stalin did, but I do believe in sweeping dead wood away with a big broom."

"By dead wood I assume you mean anyone who disagrees with you."

"That's the general idea. I can see that you've become enamored of democracy. You know, Vladimir, democracy is an extremely inefficient form of government. You waste a lot of time listening to the views of people with silly sentimental ideas. Admittedly, my way can be a bit unpleasant initially, but once you have things straightened out, your government runs far more efficiently."

"You like that word, don't you?"

"Efficiency? Yes. When you're in power, it's a much-appreciated virtue. When you're out of power, struggling to get in, democracy sounds a lot better, and can actually be useful."

"I always sensed this about you, Yuri, but now you've confirmed it. Your religion is power, and you worship the icon of efficiency, or is it pragmatism? You must have a very dim view of your fellow human being."

"The dimmest. I have seen very little to persuade me otherwise. But enough of this. It's been interesting hearing of your conversion to democracy, but we have more important things to attend to here. And despite your treachery, our plans will not be deterred. We're sending another pair of agents to eliminate this Chandler fellow. I'm sure you knew that we wouldn't let your interference discourage us. They should arrive in Washington today and be ready to take care of business within the next day or two. So you see, your betrayal has only been a minor inconvenience." He beamed with satisfaction as he said this.

"You bastard."

"I suppose you had to get that out of your system. It's a pity, really. You're a talented operative. You could have been a useful member of the team. But you've made your choice, and there's no turning back. I rather liked you, Vladimir. Just goes to show that even I can be a bad judge of character on occasion. Ah, so be it." He winced and glanced at his shoulder. "And since you shot me in the shoulder you can't blame me if I consider myself the victim; not you.

"Now then, I need some information from you and your friends. I'm sure Anatoly has already explained to you your options. Not very good ones, I'm afraid." A smug expression came over him. He drew in a deep breath and expelled it slowly before continuing. "Anyway, I need to know why you and these two Americans have been spying on us. Now don't waste my time denying this, because you know that we caught you, if you'll excuse the expression, red-handed." He smirked.

Joanna, who'd been trying to follow the dialogue between Sorokin, Bulgakov and Vyugin in Russian, yelled, "I already told them that we're on special Interpol assignment in cooperation with the Russian government. That's all they know."

"That's all they need to know," chimed in Vyugin.

"A fairly inept try at deception, if you don't mind my saying so," said Bulgakov. "I doubt very much that you are working for this government or any other. Now what the hell were you doing here? Boris, here, has already demonstrated that we are not in the mood for playing games."

"Screw you," yelled Tony, instantly regretting the taunting remark because it was more than likely that these bastards would take it as a challenge and demonstrate their resolution by torturing one of his colleagues.

"Ah, the brave American speaks up. We shall see how brave he is when we cut off one of his lovely associate's fingers." He turned to Boris, who'd been hanging back in deference to his superiors. "Perhaps you should remove one of this young lady's digits. I'll leave it to you which one."

A smile came over Boris' face at the prospect of doing something he was quite good at and rather enjoyed. "Felix, the wire cutters, please."

Vyugin bit his lip.

Tony's heart sank. He looked at Joanna, and he saw the fear in her eyes, though she voiced nothing. Somebody had to do something. But what?

"Let me see, which one shall it be?" said Boris, making the most of his opportunity. He enjoyed seeing other people suffer. Indulging this pleasure was done with a clear conscience because he was one of those sociopathic types who had no conscience. He'd first realized how much he enjoyed the suffering of others when he was a child. He loved to cut the wings off butterflies. He'd soon graduated to trapping small animals and torturing them. Cats were a personal favorite. He got double the pleasure from torturing cats because he first got to see the animal suffer and later to see the owners suffer when they discovered what had happened to their pet.

Boris was zeroing in on Joanna's right hand. "Ah. The index finger is a good choice. Yes, this finger has to go." He reached for the wire cutters. He was playing this to the hilt. So far, Joanna had not flinched, and Tony knew she was fighting the internal struggle of her life. Would her emotions win out, or would her steel will rule? He knew she didn't want to reveal weakness to the sick bastard with the wire cutters. He'd only prolong her agony. Tony didn't know how she did it. He doubted if he had the mind control to remain stoic in the face of such evil.

The color had drained from her face now. Boris called Felix over.

"Hold her while I perform the amputation. Or would you prefer....No, I think I'll do the surgery. You just keep her from moving." Felix looked disappointed, but said nothing. He grasped Joanna's arms and pinned them to the wooden arms of the chair. Boris smiled at his assistant and opened the wire cutters in preparation to cut.

Then the lights went out, throwing the room into darkness. Boris looked up with a startled expression, though it was too dark for anyone to tell. Bulgakov took charge. His voice boomed from across the room.

"Leave that for the moment, Boris......until we figure out what's happened here."

In the darkness, Vyugin craned his head down and with his teeth withdrew a narrow, four-inch razor-sharp blade that he'd secreted in the collar of his shirt. It was a blade of his own design. The tang or haft of the blade had been formed to conform to his molars so as to provide a firm grip. This allowed him to bend down close to his right arm and cut through the rope with about a dozen firm strokes. When his right hand was free, he grasped the blade and cut through the ropes securing his left hand and then the ropes around his legs. All of this took less than fifty seconds. Vyugin had perfected this system years earlier and had practiced it many times. It took skill and practice, but it was a skill he'd mastered long ago. It was no accident that, for decades, he had survived virtually unscathed as a spy in the international big leagues.

Because it was nearly pitch dark in the room, his captors were oblivious to his newly secured freedom. From inside his lower pant leg Vyugin pulled a miniature nightscope, which would enable him to see his captors, though they would not be able to see him.

Bulgakov barked orders: "Boris, you and your assistant—I don't know his name—go into the corridor and see if you can find out what's going on. One of you find your way to the conference room. See if anyone's still in there." He then searched the darkness for Sorokin, finally making out his vague outline in the darkness a few feet away. "Anatoly, keep an eye on these four. Not that you can see them very well in this darkness."

"Yes, I can barely see my own hand. Don't worry, they're not going anywhere," said Sorokin, confidently.

"No doubt you're right," agreed Bulgakov, "nevertheless, someone should be here until we find out what happened to the power. I'm going out. Back in a minute."

Sorokin was now alone with the four prisoners. He slowly worked his way from one prisoner to the next, bending over them to check their bindings to be certain that they were still securely tied. His movements were slow, not out of any desire to be leisurely about what he was doing, but because the darkness was almost total, and he had little choice. As he approached Vyugin, he felt for the older man's arms to be sure they were tied tightly. Vyugin, whose nightscope allowed him to follow the other man's movements clearly, waited for the precise second when Sorokin realized that his prisoner was no longer tied to the chair. In a split second, Vyugin jammed the point of his carefully crafted blade into the thigh of his captor. As Sorokin gasped and reflexively reached down to his leg, Vyugin rose, and gave him a mighty karate chop to the neck. Sorokin never knew what hit him. He was out like a light. Vyugin then rushed over to Tony to cut his ropes.

"What took you so long, Vladimir?" said Dantry jocularly. "Hey, you're getting blood on me."

"Be glad it's not yours. Here, free the others while I tie our friend up." Vyugin raced back to where Sorokin lay bleeding on the floor. He was beginning to stir, so Vyugin gave him another chop, and then set about tying his arms behind his back and securing his legs to the adjacent chair. He then took the man's handkerchief from his pocket and stuffed it in his mouth. When he was finished, he took up his nightscope and saw that Tony had finished freeing the other two. Vyugin spoke in a low voice so as not to attract someone from outside the room.

"Let's get out of here. They'll be back any second. Tony, take Sorokin's gun. It's inside his suit coat. I've got a knife.

Joanna, you and Lubov stay right behind Tony and me. We're going to need some luck to make it out of here."

"How did you get free?" asked Lubov, looking pale despite the nearly total darkness. He'd lost a lot of blood, and was suffering from both physical and psychological shock.

"Later, no time for that now. Follow me."

Vyugin, thought Tony, seemed ten years younger than he had back in Washington. Must be the work agrees with him. Vyugin had opened to door now, and cautiously entered the corridor. The familiar voice of Bulgakov bellowed from down the hall.

"Get someone back to that room," he was saying to someone. "We can't afford to have them get away. If they give you any trouble, kill them."

Chapter 50

"Silence," roared Bulgakov authoritatively to the panicky gaggle of conspirators awkwardly bumping into each other in the darkened room. Since the lights had gone out, they had become increasingly apprehensive. By their very nature, most of them were inclined to think the worst. It would not surprise any of them if they were subjected to an armed attack in the next few moments.

"Silence," repeated Bulgakov to the fidgety group. Slowly, they quieted down. Nervous murmuring could still be heard from the nearly invisible assemblage, but Bulgakov decided to plow ahead anyway. "There is no need to panic. The lights went out. That's all. Our prisoners are still under control, and there is no sign of anyone outside the building or outside the compound." The murmur subsided slightly. Bulgakov released a sigh of relief. He had no idea why the lights had gone out, but he couldn't afford to lose control of his supporters. "Just as soon as we know what caused the power failure, we'll inform you. I know that it's difficult to continue meeting under such circumstances. Fortunately, we'd about concluded our meeting when the lights went out. If anyone wants to say anything else before we break up, speak up. Just be sure to identify yourself, since it's almost impossible to see you." Nervous laughter at the absurdity of the situation.

A voice boomed from the back of the room. "Why don't you have a backup generator? We're planning to run the largest country in the world and we don't have provision for an emergency such as this?"

Bulgakov had hoped no one would think of this. "We do have an emergency generator." He cleared his throat nervously. "Unfortunately, that is not working, either." An undertone of mumbling and muttering in the crowd. This was not something Bulgakov had bargained for. If he was to be the leader of the new Russia, he should be totally in control, and he was not. He needed to demonstrate his authority, and fast.

"You have three prisoners, yes?" inquired an imperious voice somewhere out in the crowd.

"Four."

"How did this come to pass? This compound is supposed to be secret, yet four people were able to find it and spy on us. Where is the leak? What do they know?" Bulgakov felt a tightening in his stomach. Something had to be done.

"Sorokin and his men are dealing with them now. He and his people are very good at extracting information. We shall have answers shortly, I assure you." He was saying things he wasn't sure he could back up. Sorokin had better not let him down.

"We have just voted our approval of the final stages of your plan," said a voice from the left. "We have demonstrated our support. We have supported your elimination of one more American I.M.F. official. Killing Americans is a risky business. If word of this gets out, we are all doomed. We've been willing to do this, Yuri, because we have faith in you and in your ability to pull Russia out of its present morass." He paused briefly, no doubt, for dramatic effect. "But what's happened here has to give one pause. You don't seem to be in control."

Bulgakov drew in a long breath. "Then, if you don't mind the dark for a little while longer, I suggest that you stay around and see who's in charge here."

Chapter 51

The corridor was dark. They could hear voices coming from
somewhere in the building. Orders were being given and the
sounds of disarray could be heard. They couldn't afford to waste
time. They had to get out of the building and away from the
compound before someone discovered they were missing. The
sound of a door opening and footsteps coming toward them. Tony
grabbed the nightscope from Vyugin's hands. "Let me take a look.
I need to orient myself." The corridor was even darker than the
room they had just left. Without a flashlight, it was impossible to
see even your own feet.

The footsteps were approaching rapidly. Apparently
whoever it was had no light because there was no sign of any
illumination ahead of the approaching sound.

"Squat down behind me," said Tony as he squatted down
himself. "I've got Sorokin's gun and I've got the scope."

As the figure rounded a bend, Tony saw that it was Boris,
their original captor. He continued coming, though his former
prisoners were only a few feet ahead of him. It was simply too dark
to see them. Tony, however, saw him. When Boris was even with
him, Tony rose, locked his left arm around the Russian's neck and
brought the butt of Sorokin's gun down on the side of his head.
The man dropped to the floor without a sound, guided there by
Tony to ensure that there was no thud.

He then spoke in a low voice to his three cohorts. "Okay, out the door and try not to make any noise. These guys will be antsy, and they'll probably shoot first and ask questions later." He looked at Lubov through the nightscope. It was clear that he wasn't doing well. Losing one's finger the way he had wasn't particularly good for the system or the psyche. "Can you make it?" he asked.

Lubov nodded. He'd make it.

They were outside the darkened building now. Tony did a quick 360-degree scan with the nightscope. No one to be seen. So far, so good. He returned the scope to Vyugin, who said, "Okay, let's go. Head for the third fence post. There's a hole in the fence just to the right of it." There was a moment of hesitation. They each wondered who should go first. Tony sensed the dilemma. It wasn't that anyone feared going first. Rather, each of them felt as if they'd be leaving the others to face whatever might happen. Vyugin also sensed the problem.

"Joanna, you go first. Take Lubov. Show him where the hole in the fence is. Then you go, Tony. I'll follow behind you." This was all they needed. Joanna squeezed Tony's hand, looked into his eyes for a prolonged moment and darted toward the fence. It was a cloudy night, and there was no moonlight. It wasn't as dark as it was inside the building, but it was dark enough to have trouble with your footing. About a third of the way to the fence, Joanna stumbled and fell. Tony started to go after her, but Vyugin put a firm grip on his arm and held him back.

"She's okay. Look, she's already up and running again. All right, Lubov, go."

Lubov had lost considerable blood. He wasn't a physical man to start with, and now he appeared quite feeble. He rose shakily and started toward the fence in a slow, disjointed trot. Vyugin and Tony prayed that he'd make it. Even if he made it to the fence, he had to get through the hole and then make it through the woods to their car—not an easy trek, even for someone who was fit and healthy. Lubov lurched and almost fell, but recovered and forced himself to go on. As he neared the chain-link fence he moved faster, eager to get to the opening and through. The acceleration was a mistake. He caught his foot on an exposed root and tumbled forward.

Joanna had reached the fence and was waiting for Lubov. She'd been silently urging him on. When she saw him fall, she ran back to him and helped him to his feet. She could see that he had very little left in his tank. There was only a few feet to go now, and she wrapped one of his arms over her shoulder and slowly got him to the fence. She glanced out at his hand at the end of the arm she was supporting. It was the hand with the severed finger. It was still bleeding, though the flow seemed to have slowed considerably. She looked up, trying to zero in on the part of the fence where the hole was. It had gotten darker now, and it was extremely difficult to make out details. She headed slowly, but inexorably for where she hoped the opening was.

Back at the side of the building, Vyugin gave Tony a light shove on the back. "Looks like they might need help. Go! Leave me the gun, though. I'll cover you." Tony took off for the fence, only too glad to be able to help Joanna and Lubov. After a few steps, he slowed and looked back at Vyugin, motioning for the Russian to join him. Vyugin nodded, and mouthed the words, "I'll be right there. Don't worry about me."

When he saw that Joanna and Lubov had made it through the opening in the fence, and that Tony had reached the fence without raising any alarums, Vyugin took off for the fence. They'd been lucky so far. No one had discovered their escape. They couldn't count on that much longer, though. As soon as someone returned to the room where they'd been held captive, all hell would break loose. It behooved them to get as far away from the compound as possible before Bulgakov's goons realized what had happened.

Outside the fence, Vyugin checked to see how Lubov was doing. "Can you make it?"

"I, I don't know. I'll try. If I'm too slow, go on without me. There's no reason they should take us all."

"Bullshit," blurted Tony. "We're not leaving you. Come on, I'll help you. Put your arm over my shoulder. Let's go, though, these guys may be slow on the uptake, but they're not catatonic. As soon as they discover we're gone, they'll send the cavalry out for us."

"We've got to stick to the woods," said Vyugin. "We can't afford to take a chance on the road. Unfortunately, it will take us at least twice as long this way, but there's no choice. You all right, Joanna?"

"Yes, I'm fine. I'm worried about Lubov, though. I don't know if he can make it."

"I share your concern. He has to make it. Come, we must go."

Their progress was slow, made even more difficult because of the enveloping darkness and the constant need to swat at mosquitos. Vyugin, took the lead, and with his nightscope, was able to avoid major obstacles. Behind him, the others, without benefit of a scope, still stumbled and fell frequently. With Vyugin just ahead of them, they were able to keep to the correct general direction, but it was impossible to make out most obstacles.

As they passed the point where they'd hidden the car on their previous trip, the silent knot of fleeing ex-prisoners was startled by a sudden uproar back at the building they had so recently escaped from. Doors were slamming, and the rattling of guns being made ready for action disturbed the quiet evening. Stentorian voices bellowed orders, unsettling what had until seconds before been a calm night in the Russian back woods.

"What now, Vladimir?" asked Tony.

"Keep as low as you can, but keep going. They'll probably spread out searching. We must get away from here before they get this far." As he said, this, he remembered something. "Wait a moment, though. I need to get some of the stuff we left here on our way in." He set off to the right by himself. In less than thirty seconds he was back. "Okay, follow me."

They could hear voices behind them now. Their pursuers were gaining on them. Glancing back, Tony saw that some of the guards were on the road and some were in the woods behind them. Flashlights swept in wide arcs across the road and through the woods. Occasionally someone swore as he stumbled or as he was hit in the face with a branch. If they caught up with the escapees, they'd be in a mean mood. Then, the exhausted escapees heard a yell from deep in the woods behind them.

"This way. Broken branches and footprints. Hurry, they can't be too far ahead."

Joanna heard the crashing of dead branches and of leaves and the swishing of supple limbs behind them as the pursuers sensed they were getting close to their quarry. They were closing in, and both hunters and hunted knew this. She looked at Lubov. He was slowing down. His breath was coming hard now. She feared that he wouldn't make it. Funny, she suddenly realized. Until a few days ago, she'd never even met this man. Now she was more concerned with his fate than she was for her own. Right now, they were all feeling the fatigue that comes as a natural byproduct of stress. Surprisingly, she felt that she could still go on. Somewhere from within, she'd found renewed strength.

She glanced back at Tony. It was so dark in the forest, she could barely make out his face. "You okay?" she asked in a low voice, her concern showing.

He grinned. "I'm supposed to be asking questions like that. Yeah, I'm okay. How's he doing?"

"Not well," she whispered so as not to be heard by Lubov. She dropped back a pace and added, "I don't know if he's going to make it."

"Shouldn't be much more than a quarter of a mile."

"I know, but he's lost a lot of blood, and he's not a strong man to begin with. And those guys behind us seem to be gaining."

"I know, keep urging him on. If we have to, we'll carry him."

"Once we get out of the woods. We can't carry him in here, with these branches in the way."

"Come, we must go faster." It was Vyugin, looking back at them from the lead.

Tony ran past the others and said to Vyugin, "Vladimir, I don't know if Lubov can make it. He's lost a lot of blood, and he's getting weaker by the minute."

"Yes, I know. Well, we still have one more trick up our sleeve. Before I went into the building, I planted a bomb on the far side of the compound. Thought we might need a distraction."

Dantry grinned. "Well, what are you waiting for?"

Vyugin came to a stop and pulled a small wireless device from the heel of his shoe. He was breathing heavily. As brilliant as ever, thought Dantry, but not as fit. The years had taken their toll. Then Vyugin depressed a button on the device. At first, Tony thought that it hadn't worked. Then he saw the flash. A split second later he heard the explosion. The blast reverberated throughout the forest. From several hundred yards behind them they heard voices, excited, yelling, confused. Then the sound of people crashing through underbrush, changing direction. Through his nightscope, Vyugin watched as their pursuers changed course and headed in the direction of where the blast had just occurred.

Vyugin beamed, a rare show of ego on his part. Dantry grinned back. Joanna just said, "You did that?"

Vyugin dipped his head slightly and tried to not to show self-satisfaction on his face. "Come, this is only a temporary distraction. Lubov, can you make it?"

Lubov swallowed hard. He worked to muster the strength to get words out. "I, I hope so. I'll try." Joanna noticed that the bloody stump of his severed finger, still wrapped in a dirty rag, was still dripping blood. The man wouldn't be able to go on much longer.

The moon slipped from behind a cloud, bathing the landscape in a cool, revealing light. The four escapees were now able to see somewhat better. They picked up the pace. If it weren't for Lubov, they'd have been able to move even faster. With the increased visibility, Dantry was helping the wounded editor by sharing some of his weight. It was still slow going, but better than it had been.

"Only about a hundred meters to go," encouraged Vyugin. "We're almost to the car."

Then they heard voices behind them again. Their pursuers had realized they'd been tricked, and once again were in hot pursuit. Only now the voices sounded closer. As Dantry and the others resumed their erratic escape through the unsure footing of the Russian forest, the outcome became increasingly uncertain.

"Halt up there," bellowed a voice on a bullhorn. "You cannot escape. Make it easy on yourselves, and we will work something out. There is no need for anyone to get hurt."

Vyugin looked at Dantry and raised his eyebrows. "Keep going."

"I hear you." He turned to the other two and said, "Ignore the bullhorn. Keep going. We're almost there."

Without warning, the moon disappeared behind the cloud bank overhead. Visibility went from mediocre to closet black. Lubov stumbled and fell to the ground. "I'm sorry. I can't go on." His breathing came in short, laborious gasps. "I'm too weak. Go on without me, please. Maybe they won't see me anyway." Joanna kneeled down beside him. His eyes were dull and lifeless, and his skin felt cold. He wasn't going to make it much longer. In the distance she could hear the approach of the hunters as they broke twigs and snapped branches in their ceaseless pursuit of their weakening prey. Joanna wasn't a quitter, but the situation was beginning to look hopeless. Lubov couldn't move, and they couldn't leave without him. It seemed only a matter of a couple of minutes before they'd be overtaken and subjected to God only knew what indignities. Most likely indignities ending in death.

"Bullshit!" said Dantry in an explosive susurration. "You're coming with us." He bent down and, with an enormous effort, put his two arms under the wounded editor and lifted him off the damp ground. "We'll get you out of here," said Tony, cradling the feeble man in his arms in front of him. "C'mon," he said to the others, "let's go."

Seeing this, Vyugin and Joanna felt revitalized and pushed on ahead to help blaze the trail for Tony and his human charge.

"I think I see where we hid the car." It was a welcome whisper from Vyugin as he lowered the nightscope from his eye. "Just twenty-five or thirty meters. We'll make it now."

"Jesus, don't say that," said Dantry under his breath. He'd never believed in tempting fate. Still, he, too, now thought that he could make out the clearing where they'd left the car. Drenched with sweat and near the point of exhaustion, he hoped against hope that he and Vyugin were right. If they were wrong, there wasn't much they could do at this point about evading their former captors.

Joanna could just make out the outline of the car now. She breathed a silent sigh of relief. It wasn't over yet, but at least there was a vehicle at the end of the tunnel. The tired foursome, virtually drained of their last reserves of stamina, stumbled into the small clearing, leaning on or clinging to the exterior of the vehicle as if it were the very fount of life. Vyugin turned and directed his scope back in the direction from which they'd just come. "I see them. They're coming this way. Get in the car fast—everybody." They were glad that they'd backed the vehicle into the space so that they could now head straight out. Vyugin held the rear door open as Dantry helped the failing Lubov into the back seat.

CRACK! Joanna was startled by the sound. She immediately realized it was a gunshot. CRACK! CRACK! CRACK! "Hurry," urged Vyugin. "And keep down as low as you can."

"This is your last warning!" roared the bullhorn, sounding much closer than it had the last time. "Stop where you are and you won't get hurt. I repeat, this is your last warning."

"Screw 'em," shouted Dantry. C'mon. Let's go." Joanna had run around to the other side of the car and was scrambling into the front seat. As Dantry jumped into the back next to the ailing Lubov, Vyugin gunned the engine, and the car leaped forward. The vehicle plowed ahead, and the passengers suddenly became aware of how rugged the terrain was. On the way in they had driven slowly, and the ruts and holes had not been quite so noticeable, but now, Vyugin had to restrain the car for fear it would become so severely damaged from bumping and jolting in and out of ruts that they might not be able to go on. As he reduced speed, the sound of gunfire grew louder. The vehicle was about to enter the main road when a bullet pierced the rear window, sending tiny splinters of glass into the back seat, stinging the necks of Dantry and Lubov. Vyugin jammed on the brakes. "Hold on. There's a tree across the road. Damn! Wasn't there when we drove in here. Of all the Goddam luck, a tree would fall after we pull in. Tony, help me move it out of the way. Quickly. Here Joanna, take this gun and fire back at them until we get that tree out of the way. The other guns are in the back."

Joanna gulped a deep breath of humid summer air and felt her heart race as she opened the front side window and aimed the gun backward, getting off three quick rounds. The firing from the woods stopped. She turned to see how Vyugin and Dantry were doing with the tree in front of the car. Her heart sank as she realized that the tree hadn't budged. Apparently the fallen trunk was heavier than they'd expected, as it was barely moving, despite their straining and tugging. Without hesitation, she reached over the seat back and retrieved one of the automatic rifles. Then, with two guns under her left arm, she opened the door, got off a couple more shots in the direction of the unseen pursuers, and made a dash for the fallen tree.

"Get back in the car," yelled Dantry.

"This is not exactly the time for chivalry, c'mon. Maybe the three of us can move this thing." She dropped the two weapons at her feet and grabbed hold of the tree. Dantry rolled his eyes in exasperated resignation and bent down for one more try.

"All right," said Tony. "On two. One, two, heave!" Slowly, the massive tree moved. "Okay, just a little more. Just enough so we can get by." As he said this, a fusillade of gunfire clattered against the car behind them. Their pursuers were closing in. Vyugin and Dantry grabbed up the two guns that Joanna had dropped and unleashed a hail of bullets in the direction of the woods. Without waiting to see how effective their counterfire had been, they scurried back to the tree, and, with Joanna's added help, tugged and grunted until they had dragged one end of the tree another few feet off the rutted dirt path.

"Enough," said Vyugin. "Back in the car. Let's get the hell out of here." The pursuers had resumed firing now. Getting back into the vehicle was a harrowing experience, as lead ricocheted off nearby boulders, sending rock chips into the air and peppering the three with a hail of stinging projectiles. The engine was still running so when they tumbled into the car, Vyugin was able to send it careering ahead toward the main road. Right now, Vyugin wasn't worried about scraping the bottom of the vehicle on something as they bumped and jolted forward toward safety. If they didn't make it now, they weren't going to make it.

Two bullets tore through the rear window, spraying more bits and pieces of glass into the car's interior. One of the rounds grazed Joanna's ear. Reflexively she put her hand to the side of her head. It wasn't painful, but she had felt something —a warm liquid. Pulling her hand down she could see, even in the darkness of the car's interior, that she was bleeding. The warm blood reminded her of Lubov's missing finger and how much he had bled since that sick monster Felix had severed it. She peered through the murkiness into the back seat and saw that Lubov had blacked out or fallen asleep—whatever. It wasn't a good sign. Her eyes met Dantry's. Without speaking he confirmed that he, too, was concerned. They had to get Lubov to a doctor soon, or he wouldn't make it.

Chapter 52

They decided after a quick discussion in the car to go back to Noginsk. There was a risk in going back there—Bulgakov and his cronies might have checked hotels and inns in the city—but it seemed a small risk by comparison with going all the way back to Moscow with Lubov in dire peril of expiring if they didn't get help as quickly as possible.

On their first visit, they'd checked into the Internationale in Noginsk under assumed names. They checked in again under the same names using the fake credentials provided by Vyugin, but not before going to the nearest hospital emergency room.

The doctor, a Central Asian named Makarov, had come to Noginsk from Tashkent back in the mid-'80s, not out of choice, but because he'd been sent there. He wasn't happy with his night shift and was inclined to be impatient with anybody who disturbed his reading. He was suspicious when he saw Lubov's vicious wound.

"How did this happen?" he asked Vyugin, since Lubov was still out.

"An accident. He was cutting firewood. We have a small dacha—cabin really." Vyugin smiled self-consciously. "Just north of here. He's a journalist from Moscow. We were with him when it happened. It was supposed to be a good time. Our two journalist friends here had joined us for a few days." Vyugin allowed the doctor to think what he wanted to about the sexual preference of Vyugin and his unconscious patient.

"Firewood? In this heat?" The doctor remained unconvinced.

"He's a nervous person. It keeps him occupied. He says you can't have enough wood when winter comes." The doctor raised his eyebrows, shrugged, and leaned closer to get a better look at the blood stump on poor Lubov's hand.

"Did you disinfect it?"

"No. We rushed here as soon as it happened. Is it infected?"

"Probably. I'll sew it up and give him some antibiotics. Some painkillers, too. He's going to suffer for a week or two—physically. Psychologically, it'll take longer for him to get used to the loss of his finger. No telling how he'll deal with that. He's in shock now. Why don't you people leave him with me overnight. We'll get him back on his feet in the morning."

"Do you mind if I come back later tonight and sit with him?" asked Vyugin, sounding concerned about his friend. He wanted to be there when Lubov came to in order to be sure he didn't say something that contradicted the story they'd given the doctor.

The doctor smiled. "No, I suppose not. Come back in two hours, and you can stay with him. Visiting hours will be over, but tell the nurse at the front desk that I said you could come up."

"What floor will he be on, doctor?"

"The fourth. The nurse at the front desk will give you the room."

On their way from the hospital to the Internationale, Joanna broke the silence.

"Quick thinking, Vladimir. When Lubov wakes up, he won't know what to say."

Dantry grinned. "I'd be surprised if he came up with the firewood story."

"Precisely," said Vyugin with a sigh. "We don't need complications or dealings with the local police now—unless we're the ones who contact them."

"So what do we do now?" asked Joanna. "They'll be looking for us. I assume between them they have a lot of resources."

"They do," affirmed Vyugin. "Yes, they probably have people out looking for us now. We'll have to stay one step ahead of them."

"If Lubov spends the night in the hospital, they'll probably find him," said Dantry. "They'll check all the hospitals in the region, I'm sure."

"Another reason why I want to go back there tonight. Hopefully he'll be well enough to travel. I want to get him the hell out of there in the next few hours. Even a few hours put us at risk, but overnight they'd be sure to find him."

"Agreed," said Dantry. "Once we get him out of the hospital, what are you thinking?"

"I'm thinking we have to go on the offensive. We know they've already sent two more operatives to the States to assassinate Chandler. We have to act fast. Not to mention their plans to cause rioting and civil disorder in the streets of major cities. These people have to be stopped."

"I'm with you, Vladimir, but how are we going to do that? We're heavily outnumbered, and we have very little evidence to make a case with."

"Let's check into the hotel, and I'll show you what we have. It may surprise you."

Chapter 53

The clerk behind the desk recognized them, though not by their
real names.

"Ah, good even Mr. Vishinsky," he said, addressing Vyugin
as if he were a frequent patron of the establishment. You're
arriving late. I'm sure you and your party are tired. We'll get you
settled quickly." He took the credit card proffered by Vyugin and
efficiently found two rooms—one for Vyugin and one for Dantry
and Joanna, who once again registered as Mr. and Mrs. O'Brien
from Chicago.

"Are there any messages for us?" asked Vyugin, casually.

"No, sir. Are you expecting any?"

"It's possible. If someone calls or inquires, give me a call
immediately, will you. Even if it's at an ungodly hour." He smiled,
as if sharing a secret with a fellow conspirator.

"Of course, sir. Do you need help with your bags?"

"No, I think we can handle it. We're travelling light, as you
can see."

It was after ten when they finally got settled in. They met in
Vyugin's room to plan their strategy.

"I'm starving," said Tony. "After we talk, I want to go
downstairs and get something to eat. But first we need to map out
our strategy." He looked at Vyugin. "So, Vladimir, what have you

got up your sleeve?" At first, the expression threw the Russian. Then he caught Dantry's meaning.

"We aren't without ammunition. If we work this right, we may still be able to topple this cabal. First, we have our friend, Lubov, who, I'm sure, will testify to his being taken captive by these power-hungry plotters."

"Assuming he's healthy enough," said Joanna. "He doesn't look good."

"I'm going back to the hospital later to make certain that he's all right."

"Then we have my own testimony about my the assignment Bulgakov gave me."

"You sure you want to go into that, Vladimir?" asked Tony. "It implicates you, you know."

"It's a risk I'll have to take. There's too much at stake here to worry about myself. There's the future of my country and maybe even the world, if my assessment of these people is right. Bulgakov and his supporters are power hungry. This is not just a group of idealistic politicians trying to correct a mistake. It's just the opposite. It's a group of self-serving former KGB and military types looking to gain power and glory by conquering as much territory as they can. And they don't care who they destroy in the process." He stopped and waited for reactions from Tony and Joanna. "Maybe you think I'm wrong?"

Tony answered him in a subdued voice. "No, I don't think you're wrong. Unfortunately, I think you're right on target, and it scares the hell out of me. I've seen first-hand just how ruthless these bastards can be."

"I agree," said Joanna. "But I do think you'll be sticking your neck out, if you cite your own part in this as evidence."

"I have to take the chance that the Kirov government will appreciate my coming forth with what I know. If we save Kirov, he has to show some gratitude. At least I have to take that chance."

"He is a politician, Vladimir. With politicians you can't be sure of anything."

"Yes, but I have to go by what I know of him, and that is that, while he can be ruthless and tough like most politicians, he also has a reputation for fairness and a desire to bring something like Western democracy to Russia. What else do I have to go on?"

"Nothing, I suppose," said Dantry. "Anyway, God knows we're glad you feel the way you do, and we support you all the way. Okay, back to what ammunition we do have to fight these people. One, we've got Lubov—or may have, depending on whether he makes it or not." Vyugin and Joanna nodded. "Two, we've got your testimony, and three. What else have we got?"

Vyugin grinned broadly, as he reached into his graphite-gray canvas duffel bag. "Let me show you something." He held up a small black metal object about the size and shape of a package of gum. Dantry took it and began to examine it.

"A camera." He broke into a broad smile. "You son-of-a-bitch. You got these guys on film."

"Not all of them, but a quite a few. Enough to make our case."

"Who've you got?"

"Bulgakov, Sorokin, Marshal Suchinov—"

"Bulgakov and Suchinov. Hot damn!"

"That's not all. I also have a fairly decent shot of Commissar—or I should say, ex-Commissar Zlotov. Plus three or four others. A pretty good rogues gallery, I think. Of course, I haven't seen them yet, but I think they should be good enough for our purposes."

"How will you get them developed?" asked Joanna.

"I have a friend in Moscow who will do this for me, no questions asked. A few American dollars will show my appreciation."

"I'm beginning to feel better about this," said Dantry. "We just might pull this off."

"Wait, I haven't shown you everything." He reached back into the duffel bag and pulled out a digital recorder slightly smaller than a cigarette case. "I used a 12-inch parabolic mike back there. Recorded it all on this little fellow." He patted the tiny recorder. "Listen to this:"

"Our goal is to replace Kirov with Mr. Malenkov within the next two-to-three months. I expect that the I.M.F. is going to turn down Kirov's request for the loan. We have taken steps to insure

that that happens. When the loan fails to come through, our cadres of activists will go into action. First, there will be protests in Moscow, St. Petersburg, and Novosibirsk. These will escalate within days to riots. Cars overturned, shop windows broken, work stoppages in the Metros and other public transportation."

Vyugin watched as smiles broke out on the faces of his two associates. Dantry was the first to speak.

"How'd you get that? You weren't in the building until you joined us."

"The microphone is of the latest design. It registers the vibrations of a person's voice on window glass. The range is over 100 meters, if the conditions are just right. Today, they were very good—except for one interruption. Who knows what that might have been. Perhaps someone closed a door to the meeting room. Whatever."

"Who is that speaking?"

"Bulgakov. Good stuff, eh?"

"Very good. Got anything else?"

"Listen."

"Key newspapers and TV stations under our control will call for a government that can bring back the glory and respect that we had during the Soviet era. They will couch it carefully so as to imply that it would not be a replica of the Soviet Union with its flaws—"

"Something interfered with the reception here, but I have more. Listen."

"The papers we control will write about how once again Russia must control the inferior ethnic minorities of Central Asia and the Balkans. Just since 1991 it's become clear that, if you leave these tribes to their own devices, they create all kinds of social and political mischief. It is better that we control them and use their labor to further the ends of a new Russia." Burst of applause.

"This will do it," said Joanna, beaming with intensity. "This will destroy their little plan to create a new Soviet Union—or whatever they intend to call it."

"I hope so," said Vyugin. "But just in case that's not enough, listen to this:"

"Once we have rebuilt our new Sov— er our new Union of Mother Russia, the Central Asian Countries, and several Balkan states, there is no reason why we should not build on that. This cannot be done overnight, but it need not take long. Within a few years we should be able to incorporate additional countries from Southeast Asia and even begin to move into Eur—"

"Unbelievable," declared Dantry. "That's exactly what they plan to do. First another USSR. Then, the world. Son-of-a-bitch, Vladimir. You're a one-man intelligence organization. This'll do it. This'll do it."

Joanna cleared her throat. She wasn't smiling. The two men looked at her, wondering what had transformed her mood so suddenly.

"What is it?" asked Vyugin.

"This is excellent stuff, Vladimir. Almost too good to be true." Vyugin frowned, as if expecting an insult, or comment belittling his efforts. Joanna continued, oblivious to the look of concern on the Russian's face. "My concern is that no names are mentioned in any of these recordings. How do we prove that it was Bulgakov? If we play these for someone in the Kirov government, they could say we recorded this ourselves."

Vyugin breathed a sigh of relief. He was afraid she'd thought of something he hadn't anticipated. "I doubt it, Joanna, but, you're right, it is possible. I doubt it will happen, though, because Kirov doesn't trust Bulgakov, and wouldn't be at all surprised if he were to plot behind his back. He'll be happy to accept evidence that he can use against Bulgakov." He stopped to consider any other possibilities he could imagine before he went on. "But let's suppose one of his aides or he, himself, is suspicious. Worse case scenario, let's say they suspect that we're working for Bulgakov or his people in some elaborate Machiavellian scheme to embarrass him with a phony plot that he could then easily discredit. But—"

"I could see them thinking that," interrupted Dantry.

"That's kind of what I meant," said Joanna. "Not that it will happen, but what if it does?"

"You're right, you're right," said Vyugin impatiently. "Of course we need to be ready for such an eventuality. I was about to get to that before you interrup—." He realized he was so involved with his own thoughts that he was letting these perfectly reasonable interruptions annoy him. "Sorry. What I was about to say was we could easily do an electronic voice comparison of what we have with a recording of Bulgakov's voice that they come up with. If we need scientific proof, we can come up with it."

Dantry could feel the possibilities now. "Good. What we need now is a plan of attack. We've got to make sure we go to the right people. Any ideas, Vladimir?"

"Yes, first, I must go to the hospital and retrieve Lubov. Let's hope I get there before Bulgakov's thugs do. In the meantime, you two get some food and rest. You'd better make a call to that cop in Washington and alert him about possible new attacks on Chandler. Let him know that new operatives have been sent from Moscow. I wish we could do more, but at least we can do that much."

"We'll take care of it," said Dantry. "And we'll make the call from another hotel, just in case."

"Yes, good idea."

"Er— Vladimir?"

"Yes, Joanna?"

"Question."

"Yes?"

"How did the lights go out?"

He grinned. "I assume you mean back at the compound."

"You know that's what I mean. Well?"

"Well, as you know, Tony surrendered himself before I did. I'd told you, Tony, that I had something to do before I came in."

"Which was?"

"I places two bombs with time fuses set to detonate after I was inside with you. I attached one to a power line coming into the compound. The other I placed near what appeared to be a generator. I hoped that it was a back-up power source. I wasn't sure, but it looks as if I guessed right." He grinned again.

"You son-of-a-bitch."

* * *

As much as he enjoyed the approving comments of his new associates, Vyugin realized that they couldn't afford to luxuriate in their good fortune for long.

"Now we're going to want to hide our evidence. I checked these floorboards. None of them budge, so I can't do what I did back in my little Moscow hotel. Help me come up with a suitable hiding place."

"How about the ceiling," offered Joanna. "The ceiling tiles look like they're removable."

Dantry smiled. "You may be on to something. Here, give me a chair."

Five minutes later, with their evidence, weapons, and electronic gear safely stashed above them, Vyugin left for the hospital, while Joanna and Tony went down to the lobby to find a restaurant.

The café off the lobby wasn't much, but after the day they'd had it was more than adequate.

"I'd forgotten how bad Russian beer can be," grinned Tony. "Still, the food wasn't too bad. How about you?"

She smiled. "It was fine. Just glad to sit down in a comfortable place without those goons hanging over me. I hope Lubov is okay. The poor guy. My God, how can people be such beasts?"

"He should make it—physically, anyway. How he handles it psychologically is another story. Only time will tell."

"Do you think we can get these guys?"

"Vyugin's got some pretty convincing evidence. I just hope we can get to someone high enough up, and before Bulgakov and his gang get to us. Jeez, Jo, I am so sorry I got you into this."

"We've been there before, Tony. I volunteered, remember. I'm glad I came, too—despite what we've been through. Think what I'll be able to tell my grandchildren."

"Yeah, if we get through this in one piece. This is not a game. These guys will not let anything or anyone get in their way."

"They're desperate, but so are we, now that we know what the stakes are. We can't afford to fail.

* * *

Vyugin pushed his way through the revolving doors and entered the well-lit reception area of the hospital. The large waiting area was empty. He was about to go up to the reception desk when he noticed two large men standing there.

"I'm sorry, visiting hours are over until tomorrow morning. You can come back then," said one of the nurses behind the desk to the two burly men, who fidgeted impatiently as she spoke. She was a hefty woman herself—probably in her mid-forties—and clearly sleepy. She had little patience for these two, who had the temerity to challenge standard hospital policy. What she liked about the night shift is that it wasn't busy.

Instantly Vyugin's senses went on alert. These two had to have been sent by someone back at the compound. And by stopping at the desk to inquire about Lubov, they'd lost their advantage over Vyugin. If they hadn't stopped, they might already be in Lubov's room. Of course they'd had to stop because they didn't know what floor the editor was on. And they certainly didn't know the room. Vyugin at least knew the floor. That would have to do now. He couldn't afford to go to the front desk with those guys there, and if he waited till they were gone, they could beat him to Lubov's room. He hoped that the presence of the two men at the desk would continue to distract the two nurses long enough for him to pass by unobserved.

The goon doing the talking played right into Vyugin's hands. He raised his voice, obviously angry. Good, thought, Vyugin. Things were heating up. Both women behind the desk now were remonstrating vehemently. Vyugin saw his opportunity and quietly headed toward the elevators.

He could hear the loud voices arguing vociferously in the reception area behind him. He reached the elevator area. One elevator door was opened, and he quickly got in and pressed the four button. He knew he didn't have much time. If those two men were who he thought they were, they wouldn't be put off by the two women at the desk—at least not for long. While these toughs might prefer not to call attention to their mission, they'd risk it rather than fail and then have to go back to face Bulgakov or Sorokin empty handed.

The elevator opened onto an antiseptic, pale green corridor. He looked up and down the length of the hall and saw no one. So far, so good. For no reason other than the likelihood that it had more room choices, he started down what appeared to be the longer part of the corridor. After going about 100 feet, he came to a nurses station. A nurse with her back to him was checking a chart. She was petite, barely five-feet tall. Her short ash-blonde hair was cut stylishly in the latest mode of cuts he'd seen in Europe and the States. What the hell, he had to find Lubov's room, so he cleared his throat to get her attention. She whirled around, startled. Not expecting anyone at this hour.

"Yes? You're not supposed to be up here."

"Actually, I am. Dr. Makarov said I could come and stay with my friend. He's the one with the amputated finger."

Recognition flashed in her azure eyes. "Oh, yes. Mr. Lubov." She looked at a sheet on the desk in front of her. "Yes, Dr.Makarov left a note here. He said someone would be coming to stay with Mr. Lubov. He's in Room 421—across the hall and down two doors."

"Thank you. By the way, how's my friend doing?"

"The amputation will heal. The doctor gave him an antibiotic. He'll need to take them for ten days. If he has a problem, I think it will be depression. Losing any appendage is mentally traumatic. And this, because it was an accident, and not something he'd prepared himself for mentally, will be quite hard for him to accept. But you can go see him now."

"Thanks again."

Chapter 54

Lubov looked up when he entered the room.

"It's you. They said someone brought me in here, but I was in such a fog. So confused. Thank you. Thank you for getting me out of that hellish place."

"I'm afraid I'm going to have to get you out of this place, too."

"They should release me later today or tomorrow."

"We have to go now. Some of Bulgakov's thugs are downstairs in the lobby. Can you walk?"

"Uh, yes, I suppose so. You think they'll come up here?"

"I'd bet on it. Come, put your clothes on fast. Don't be fastidious. We've got to get out of here right away." As Vyugin's words registered, Lubov shook himself and threw off the covers. Vyugin went to the closet and grabbed the editor's clothes. "These yours, or his?" He nodded in the direction of the other bed in the room where an old man appeared to be sleeping soundly.

"Mine." He took them and rapidly pulled on his pants, wincing in pain as the stump of his missing finger brushed the fabric. To Vyugin it seemed like hours, but it actually took Lubov less than sixty seconds to get dressed.

"Okay, now I'm going to peek outside to make sure no one's there. Not even a nurse." He peered into the hall and scanned its length. "Okay," he said. "Right now, it's all clear. Come quickly and don't talk. Just do as I do. If someone sees us, you're just taking a brief walk. Got that?" Lubov nodded.

The nurse he'd spoken to on the way in was not to be seen. Vyugin did a slow trot toward the bank of elevators. He pressed the down button and held his breath.

The lighted numbers for one of the two elevators indicated that the left-most car was ascending and was about to open on their floor. A second elevator was descending and was still two floors above them. He prayed that the ascending car wasn't occupied by the two toughs he'd seen in the lobby. As the doors of the car on the left opened, Vyugugin berated himself for not using the stairs. He was losing his edge.

A woman doctor got off, forcing a professional smile at Lubov and Vyugin before she moved purposefully down the corridor. Vyugin gave a sigh of relief. The second car had arrived now and was starting to open. Vyugin held his breath. The door opened and a tired-looking nurse got off without even glancing at them. Good. Vyugin pushed Lubov into the car and hit the button for the basement.

"We'll get off in the basement and find our way out. We don't want to meet our nasty friends in the lobby. Let's hope it doesn't stop there first." Again, he chided himself for his stupidity in not using the stairs. Lubov barely nodded. He was struggling to keep up. Whatever Vyugin said was okay with him.

The basement was crowded with laundry hampers and miscellaneous hospital paraphernalia. The lighting was poor, and there was no one to be seen. Good. Vyugin followed a narrow corridor, hoping it would lead to an exit. They wound around and between ancient clutter, the likes of which would surely have frightened most patients on the floors above were they to know of such disorder and messiness.

Right now, though, clutter wasn't uppermost in the minds of Vyugin and Lubov. They just wanted to get as far away from this hospital as possible. They'd been making their way through this underground maze for several minutes now and not seen a single exit door or even a sign indicating where one was.

They heard men's voices from somewhere behind them. Faint, but agitated. Vyugin couldn't make out what they were saying, but he had the feeling they were Bulgakov's two thugs. The voices were louder now, and still there was no sign of a way out.

Then Vyugin felt a slight gust of fresh air. They must be near a door. They pushed ahead, though Vyugin could see that Lubov was flagging. They turned a corner, and there it was. A loading dock with its huge overhead door raised. Two men were unloading a truck. There was no way Vyugin and Lubov could leave through that door without these two seeing them and then telling Bulgakov's men that they had. Vyugin got an idea. He scanned the area, desperately searching for something he could use. Then his eyes lit upon something that would be perfect for his needs. Two empty water glasses. Looked like they hadn't been washed in weeks. He grabbed one of the glasses and heaved it down the corridor, well past the open loading dock.

The crash of breaking glass startled the two workmen. They both looked in the direction of the sound they'd just heard. They stared down the corridor, speaking in an agitated manner. Finally, they shook their heads, apparently dismissing the noise as nothing important and went back to what they'd been doing on the truck.

Vyugin threw the second glass in the same direction as the first. Its crash seemed louder than the first. The two workers dropped the large box they were carrying and started off in the direction of the noise.

Vyugin winked at Lubov and motioned for him to follow. They made a dash for the open door. It was a slow dash, as Lubov was extremely weak, but they got through the door and down a short flight of steps and disappeared into an alley.

As the darkness of the Russian night enveloped them, two men stood catching their breath on the loading dock looking out into the blackness. Then they saw the steps leading down to the black-topped surface below.

Chapter 55

The Lada started on the first try. Vyugin rammed the stick shift into first gear and tore out of the parking lot. He quickly headed into the flow of traffic before looking back. He wasn't sure that, even if he were being followed, he'd know what car it was. After a few glances back, he began to relax a bit. The traffic was moderate, but nothing about the vehicles behind him stood out. He'd probably eluded the two Bulgakov henchmen. If he hadn't, he'd have to deal with them when they made their move. He looked over at Lubov. The man was pale and silent.

"How you feeling?"

"Okay," came the feeble reply.

"The nurse said you were going to be all right."

"Yeah."

"It'll take some time to get used to what they did to you. I know that. If we can bring these guys down, maybe you'll feel a little better about it."

Lubov turned to meet Vyugin's eyes. "It would help."

Vyugin pulled over to the curb about ten blocks from the Internationale. He waited to see if a vehicle with the two gunmen pulled over or went by. The traffic was light enough now to check out the occupants of every car. After waiting a full three minutes without seeing anyone who looked the least bit like the two men, he pulled back into the flow of traffic and went on to the hotel.

He knocked on Dantry's door and waited. An eye peered through the peep hole, then a clatter, and the door opened.

"Thank God you made it," said Joanna. Then she addressed Lubov. "Are you okay?"

He smiled wanly. "Yes, I'll make it. Thank you."

"All clear, Vladimir?" asked Tony.

"I think I saw two of their men at the hospital. We got out before they could follow us. They won't give up, though. I'm sure they'll be checking all the hotels."

"We should be okay here at the hotel. We checked in under names they'll never connect with us."

"You're probably right. All the same, I think one of us should keep an eye out for them in the lobby. You know, hang back as far from the front desk as possible. We can work up some sort of middling disguise. I'll take the first shift. I need a quick bite to eat; then I'll be on watch from midnight to two." Then, realizing they couldn't afford to be sidetracked from their reason for being there in the first place, he added, "In the morning, over breakfast, we'll decide how we're going to prevent this *coup d'etat*."

"Sounds like a plan," said Dantry agreeably. "For tonight, I'll take the two-to-four a.m. lookout."

"I'll take from four till we leave," said Joanna.

"Somebody should be down there now," said Tony, "until Vladimir gets there. I'll go down while you get some food, Vlady. First you better tell me what these guys look like." Vyugin quickly described the two men, told Lubov he could take one of the beds in his room, and dashed off for the lobby and his quick supper.

The night passed uneventfully. The only downside, thought Dantry, was that he got about two hours sleep. After his middle-of-the-night watch, he couldn't get back to sleep. All he could think of was how they were going bring down the *coup* without getting themselves accused of being involved, or worse, getting themselves killed. He'd seen too much death. And he'd seen more than enough vicious, cruel men.

Dantry sighed, letting his tired mind roam six thousand miles across Russia, Europe, and the Atlantic to City Island, Long Island Sound, and a life with Joanna. It was a life that beckoned loudly in his exhausted mind—a mind nearly as tired as his body.

He knew now that he wanted to spend the rest of his years with her. It would take him that long to get over the guilt of letting her come along on this venture, risking her neck more times than most people did in ten lifetimes. God, she was amazing.

And he knew, too, that life with her wouldn't be just lazing away on the sunlit water. If they got out of this alive, they'd both have a new appreciation for what mattered. Funny, until now, he really never knew what mattered. He knew now that they both wanted to do something with their lives, accomplish something—something their kids could point to with pride. He smiled at this. Where'd these kids come from?

At breakfast, each of them seemed nervous, restless—as if they were closing in on the final chapter of their daring venture. Each in their own minds knew that final chapters can have good endings and bad ones. The outcome of their final chapter clearly was in question

"We can proceed in one of two ways, I think," said Vyugin. He looked around the table to see if they were with him. He saw that he had their attention. He couldn't tell what they thought, but they were listening. "We can go directly to Kirov and try to convince him that his administration and the very future of Russia are in serious jeopardy—that this *coup d'etat* attempt is going to be made soon, very soon." He scanned the table. All eyes were on him. He continued. "Or we can conclude that it would be easier to convince his aides, on the assumption that two or three of them, if convinced, would be more persuasive, and therefore more likely to get results, than would Kirov trying to convince people below him. It's not inconceivable that people in his government might think that the president was paranoid. So, those two approaches, I think, are our two best options. Tell me, what do you think?"

"There's a risk either way," said Dantry, "but I'm inclined to go right to the top. Kirov has the power. He can make the decisions. If we convince him, we've succeeded."

"True," said Joanna, "but Vladimir has a point. Even if we do convince him, will his staff support him—or will they think he's paranoid, and try to talk him out of it or just humor him? I suppose a lot depends on what kind of man he is and how much respect he commands among his own staff. Vladimir, you know him, don't you?"

"I've met him, and I know people who know him. He is respected, but I do think there's a real danger in going to him first. Besides, it may not be that easy to get to see him anyway. I'm leaning toward meeting with his staff or one of his chief aides. We can always go above them if they don't buy our story."

"You just said you're not sure we could even get to meet with him," retorted Dantry excitedly.

"True, but at least we would have the possibility of a second appeal. If we start with him, there is no higher level to which we can appeal."

"Okay, I'll buy it. Do you know anyone close to Kirov that we could meet with?"

"I know Gennadi Potemkin."

"Who's he?"

"Kirov's chief of staff. Young, brilliant, and ambitious."

"Can you trust him?"

Vyugin smiled wryly. "Can you trust anyone in government?" He brought his open palms up to his face and exhaled slowly. Then he dropped his hands to his knees, leaned back and said, "Probably. I think he believes in Kirov. And he's already in a position of considerable power. Why risk that? Yes, I think he can be trusted. Besides, I can't think of anyone else."

Joanna nodded her endorsement. Dantry seemed alone with his thoughts.

"What's bothering you, Tony?" asked Vyugin. "You don't like the idea?"

Dantry sniffed. "No, I guess not. I'm just picturing how this might go. The three of us meeting with this Potemkin guy, trying to convince him that his counterpart in the prime minister's office is plotting to overthrow his boss. I wish we knew something about how Potemkin and Bulgakov get along."

"Unfortunately, we know next to nothing about that. I can tell you that they come from totally different backgrounds. You know about Bulgakov's KGB background. Well, Potemkin comes from academia."

Joanna's eyes suddenly lighted up. She slapped her forehead and blurted, "My God. I've met him. I was up in Boston for a conference. On Soviet studies. I was still a student. I'll never forget it. It was the most confusing experience of my life." She laughed. He was this young, good-looking professor from Russia. He was very charming, and I remember liking him and at the same time feeling guilty about it because he represented the other side."

Vyugin smiled at the irony of it all. "I suppose he was, and no doubt still is, charming. He taught at the University of Moscow before Kirov asked him to join his staff. Within six months he'd been promoted to chief of staff."

Tony grinned at Joanna. "You just realized it was the same Potemkin?"

"I know. Dense. But I just put two and two together. It must be the same guy."

"What did he teach at Moscow U?" asked Tony.

"Economics. He's studied at the London School of Economics. Spent a year at the Harvard Business School."

"Then he must be a free-market guy."

"One would think so."

"How do you come to know him, Vladimir?"

"After I retired, I took some courses at Moscow University. I ran into him there."

"Were you in any of his courses?"

"No, as a former intelligence agent I'd been invited to participate in a seminar in something called the Soviet Role in 20th Century History." A grin flashed across his normally stoic face. "Not the kind of seminar I would have been invited to—nor permitted to—attend while I was actively involved in my intelligence career. In any event, Gennadi Potemkin came to the seminar to observe. Apparently he was just curious. Anyway, afterward, he introduced himself to me. Told me he was surprised to know that at least one former KGB person had, as he put it, so much depth. Said he never would have believed that a spy could also be a humanist." Vyugin smiled, obviously pleased to be able to relate this experience.

"So we can conclude from this that Potemkin, too, is a humanist," said Joanna.

"I suppose it's a reasonable deduction, though, not conclusive."

"It's all we have to go on," contributed Tony. "We'll have to risk it."

"Let's not lose sight of one thing, though," said Vyugin. "Even if he's a decent, fair-minded person, there's no guarantee he'll be persuaded by what we present to him. He may either not be convinced or suspect that we have some sort of agenda of our own."

"Such as?" It was Joanna asking the question.

"Such as," said Vyugin, "trying to embarrass Kirov by sending him and his staff on—what do you Americans call it?—a wild duck chase."

"Goose," said Dantry, smiling.

"Goose?" Vyugin seemed puzzled.

"It's goose; not duck."

Vyugin processed this a moment, then laughed. "Ah, yes, wild goose chase. Whatever."

"Okay," continued Dantry, "but I would guess that, if we get an audience with this Potemkin, we have a pretty good chance of getting his attention and making him see the threat to his boss is real. Hell, Vladimir, you've got enough evidence."

"Which reminds me, I still have to get this film developed."

"When we get to Moscow."

"We going there today?" asked Joanna.

"I think we should. Noginsk is too close to the compound for comfort," said Vyugin. "Our friends didn't find us last night, but you can bet they'll keep trying. Bulgakov may even send others to help. Let's finish up here and leave within 30 minutes. When we leave the dining room, we should each leave separately. They'll be looking for four of us. Let's not make it too easy for them. And keep an eye out for anyone who looks suspicious. The sooner we leave here, the better. We should also leave our rooms separately when we go down to the car. We've gotten this far safely." As soon as the words had left his mouth he realized that Lubov might not agree with this conclusion. "Sorry, my friend, that was insensitive."

Lubov, who'd remained silent throughout the breakfast conversation, forced a weak smile. "That's all right, it could have been much worse for all of us. And, as you've observed, we're not out of the woods yet."

Chapter 56

Vyugin was the first one to the car. He'd called for it before leaving his room. When he appeared in front of the hotel, the Lada was just pulling up. It had been parked somewhere near the hotel, though he had no idea where. The hotel had no underground garage, so it had to have been somewhere off the premises. No matter, really. The car was ready when he needed it. Far more efficient than he'd come to expect Russian service to be. He felt a small flush of pride. Maybe we are making some progress, he thought.

"I see the car's here," said Dantry as he came out the front door of the hotel. For a brief moment, it seemed to Vyugin that the man behind the wheel looked vaguely familiar. Then, hearing Tony's greeting, he brushed it off as the usual paranoia one feels on a mission.

"Yes, just pulled in. As soon as the others are here we can go. So far, so good."

"Here they are."

"Good." Vyugin tipped the driver as he got out of the Lada. The man broke a quick smile and mumbled his thanks.

It was only 8:30 a.m., and it already warm for this part of Russia.

"Gonna be a scorcher today," said Dantry.

"Yes." Vyugin seemed distracted. He waited patiently for Joanna and Lubov to stow their luggage and get in the car. When they were finally on the street, Dantry noticed that he kept looking into his mirrors.

"Somebody following us?"

The two men in the rented Proton—a recent import from Malaysia —had a smug look on their faces. They'd finally gotten smart. Hearing the words from the speaker they'd placed on the front seat between them confirmed to them just how smart.

Viktor, the shorter of the two men, the one sitting on the right side, couldn't resist a comment.

"Yes, you stupid shits, somebody is following you."

Grigori, the driver, merely smiled. How quickly his cocky partner forgot how inept they themselves had been until they'd finally screwed up their courage and called Sorokin. The gist of the call had been that they'd finally tracked Vyugin, his American friends, and that annoying editor to the Hotel Internationale in Noginsk. Unfortunately their quarries were already in their rooms, *in a* and the hotel was so big it could take all night and much of the *small* next day to find them—since they didn't want to take the more *city?* direct approach and force the information out of the hotel clerks. Sorokin had warned them from the start not to attract unnecessary attention.

Sorokin had then asked how they'd found Vyugin and his companions, and Grigori had told him they'd talked to parking attendants at each of the few hotels in town, describing the Lada and its four occupants. One attendant became very cooperative when shown a handful of rubles. He'd taken them to the parked car and left them with it, whereupon they'd planted a bug under the front seat. Sorokin had been impressed. He'd not thought Grigori or his partner had the imagination or the brains.

"I'm not sure," said another voice from the small speaker. "I wouldn't rule it out. Keep watching."

"Two guys, huh?" It was Dantry.

"Probably. I would imagine it would be the same two I saw last night at the hospital."

"They're three cars back—if it's them."

"Keep an eye on them."

* * *

"They've spotted us," said Viktor. "What should we do?"

"Nothing. They don't know for sure."

"Yeah, they do."

"Well, even if they do, we still have the advantage because we can hear them. We'll follow them till we get out of town. Then we make our move."

Viktor smiled. "I'm gonna enjoy that."

"Yeah, but let's not underestimate them. They're not stupid. Beside, there are four of them and two of us."

"But we have the advantage of surprise. We're not going to negotiate."

"True, we'll do this fast, and get the hell back to the compound."

* * *

Vyugin reached over and tapped Dantry on the shoulder. Before Dantry could say anything, Vyugin put his index finger to his lips, indicating that Tony shouldn't respond verbally. Seeing the light of recognition in Dantry's eyes, he then said, as casually as he could make it, "I need to look at that map."

Vyugin eased the Lada out of the mainstream of traffic and pulled to the curb. He then stared at the flow of traffic they'd been in and saw that Tony had indeed been right about their being followed. The Proton passed by with its two male occupants staring straight ahead.

Meanwhile, Dantry had come up with a piece of paper from the glove box. He handed it and a ballpoint to Vyugin, who proceeded to scribble a quick note. He handed the paper back to Tony.

The scribbled message said, "You were right. They just passed us. Pulled over up ahead. Have to watch what we say. May be bug in car. Get weapons out and be prepared. When we pass them, if they pull out and follow, we can expect an attack. Probably on open road in countryside. Make conversation normal. In the country, I'll find a building or some shelter to make our stand. Be ready."

Dantry passed the note to Joanna and Lubov in the back seat. They read it together and slowly, as the full impact hit them nodded their understanding. Joanna proceeded to pull their three automatic weapons from a duffel bag on the floor by her feet. She gave two to Tony in the front and refamiliarized herself with the Uzi she'd kept in the back seat.

"Okay, I think I've got it now," said Vyugin. "Better keep the map handy, though."

"It's not going anywhere," said Tony, trying to set a nonchalant tone for their pursuers, who very likely were listening.

"It should take us four or five hours to get to Zagorsk,"

"On these roads, it could take a day," quipped Dantry.

For the next ten minutes Vyugin headed for the outskirts of Noginsk. They kept conversation to a minimum. What they did talk about was unrevealing, or at least they hoped so. As they approached the open countryside, both Dantry and Vyugin noticed a car about a half mile behind them. They were pretty sure it was their pursuers. They nodded to each other, and Dantry leaned back over the seat and used hand signals to indicate to Joanna and Lubov that they were being followed. Then Dantry scribbled a note and showed it to them: "Get ready. Be ready to fire, Joanna. It's going to be messy. If we have time, we'll take cover behind a building or something. If not, we fight from the car."

Lubov didn't need this. He looked as if he were going to faint. He'd already gone through more than most people had in a lifetime. And he clearly wasn't a warrior type. Joanna took a deep breath and rechecked the Uzi. She knew how it worked. She'd already used it when they were escaping from the compound. She just wasn't sure she could pull the trigger again when the time came. She swallowed hard and looked out the rear window. The car was closer now, no more than a quarter of a mile.

Vyugin checked the mirror. He wasn't going to try to outrun them. No point. Good way to get killed without a bullet being fired. No, if they had a chance, it was the element of surprise. The very thing their pursuers were no doubt counting on. But what the two men in the car behind them didn't know was that their intended victims had guns. He had to say something now. It would be too obvious if they didn't mention their pursuers any more. Not after having identified them already.

"I think that's them coming up on us."

Dantry did a double take at this; then quickly realized why Vyugin had said it. If there was a bug in the car, the other car already had heard them. If there wasn't, it didn't matter. The important thing was to avoid referring to their guns or their strategy.

"Let's hope they don't have guns or we're goners. Let's just hope they want to talk."

Vyugin raised his eyebrows and said, "Yes, let's hope that."

They'd broken out into the countryside now. The transition from city to country happened suddenly, as it so often did in Europe and Asia. There was virtually no suburbia in many cities on either continent. It had been Vyugin's observation that suburbia as a major phenomenon was an American phenomenon, no doubt engendered by good highways and inexpensive petrol.

The pursuing vehicle was now just a few hundred yards behind them and accelerating rapidly. Vyugin looked over at Dantry to be sure he was prepared for what was about to happen. Tony nodded his readiness. He glanced at the two in the back seat. They met his eyes knowingly.

Up ahead on the right, perhaps three hundred yards, was what appeared to be an abandoned stone farm building. Probably an old barn. The signs of neglect were everywhere: grass growing waist high, missing stones from the walls, and a roof that looked like a sieve. A neglected barbed-wire fence paralleled the road in front of the old barn. As they neared the building, Vyugin noticed that in front of it the fenced sagged nearly to the ground. He knew then what he would do. He poked Dantry on the arm and pointed to the stone barn. Tony nodded.

The car with the two Bulgakov lackeys was no more than a couple hundred yards behind and gaining fast. The stone barn was close now. Vyugin braked, throwing up a cloud of dust behind them. He wrenched the wheel to the right, and the car lurched and skidded until he was able to bring it under control sufficiently to head directly for the low point of the fence. As the Lada made contact with the wire it threw up stones, pebbles, and dust, jolting and bumping through the opening and over the gaping gutter. There was a screeching sound as the sharp, rusted ends of the wire fence caught on the undercarriage of the car, and then it came to a sudden stop in front of the dilapidated old building. Vyugin looked back at the road and saw that their pursuers had flown past, unable to stop in front of the building because they were going so fast. They'd be back.

"Out, everybody," barked Vyugin. Into the building. Fast!"

The doors of the car flew open and the four occupants made a mad scramble for the building. Inside, Vyugin said, "Lubov, you keep down. The rest of us will station ourselves at the two windows. Joanna, break the glass out of that one. The glass in this one is missing."

Dantry suddenly had an idea. "Got an idea. Gonna give these guys at taste of their own element of surprise." He darted out the door.

"Where the hell is he going?" yelled Vyugin.

"He knows what he's doing," said Joanna.

"He better. There's no turning back now. Their car just pulled up. Be ready Joanna, and if they're carrying weapons, shoot before they do."

"Before?… " She was uncomfortable shooting first. What if they weren't intending to shoot?

"Yes, before. You won't get another chance." Vyugin knew what was going on in her mind. He'd seen it before. Survivors couldn't afford to think like that.

The two men were getting out of the car now. They both had automatic rifles—Kalishnikovs. Vyugin opened fire. Joanna followed suit. The two men dived for the ground. They exchanged a few words and began to scramble in opposite directions. They would attack the building from both sides. Obviously they hadn't been hit.

Vyugin surveyed the situation. The barn had two windows facing the road. These were the two windows he and Joanna were manning. There was another window in the rear wall of the building and the one door in the side wall. The fourth wall was solid stone. He and Joanna would somehow have to cover all three openings to the outside, since they could no longer see where the two gunmen were. The advantage was once again with the enemy.

"Joanna, cover the rear window. I'll watch the front and the door. Let's hope Tony isn't caught by surprise." As he was speaking, a gun barrel was inserted near the sill of the doorway.

A staccato burst of fire reverberated throughout the hollow interior of the building. Joanna felt a stinging sensation on her forearm. She looked down. A bloody line about two inches long was forming, but it appeared that it was only a superficial wound—much like the one on her ear. She aimed her Uzi in the direction of the doorway and let loose several rounds. There was no one there. She turned to check the rear window. As she did a gun barrel came into sight. She was about to fire when she heard two short bursts. Vyugin had covered her. Someone just outside the window swore in Russian.

Vyugin realized that they couldn't survive in the barn for long. One of these times, the gunmen would guess right and score a hit. Vyugin forced himself to scan between the doorway and the front window, counting on Joanna to cover the rear window. But he knew he'd have to make a preemptive countermove soon, or their attackers would win the deadly game they were playing.

Another blast, this time from one of the front windows. Their attackers were smart. They kept their faces out of the line of fire as they stuck their gun barrels into the windows and doorway. They couldn't be accurate, but they were obviously counting on getting lucky while at the same time minimizing their own exposure. Even if they didn't score a direct hit, there was a good chance a round would ricochet off the stone walls and hit home anyway.

Suddenly he heard a thunk, followed by the sound of something solid rolling across the stone floor. He whirled and saw what it was.

"Grenade!" yelled Joanna. Hesitating for only a second, she bent down to pick it up and with one smooth motion hurled it out the rear window. It had barely cleared the sill when it exploded with a resounding earsplitting blast. A solid wall of air knocked her off her feet and onto her back on the hard floor.

Vyugin unleashed a series of bursts from his Kalishnikov, first through the doorway; then through the front windows. He then kneeled down to check on Joanna. As he did so, he heard two short bursts from an automatic rifle followed by a scream from somewhere behind the building. Joanna's heart stopped. Had Tony been hit? Was this how it was all going to end? She stepped toward the back window and was about to peer out, when Vyugin grabbed her and yanked her out of the way.

"Good God, do you want to get yourself killed?"

"Tony—"

"You don't know. Stay alert. This'll be over soon enough."

"Hey guys. Can I come in?" It was Dantry, just outside the doorway.

"You got 'em," said Vyugin. "Good work."

"Jesus, Tony," cried Joanna. "I thought you were dead."

Dantry stepped into the barn. "Not this time. Our two friends, though. That's a different story.'

"Let's get out of here," said Vyugin.

Before leaving, Dantry pulled the gunmen's car off the highway and parked it behind the barn so it wouldn't be noticed from the road. He and Vyugin searched the vehicle for any evidence or information they might find useful. They also wanted to be sure there was nothing that mentioned any of them. They found the radio receiver on the front seat. The only other thing they found was a notebook with Vyugin and Lubov's name in it. Dantry grabbed the radio and Vyugin stuffed the notebook in his pocket. They could examine the notebook more closely later. The important thing now was to get clear of the barn and the two bodies behind it.

Chapter 57

"Have you heard anything from the two men you sent out?" asked Bulgakov.

"I spoke with Grigori a few hours ago," said Sorokin. "They found Vyugin and the others."

"And?"

"They know what hotel they're in, and they know where their car is parked. They've placed a listening device inside the car, and they plan to follow them out of Noginsk. Once they're in the country, they'll kill them. Better not to do it in Noginsk."

"Good, at least it's a good plan. You sure these two won't bungle the job?"

"They're good men. Consider it done." As he said this, Sorokin prayed to the ghost of Lenin that the two clowns wouldn't screw up the assignment. In his opinion, Grigori was fairly competent, but Viktor was basically an idiot. Strong as an ox, but dense as an oak tree. He sighed and smiled confidently for the benefit of his boss.

* * *

Joanna's spirits had soared in the immediate aftermath of their harrowing experience back at the crumbling stone barn as she realized how close they'd come to being killed. The rush of elation had come from the sudden relief she'd felt as she realized that Tony had saved them all when he killed the two gunmen. If

Tony hadn't gotten them first, the gunmen assuredly would have killed all four of them.

But her elation had quickly dissipated as she considered what Tony had done. She'd gone there before with her thoughts—a number of times. She'd always known that Tony had killed—or might have killed—people in his past line of work, but to be with him as he'd actually eliminated two lives somehow made it all too real.

She hadn't gone behind the barn to look at the two bodies. There'd been no point, and besides, she hadn't the stomach for it. It would have made what she already knew even more indisputable. By not seeing the corpses, what Tony had done was somehow a little less real.

She knew it was unfair to Tony to judge him like this. Good God, he'd save their lives. She was going to have to get over this. Damn! Here she was, halfway around the world, with one of those rare men who actually make a difference. She shook her head disdainfully. How loosely people use that expression. But Dantry really was one of those rare individuals. Vyugin, too, she'd come to believe. Hell, Lubov might not be as physical, but he, too, had put his life on the line to defend what he believed in. So here she was, associating with three men of real substance, and she was shrinking like a moralizing academic because these three men had done more than merely curse or bemoan a situation they didn't like. They'd actually taken action.

* * *

As they crossed under the outer ring road around Moscow, Vyugin broke the silence.

"First I want to take the film to my friend to be developed. Then I think we should check into our little hotel off the Arbat. We can clean up and leave most of this stuff in our hiding place. Then we'll eat and pick up the pictures."

"And then we go see Potemkin?" asked Dantry.

"Yes, then we go see Potemkin. I'll need to call him first. Let's hope he's in."

"And let's hope his boss is in, or at least reachable."

"Yes."

* * *

"Have you heard anything from your two men?" asked Bulgakov anxiously. He wouldn't relax until he had confirmation that they'd finished their job.

Sorokin had dreaded the question. He'd been trying desperately for an hour-and-a-half to make contact with Grigori or Viktor.

"Not yet. They're probably in the middle of the assignment right now. I should hear from them soon. I told you, they're quite reliable."

"Be that as it may, I want to know personally. As soon as you hear something, I want to know. Even if you have to interrupt me. Clear?"

"Very clear, sir. Just as soon as I hear, you'll hear."

"It's even more important now that these people be eliminated. I've decided to move up everything. Whether we succeed in killing that I.M.F. loan or not, we're going to start the civil unrest next week. We cannot afford to let too much time go by before we act."

"But you felt that killing that loan was so important."

"It would help a lot, but we can't put all of our eggs in one —, how do the English say it?"

"One basket."

"Yes, one basket. One way or the other, we must proceed with our plans. If the loan fails to go through, that will be a big help. The new team we sent to the States should take care of that. But even if they fail, and for some unforeseen reason the loan passes, we must still proceed with our plans." He paused to see how Sorokin was accepting this. Sorokin nodded, though Bulgakov couldn't tell for sure whether he was agreeing or simply indicating that he was following the conversation. "I'm counting on your help, Anatoly. Together we can rule the world."

Anatoly Sorokin was not a timid man. His ruthless ambition was apparent to all who came in contact with him. But despite his self-aggrandizing character, he loved his country. In the last analysis, he wanted what was best for Russia. Needless to say, he wanted to have a lot to say about how Russia was run. That's why he was involved with Bulgakov's movement in the first place. But from the start he'd been under the impression that Bulgakov was leading the cabal in order to put Malenkov in power and get Kirov out. The general understanding had always been that Russia needed strong leadership to bring it back to its glory days. There had never been talk about ruling the world. And there had never been talk about Bulgakov being the one to replace Kirov. Well, that wasn't exactly true. In the unlikely case that Malenkov wouldn't or couldn't accept the presidency, it had been generally understood that Bulgakov would be the logical next choice. But virtually everyone had just assumed that Malenkov would want the top job. After all, wasn't he behind all this?

"Rule the world, sir? Isn't that a bit ambitious? I thought our goal was to get Russia back on its feet?"

Bulgakov gave his lieutenant a look of disdain. "Listen, Anatoly. An opportunity like this only comes around once every few generations. History has been kind to us. It has placed us squarely in the middle of a situation thousands of men of ambition around the world would kill for. We're here and the time is ripe. You and I, with the help of our cadre of supporters, have a chance to make history. You can be the second most powerful man in Russia. Someday, someday soon, I believe, you can be the second most powerful man in the world. But we must act swiftly. These situations don't present themselves for long. Conditions can change overnight. Hell, the economy could improve here and where would our opportunity be?"

Sorokin was too ambitious to say what he was thinking—that if the economy improved, Russia would be better off and maybe there'd be no need for a *coup d'état*. But as much as he questioned Bulgakov's newly revealed motives, the thought of losing the opportunity to gain what until now he would have considered unimaginable power persuaded Sorokin to keep his thoughts to himself. Sorokin was a pragmatist above all else.

Bulgakov continued. "Remember, Anatoly, I want to know about the fate of Vyugin and his associates as soon as you hear."

The meeting was over. Sorokin wilted as he left the room. He wasn't at all as confident as he'd been a few hours ago. The success of Grigori and Viktor's mission could have a direct impact on his own future.

Chapter 58

"The pictures are better than I'd hoped for," said Vyugin. "See for yourselves." He handed the prints to Joanna.

It was true, thought Dantry as he poured through the stack of prints that Joanna had passed on to him.

"Yeah, most of them are clear and recognizable. I'm assuming they're recognizable anyway. You know these people better than I do."

"Zlotov is very clear to anyone who knows him. So is Marshall Suchinov, and Bulgakov and Sorokin. Yes, there are at least six or seven people that I recognize here. Some of the others I don't know, but I'm sure we can find someone who does. Potemkin will probably know most of them. These are good. Very good."

"These will only be convincing, though, in conjunction with the digital recordings you have of Bulgakov. Without the audio, Bulgakov and the others could make up some bullshit story about being on retreat or at some kind of think tank or something."

"True. Taken together they become convincing evidence. By themselves—especially the photos—they are less convincing. Fortunately, we have both." Vyugin smiled.

Joanna said, "I'm impressed. You were a one-man intelligence team back there."

"We did it together," beamed Vyugin. "Besides, the job is far from over. Did you call that detective in the States?"

"I spoke to Markowitz. He's the guy who gave me a break. Good guy. Lucky he was on duty when I called. He was just coming on duty. Anyway, I told him that two more operatives had been sent to kill Chandler. He'd better warn him and arrange for protection. He tried to quiz me about how I knew all this. I told him he'd have to trust me, and we almost came to blows on the phone. Finally left it that I'd fill him in back in the States. He didn't like it, but he didn't have much leverage. Frankly, he couldn't afford not to take me seriously."

Lubov, who typically had laid back and kept his own counsel, now spoke up.

"May I make a suggestion?'"

"Of course," said Vyugin.

"Perhaps we should take what we have to the papers instead of to Kirov or his chief of staff. By giving this to them, we place them in a difficult position. If we are able to persuade them to take action, Bulgakov and the generals in his cabal could turn it around to make it look as if Kirov, himself, is pulling some kind of political plot to get rid of his competition. And if Kirov does nothing, he'll know he and his government are doomed. His only chance of defeating Bulgakov is to put together a coalition of his own supporters before he takes action. This would take time. Probably too much time. Bulgakov may have already started his riots before they are ready to act." He paused to study his three listeners to see how they were taking this.

Dantry said, "Makes sense." Vyugin and Joanna nodded their encouragement.

"Continue," said Vyugin.

Lubov took a deep breath before continuing. "I'm pretty sure I can get my paper to run a story, but I'd like to get at least one Russian-language paper to run it, too. I'd like to try *Pravda*. Since the break-up, they've been the voice of the opposition. They're always trying to keep the politicians honest. There are others we could try, but, as I said, we're running out of time. I know the managing editor over there. We could start with him."

"Won't they wonder why a competing paper wants to give them a story?" asked Joanna.

Lubov smiled for the first time since his awful experience out at the plotters' compound. "Very insightful, miss Barbeau. Yes, they will think something funny is going on. I will have to convince them that national security is at stake." His expression turned serious again. "I'll also have to convince my own editor-in-chief that we should share this story. We don't make it a practice to help our competition. But I think I can do it. I think we must try." He looked up and asked, "How do you feel about this?"

"I like it," said Vyugin. "How about you two?"

"Makes sense to me," said Dantry, repeating his initial sentiment. "Joanna?"

"I like it, too, but—"

"Yes, what is it?" asked Vyugin.

"As long as we're considering alternatives, shouldn't we be thinking of going to the police with this?"

"Vyugin's mouth curled into a smile. "No, Joanna. I don't think that would be such a good idea."

"You mean the police are in on it, too?"

"Not necessarily. But I would expect them to be sympathetic. Most of the police in this country think we need a firmer hand at the top. Both Malenkov and Bulgakov would appeal to them. In fairness, I'm sure there are policemen who would see the danger in handing over the country to such men, but they're probably in the minority. I wouldn't take the chance. I think going to the newspapers is our best bet."

"Okay, let's do it," said Dantry. Then turning to Lubov. "Can your editor-in-chief make this decision?"

"I think so. He's very close to the owners. He may call them to tell them what he's going to do, but they trust him." Lubov hesitated before adding, "I don't particularly like him, but that's not important."

"You don't like him? Should we know why?"

"Just a difference in how we go about things. It's probably me as much as it is him. This is much bigger than our differences in style and personality."

Dantry considered this for a moment and then proceeded. "Are the owners Kirov supporters?'

"Yes. That will help."

"How about *Pravda*? Who do they support?"

"They lean toward Kirov, but they like to pick at all of them. I suppose they'd say he's the least bad of the major politicians. Under the Soviets, of course, they were a puppet paper. Whatever the Kremlin wanted said, they said it. Today, though, they like to think of themselves as the voice of truth. They're a good paper now. But neither *Pravda* nor the *Moscow Times* will want to attack Bulgakov unless they're damned certain of their facts, because he's Malenkov's right hand man and Malenkov is no one to be trifled with, nor is Suchinov, for that matter."

"Well, we have the facts and the proof," said Vyugin.

"Yes, that's true, but sometimes that's not enough. Even with the facts, my editor and the owners are going to need courage to take on Malenkov and these other guys. And so will the people over at *Pravda*. They have to be willing to risk everything. If they guess wrong, they could lose their jobs—or worse."

Chapter 59

"Are you sure it's them?"

"Yessir," said Boris. "Both dead. They've been identified by our own people."

Sorokin put his hand to his head and frowned.

"This is turning into a fucking nightmare. They were supposed to take care of Vyugin and his accomplices, and instead, they're dead and those traitors got away. What happened?"

"They were shot. Both of them. They were found behind some old barn on the road from Noginsk to Moscow. There was evidence of a lot of gunfire. Must've been a hell of battle."

Sorokin squinted and frowned. The implications of this were already beginning to set in. "Do we know where Vyugin and the three others went? No, I don't suppose you do."

"No, sir, they found tire tracks next to the building. It looked as if they pulled out in the direction of Moscow, but that's all we know. In fact, before this happened Viktor radioed us that they'd overheard the fugitives say something about going to Zagorsk. Why would they go to Zagorsk?"

Sorokin sneered. "They wouldn't. It was a ruse to deceive us. They probably went to Moscow. If they want to hurt us, that's where they'd go. There's nothing in Zagorsk. All right, you can go.

But let me know if you learn anything else—immediately. Now go."

This was really bad. He was convinced Vyugin would go to Moscow to do what he could to undermine Bulgakov's plan. Sorokin dreaded telling Bulgakov what he'd just heard. He wracked his brain for an idea—some way he could turn this around before Bulgakov learned about what had happened. If he only knew what Vyugin and his friends intended to do. Would they go to the police? Would they go directly to Kirov? Would they go to the media? There was no way he could cover all these possibilities before Bulgakov found out about Grigori and Viktor. Right now he wished he were in the middle of the Atlantic ocean on an island. Somewhere, anywhere but here. When he got his hands on Vyugin and the other three, they'd wish they'd never fucked with him. Their death would be inevitable, but nice and slow—slow so they'd be aware of what was happening to them. Slow, so they could reflect on who they were dealing with.

Chapter 60

Igor Godin was the editor-in-chief of the *Moscow Times*. He was a bear of a man. Everything about him was oversized. His shiny dome-like head shone in the late-afternoon light streaming in through the massive windows. He was the sort of man who, by his very presence, took over a room.

"Good God, man. What a fright you've given us. We've had the police looking for days. Your wife has been frantic. Did you call her?"

"Yes, I've already spoken to her. I'm going home after I leave here."

"Tell me, man, what happened. First tell me who your friends are here; then tell me what happened. I hope you don't mind if I record this."

* * *

Godin leaned back in his seat and slowly expelled the breath he'd taken in as the full impact of Lubov's story hit him. He'd let Lubov talk for twenty minutes without interruption. When Lubov told him about his finger and showed him the bandaged stump, Godin gasped in shock. Vyugin, Dantry, and Barbeau remained silent during the telling. Now Godin began to talk.

"You say you have evidence?"

"Yes, we can show you now."

"I think you'd better."

* * *

"These pictures, together with the voice recordings, are devastating. I hope you have copies of all this."

"Not yet, we just got into town. We will."

"We can make copies here while we're talking. Give me what you have, and I'll have someone take care of it while we're talking." He rose and stood waiting for Vyugin to give him the pictures and the digital voice recorder.

Vyugin hesitated. "We can do it right after we leave here. Don't bother."

"No bother. It'll save you a trip. Come, give me what you have. I'll have Tasha do it, Alex. She can be trusted."

Lubov nodded. "Yes, I suppose that would be all right. Make sure she tells no one." He gave Godin the pictures and the voice recorder. "She'll have to record from this to another recorder. I hope she has something that she can use."

"We have everything here. You know that, Alex. Please, please, everyone. Talk among yourselves for a moment. I'll be right back." He left the room.

Three minutes later Godin returned beaming. "It's being taken care of. Now, back to our discussion. You think we should run a story on this, I assume?"

"Definitely," said Lubov. "We had considered going directly to Kirov or to the police, but thought better about it. It could take Kirov or his staff too long to muster support among their own people. The police very likely are Bulgakov supporters."

"I agree with your thinking. Far better that we run a story."

"When will you run this story?" asked Dantry.

"In tomorrow's edition, of course."

"Can you give us some idea of the tone of this story?" asked Vyugin.

"The tone? The tone will be just as I have gotten it from you," he said unctuously. "It will underscore the seriousness of the threat of this cabal. Don't worry, it will be just what the doctor ordered." He leaned back with a satisfied expression on his round face. Then, as if it had suddenly occurred to him, he turned to Lubov. "By the way, Alex, take as long as you need before returning to work. I realize you've been through a terrible trauma."

"I'll be in tomorrow."

"As you wish. Now, can I do anything else for you people?"

Something was bothering Lubov. Was it the cavalier attitude of Godin? Was it that he hadn't brought other editors in to the meeting? Was it that he hadn't seemed as shocked by their revelations as he should have been? He decided to act on his intuition.

"Before we leave, I think I'll visit the men's room."

"Yes, of course. We'll wait for you here," said Godin.

* * *

Lubov walked swiftly past the men's room and headed for a small office diagonally across the building from the small conference room he'd just left. He'd been one of the first people hired at the paper, so the layout was as familiar as his cramped apartment where he and his family lived. Yet today, he felt like an outsider visiting the paper for the first time.

The door to the office was ajar. He peeked in and saw that Tasha was working busily on something. She was always busy. Tasha had something of an all-purpose job at the paper handling multimedia and anything to do with communications. She knew everything there was to know about cameras, computers, scanners —not to mention audio and video recorders. If a photo was of such bad quality that you could barely make out the subject, Tasha could work her magic and turn it into a usable print. If something needed scanning, she did it. If someone brought in an old reel-to-reel tape, she had the equipment to transcribe it either to cassette or digital format. She was a whiz—a person the paper could not do without. She'd come to the *Times* the same year as Lubov—1992—and they'd quickly become fast friends. Lubov knocked and pushed the door in a few inches.

"You busy?"

Startled, she turned, and seeing who it was, winked and said, "What's on your mind? Hey, where've you been? Haven't seen you around here the last few days?"

"It's a long story, love. Tell you about it when there's more time. Say, what'd you do with those pictures and that recorder Godin brought in?"

A puzzled look came over her plain, but pleasant face. "When was this? Godin hasn't given me anything but the back of his head in weeks. He doesn't have time for us peasants."

"You sure? Could he have dropped something off that you missed? He just came back here a little while ago. Less than an hour."

She quickly scanned the small room, moving things on her work surface, checking the top of her desk, and even the floor. "No, if it was here, I'd know it. Wish I could help you, Alex."

"I wish you could, too. Guess I made a mistake. Thanks for checking, love. Gotta run."

Lubov didn't like the picture he was getting. Godin had been a recent hire at the *Moscow Times*. The rumors had it that he consorted with a lot of military types, though Lubov had never actually seen him with these people. He was a good editor, a well-organized manager, and generally fair-minded when it came to dealing with the staff. Still, Lubov never felt that his boss shared the same commitment to the paper's democratic editorial policy that he and the other editors did. It wasn't anything you could put your finger on. He generally adhered to the paper's editorial philosophy, though on more than one occasion Lubov thought that he'd let opportunities go by that he should have jumped at. And there were times when he actually seemed to lean in the direction of the military hard-liners. Nevertheless, the paper was making money, and most of the mail it received indicated that the readers were pleased. At least most of the mail he saw.

But Godin had just lied to them. If he hadn't taken the pictures and the voice recorder to Tasha, where had he taken them? Lubov intended to find out.

Chapter 61

As he approached the conference room where he'd left his
associates and Godin, Lubov felt a tightening in his gut. He wasn't
the type of man who enjoyed confrontations. He wasn't a highly
aggressive type. At 52 years of age, he knew himself well, and he
knew that confrontation was not his thing. Intellectually he knew
that half his gender—maybe more than half—had more than
enough testosterone, but emotionally he just couldn't fathom why
people couldn't resolve their differences through peaceful
discussion of issues. It was not that he was afraid to defend what
he believed in. It was just that he'd found that with reasonable
people it didn't usually have to be unpleasant. Now he'd see just
how reasonable he himself was.

As he entered the room, Godin, Vyugin and Dantry rose.
Joanna started to get up. Lubov motioned with his hands for them
to keep their seats.

"Not yet. We're not finished here." Then he turned to
Godin and stared him in the eyes with a vehemence the editor-in-
chief had never before seen in his mild-mannered second-in-
command. "Igor, this is painful for me to say, but you lied to us."

Godin's face turned red. Lubov had never spoken this way
to him. For that matter, no one had. He was fuming. His anger,
however, was tempered somewhat by guilt. "What in God's name
are you talking about, Alex? Have you lost your mind?"

"I just spoke with Tasha. She said you didn't give her the
pictures or the recorder. You told us you did."

"She wasn't in her office. I left it there for her. I intended to talk to her as soon as you left."

Lubov put his hands to his head in a frantic gesture. "My God, why are you lying? That's simply not true. Tasha looked for the pictures and recorder. I was with her when she did it. There was nothing there."

Godin thought fast. "Then someone must have taken them. I'll look into it."

"You lying son-of-a-bitch," roared Lubov uncharacteristically. "I can't believe this. I respected you, Igor. How can you lie like this? You must be working for that power-mad monster Bulgakov. What the hell did you do with our pictures?"

Godin seemed confused. He had not bargained for this. While he was a competent newspaper administrator, he had no experience with international intrigue. He'd been found out by an employee and several people who seemed more experienced in dealing with this sort of thing than he was. He was clearly out of his league.

Vyugin spoke before the editor-in-chief could respond. His tone was ominous. "We are now going to accompany you as you retrieve our material. Believe me, sir, we are not people you want to trifle with. Do I make myself clear?"

Godin looked down at his feet. "Yes, perfectly."

"Good, then let's go find our pictures. By the way, do the owners of the paper know of your association with Bulgakov and his plot?"

"It is not a plot. It is a plan to bring order to a chaotic nation. Russia cannot go on this way."

"You can rationalize it anyway you want. You didn't answer my question. Do the owners know that you're helping Bulgakov?"

"No." Godin's answer was barely a whisper.

"I see. I imagine they'd find that interesting information. We can talk about that later. Now, take us to the pictures."

What little color was left in Godin's face drained, leaving a sallow, frightened countenance. The shaking shell of a man slowly rose and headed for the door.

Less than a minute later he led them into his office.

"What a surprise," said Dantry. "They're not lost after all. They're right here in your office." Godin pulled a ring of keys from his pocket. He sorted through what appeared to be close to a dozen keys, and finally unlocked the door to a closet directly across from his desk. He reached up to a shelf that was slightly above eye level and pulled down two large manila envelopes.

"Here."

Vyugin opened each envelope, one at a time to make sure everything was there. When he was satisfied, he looked at Godin and said, "What did you hope to gain by collaborating with Bulgakov? A minister's position in his cabinet. Director of communications for his new government? What?"

"I believe in what he's doing. I would do it for no reward other than the satisfaction of seeing him bring order and respect back to Russia."

"Yes, yes. But what did he offer you?"

Godin sighed resignedly. "A cabinet position. But that is not why I got involved."

Vyugin stared the broken man in the eyes and spoke in a measured, frosty voice.

"I advise you not to inform Bulgakov or any of his people that we've come to see you. Ignore that advice at your own peril. Good-bye Mr. Godin."

Chapter 62

"Do you think Godin will tell Bulgakov about our visit?" asked Joanna. "After your threat."

"Of course he will." Vyugin smiled and proceeded to explain, "You probably wonder why I bothered to threaten him at all. It was to make him fear us, of course, but I don't think it will frighten him enough for him to keep his mouth shut. He probably fears Bulgakov as much or more than he fears us. Still, he *will* fear us now, and we may need him again. If he believes we are not to be trifled with, it will be a bit easier for us. And then, if Lubov here should want to return to his job, I think he'll let you—especially if he thinks your friends want you to work. If I'm any judge of character, our Mr. Godin is ambitious, but no hero. He can be intimidated. And don't forget, he still has to wonder if you or one of us will tell his owners about his part in this illegal plot."

"I agree," said Dantry. "Keep the pressure on and there's no telling how useful that creep might be. Okay, so now what, Vladimir? We just lost our newspaper."

"Now we go to *Pravda*. You know what Pravda means, don't you, Joanna?"

"Truth, I think."

"Right. A big joke back in the Soviet days. Today, let's hope it is aptly named." He glanced at Lubov, and became serious. "You don't look so happy, my friend. What's troubling you?"

"Aside from my finger?"

Vyugin looked contrite, "Forgive my insensitivity. Yes, aside from your finger?"

"I'm not sure I want to go back to my job at the paper."

"I can understand that. Still, I think it might be good if you did. I know it will be unpleasant, but more for him than for you. Besides, you can keep an eye on him."

Lubov looked dejected. Vyugin caught this and said,

"I don't think he'll be there for long, anyway. What do you say? You've already gone way out on a limb for Russia. You can do this, too. No?"

"Yes, you're right. I'll give it a try."

"Good, so let us pay a visit to *Pravda*."

Chapter 63

The trim, athletic figure of Yevgeny Ivanov presented a stark contrast to the appearance of most male Muscovites, who somehow seemed unconcerned about fashion. At well over six-feet, his full head of lustrous black hair was parted just to the left of center and combed almost directly back. It reminded Dantry of the dashing and dissolute males of the American twenties he'd seen in old movies. That Ivanov was conscious of his appearance was manifest by the fashionable Western-style suit he was wearing. And he was clearly proud of the fire-engine red suspenders he wore over his graphite-gray, neatly pressed dress shirt.

Ivanov was the editor-in-chief of *Pravda*, the newspaper that had so enthusiastically earned its reputation as a house organ for Soviet communism. Since the break-up, though, the paper had zealously cultivated a reputation of seeking out corruption and scandal wherever it found it. Russians read it to get the inside story on things they knew were wrong. *Pravda* told them why.

Despite his sartorial flair, Ivanov's smile was warm and seemed genuine as he greeted his four visitors.

"Please don't construe this as resentment on my part, but you're hitting me at a bad time. Deadline and all that." He smiled again. "But I wouldn't have missed this for anything. Would you like to know why?"

"We're all ears," said Dantry. Ivanov seemed puzzled. So did Vyugin and Lubov, for that matter. Dantry realized why, and added by way of explanation, "It's an American expression. Means we can't wait to hear why."

"I see," grinned Ivanov, still not certain that he did, but not wishing to pursue it further. He liked being the one in command, and anything that even hinted at his not knowing something that he probably should know, made him uncomfortable. "Very well, I'll tell you why. I received a telephone call not long ago from Yuri Bulgakov, Mr. Malenkov's chief of staff. He told me that I might be contacted by Lubov here, plus a Mr. Vyugin and two Americans. He said these people—you people obviously—were some kind of political fanatics who should be avoided at all cost, if they attempted to tell me a story about some very upstanding men in the government and the military. I said to him, why would they do that? He more or less said that you were all a bunch of lunatics. He said that he and some of his associates had had a very unfortunate meeting with these four people—you four—and they had gone away with a lot of misunderstandings and crazy ideas." He paused and eyed his four visitors. "So you are these crazy people." He laughed.

"And did you believe him?" asked Lubov.

"I am not inclined to believe much that Mr. Bulgakov says. He is known to be deceitful and vicious. Still, other than you, Lubov, I don't know you, either. For that matter, I've never met Lubov in person. We've spoken on the phone a few times at most." His expression softened. "But I do know that your reputation is good. You are well respected in the profession. Anyway, you see that I have been forewarned about all of you. I suppose it would be good to hear your side of this. Why don't we make ourselves comfortable. Would you like some tea?" As an afterthought, in deference to the two Americans present, he added, "Or coffee?"

* * *

A half hour later, after Lubov, with contributions from Vyugin, Dantry, and Barbeau, told their story, he pushed back from the conference table.

"So there you have it. Our side of the story."

Ivanov's expression was grave. The impact of what he'd just heard had obviously given him cause for serious concern. Dantry wondered to himself what that concern might be. Was

Ivanov concerned for the health of his country or was he concerned that four "lunatics" were running around giving Bulgakov a bad name? He decided to find out.

"What do you think?"

Ivanov smiled. "What do I think? I think it's time we put that bastard in his place. Kirov may not be perfect, but he's a decent man. Clearly, Mr. Bulgakov would like to become the latest in a long line of Russian dictators. I have felt this about him for several years. Now, I have proof. The man is a snake. We shall expose him in tomorrow's edition. Unless you have some objection." He made eye contact with each of his guests. "I thought not. Good, then, it's decided. I need the four of you to spend a little more time here, though. If you don't mind, I'd like for you to repeat what you've just told me to my editorial board. One, to inform them, and two, because some of them will be writing stories about this. Can you spare another hour or so?"

"That will not be a problem," said Vyugin.

Ivanov started to leave the room, then stopped and spoke to Lubov. "I imagine it will be difficult for you to go back to your job at the *Times*." Lubov nodded, and Ivanov continued. "I think we might be able to find something for you here. Perhaps not the managing editor's job—I have a fine managing editor now—but I think we might find something suitable for your talents, something that could grow into a very interesting position. Would you be interested in talking when this is over?"

Lubov beamed. "I would indeed."

"Good. But as you well know, this isn't over."

Chapter 64

"Yes, Anatoly, what is it now? I hope you have something that will make me happy. Lately you've brought me nothing but bad news." Bulgakov's tone was menacing. Sorokin, a man who had more than once made other men tremble in terror, found himself tensing up. Bulgakov had been known to act impulsively when he wasn't pleased. A story had circulated a few years back about the time when one of Bulgakov's assistants had brought him bad news and he'd lashed out with the butt of his gun against the side of the poor man's jaw. On more than one occasion he'd sent subordinates off to remote posts because of his displeasure. The Soviet days were behind them now, but Bulgakov was the same man. Sorokin tried not to let his apprehension and resentment show as he responded to his boss.

"They've shown up in Moscow. They went to the *Moscow Times*, Lubov's paper, and told their story to Godin." A smile flickered across his hard, angular face. "Stupid bastard. Lubov's been working for him for over a year and apparently had no idea Godin is one of us. Godin's a good man. Called me as soon as they left."

"And how did they leave? What did Godin tell them?"

Sorokin was afraid Bulgakov would ask this. "Well, that's where Godin was stupid. He took their pictures—said he'd have them copied. Turns out Lubov is not as stupid as I thought he was. He excused himself to go to the toilet. Used that as an excuse to check up on what Godin had told him about the pictures. He found that Godin had stashed them away."

"So what. All he had to do was tell Lubov that he hadn't gotten to it yet. That he was going to have them copied as soon as they left. I don't see the problem."

"Godin made it a problem. When he took the pictures he said he was taking them to a woman who took care of such things for the paper. She was only a few offices away. Lubov went to her and asked her about the pictures Godin had given her. She said Godin hadn't given her anything. When Lubov and the others confronted Godin, he produced the shots from his office closet. Really badly done. When I spoke with Godin, he was a nervous wreck. Man doesn't have the nerves for this. At least he called me."

Bulgakov rolled his eyes. "Anatoly, I told you I needed good news." He closed his eyes and drew in a long breath. Then he exploded. "Is this what you call good news? Do you realize that we're losing control of this whole operation?"

"I don't think it's that bad."

"Oh you don't, eh? Tell me, do you have any idea where these four troublemakers are going next?"

"My guess would be another newspaper. Most likely a prominent Russian-language paper."

Bulgakov's eyes lit up. "Yes, I think you might be right."

Chapter 65

"By order of the prime minister. You must stop the presses until this has been resolved," snapped Sorokin, knowing as he spoke that what he was doing would put his career in serious jeopardy. Hell, it was more than his career. He could go to prison for this—if it backfired. Back in the Soviet days, there would have been no one to answer to, but today, as chaotic as the Russian government sometimes got, there was still the risk—a very serious risk—that he would be called upon by someone in the government to justify his actions. As screwed up as things were in Russia, you couldn't just go threatening newspapers the way you used to. The only way he'd survive this, he realized, was if Bulgakov were successful in pulling off his *coup d'état*. And Sorokin was far less certain that that would happen than he was just a few days ago. The man he'd just given the order to didn't appear to be shaking in his boots. Sorokin had just met the man and already he hated him, dressed like some Western dandy, all smug and superior.

"I'm afraid you're a few minutes late," smiled Ivanov. "The trucks have already left the printing plant with the papers. They're being delivered around the city as we speak. They're also being delivered to airports for distribution around the country and into Europe. So you see, you're a bit too late. Pity isn't it?" He was clearly enjoying this, as he paused to see the effect on the visiting storm trooper. When he continued, his voice was more serious.

"I want you to know, though, that I wouldn't have stopped the presses for you anyway. You can tell the prime minister to go to hell. In fact, I think our readers would love to hear about how Mr. Malenkov, the man who would be president, has resorted to the methods of the Communists back in the Soviet days. Yes, that will make a good story for tomorrow's early edition."

Sorokin winced at Ivanov's words, knowing as he did that Malenkov was not involved in Bulgakov's plans to take over the government. Now Sorokin had a bigger problem. Malenkov would come down hard on Bulgakov when the story in *Pravda* reached him. When tomorrow's *Pravda* named Malenkov as the man behind it all, the game would be over. Hell, If Malenkov didn't get Sorokin, Bulgakov would on his way down.

Sorokin made one last effort. He'd try a different approach —tact—an approach with which he had very little experience.

"I'm sorry, please forgive me for being heavy handed. I was wrong. Please let me explain why you must help us with this."

Ivanov rolled his eyes. "This ought to be good."

Sorokin, who had little sensitivity for irony, proceeded. "These four people are making outrageous and unpatriotic statements about respected men in the Russian government. The things they have said are scandalous and defamatory. If you print this—I realize that one story is already on its way to the news vendors—it could do irreparable harm to the reputations of these good men. But, if in tomorrow's edition you could say something to the effect that the information given you for today's story was inaccurate, you could still salvage the reputations of these good men. I know that you consider yourself a good journalist, so I appeal to your sense of justice, sir."

"This is insulting, Sorokin. It is not just on the word of these four people that today's story is based. It is also based on the recorded words of your Mr. Bulgakov. His words, sir. His!" He paused to let this sink in. "And don't forget the photographs. They speak a thousand words themselves. Don't talk to me about justice when you defend this kind of treachery on the part of the people you work for. You should be ashamed of yourself. I've seen enough of you, sir. Please leave."

Sorokin's nostrils flared and his cheeks flushed. He did all he could from strangling this arrogant holier-than-though intellectual. He knew if he didn't leave, he would do something violent.

"You haven't heard the last of me, Ivanov," he roared as he turned to leave. "Keep your back to the walls."

"Don't threaten me, Sorokin. Your ship is sinking, and if I were you, I'd reach for a life raft."

Chapter 66

Antonin Kirov put the early edition of Pravda down on the side of his highly polished desk. After reading the lead story in the paper he'd summoned his chief of staff to his office. Kirov poked a finger at the story as he spoke.

"You've read this, of course, Gennadi?"

"Yessir." Potemkin's expression remained impassive.

"And what do you think we should do about it?"

"I just read it, sir. I've been considering the possibilities."

"Yes, yes. Tell me how you see those possibilities.

"At first blush, it would seem that you should take immediate and forceful action. It would show that you can't be trifled with, that insurgent forces can't resort to illegal means to gain power."

Kirov pushed out his lower lip and nodded. "And at second blush?"

"If you take action against Malenkov and Bulgakov, before you investigate, it could make you appear extremely partial and—"

"But I am partial. Partial to the presidency. Partial to preserving this fragile democracy we're trying to create here."

"I was about to add hasty, impulsive. Your critics could say that you seized upon the first hint of a coup and treated it as if it were already proven to be a coup." Potemkin was fairly certain that his boss wouldn't be acting impulsively. He had no doubt that Malenkov and Bulgakov were capable of such actions. Especially Bulgakov. He felt comfortable talking to Kirov this way. They'd developed a close working relationship since Kirov had come to office, and Kirov tended to respect, if not always agree with, his tendered opinions. Kirov knew that Potemkin was simply telling it as he saw it—something most people didn't do when they addressed the president.

"If it turned out to be that these people were pure as the driven snow, I would be vulnerable, I agree. But, I think, Gennadi, that I am clearly vulnerable now. If I do nothing, I play right into their hands. For all practical purposes I would be handing over the government to them. And even if we are wrong, though I doubt that that is the case, at least I would establish that the office of the president is not to be taken lightly. It would discourage such plots in the future. Tell me where my thinking is wrong here, Gennadi."

"I don't think you're wrong, sir. I was leading up to the same conclusion....with, perhaps one small suggestion."

Kirov squinted and eyed his advisor cautiously. "Yesssss. And what is that?"

"Before you take any action, I think you should talk to these four people mentioned in this *Pravda* article. You may gain some insights, which could be useful...maybe even invaluable. But if you do this, I think it should be right away."

"Can you get them here quickly? I think your idea is a good one, but only if we can get them here within hours. If it takes longer than that, we can't chance it. As you say, I must act quickly. Hell, not only as a show of strength, but to head off any precipitous actions by these would-be revolutionists. Now that they know the cork is out of the bottle, they may see the need to accelerate their plans, figuring if they don't move first, it will be too late."

"Yes, I agree. Let me get on it right away." Potemkin rose from his chair and started for the door. Then he stopped and addressed the president somberly. "I think, sir, regardless of whether I find these people in time or not, you should be thinking of what action you will take against Malenkov and his followers."

Kirov dropped his head slightly. At that moment, to Potemkin, he seemed to have aged by ten years. He didn't envy his boss right now. It's not easy to move against men of high rank, especially when they're in your own government. If Kirov botched this, he would never survive it. At the very least, he'd be driven from office in humiliating disgrace. At worst, he'd be imprisoned or even assassinated by the vindictive forces he was trying to subdue. Potemkin would do all he could to help, but right now he could see Kirov and his government slipping away. And with it, he realized, would be his own career, or worse.

Chapter 67

Bulgakov gripped the receiver so hard his knuckles turned white.

"Tell me, Anatoly—tell me that this is your idea of a joke. You, the one who must always be in control of a situation, you, of all people, couldn't have lost control of things this badly."

Sorokin's voice on the line had lost it's usual forcefulness.

"We have completely underestimated these four people, Yuri. They anticipate our every move. Now, I think, *Pravda* is going to run a new story—in tomorrow's paper. It will say that Malenkov is heading up our activities, and that you are working to support him." As he reported this, Sorokin realized that what he was telling Bulgakov was bad on several levels. The obvious thing was that more of their plot would be exposed. If anyone had missed the story in today's *Pravda*, they'd undoubtedly read about it tomorrow. It wasn't going to go away.

On another level, he knew Bulgakov would be livid to hear that Malenkov was being given credit for something he'd had nothing to do with. It diminished Bulgakov, and Bulgakov had a huge ego. He wouldn't like this at all.

Worse, tomorrow's story would make an enemy of Malenkov. Not someone you want against you. And Bulgakov and his followers didn't need any more enemies. They'd outlined in their planning sessions who they saw as their enemies, and Malenkov was not one of them. Bulgakov had, all along, hoped to side-step around Malenkov on his way to the top. At the very worst, he planned to eliminate him. At best, he might have kept him on as prime minister. But now, now he would be their enemy. Sorokin didn't want to give this report to Bulgakov, but he had no choice. He waited for the other man's reply.

"How fast can we mobilize the rioting in the streets?" As angry as he was, Bulgakov was above all a pragmatist. The exigencies of the situation called for action. He could deal with Sorokin later.

Sorokin exhaled in relief. At least for the present, his leader was more interested in taking action, than in venting his spleen. It took him fifteen seconds to collect his thoughts before he answered.

"Forty-eight hours. Maybe twenty-four in Moscow and St. Petersburg. You think they'll still come out in the numbers we counted on?"

"It's our only chance. If we have a good enough showing, it can be seen as a justification for the 'plotting,' we're been accused of. The average citizen may conclude that our planning was necessary and come to the realization that Kirov and the Western-leaning press have been covering up the disastrous incompetencies of the Kirov government."

"It's a stretch, Yuri, but worth a try. As you say, it's our only chance."

"Yes, but let's make it happen as quickly as possible. Forty-eight hours could be too late. Make it twenty-four. If Kirov has any balls, he'll send the FSB out to round us up. If they come after us, it could be difficult. Just between you and me, Anatoly, I don't think the old man has the balls, but just in case, we'll need to keep a low profile."

"Uh, Yuri?"

"Yes?"

"I think bringing out the agitators is a good idea, but do you think that's going to be enough?"

"Of course not. After they've made a satisfactory impact on the public psyche—that is, after Russia sees what terrible straits we're in—we make our move on Kirov." Bulgakov was being viscerally aroused by just talking about it. He got off on power, and just talking or thinking about it gave him a rush.

Then a thought hit him in the pit of the stomach. "Anatoly, you are using a secure phone aren't you?"

"I'm calling from a phone box. Should be fine."

"I hope so. I hope so. All right, get those agitators activated now. As soon as you have a more accurate idea of how many you can get out, get back to me. We're going to make a revolution." Bulgakov hung up before Sorokin could say what was on his mind.

Chapter 68

"Come, come," beckoned the president. "Please, I'm interested in what you have to say. Here, make yourselves comfortable. I hope you'll forgive me if I skip the usual courtesies. Under different conditions I would like to get to know each of you better. But I think Mr. Potemkin has already briefed you on why I asked you to come. I'm afraid we don't have a lot of time."

Vyugin and the others nodded. They understood.

"So I hope you can appreciate that it is a matter of some urgency that we get down to business." His summoned guests nodded again. "Good. I read the account of your experiences in today's Pravda. Then Gennadi," he nodded in the direction of his chief-of-staff, "Gennadi received a phone call from the editor of the paper. His name escapes me now—"

"Ivanov," interjected Potemkin. "Yevgeny Ivanov."

"Yes, Ivanov. Anyway, this editor tells Mr. Potemkin that a Mr. Sorokin had been sent to the newspaper by the prime minister. The implication being that the prime minister is behind this dastardly plot to overthrow the legally elected government of Russia. If this is true, I think you can see that it presents me with a very difficult situation. It is bad enough that this Sorokin and Bulgakov, not to mention field Marshall Suchinov and the others could be involved in such a plot, but my own prime minister...."
He put his open palm to his forehead and sighed.

Vyugin cleared his throat. When the president looked up he spoke.

"Mr. President, we don't think Mr. Malenkov is involved in this. We don't think he even knows about it. We believe Bulgakov is behind the whole thing." Kirov nodded, but didn't interrupt. Vyugin went on. "My associates and I," he turned and indicated Dantry, Barbeau, and Lubov with a sweep of his arm, "believe he is a desperate, power-hungry man. We believe he will stop at nothing to rule this country. And we have evidence that, once he gains control, he would follow a policy of political aggrandizement. He intends to gobble up as much of Central Asia and Europe as he can. He is a very dangerous man, sir."

Kirov nodded silently and considered what he'd just heard. After a moment, he addressed Dantry and the others.

"Are you all in agreement on this?"

"Yessir," they said almost in unison.

Vyugin decided their best chance of convincing Kirov that they were for real was to level with him. He knew, too, that leveling with the president meant that he'd have to reveal that he'd originally gotten involved in this mess when Bulgakov had given him the assignment to assassinate Tony Dantry's brother. By revealing this, he'd be confessing to having been willing to commit a capital crime. This, he did not want to do. But if he didn't, how were they going to explain why the four of them were involved in all of this. When all was said and done, Vyugin was a patriot. He loved his country, and he believed Kirov was its best hope for the future. In the end, the choice was easy. He would risk it. He could not stand by and watch Bulgakov destroy Russia and much of the Eastern Hemisphere.

"Mr. President, as you know, Miss Barbeau and Mr. Dantry here are Americans. They got involved in this because Mr. Dantry's brother was killed by people sent by Bulgakov. I know that this is true because I was the first person sent by Bulgakov to kill Mark Dantry. At the time, I was under the impression that it was at the behest of you and Mr. Malenkov. I happen to believe in what you're trying to do, sir. I'd like to see you get the chance to accomplish what you've set out to do. When I came to realize that Bulgakov was deceiving me about the mission, I had a change of heart. Unfortunately, though, Bulgakov sent others to kill Mr. Dantry—and they succeeded. I won't go into the details, but that's when Tony Dantry here and I met and decided to work together to try to stop Bulgakov."

"You realize, sir," said the president, "that you have just confessed to being a paid assassin?"

"There was to be no pay, Mr. President. Bulgakov did tell me that my pension would be guaranteed. But that was all. I did it because he had convinced me that it would help to keep you in office."

"I've done a little investigating, Mr. Vyugin, and I know that you are retired from the KGB. I appreciate that you had my survival in office in mind when you took your assignment, but if you believe in me as you say you do, you should know that I don't approve of assassinating those I don't agree with or those who present a problem. You should know that I'm working toward a new Russia, where we solve things diplomatically or through law, not through force and terror."

Vyugin looked down at his feet. He felt thoroughly chastened. Funny, he thought, he was not so concerned with his fate in the legal system, but he was more embarrassed than he'd ever been in his life. Suddenly that life, the life that he'd so willingly devoted to serving his country, seemed tawdry and mean. Since his retirement, he'd reflected often on what he'd done while in the service of the KGB, but he'd been able to see it as a somewhat honorable, if not noble career. This, he realized now, because he'd spent much of his time in retirement sharing old war stories with fellow KGB retirees. But now, under the glare of Kirov, a man he considered truly admirable and honorable, the half of his life spent in the KGB made him uncomfortable. Was it because he respected Kirov more than any man he'd ever met? Was it because Kirov's nobility conveyed a purity of purpose he'd rarely encountered before? Or was it that the president's words had shocked him into a wisdom that somehow escaped him during the last six decades of his life? He looked into the steely eyes of the president, who was waiting for Vyugin's response.

"I do know that, sir. Old habits and old methods die hard. When I took the assignment, I suppose I was a product of my background. I make no excuse for it, other than to say, that at a certain point I knew that it was wrong."

"You knew that you had been lied to. That is not the same as renouncing killing as a method of solving problems."

Dantry, who'd been following this colloquy with interest, was impressed with Kirov. He also felt a growing admiration for Vyugin, who responded valiantly.

"No, you're right, Mr. President. And I realize that's a big distinction. I think maybe I'm beginning to see that, too. In any event, sir, I'm at the mercy of the state. But I hope you'll let me continue, first."

"Of course. Go ahead."

"You should know, sir, that Mr. Lubov here, risked his life to defend what you believe in. Bulgakov's people kidnapped him and held him captive. To try to make him give up information they severed one of his fingers." He pointed to the still bandaged hand of the editor. "He's a brave man, sir, as are Mr. Dantry here, and Miss Barbeau. They both have repeatedly risked their lives trying to expose Bulgakov's treachery."

A half hour later, Kirov thanked them and asked them to keep in contact with Potemkin. He said they were pledged to secrecy from this point on until the matter was resolved. He also offered them protection, which they refused.

* * *

Malenkov didn't like to be summoned by the president. He didn't like Kirov. He didn't like his politics—too soft and trusting—and he resented his becoming president. They had both vied for the job, and Kirov had won. It was strictly personality, realized Malenkov; not accomplishments or agenda. Hell, most of the old-line party types preferred him over Kirov. But the younger members of parliament liked Kirov. He had an engaging personality that appealed to these naïve younger types. The seasoned old pros knew that accomplishment and agenda were what counted. And so it had happened. Kirov had been elected by a handful of votes, and he, Malenkov, clearly the superior leader, had to play second fiddle. Still, he had to admit to himself that the president had not done anything really outrageous, and that he had always treated him with the proper respect. And, it hurt the old pro to admit this, even to himself, but the president was sort of likeable in an offbeat, disarming sort of way.

Kirov was reading something as the prime minister entered the huge office. He stood a few feet inside the doorway and waited for the man to acknowledge him. The president noticed him immediately and looked up.

"Ah, Mikhail. Please come in. No, over there. Try the couch. Let's be comfortable. There is something I must speak to you about."

Chapter 69

The Cabinet Room was buzzing with conversation when Kirov entered. When they saw him, the room fell silent. The president slowly and deliberately made his way to the head of the table. When he reached the end of the table he faced the ministers assembled before him and paused there for a moment, surveying each of their serious faces.

"Gentlemen, I've called this emergency meeting because a grave threat faces this government and this great country. Earlier today, I met with prime minister Malenkov." He dipped his head in the direction of the prime minister who was seated at the opposite end of the long table. "We both agree that the matter I'm about to share with you is of the utmost importance." Malenkov nodded his confirmation. The room erupted again in agitated, whispered conversation. Kirov ignored this and continued.

"At this most difficult time, I appreciate the support of the prime minister. We are both here to ask for your support in dealing with the dangerous situation facing us." The level of the subdued murmurings increased. Every man in the room knew how enormous the stakes were.

Twenty minutes later, Kirov paused to take a drink of water. Yevgeny Chernenko, the minister of transportation spoke.

"Mr. President, what you have told us is very disturbing. It would seem to confirm the report most of us have read in *Pravda* —a report that I read with skepticism, since lately *Pravda* has made it a practice to publish stories that seem designed to shock. Lately they've been doing stories like those you read in the British tabloids—stories written to appeal to the masses in order to increase circulation. But from what you've said, it would seem as if this story is accurate—especially if as you say, you have evidence to prove it. I, for one, support you if you can share this evidence with those of us in this room."

"That can be done as soon as we conclude this meeting," said Kirov.

From the other side of the table a squat man with virtually no hair and with more neck than he needed spoke next. It was Andrei Lubin, minister of education.

"I think we should expect Mr. Bulgakov to take action very soon, Mr. President. Now that he's been exposed in the papers, he'll be desperate. He obviously is not going to surrender to you or to Mr. Malenkov, so, if you plan to intercede, I urge you to take action preemptively. I would support such action."

"Mr. President, I consider this discussion impulsive and unjustified," complained a white-haired man next to Lubin. This was Alexander Medved, minister of defense. A lot of his friends were anti Kirov. They felt the president was too tolerant and too patient. Many of them considered Kirov too soft, despite the man's outstanding record in the military when he was younger. Unlike most of Medved's associates, though, Kirov had left the military and entered the diplomatic corps. Prior to becoming president he'd served stints as ambassador to the United Kingdom and to Canada. Medved and his associates somehow had convinced themselves that the president had become brainwashed by his years in the

West. Medved chose his words carefully now, aware that some of the ministers around the table did not share his views; yet knowing that some of them did. He had to be careful that he didn't alienate those who sided with him while he attempted to win over some of the ones who didn't. "Mr. Bulgakov has been a dedicated patriot throughout his career." He stared down the table at the prime minister. "I'm shocked that you, sir, would turn on Bulgakov this way. Are we going to ruin a man's career based on the rantings of a radical newspaper? Let's at least give the man a chance to explain before we take action against him."

"I agree with Alexander," intoned a lean, raw-boned man in his late forties. His thin, sandy hair was buzzed short and what there remained of it receded dramatically, revealing a prominent shiny forehead. It was Konstantin Nicholayev, head of the FSB. "Give the man a chance," he entreated his fellow ministers. "He's a proven patriot. I suggest we invite him to meet with us here next week for an unofficial, private meeting. It will give us a chance to learn more about this and give him a chance to prepare his case."

"I don't think we can afford to wait till next week," said Kirov. "Based on the information I have, Bulgakov could set off rioting in Moscow and Petersburg as early as tomorrow. And in other cities by the next day. We cannot afford to wait. Gentlemen."

"The president is right," said Lubin. "The evidence is quite clear. There is no confusion on this. I say we round up Bulgakov and his collaborators first and then give them a chance to explain. If, by some strange chance there has been a mistake, we can apologize later."

Medved interrupted abruptly. "You claim to be a supporter of democracy and you would resort to such tactics," he roared. "Shame on you Andrei Lubin. That is the kind of thing the KGB would have done back in the old days."

"You have nerve, Medved, I'll give you that. You have nerve to invoke democracy on your behalf. You, who has all along supported the methods of the Soviets, you who continues to encourage the Communist Party, even when its ignominious seventy year track record of abject failure and waste has been acknowledged by the world. You, who bragged about your role in putting down the Chechnyan uprising, when all they sought was freedom to live their own lives." Lubin paused for dramatic effect. "The only reason you invoke democracy now, sir, is because you think it can be helpful in pulling your friend Bulgakov out of the fire. Well let me set you straight on this, sir. The president was fully consistent with democracy when he called this emergency meeting and put the question to us. If we vote to support his efforts to squelch this traitorous *coup d'état*, then that is democracy in action. If the president had acted unilaterally, that would have been the way of those you admire so much. I think all of us in this room owe the president thanks for respecting democracy and for respecting each of us in this cabinet. He did not try to circumvent us as so many of his predecessors would have done. He came directly to us and laid the matter before us. Now we owe it to him to give him our support. We owe it to the future of democracy in Russia. We cannot afford to delay, or his forthrightness will have been wasted. I call for an immediate vote on the matter."

Kirov welcomed the support, but he was afraid that the call for a vote was a bit precipitous. He had planned to take more time during the meeting to build his case. He wasn't at all sure he had the votes at this point. But to intercede and put off the vote would be perceived as a sign of weakness, so he took a deep breath and hoped for the best.

Chapter 70

The vote was 11 to 7 in support of the president. Medved and the six others who opposed the president, left the room fuming. It was not a satisfying victory for Kirov, for several of his supporters admonished him, saying ominously that he'd better be right, or he could not expect their support the next time. Still, if he was right, Kirov knew there at least would be a next time.

* * *

"Our people in Petersburg and here in Moscow say they can get something started by three tomorrow afternoon," said Sorokin. "They can't promise how big the turnouts will be, however. The *Pravda* story has made a lot of our supporters jittery."

Bulgakov exploded. "You mean they're running at the first minor obstacle! I should have expected this. Today's Russians are weak and spineless. This just shows how much we're needed, Anatoly. This country needs a backbone."

At the other end of the line, Sorokin shook his head. Sometimes Bulgakov's singleness of purpose could make him oblivious to the real world. This was one of those times. "I don't think they've lost their zeal, Yuri. It's just that some of them feel that if they riot they'll be playing right into the hands of Kirov. They'll essentially be confirming the *Pravda* story."

"Listen. We're beyond denying the truth of the *Pravda* story. Now that the cat is out of the bag, so be it. Look on the positive side. Many who've read it will undoubtedly be heartened to know that someone of my stature is giving breath to the thoughts they've had for years. The story will give them hope. Many of them will be on our side."

"Perhaps. Perhaps. But Russians tend not to be activists. They bitch and moan about bad conditions, but most of them accept whatever happens. Most of them are stoics; not revolutionaries. Besides, the story was not that flattering, and I suspect even our supporters out there would not approve of our methods with that I.M.F. man in Washington and with that editor Lubov. No, Yuri, I don't think we should be euphoric just yet. Let's just hope that the demonstrations in Petersburg and Moscow are effective."

Bulgakov was furious. He was not used to be being lectured to this way. Still, he needed Sorokin's help. Through a superhuman effort he managed to control his ire. "Anatoly, I think you underestimate the dissatisfaction in this country. Wait until tomorrow, and you shall see. In the meantime, what has been done about eliminating Vyugin, Lubov, and the two Americans?"

"Since this has all come out in the press, nothing. It would seem ill advised to kill them now. Everyone would know it was us. I think we have more important things to attend to now, Yuri."

Bulgakov was livid. This was the last straw. Bulgakov would take no more of this insubordination from Sorokin. Lately the man had taken to using his first name as if they were equals. Bulgakov had never tolerated this level of familiarity from anyone outside his own family and he was not going to now. Only rarely did Bulgakov's temper take control of his judgment. This was one of those times.

"I'll be the one to decide what our priorities are. What I want from you is accurate information and prompt execution of my orders. Right now, I'm ordering you to eliminate those four troublemakers. Is there anything about that that you don't understand?"

A red flush crept up both sides of Sorokin's neck. He hadn't become one of the most feared men in Russia by being timid. The only reason he'd obeyed Bulgakov's orders thus far was because he happened to think the man was Russia's best bet to reshape the chaos of the nation into a well-disciplined superpower. He had been counting on being an important part of the administration of the future superpower. But he could only swallow his pride so long as his leader gave him the proper respect. Until today, that had been the case. But this, this was intolerable. He took several deep breaths to control himself before he spoke. His relationship with Bulgakov would never be the same.

"Unfortunately, Yuri, I understand only too well."

Seemingly oblivious to, or contemptuously unconcerned with, Sorokin's resentment, Bulgakov asked, "You will take care of these four people?"

"It will be taken care of," hissed Sorokin as he hung up.

Chapter 71

When Lubov returned to the *Moscow Times* to retrieve his personal possessions, he was confronted by an unctuous Igor Godin.

"Look, Alexei, I know you are disappointed in me. Such is the way with the world. We each have our own loyalties, and I suppose it will remain that way. I certainly do not expect you to see why I behaved as I did. Frankly, I don't understand how you can defend that Western pawn Kirov. But as I said, we're not going to persuade each other to change." Lubov was impatient and had no desire to listen to a speech by his former boss. Not after the treachery he'd witnessed on their previous meeting. Godin went on undeterred. "I wish you would remain on staff. I'm sure we could work together. Give me a chance to prove that true gentlemen can disagree and still work together in a civilized manner."

"I'm sorry, I don't think it would work. Now if you don't mind, I need to finish packing up my things."

Godin didn't pretend to look disappointed. He hadn't expected a reply in the affirmative. He was really just probing for any information Lubov might divulge before he dropped his bomb. "Very well. Then shall we forward your personal mail and messages to your home?"

"I'm moving to a new place. I'll let you know when I've moved in. I'll only be at my present apartment for a few days more."

This was useful information for Godin, who knew that Lubov was a bachelor who lived alone. He would have to forward this information to Sorokin immediately. It would only strengthen his standing with the Bulgakov movement. God forgive him, Lubov was a nice fellow, but one could not let sentiment stand in the way of progress. Then, as Lubov once more started to leave, Godin dropped his bomb.

"By the way, Alexei, the Bulgakov people believe that the piece in *Pravda* did them a big injustice." Lubov frowned scornfully at this. He really didn't care what the Bulgakov people thought. Godin pressed on. He was enjoying this. "They have not appreciated the interference from Vyugin, not to mention you and the Americans."

"Igor, I don't really care what they think. Please get to the point."

"Sorokin's people have found where Vyugin's wife is staying. In St. Petersburg, with his daughter and son-in-law. They're under surveillance now. Bulgakov wants Vyugin to persuade Kirov to call off any efforts to interfere with the planned people's demonstrations in Moscow and St. Petersburg. They also want him to allow Bulgakov and his followers freedom of movement. In other words, to be treated like any other citizen." The look on Lubov's face was one of incredulity. "It is not unreasonable, Alexei. True, it's unfortunate, but they now believe that the only way Vyugin will agree to such terms is if he knows that his wife and family could be at risk."

"You son-of-a-bitch. You people are monsters!"

"I'm not interested in your moral judgments. I'm simply delivering a message. I'm afraid the only thing you can do is convey this message to your new friend Mr. Vyugin."

While he wouldn't trust Godin or the conspirators with his pet cat—if he had one—Lubov realized that he had no choice. He had to give Vyugin their message.

"I'll give Vyugin and the Americans the message. One of us will let you know the decision."

"Wait, I'm afraid nothing these days is simple. First, forget the Americans—for now, at least. Just tell Vyugin. But tell him that before he acts, he must get specific written instructions. Bulgakov cannot afford to have Vyugin or the Americans mishandle this." An expression of disgust and annoyance came over Lubov's tired features. Godin didn't notice.

"Vyugin will have to pick up these written instructions in a place of Sorokin's choosing—a place that is accessible enough, yet remote enough to make the pick-up so that neither side can interfere with the other. Do I make myself clear?"

"Yes. What you mean is a place where the transfer can be made without Bulgakov or Sorokin getting caught."

"Then I have made myself clear." Godin grinned smugly.

Lubov was on the verge of losing his self control. "Just tell me where."

"The Novodevichy Convent."

"On the river? Southwest of the city."

"Yes, the Smolensky Cathedral is there," explained Godin, as if her were talking to a schoolboy and not an experienced editor. "The convent is now a museum."

"Yes, yes. I know."

"Of course. Well, there is a phone box—between the convent and the cathedral, but closer to the convent."

Lubov nodded and Godin continued, "He should go there within the next two hours. He should enter the phone box. Behind the phone itself, if he looks carefully, he will see the edge of an envelope. Just the bare edge. For obvious reasons it cannot be too visible. Vyugin will need something to pry it out with. Something sharp like a knife. Once he has the envelope, the instructions will be quite clear. Essentially they are the approach he should follow to insure that he makes contact with President Kirov. Bulgakov fears that if Vyugin mishandles this, he might not gain access to the president. That would be bad for everyone—especially Vyugin's wife and family." He leered wickedly.

Chapter 72

"It could be a trap, Vladimir. You know Bulgakov and Sorokin would love to get their hands on you."

"I doubt it, Tony. I may have caused them a great deal of trouble, but now they have bigger concerns. They can't be bothered with me right now. What they do need is time. And they think I might be able to get that for them. If I can get to Kirov again and talk him into postponing any actions he's planning to take, that would be far more important to Bulgakov than getting revenge on me for being a nuisance. Besides, they have my wife and family under surveillance. What choice do I have?"

"Tell the police. Let them handle it for you."

"And what if Sorokin or one of his gangsters decides to kill my wife or daughter to teach me a lesson. No, I can't take that chance. Besides, I don't even know who's side the police are on. Don't worry. I'm counting on Bulgakov seeing me as more useful alive than dead."

"Then you intend to try to talk Kirov into calling off the troops? You know what that will mean, don't you? My God, it could allow Bulgakov's street fanatics the time they need to set off the rioting. It could mean helping Bulgakov become dictator of your country."

"Of course not. That's precisely what I don't intend to do. I'm hoping that if I get the president's ear, I can erase any doubts he may have about the need to take immediate action. At the same time I hope to enlist his help in removing Sorokin's goons from

their surveillance of my son-in-law's house. Wish me luck, Tony."
He then turned to Joanna and smiled. "I could use your luck, too,
young lady."

Tony shook his head in resignation. He knew that, if the
situation were reversed, he'd do exactly as Vyugin was doing. He
wasn't going to change the mind of his new friend.

Friend. How strange things had turned out. He was now
thinking of Vyugin as his friend—the same man who'd been sent
to kill his brother. But he couldn't deny the developing affection he
felt for the man. He really did feel that way toward the Russian.
And he was concerned now for his safety. And the safety of his
family. Christ! The poor bastard had no good options. If he did
nothing, Sorokin's goons might kill Vyugin's wife or daughter. If
he did what Bulgakov wanted and went to this convent to retrieve
the instructions, they could capture him and do God knows what.

Damn! The more he thought about what Vyugin was being
asked to do, the more he realized it had to be some kind of a trap.
Shit, if Bulgakov wanted to plead with Kirov, he would have done
it himself. Vyugin was being set up. Tony had to stop him before it
was too late. Unfortunately, Vyugin had already left for the
convent.

Chapter 73

"I still think this is a mistake, Yuri. I understand your need for revenge, but this man is more useful to you alive. Hell, you can kill him later. Besides, we're wasting good men in two different cities to satisfy your need to get even." Sorokin had never spoken to Bulgakov this way before, but these were desperate times and called for desperate measures. Time was running out, and he couldn't afford to worry about Bulgakov's ego now. Hell, it wasn't just the leader's neck that was on the line. Everybody's was— including his own. "I've got four people in St. Petersburg and another two here in Moscow. Right now, they could be helping the organizers with the street volunteers."

Bulgakov was furious. People didn't speak to him this way. Not even his most trusted ally, Sorokin. He bit his lower lip. He hadn't become the most feared man in all of Russia by losing his self-control. Through a supreme effort of will, he counted to ten. He needed to stay in control. He knew Sorokin was right. It was just that victory had been in his grasp until that prick Vyugin and his friends began to interfere. He knew he'd lashed out—atypical behavior for him. He'd prided himself on his self-control and on his ability to use anger as a weapon that he controlled at all times. This was the first time that anger had controlled him. His eyes met the slate-gray eyes of his iron-willed lieutenant. Sorokin was waiting for his reaction.

"You're right. I did let my emotions get away from me. Call off the men in St. Petersburg and Moscow. You're right about needing them to help organize our street efforts. We can deal with Vyugin and the others later."

A look of relief came over Sorokin's stern face. At least Bulgakov had regained his senses. Things were still in bad straits, but at least the boss had regained his self-control. Still, his decision to call off the dogs may have been too late to help Vyugin.

"Good. You realize, though, that it may be too late for Vyugin?"

"Whatever. Call the men off, but if they've already taken care of the traitor, I won't lose any sleep over it."

* * *

Vyugin hadn't been out to the Novodevichy Convent since he was a child, but as soon as it came into view, the exquisite structure and the majestically beautiful Smolensky Cathedral adjacent to it were as familiar as if it had been yesterday. He parked the car and took a minute to stand and admire the lovely setting. Magnificent. It was one place the Soviet Neanderthals had left untouched. The gold-domes of the cathedral's several spires sparkled in the bright sunlight of the brilliant summer day. As he looked upon this treasure from a different era, his problems, at least for the moment, faded into the distance.

The cathedral had been built in 1525. It had survived the years handsomely, thought Vyugin, succumbing momentarily to nostalgia. If buildings could speak the convent would have a lot to say. Buried on the grounds were such notables as Chekhov, Prokofiev, Molotov, and Khrushchev. Under the Soviets, the Convent had become a museum, a status that continued to the present. It might not be serving its original purpose, but at least it paid homage to it. Vyugin was moved as he stood there in the sun. He wished he could afford the luxury of more time to take in the memories and ghosts of the past that this carefully preserved corner of the capital offered anyone who took the trouble to immerse themselves in.

But this was not the time. He shook himself out of his reveries. The lives of his loved ones were at stake. He scanned the grounds for the phone box he was supposed to enter. There, less than a hundred meters away he saw it. It was nestled against the outer side wall of the cathedral, in the shade of a large oak tree. He headed briskly toward the phone box. As he neared the box he could see that there was someone in it. It was an older woman, probably in her late seventies or more. He slowed his pace. He'd wait. She was leaving now. Vyugin moved quickly. He wanted to get to the box before someone else occupied it. The sooner he got this over with, the better. It was a warm day. Quite warm for Moscow. Vyugin was feeling the heat. He wiped his brow and stepped into the box. He left the door open so he'd at least have some air.

The phone itself was a metal, gray rectangular affair. The paint was scratched with phone numbers, initials, coarse graffiti, and childlike messages from callers long gone. Vyugin allowed himself a smile. The phone was so old, it looked as if Stalin himself had installed it. It was just one more vestige of a 70-year period of neglect. But the sorry state of the former Communist state was not his concern right now. Right now he had more pressing matters to concern himself with.

He examined the loose-fitting seam where the rectangular phone base unit met the wall of the phone box. Yes, there was something there. It looked as if it could be the edge of an envelope. Very cleverly done, he had to admit. It was visible—if you were looking for it, but it certainly wasn't obvious. A casual user of the phone would never notice it. The envelope could probably go unnoticed for months. He pulled a small pocket knife from his trousers. He opened it with his thumbnail and carefully probed the narrow crack. God forbid he push the envelope too far in and thus out of reach. What would he do then? Under the circumstances, he realized, he'd have to pull the phone off the wall and hope to hell no one was watching.

There, he had it. Slowly, slowly. Yes, it was an envelope. Vyugin began to relax a bit. Maybe he would see his beloved Ludmilla soon. The envelope was perhaps a third of the way out now. He reached with his fingers and pulled.

The coruscating flash of light became his only, if fleeting reality. The last thing Vladimir Vyugin remembered beside this overpowering whiteness, was how close he was to saving his wife. The blast blew the two small side walls of the phone box outward and somewhat upward before they landed ten feet away, shattering their dirty glass panels. A shard of glass creased the skull of young woman more than 50 feet from the explosion. The few people on the grounds of the convent at that moment remained motionless, stunned by the blast from hell. Only later did they reflect on the irony of such an evil thing happening on such sacred grounds.

Chapter 74

"Oh my God!" cried Joanna, as her hands flew to her face. "Oh my God! They've killed him." Dantry grabbed her and pulled her to him, holding her tight.

Lubov hissed something under his breath in Russian that Tony didn't understand. A few days earlier, the editor's expression would have been that of a frightened child. Now, there was anger in his intelligent eyes.

"Those bastards!" muttered Dantry. "Those fucking bastards."

They were standing a little more than a hundred yards from what until a minute ago had been the phone box. They'd kept out of sight because they hadn't wanted their friend to know they were following him, nor had they wanted a possible observer working for Bulgakov to notice them. A diaphanous cloud of smoke remained where moments ago their friend had been. They edged closer now. A small crowd was gathering near the site of the explosion. The police had not yet arrived.

When Dantry and the others were within about seventy-five feet of the site, Tony stretched out his arms to keep Joanna and Lubov from going any closer. He felt a wave of nausea come over him. How much grotesqueness could he tolerate? The turbulence in his life since learning of the death of his brother was beginning to take its toll. While his life at City Island had not been wholly satisfying, it had been a welcome contrast to the coldly calculated machinations and occasional killing in his professional life. But the events since his brother's death were more than a match for the horror of his days as an intelligence agent. These past two weeks were worse, in that innocent people were suffering and dying. First his brother is killed. Then Joanna gets involved. Then the Russian editor Lubov loses a finger. Now, Vyugin, while not totally innocent, but certainly as reconstructed as he himself was, is brutally executed. Dantry tried to block out the horror. For a moment, he was transported back to his dependable, if slightly battered boat on Long Island Sound. The screeching of gulls and the smell of the water beckoned him. A voice shook him out his thoughts.

"I'm going to see if he can be helped," said Lubov, taking a step forward. Dantry grabbed the editor's sleeve and pulled him back.

"No. Believe me, there's nothing left of him. Don't go there. Stay here."

They'd followed Vyugin here without telling him. Tony had not been as convinced as Vyugin that Bulgakov's people wanted to keep him alive. Dantry had had too much experience with fanatics to expect logic when dealing with such people. He and Joanna had persuaded Lubov to join them. Lubov had invested everything in this. He deserved to be in on it to the end—if that's what he wanted. He did, and he was with them now. But Lubov appeared to be off in his own world.

"From here we look like any other bystanders," said Dantry in a low voice. "We get any closer, and we look suspicious. From the looks of things, unfortunately, we don't have to get any closer to know what happened. Vladimir couldn't have survived that blast."

Lubov, who minutes earlier seemed to have gotten back some of his color, was ghastly white and once again appeared to be in shock. Joanna's eyes were red, and she was trying valiantly to control herself. Dantry's eyes were blazing. The nightmare that had started back in Virginia would not let up.

Tony turned and said, "C'mon, let's get out of here."

"You think this was intentional?" asked Lubov, emerging from his private thoughts.

"You bet your ass it was intentional," snorted Dantry. "C'mon, let's go."

"What do you intend to do?"

"First we get away from here. If they still have time for revenge against Vyugin, that means they probably haven't forgotten us, either."

A look of understanding came over Lubov's pallid face. His mind wasn't used to thinking this way. Joanna seemed drained as the full realization sank in.

"Christ, Tony, you're probably right. My God, these people are monsters. What do we do?"

"First thing we do is go on the offensive."

Chapter 75

Bulgakov picked up the phone on the first ring. For the past two days he'd done that. While those around him didn't notice, he was beginning to feel the pressure of events.

"Yes?"

"It's me," said Sorokin, not even bothering to hide the fatigue he was feeling. "It's done. The blast reduced him to a hundred pieces."

"Excellent." This was the first good news Bulgakov had received in days. "How about the others?"

Sorokin was not exactly a caring person, but he shook his head as he realized that Bulgakov had not even asked if anyone else had gotten hurt. Sorokin had always thought of himself as self-absorbed and hard, but Bulgakov was ice.

"We'll get them if you feel it's important. You're sure you want to waste the men on this?" As soon as he'd uttered the words, he regretted them.

"I'll decide what's important and what isn't. Just get the job done. Or should I get someone else to handle it?"

Sorokin was burning. "I thought you'd decided against going after these people?"

Bulgakov looked as if he were about to boil over. He didn't like being challenged. "For a brief time I was willing to let them go. But the more I thought about it, the more I realized how foolish that would be. I want them dealt with." His voice was rising now as the intensity of his feelings took over. "Do you have a problem with that?" he roared.

Sorokin fought the urge to hang up, but he realized what a mistake that would be. He had enough people who hated him. He didn't need Bulgakov as an enemy. He turned away from the phone and sighed. Then he spoke directly into the receiver. "I'll take care of it."

* * *

"Thank you, Mr. President, for seeing us," said Dantry. It had not been easy getting in to see Kirov. The guard in the downstairs lobby of the imposing Kremlin building had tried to turn them away. He'd pointed out what should have been obvious—that you couldn't just come in off the street and see the president. Of course it was obvious to Dantry and the others, but they couldn't afford to be sent away. Dantry had persisted.

"Look," he'd said to the guard, "this is one of those times when making the wrong decision could mean not only losing your job, but everything that's important to you. Call up to Potemkin and tell him it's three of the people he met with yesterday." He gave the guard their names. By this time a second guard had come over to see what the problem was. He listened as Dantry outlined his case. "Tell him that it's only three of us because the fourth was just killed by the people we spoke to him about in our last meeting."

The two guards raised their eyebrows and stepped aside to discuss how they should handle these three curious nobodies. After a couple of minutes, the first guard returned and said he'd make the call. Now Dantry and the others prayed that Potemkin would be in to take the call. Fortunately, he was.

Potemkin ushered them into Kirov's office. Kirov indicated that he should stay. As Dantry sat down, he noticed that the events of the past few days had taken their toll on the president. The Russian leader's eyes were dark and sunken. He'd clearly been having a rough time. Despite his obvious fatigue he was courteous.

"This is most distressing. You are telling me that Mr. Vyugin, who was in this very office yesterday, has been murdered by Bulgakov's people?"

"I'm afraid so, sir," said Dantry.

"Tell me about it."

Dantry proceeded to describe what had happened at Novodevichy Convent and how they had come to be there in the first place. He didn't spare the details. The president appeared to be shaken by what he was hearing.

Kirov directed his attention to Lubov.

"You observed this, too?"

"Yes, Mr. President."

"And it was as Mr. Dantry describes it?"

"Exactly, sir."

Kirov now looked at Joanna.

"And you, Miss Barbeau is it?"

"Yes, Mr. President. Barbeau."

"You were there, too?"

"Yessir. It happened as Mr. Dantry says. It was horrible."

"Yes, it sounds as if it was. I don't wish to alarm you, but I think we should be concerned for your safety now. If these people would kill Vyugin, there's no reason to think they would stop with him. Not if they view you as all being inimical to their interests. I think you should stay here in the Kremlin until we have this under control."

Lubov and Dantry exchanged looks. Then Dantry looked at Joanna, who said, "I don't think that will be necessary, sir. We can take care of ourselves."

For the first time, the president smiled. "I would hazard a guess that Mr. Vyugin would have said the same thing. How do you think you can protect yourselves from a cabal of trained assassins?"

Dantry responded. "You could be right, sir. I've had a little experience there myself. And we definitely are outnumbered. Do you mind if I ask what you intend to do about Bulgakov and his plotters? I know you can't be specific, but I think we've earned the right to some information."

"You're right, Mr. Dantry. You have earned our gratitude, but you're also right about my not being able to tell you what I intend to do. You must understand, that I can't tell very many people that." The president looked off to the right, seemingly deep in thought. When he turned back to face his three guests he said,

"However, if you were to stay as my guest here at the Kremlin for a few days, I think I could give you a general idea of what might happen." He glanced at Potemkin, who nodded.

"In other words, you could keep an eye on us," said Dantry grimly.

"Yes, but certainly you must understand that, Mr. Dantry." He hesitated, as if not quite sure how to qualify this. "In view of your professional experience."

"Yeah, I suppose."

"Good, then if I have your pledge that you and your colleagues will remain here until our initiatives have been set in motion, I'll have Gennadi brief you. Before we do that, however, I need to talk with him alone. If you'll excuse us, please make yourselves comfortable in the outer room there. Then Gennadi will see that you're provided with rooms and food."

"And a briefing," reminded Dantry.

"Yes, and a briefing."

* * *

The two rooms for which the president had arranged made Joanna envious of the other guests who'd occupied these quarters over the past centuries. She conjured up visions of relatives of czars and visiting royalty, for the accommodations were nothing short of spectacular in their elegance and comfort. No wonder the masses had risen up against the czar. The disparity between these quarters and the cramped apartments most Russians shared with their families and even other families was shocking. They weren't really rooms. They were suites with rococo décor inspired by 18th Century French architecture. The delicate gold inlaid filigrees of the furniture and the superficial elegance represented by these two suites, if converted to rubles, could have paid for the housing of a hundred Russian families for a year.

An ample, if less than elegant spread of food had been brought into the larger of the two suites. The three guests suddenly realized how hungry they were and found themselves putting away the food as if this were their first meal in days, which wasn't that far from the truth.

"I didn't get the impression that the president plans to do very much, did you?" asked Joanna.

"He's hard to read," said Lubov. "He's not known as a man who would turn to force to solve the country's problems. That's why we elected him. He was a breath of fresh air. But I know what you mean. If he's too much of a pacifist, he might give these bastards too much leeway. I hope he doesn't think he can win them over with appeals to their good nature."

"Let's hope not," said Dantry. "If he does, I pity Russia. Jesus, this is frustrating. I feel we should be doing something. Do you think this Potemkin guy will really fill us in on what's going to happen?"

Lubov knew something about the Russian character, and he knew something about Potemkin. "I think he will. He has a good reputation, which is unusual for a Russian bureaucrat. I doubt if he'll tell us much, but I think he'll tell us something."

"I hope it's soon," said Joanna. "Not knowing anything is awful."

"Yeah, it's a bitch," agreed Dantry. "If we don't hear something soon, maybe we should leave."

"And do what, Tony? We've given our pound of flesh. We can't do anything now. Let's just wait and pray."

"Ah, pray. Yes, that's always good. We can use your prayers." The rich baritone voice of Potemkin interrupted their frustration as the tall chief of staff entered the room. "You must be wondering what is happening?"

"That, sir, is an understatement," said Dantry. "What can you tell us?"

"May I sit down?" He didn't wait for their reply. He reached for a glass and poured himself a glass of robust red wine from Georgia. "I can tell you this. We have ordered the national militia to be on standby in St. Petersburg and here in Moscow. We've also alerted the police in both cities. At the least sign of a street disorder and organized group, they will go into action and break it up."

"Are you sure the national militia and the police will side with the president?" asked Lubov.

"Good question. No, we are not certain, but we believe most of them will do as the president requests," a gleam came over his eyes now. "Especially since we have told them that as we speak we are arresting Bulgakov, Sorokin, Marshall Suchinov, commissar Zlotov, and most of the people you saw at that compound outside Noginsk."

Dantry exchanged looks with Joanna and Lubov. The president was not a paper tiger.

"What will the president charge them with?" asked Lubov.

"Treason...and murder to begin with."

"Can you make the charges stick? What I mean is, a lot of people in your government probably side with Bulgakov."

"Yes, I know what you mean. The answer to your question is yes. We think we can—especially with the help of the press." Lubov raised his eyebrows. Potemkin took note and continued. "No, I do not mean control of the press. What I mean is, I hope that journalists like you, Mr. Lubov, will tell the story of Bulgakov's perfidy and brutality and when that gets out, it will be a lot more difficult to defend the actions of the cabal."

"I'd love to tell the story," said Lubov with a rueful smile, "but I don't have a job."

Potemkin smiled. "Don't be too sure about that. Your boss Godin is one of the people being arrested. The owners of the *Moscow Times* knew nothing about his activities, and, in fact, were shocked to learn of them. They've already sacked him. If he hadn't been arrested, they would have anyway. They want you back, Lubov. In Godin's job."

For the first time since they'd met him, Joanna and Dantry saw Lubov smile. Color began to suffuse the pale features of the beleaguered editor.

"You'll have your story. When can I get back to the paper?"

"For your own safety, I suggest you wait till morning. By then, most of the key conspirators will have been rounded up."

"This should be in tomorrow's paper," said Lubov with conviction. "It cannot wait. With all due respect and appreciation, sir, I must get back now. You can't afford to wait for this story." He pursed his lips and added, "I've never done this before, but my country comes before my paper. I think you should inform Ivanov at *Pravda*, too. We need this story even more in the Russian language."

"Yes, of course you are right. The president wanted you here for your own safety. You realize, that if you leave here and go to the paper you will be putting yourself in grave danger. I don't have to tell you how vicious these people are."

"I understand the risk. Still, I must go. The very future of Russia is at stake. I don't think of myself as a risk taker. All my life I've chosen the safer course. You might say that my life has been guided by a risk- avoidance philosophy. Well, I've seen the devil this week. I've seen the hell he could bring to this country. It's time I took a risk."

"I'll speak to the president. I'll recommend that he provide you with some protection. Give me a moment." Potemkin left the room.

Chapter 76

The stories the next day were devastating to Bulgakov. Most political observers believed that, without the stories, the outcome might have been different.

The unrest and disaffection in the great sprawling nation had been growing with every passing day. However, no one living could remember a time when the people were not unhappy with conditions in Russia. It had been ever thus. Still, much of the press in recent months had been coming down hard on the idea that Kirov was too weak to control the unrest in the country. Many believed that, while intelligent and basically decent, the president was perhaps too cerebral for the job. Russia was, and always had been, a rambunctious country. It needed a tough, no-nonsense type leader at the top.

The stories in *Pravda* and the *Moscow Times* not only exposed the plot to overthrow the government, they also exposed the true nature of the conspirators. Plots to overthrow the government were nothing new to Russia. Usually, though, they were presented in the press as something positive. Russians were so used to being ignored or abused by their governments that virtually any hint of change was seen as an improvement. It wasn't that Russians stopped being cynical. It was just that most figured that any change represented at least the possibility of a slight improvement. But when people read of the assassination of Mark Dantry and the continued efforts to assassinate a second I.M.F.

official they balked. And reading first-hand accounts of Lubov's finger being amputated, and Vyugin being blown up turned the stomach of more than one miserable Russian citizen.

Many who read the morning papers were citizens whose relatives had survived Stalin's horrors and Khrushchev's abuses. A few of the older ones remembered those times first-hand. Their parents and grandparent had been in food lines and lived huddled together with a dozen other people in two rooms. Many still lived in intolerably crowded conditions. They weren't easily shocked or discouraged. They'd either seen or heard it all. But to know this much about a group of people who would rule them if they succeeded in their coup was too much even for them. The turnouts for Bulgakov's planned street demonstrations were disappointing to say the least. There was, effectually, no show of support. Peripheral supporters disappeared into the woodwork. Unfortunately for those closest to Bulgakov, it wasn't that easy to disappear. Nearly everyone who'd been at the meeting at the Noginsk compound was rounded up. These were not men who could blend in. They were high-profile people—something that most of them enjoyed immensely. But in the last 24 hours their high visibility had made it relatively easy to find them. At least most of them. The only one of significance still missing was Sorokin. The police and federal officials assured Kirov that he'd be found soon.

Bulgakov had outsmarted, or more accurately, out-egoed himself. He'd been the first one to be apprehended. It had been a stupid move for someone so smart. He'd tried to sneak into his office late at night to retrieve personal belongings. He'd wrongly concluded that no one would expect him to risk such a visit. His boss, Malenkov had confronted him with two agents sent by Kirov. They'd been in turn accompanied by two Moscow policemen. Kirov had gambled that the police would not turn against him. It had been a good guess.

Chapter 77

When Dantry and Joanna arrived in St. Petersburg, they took a taxi directly to Octyabreskaya Naberezhnaya. Now they mounted the eight steps leading up to the three-story brownstone building where Vyugin's wife was staying. Dantry paused on the top step and looked into Joanna's tired eyes.

"I'm really not looking forward to this."

"I know."

He sighed. "Okay, let's get it over with." He rang the bell.

*   *   *

"Someone's at the door, Sonia," said Ludmilla Vyugin to her daughter. "A man and a woman. I don't recognize them. Be careful."

"Those people are gone, Mother. Don't worry." As Sonia approached the front door, she secretly admitted to herself that she still felt some concern. She'd never seen the two people standing on the front stoop. She opened the door cautiously, ready to slam it at the least indication that something was wrong.

"Yes," she said, holding the door slightly ajar.

Dantry spoke first.

"Is this the Yachenko residence?"

Sonia hesitated before saying in a voice only slightly more than a whisper, "Yes."

"My name is Tony Dantry. This is my friend, Joanna Barbeau. We were—" He caught himself, then said, "We're friends of Vladimir Vyugin. You must be his daughter."

"Yes. What do you want?"

Dantry sensed her nervousness.

"Please believe me. You have nothing to fear from us. I'm afraid, though, that we have some bad news. May we come in?"

"Who is it?" called Ludmilla from somewhere in the house.

"They say they're friends of papa. They said they have bad news."

Ludmilla entered the room breathlessly, her face a grim mask. "I knew it," she shrieked. "I knew it." Then, her voice dropped to a near-audible whisper. "Oh dear God, this can't be it. This can't be it." She buried her face in her hands as Joanna and Tony hesitantly entered the room.

"We are so sorry, Mrs. Vyugin," said Joanna compassionately, struggling with her Russian, and moving closer to console her. The distraught women allowed herself to be hugged by the American stranger. Joanna was that sort of woman—a woman with whom strangers felt immediately comfortable.

For the next half hour Tony and Joanna related the whole story— from the moment Vladimir Vyugin and Tony Dantry first met in Washington, right up to the fatal explosion at the Novodevichy Convent in Moscow. Sonia, the daughter, had cried. First a flood of tears, followed by wracking sobs. Now her tears were under control, though her eyes were red and her cheeks were streaked with tiny dried rivulets of mascara. The reaction of Vyugin's wife was different.

After the initial shock, Ludmilla had not cried. She'd sat nearly motionless, collecting herself and reflecting on the life of anxiety and tension she'd shared with a man who never should have entered a career in espionage in the first place. She'd never been able to fathom why this essentially good man could have rationalized such a life. And now, as she looked across the small sitting room, she found herself facing another man who'd apparently spent the best years of his life as a spy, too. Only this one had done it for the Americans. There was something disquieting about such men. But she admitted, almost as an aside to herself, that there was something about such men that attracted her, too. She stirred from her faux catatonia and forced herself to speak.

"I knew this would happen," she said in a monotone. "The only surprise is that it took this long. But when my husband agreed to this one final mission, I knew he'd never come home alive. I tried to talk him out of it, but he was convinced that it was important for Russia—perhaps the most important mission he'd ever accepted. His intentions were always good." Then, with a twisted, fatalistic smile, she allowed herself for the first time to weep quietly.

Dantry considered his words carefully, "You can be proud of what your husband did these past few days. He may have been instrumental in keeping Russia out of the hands of a very evil man."

"You mean Bulgakov."

"Yes."

"Ironic. This is the man who gave my husband the assignment in the first place. It was to save Russia from a man who would destroy Russia." She sniffed cynically. "The same mission, only the players change."

"Yes, but as we've explained, he quickly became convinced that, had he fulfilled the assignment, he would have helped put a very bad man in charge of this country. Believe me, Mrs. Vyugin, from what I've seen of Kirov and Bulgakov, I'd have to say that your husband made the right decision."

She sniffed. "But when Vladimir thought the assignment was noble, he was willing to kill an innocent man. How is it that you people can do this?"

These words cut to Dantry's inner soul. She was describing him, too. "I suppose that's true, but you must consider his training and the Cold War culture he was brought up in. Virtue in his world meant the end justified the means. Patriotism has a strong pull on a man's heart. Believe me, I know. Don't judge him harshly. He gave his life for you and his country. The people he helped stop are more vicious than you can imagine."

"Oh, I believe you, Mr. Dantry. I believe you."

Sonia came to her mother's side and hugged her.

"Mother, my God, Mother, I can't believe he's dead. When he retired I was so happy he'd survived that horrible job—that the two of you would be able to enjoy your retirement out in the country." As her daughter said this, Ludmilla Vyugin seemed somehow older than she'd appeared when Dantry and Joanna first saw her. The finality of what had happened was sinking in. Joanna sensed this and offered what little support she could think of.

"He did die for his country. I hope you both realize that he died a hero."

"Russia always demands too much from its men," said Ludmilla Vyugin dolefully.

Chapter 78

The calendar had just slid past the middle of September—less than three months since Dantry and Joanna had returned to the States and their lifestyle in New York. A light wind was blowing from out of the west. There was more than the usual chop on Long Island Sound this afternoon, and Tony, holding two cold bottles of Dos Equis, did a balancing act as he made his way past the cabin to the bow of his aging, but beloved boat. It was one of those rare days when the air quality must have rivaled what it had been back in 1525 when Giovanni da Verrazano discovered what is today New York Harbor. The sun seemed larger than usual as it burned through the deep cobalt sky—its reflected brilliance giving the Sound a magical quality that Joanna found enchanting. She put down her book and followed Dantry with her eyes as he made his way forward, a big grin on his tanned features. She returned his grin with a quizzical expression.

"What are you so happy about?"

"I've just made an important decision."

"Like what we're going to eat tonight?"

He laughed. "No, even more important than that. I know you'll find that hard to believe. But seriously, I've decided that I'm going to get a job." He looked out to the east at the vast shimmering expanse of water. "It really is true. You *can* have too much of a good thing. I love this Sound, but...now don't laugh.... I want to do something with my life. Not something earthshaking, but at least something constructive. At least something that helps bring people together."

She just stared at him. She wasn't sure where he was going with this. Finally, she screwed up her face and said, "Like joining the Peace Corps? I'm sorry, my love, but I don't see you doing that."

He laughed. "No, not the Peace Corps. I'm not that altruistic. And I do value my creature comforts too much at this stage of my life. No, I was thinking more of working with one of these relocation firms. In particular, the ones that deal internationally."

"What would you do?"

"Well, if they'd have me, I think I could help business people from various countries understand the cultures of the countries they were being sent to. When they work overseas, business people tend to be the advance guard of a nation's culture. They represent their country—for better or for worse. Remember the term Ugly American? You don't hear it much anymore, but back in the 50s and 60s it was pretty common. It represented a then commonly held American view that everyplace but here was the boondocks of civilization. The ones who were most guilty of this kind of nationalistic tunnel vision thought of themselves as better informed and more sophisticated than people from other lands, whereas, in fact, they were the most provincial among us. Basically, the only thing they had that most foreigners didn't have at that time was money. And many of them lost no opportunity to flaunt the fact.

"It's not that bad now, though some Americans still think that if they speak loudly enough when they're visiting another country, they'll be understood. It would never occur to them that they might take the time to learn enough of the other guy's language to make themselves understood. Hell, even if they weren't understood that well, the fact that they tried the language would be an icebreaker."

Joanna smiled.

"You've been giving this a lot of thought, haven't you?"

"Yeah, I have. I see so much hatred in this world, and most of it is based on nothing but ignorance. Hell, I was part of it. I can remember so many times when I used to travel for the agency in Europe or Asia. I'd mention to some local the next town I was going to, and the local would act like I was making this big mistake. I'd pursue it with him, and he'd say something like 'You won't like these people. They are not nice.'

"I'd say, 'How do you know this? Have they treated you badly?'

"The guy would say, 'No, I've never been there, but that's what people say.'"

Joanna nodded. "I know. You don't have to go overseas to experience that, either."

"Right. Anyway, maybe I'm a slow learner, but I've come to the conclusion that helping people understand each other might in some small way make a greater contribution to improving the world than being a good spy."

"This whole thing with your brother and Vyugin has made you feel guilty about working for the CIA, hasn't it?"

He pursed his lips thoughtfully before he replied.

"It certainly didn't help matters. But, no, I began to feel a little guilty long before this summer. It was one of the things that contributed to my rather early retirement. Shit, some of the things we did were right. I still feel that way. Certainly we felt that way when we did them. But what I'm feeling now goes right to the premise of much of what we do in the intelligence field. It's the presumption that you can't trust anybody, so, if you're smart, you'll get them before they get you. And I'm talking about both sides. Hell, all sides. Everybody's in the game. Not just us and the Russians."

"Well, can you?"

"Can I what?"

"Trust anybody? Not you personally, but in general. Can you trust anybody. Other than me, that is?" She winked teasingly.

"I know it sounds naïve. Sure, you can't trust everyone about everything. But most of our mistrust is based on physical and cosmetic differences. Or blind tradition passed on from generation to generation. Look at Kosovo and Northern Ireland. I've always found it interesting that when you take people from these places and put them in America, they soon end up being friends. They're the same people. Only their attitudes have changed."

"So you think you can do something about this?"

"I know I won't make things worse. Maybe, if I'm lucky, and if I do a few things right, I might be able to make a small difference." He smiled. "I hate that expression. Make a difference. People use it too loosely. But, yeah, I'd like to try to make a difference."

"You're really serious about this, aren't you?"

"Yeah, I am."

"Where does that leave us?"

"I hope closer than ever. I thought maybe you could be my mentor. I thought also that you and I could put a little more stability into our lives."

"Like?"

"Like maybe we should get married."

"Are you proposing to me?"

"I guess I am. How about it?"

"I should take some time to think about it."

"I understand. Kind of sprung it on you, didn't I?"

"You did that. Okay."

"Okay what?"

"Okay, I've thought about it."

Dantry took a deep breath.

"And?"

"And I accept. You know, I would have accepted even if you didn't have a job."

"But having a job is better."

"I didn't say that. But I do like the kind of job you're thinking about. I like that a lot."

"I hope you'll like this, too." As he said this, he pulled a small box from his pocket.

Chapter 79

"Did you see this?" asked Joanna, pointing to a small item on page nine of the *Times*.

He set his coffee down and leaned over to see what she was referring to. He gave her a peck on the cheek.

"What?"

"This."

He took the paper and read with interest the piece she had indicated with her index finger.

> MOSCOW—A former high-ranking official in the Kirov administration, missing for over two years, was found dead in his Moscow flat yesterday. The official, Anatoly Sorokin, former deputy chief of staff to Prime Minister Mikhail Malenkov and trusted lieutenant of the Prime Minister's fallen chief of staff, Yuri Bulgakov, was found shot to death in his two-room flat in one of the poorer sections of the city. Details of the shooting were not provided by the police, but it was rumored that Sorokin had been in hiding since Bulgakov's failed *coup d'état* attempt two years ago last July. Sorokin's landlord told the Associated Press that he had known his tenant as Vyachaslav Minsky, and that he believed him to be somehow involved in the Russian drug trade. The landlord said that he thought Sorokin might have been part of the Russian Mafia. Sorokin was believed to have been the only important member of the Bulgakov cabal still at large.

Dantry let the paper drop. He smiled, not a big broad smile, but a smile that indicated a final relaxation of some long-lasting burden.

"Well, I suppose you could say that's the final chapter."

"Closure?"

"Yeah, I suppose you could call it that."

"President Kirov's been doing okay lately. He's got more support in the Duma, and the Moscow press can't say enough about him."

"The ruble's improving, too."

"Getting that loan approved didn't hurt."

"He's still fighting the Mafia, though. Those guys are tough."

"At least he's fighting them. Hell, in the past the Russian presidents just gave it lip service."

"So, my darling, tomorrow you leave for Moscow in your new role. How do you feel about it?"

Since joining International Relocation Ltd., Dantry had conducted relocation seminars in Paris, Brussels, Prague, Bangkok, Hong Kong, and half a dozen other cities around the world. He'd done even more workshops in New York, Boston, San Francisco, Miami, and Seattle for incoming executives from other countries. The seminars had consisted of providing information about the local customs including most importantly, the taboos. Where he knew the language, he provided minimal language training. Where he didn't, he brought in other I.R.L. people to work the seminars with him. Tony found the work exhilarating and fun. And, most importantly, satisfying. Until now, though, he hadn't done any workshops in Moscow. Tomorrow he would take off from J.F.K. and would conduct his first Moscow seminars two days later. He shook himself out of his thoughts and answered his wife.

"Nervous, but excited. I can't wait to see the changes that have taken place in the last two-and-a-half years. It should be nice not looking over your shoulder every time you make a move."

"Wish I could go with you."

"You still can. You can explore the city while I conduct my classes. Then we can take in the nightlife together."

"Maybe I will. If I can do it without leaving the college in the lurch. Yes, I think I'll do it."

"Great, the only thing is, I was thinking that I might go up to see Ludmilla Vyugin in her country dacha. Would you mind?"

"It would be nice. Sad, but nice."

End

About the Author

Richard Scott is a retired editor, writer, and publisher, having been president and publisher of the David McKay Company and president and publisher of Fodor's Travel Publications. He's also been managing editor of *American Bookseller* and *Bookselling this Week*. In the 70s Mr. Scott was co-host with Isaac Asimov, Brendan Gill, Nat Hentoff and others of the talk show *In Conversation*. The show ran on radio station WOR in New York and eleven other stations around the U.S. He's a former trustee of Historic Salem, Inc. and of the Salem Athenæum in Salem, Massachusetts. He lives in Salem. You can contact him at richard.scott2000@comcast.net.

11544780R0025

Made in the USA
Lexington, KY
12 October 2011